*For my husband,
who has made this
whole wild ride worth
every second*

Prologue

The Dragon's Heat Novels
by Tessa Adams

Dark Embers
Hidden Embers
Forbidden Embers

Soulbound

A LONE STAR WITCH NOVEL

Tessa Adams

A SIGNET ECLIPSE BOOK

SIGNET ECLIPSE
Published by New American Library, a division of
Penguin Group (USA) Inc., 375 Hudson Street,
New York, New York 10014, USA
Penguin Group (Canada), 90 Eglinton Avenue East, Suite 700, Toronto,
Ontario M4P 2Y3, Canada (a division of Pearson Penguin Canada Inc.)
Penguin Books Ltd., 80 Strand, London WC2R 0RL, England
Penguin Ireland, 25 St. Stephen's Green, Dublin 2,
Ireland (a division of Penguin Books Ltd.)
Penguin Group (Australia), 250 Camberwell Road, Camberwell, Victoria 3124,
Australia (a division of Pearson Australia Group Pty. Ltd.)
Penguin Books India Pvt. Ltd., 11 Community Centre, Panchsheel Park,
New Delhi—110 017, India
Penguin Group (NZ), 67 Apollo Drive, Rosedale, Auckland 0632,
New Zealand (a division of Pearson New Zealand Ltd.)
Penguin Books (South Africa) (Pty.) Ltd., 24 Sturdee Avenue,
Rosebank, Johannesburg 2196, South Africa

Penguin Books Ltd., Registered Offices:
80 Strand, London WC2R 0RL, England

First published by Signet Eclipse, an imprint of New American Library,
a division of Penguin Group (USA) Inc.

First Printing, February 2013
10 9 8 7 6 5 4 3 2 1

ALWAYS LEARNING   PEARSON

Prologue

I was born on a dark night, under a Dark Moon in a sky turned bloodred with power and prophecy.

Some say it was a less than fortuitous beginning to a new life of power, but as I squalled my way into the world, none of those bound to love me were disturbed by it. Why should they have been? Magic was everywhere.

It was burning in the wall of flames that surrounded the birthing bed.

Bubbling in the vases of sacred water positioned at North, East, South and West.

Trembling in the blessed earth sprinkled all over my grandmother's prized Aubusson rug.

Even spinning in the air that whipped around the room in a frenzy.

Yes, magic was all around me. How could it not be when hundreds, thousands, of members of our coven were there, gathered right outside the walls of my grandmother's garden, straining for their first glimpse of the enchanted one? Of me.

The news of my imminent birth spread quickly—which was no surprise as it was the most anticipated, most celebrated, occasion the coven had seen in many years. Since the birth of my own mother some two hundred odd years before, probably. After all, it's not every day that a seventh daughter bears a seventh daughter, let alone does it on the seventh day of the seventh month. In fact, our historians swore that it had never happened before.

Tales of my expected power spread until they became a thing of lore. Or even worse, until all those stories—all those whispers—became the norm. The expected. I would be great, powerful, untouchable by nearly all witch standards.

It was one hell of a birthright for a scrawny, five pound baby, but my family was convinced I would live up to it. As were my coven, the Council and the entire magical world.

And when the sky split straight down the middle, when it was rent in half by the most powerful forces of Heka—of the goddess Isis, herself—I moved from creature of lore to portent of legend.

Lightning spun through the sky like a whirlwind, whipping around and around as it tore through my grandmother's roof and through the third and second stories of her house until it found me tucked safe in my mother's arms on the ground floor.

And that's when it hit, lighting up my mother and me—the whole room, really—in a strike of such brilliance that it could be seen for endless miles. It disappeared as quickly as it had come, leaving the two of us untouched—except for the golden mark that appeared on my neck and collarbone.

A circle with the outline of a pointed half circle above it, it was Isis's most sacred symbol—a magical tattoo that nothing could remove and one that no one had been gifted with before me.

The legends and the expectations grew. And grew. And grew. Until no mortal could possibly live up to them.

Especially not me.

One

My humiliation is complete.

I can see it in their faces, in the way some are trying desperately not to look at me while others can't stare long or hard enough.

I can see it in the embarrassed flush on my father's cheeks and the clenched hands, wandering gazes and tapping toes of my sisters.

And, most of all, I can see it in the way my mother's amethyst eyes have glazed over with mortified tears. In the way she keeps clicking together the heels of her favorite, ruby red pair of cowboy boots—like if she hits the perfect spot she'll spiral out of the room just as Dorothy did all those years ago.

Too bad there's never a tornado around when you need one.

I try to tune them out, to close my eyes and pretend that I'm up in my room, practicing, instead of standing here in the middle of my Kas Djedet—my magical coming out party—making a complete and total ass of myself. If I can do that, if I can just forget my audience of legions, then maybe this once I can find a way to make the stupid spell work.

The fact that it never has before is utterly inconsequential to me now. Everything is, except making fire.

Please, Isis, just this once. I beg of you.

There's no answer, but then I didn't really expect one. Except for the day I was born, Isis has been notably absent from my life. You'd think, by now, I would have learned to stop asking.

Still, I concentrate on the spell as hard as I can, repeating the words over and over again in my head like I've been taught. The charm itself is child's play—or at least, to a certain kind of child. But I've never been able to do it. Never been able to do *anything* when it comes to magic, no matter how much I study or how hard I try. Why I let my family talk me into believing tonight would be different, I'll never know.

Maybe because I wanted to believe it as much as they did.

Still, I'd warned my parents, weeks ago, that this party was a bad idea. Told them that I was going to fail. That I absolutely, positively could not do what they so desperately wanted me to.

They'd refused to listen.

"You're simply a late bloomer," my mother told me. "Your powers will unlock on your nineteenth birthday and you'll do fine. Isis knew what she was doing when she marked you. Trust me."

"You're just nervous," my dad concurred. "Once you're up there, the magic will come."

"Performance anxiety," my oldest sister, Rachael, commented with a smirk that was a long way from sympathetic. "Good luck with that." Still, despite her amusement, it was obvious that she hadn't expected me to fail either. But then, why would she? No one in my family fails. At anything. And certainly not at magic. There hasn't been a latent witch on either side of my family tree for seven generations. And if there *was* going to be one, it certainly shouldn't be me.

After all, with my birthright, I should be loaded with

power. Showered with it. It should be leaking out my pores and lighting up everything I touch.

Instead, it turns out that seven is *not* my lucky number. I can't do even the most basic spell.

I try again.

Nothing.

Again.

Nothing.

In the audience, someone clears his throat, coughs, and the small amount of concentration I've been able to muster shatters. I glance around—I can't help myself— and once again see the shock, the horror and disgust, rolling off the witches and wizards gathered in my family's ceremonial ballroom.

Even my own family looks ashamed, like they can't believe I'm one of them.

It's the last straw and more than enough to get me moving, to have me jumping off the circular stage set up in the center of the room and zooming out the French doors that lead to the patio.

Behind me, my mother shrieks my name. In a booming voice, my father demands that I return to the ballroom at once. But I'm running full out now, scrambling to get away from the pity and the revulsion radiating from so many of the guests. They've come from all over our territory, all over the *world*, to witness the Kas Djedet of the youngest, and supposedly most powerful, Morgan daughter. What they've witnessed instead doesn't bear thinking about.

No, I tell myself, nothing can make me go back there. Not when the joke that is my nineteenth birthday party is still in full swing, and maybe not even when it's over.

My black designer cowboy boots, bought by my mother especially for tonight, pound over the hard, packed earth as I flee my yard for the safety and comfort of the peach orchard behind my house. The sweet scent of the fruit tickles my nose but I'm too busy sprinting down row after row of trees to notice. The only thing clear in my head is the need to get away.

I don't come to a stop until I'm at the lake at the very end of my family's property. It's my thinking spot, the place I've been coming to brood and cry and reflect since I was a little girl. As far as I know, I'm the only member of my family to come here, and if I'm lucky, it will be the last place they think to look for me.

Frustrated, fuming, I yank off my eight hundred dollar boots—which are supposed to help me channel magic and instead have only aided in channeling mortification—and hurl them, one after the other, into the lake. As they sink, I feel an incredible surge of satisfaction welling up inside of me. The first satisfaction I've felt all day, all week. All year.

Screw magic, I tell myself as—mindless of the Dolce & Gabbana party dress I'm wearing (again courtesy of my mother)—I sink down onto the moist dirt surrounding the lake so I can dangle my feet in the water. Being a latent witch isn't the worst thing in the world. It just feels like it now because of the party.

Most days, it's actually a relief not to be able to practice magic. After all, who needs the hassle? The responsibility? And who actually wants to touch all those gross potion ingredients, anyway?

A couple of tears roll down my face and I brush them impatiently away. I will not feel sorry for myself. I. Will. Not. Feel. Sorry. For. Myself. It's stupid and useless and utterly selfish. My life is better than a lot of people's, even if it doesn't feel like that right now.

Leaning back on my elbows, I gaze up at the beautiful night sky above me. And repeat the admonishment again and again, until I almost believe it.

I lay there until the heat of the summer night sinks straight through the cold brought on by nervousness and humiliation. Until my arms fall asleep from resting so long in the same position and my neck gets a crick in it for the same reason. And still I don't move. I can't. I'm transfixed by the idea of what comes next. Or, to be more specific, what doesn't.

What am I supposed to do with my life now that it's clear, once and for all, that I am *never* going to follow in my family's boot steps.

College?

Backpacking through Europe?

Getting a job—a regular, run-of-the-mill *job* with no magic involved?

Is it too much to contemplate all three?

The possibilities stretch endlessly in front of me, not nearly as disappointing as they should be. I'm actually a little excited, to be honest, at least until reality comes crashing back down. There's no way my mother will let me do any of those things. No way my parents will just let me walk away from centuries of coven tradition to lead my own life somewhere else. It simply isn't done. At least not for me, the youngest princess in Ipswitch's royal family and second in line to the throne, right behind my only brother. Latent witch or not, my place is with the Ipswitch royal family of witches. No other choice will be tolerated.

Depressed, I pick up a handful of rocks, then skip them across the surface of the lake, one after the other. I'm lost in thought, not paying much attention to what I'm doing even as I'm doing it—at least not until the last stone goes spinning out of control. Instead of jumping harmlessly across the water, it starts to glow, to spin. Then it rises straight up from the lake—about ten or fifteen feet in the air—and hangs there, whirling, for long seconds before it explodes outward. Hundreds of small, burning red pebbles fall harmlessly back into the water.

Eyes wide, heart pounding, I scramble back from the

edge of the lake. *Did I do that?* I wonder frantically. But if so, how? I can't even light a candle using magic, let alone make a rock levitate and then explode. It simply isn't possible. No matter how much I want it to be so.

I glance wildly around, looking for some explanation, some *reason* for that rock to have done what it did. But there's nothing, no one, on either side of me.

Just to be sure, I turn to look behind me . . . and that's when I spot him. Dressed in black, he blends completely into the surrounding trees. I wouldn't have seen him at all except for the small flames dancing back and forth along his fingertips.

The show-off.

"What are you doing out here?" I demand, keeping my voice steady with an effort. "This is private property."

I can't see his face, don't know who he is, but the power rolling off him is unmistakable. Not because of the rock or the fire—both are simple spells for someone who can wield magic. There's just something about him, an electricity that fills the air between us, that overwhelms the peace and quiet of the lake with the unmistakable aura of potent magic ruthlessly leashed.

"Looking for you." He walks toward me slowly and as he does, he extinguishes the flames that have moved from his fingertips to his upturned palms. I can still see him, though. Away from the trees, the light of the full moon silvers over him.

He's tall, with broad shoulders, a narrow waist and long, powerful legs. I strain to see more of him, to figure out who he is though I am certain I've never met him before. I would remember the aura of raw power that surrounds him—it's not something anyone could easily forget.

With that realization, suspicion whispers through me—an idea so outlandish I can't begin to credit it. But then he takes a few more steps and I get my first good look at his face. Razor-sharp cheekbones where they peek through his dark, chin-length hair. Full lips curled into a sardonic smile. Midnight eyes rimmed with impossibly long lashes. And a face so beautiful, so distinctive, that it's impossible to forget.

I don't know who he is and while there's a small part of me that wants to swoon at his feet, the majority of my brain is screaming for me to run. To get as far away from him as fast as I possibly can.

I choose not to listen.

Instead, I start to ask his name, but he's even closer now. So close that I can see *his* mark. It's a stark black tattoo in the shape of Seba, the Ancient Egyptian star, and like mine, it has been magically cast into the left side of his neck. It's an unusual place for a mark and seeing it has me stumbling, though I haven't moved an inch. I catch myself, force my knees to hold my weight when they want nothing more than to buckle.

Two thoughts hit me at once.

First, that I was right about the power. The man who is even now slowly, inexorably, crossing the last few feet between us, is a warlock of almost unimaginable skill. One who straddles the line between light and dark, white magic and black. One who even my very powerful parents speak about only in whispers, despite the fact that his brother has been dating my sister for years now. Though Ryder celebrates most holidays with us, Declan has never before been invited to our house. I'm not sure he was even invited this time. After all, my mother is adamant that we don't associate with his kind of power.

And secondly, that he's even better looking than the stories proclaim. And that's saying something.

He stops only a foot or so from me and though I want to look away, I force myself to meet the burning gaze of Declan Chumomisto, the man many consider the most powerful warlock living today. Some people say that he's losing it, that he's not nearly as formidable as he once was, but the rumbles only feed the rumors about him. Especially when he can still do things that most witches can only dream of. Standing here, across from him, I see no hint that he's lost any of that power. The air around us all but throbs with it.

Which, unfortunately, makes holding my ground even harder than I expected. Being near him is intense, overwhelming. So electric that I can feel every cell in my body vibrating with the strength of it. It's also scary as hell.

"What are you doing here?" I whisper, when what I really want to ask is *why me?*

Why am *I* reacting like this to you?

What did *I* do to attract your attention?

And why did you come out here to talk to me when there are so many more interesting people back at the house?

But reading minds must not be one of his gifts, because his smirk grows more pronounced as he answers my original question. "The same thing everybody else is, I would imagine. I came for Xandra Morgan's Kas Djedet."

Of course he had. My cheeks burn with shame and I want nothing more than to duck my head and run away yet again. From him, from home, from the whole nightmare of my nineteenth birthday. Still, I might have fled earlier, but I wasn't raised to be weak. Tilting my chin, I ask, "Did you enjoy the show?"

He laughs as predicted, but there's no mockery in the sound—which is totally not what I expected. "Your family will get over it."

"You know my family?" This is news to me.

"Not really. But isn't that what people are supposed to say at times like this? When royalty screws up, royally?"

Now I'm the one who's laughing. At least he's honest. "Yeah, I guess they are."

He glances down at my muddy feet. "You want to sit?"

Do I? With *him*? I don't know. His laugh has calmed my earlier terror, but my heart is still practically beating out of my chest. Declan Chumomisto is talking to me.

He extends a hand to help me settle, but I don't take it. I don't move at all for long seconds, just stand there watching him. He's a grown man, powerful beyond my comprehension, and I'm a nineteen-year-old screwup. We don't exactly have a lot in common, even if it's only midnight conversation that he's after.

"Is something wrong?" he finally asks, letting his hand fall back to his side. There's no impatience in the question, no condescension. Just an honest concern that has me forgetting the whispers about him. Or at least putting them aside for a while. Despite my best intentions, I lower my guard.

"You mean besides the fact that I just humiliated myself in front of my entire coven?" I answer, settling down beside him as he takes off his socks and shoes.

"And what looks like a fair amount of outsiders as well, don't forget."

"Gee, thanks. I was totally in danger of forgetting that, so I appreciate the reminder."

"I do what I can."

"And not a thing more, I bet." I narrow my eyes at him. "You need lessons on how to pretend to give a damn."

"Oh, I give a damn, Xandra. I just didn't think you'd want me to lie to you. I can try, but I warn you, I'm not very good at it."

"Someone like you doesn't have to be." I, on the other hand, have spent my whole life living a lie. Trying to be who my parents want me to be no matter how hopeless I am at it.

"Someone like me?" There's a dangerous note in his voice now, but I don't care. I'm feeling reckless.

"I'm not stupid. I know who you are. Someone like you doesn't have to answer to anyone."

This time it's his eyes that narrow. "You'd be surprised."

To the side of us a peach tree bursts into flame. For a moment, Declan looks stunned, like he can't imagine how it happened. I wonder what that would be like, to have so much power that it could just leak out like that without me even noticing. I don't think I'd like it — I'm too much of a control freak.

A second later, the fire goes out as suddenly as it started. He doesn't say anything else and neither do I. Instead, we just sit here, the tension between us ratcheting up with each minute that passes.

"So, why did you come?" I finally ask. "You don't know my family, don't know me. You aren't even part of our coven. So why did you travel halfway around the world—"

"Halfway across the country, not the world. I was in New York before this."

"Whatever." I couldn't care less about semantics when there are questions I want answers to. "So why, out of all the places you could be right now, did you choose to be here?"

"Because you're here."

My gaze jumps to his. I've been careful not to look him in the eye since those first moments, scared of what I might find. Now, I know that fear is justified. Power — overwhelming, unimaginable power — swirls in the obsidian depths and I can't look away. I'm pinned, as trapped here as I was back there on that stage. More so, really, because here it feels like there's no escape route. No back door to scuttle out of. Nowhere to run.

I desperately want to look away. But the pull is intense, like he's reached out and grabbed me and there's nothing I can do about it.

I'm playing prey to his predator.

Even worse, there's a strange lethargy pulsing through me. Pulling me into him. Pulling me under. I start to fall . . .

No! I don't know what game he's playing, but I won't be anyone's pawn. Not anymore. When I jumped off that stage tonight and ran away, I started a new path for myself. A new life. Instinctively, I know that this isn't it.

I finally find the strength to wrench my gaze from his and as I do, I feel this pop, like I've ruptured something deep inside. I gasp, wrap my arms around myself in an instinctive bid for comfort. Declan doesn't react at all, doesn't move a muscle, but I think he felt it too.

When silver sparks of energy whip through the air around us, I'm sure of it.

Reaching a hand out, I capture one of the sparks. I can't stop myself. I want to know, for just a second, what that kind of power feels like. It sizzles against my skin, crackling and spitting, burning me, until I open my fingers and let what's left of the spark fall back out into the air.

My palm throbs where it touched me, white hot and painful. It takes all my energy not to flinch, but I manage it. It's my turn not to react. Except, Declan knows—just as I did with him. He reaches out, gently cups my hand in his own. Strokes the fingers of his other hand lightly over the burn.

It should have been smooth, easy, but the second his skin brushes against my palm, the entire world ignites.

Fragments of memories I shouldn't have rush at me—
terrifying, fascinating, *compelling*. I close my eyes, try to
block them out, but they're still there behind my eyelids.
Still there, deep in my mind as every nerve ending I have
lights up like it's Christmas at Rockefeller Center.

I order myself to pull away, to break the connection
this one last time, but I can't do it. The pleasure, woven
as it is amidst the pain, staggers me and I can't do anything but sit there and soak it all in.

The pain dissipates as suddenly as it came, but in its
place . . . in its place is a silver Seba, identical in all but
color to the one on Declan's neck.

"What did you do?" I gasp, looking at the new mark
on my palm. It shimmers in the moonlight, is the most
beautiful—and frightening—thing I've ever seen.

"That wasn't me, Xandra." But he looks shaken as his
fingers close around mine in a grip so possessive it
makes my breath catch in my throat. I start to pull
back—this is too weird, even for the daughter of witch
royalty—but then I realize his hand is shaking even
worse than mine. It's enough, that hint of vulnerability,
to keep me here when every instinct I have screams at
me to flee.

"What—" My voice breaks and I clear my throat, try
again. "What's happening?" The sparks aren't stopping.
In fact, they're spinning all around us like a freak mid-
summer snow flurry—growing hotter, more plentiful, the
longer we're touching.

Declan doesn't answer, just shakes his head. I get the
impression, right or wrong, that for all his power and
experience he doesn't know what's going on any more
than I do. I take a step back and electricity arcs between
us, flowing from him into me and back again.

Every cell in my body is vibrating with it, every nerve
ending screaming with the agony of it. Just when I think
it's over, that the electricity is going to rip us apart, he

does something even more unexpected. He leans forward, and slowly lowers his mouth to mine.

Rockefeller Center turns into Mardi Gras, the Fourth of July and New Year's Eve all rolled into one. Too bad I never thought to wonder what happens after the ball drops.

Two

I shouldn't have drunk the damn tea.

I'd known it even as I took the first sip, but when I'd asked my mother what was in it, she'd sworn it was completely innocuous. Chamomile. Mint. A touch of lavender for luck.

Yeah, right.

But when I'd scented all three herbs in the cup she'd handed me, I'd decided to give her the benefit of the doubt. And while there'd been something else in there—something a little sweet that I couldn't quite identify at the time—I'd just put it down to the agave syrup my mom's been crazy about for months now.

I'm not a fan of the stuff but my mother looked so anxious, and so happy to see me after my six-month absence from Ipswitch, that I hadn't been able to disappoint her. I'd drunk the entire stupid cup in one long gulp to make up for the unpleasant taste.

I'm paying for it now, big time, which makes me an even bigger fool today than I was eight years ago. Back then, I'd still been trying desperately to live up to her expectations of me, to be the witch she wanted me to be. In the last few years, though, I've given up on trying to be something I'm not and have instead built a life for myself that I'm proud of—away from my hometown.

Away from the magic that is so much a part of this place.

Which, I suppose, makes my momentary gullibility more understandable. It's been a while since I've been around the insanity and I've obviously forgotten how bad it can get. It was a mistake to think that I would be safe here, even for a couple of days.

After all, from the moment I walked away from Ipswitch and the magical legacy I had no hopes of living up to, my mother has been desperate to get me back. She'll stop at nothing to find a way to unlock the powers I'm perfectly content without, will do anything to turn me into the Magic Barbie she's always wanted me to be. Maybe if I'd remembered that, instead of thinking about how much I'd missed her, I'd be in better shape now.

Live and learn, I suppose. And just to be clear, I'd *really* like the chance to live through this. I send the thought out into the universe even as I wonder if the number for Poison Control is the same as it was when I was a little kid.

I reach for the phone, but it falls to the ground before I can wrap my hand around it—whether by accident or design, I'm not sure. The fact that it's perfectly believable that my mother would have charmed the phone to prevent me from calling for help is one more glaring piece of evidence against both of us.

Idiot, idiot, idiot . . . The word thrums through my brain, a triple-syllable repeating chorus that echoes the three-step cramping in my stomach.

Squeeze, tighten, release.

Squeeze, tighten, release.

I-Di-Ot.

I didn't know anything could hurt this much. Had my mother inadvertently given me too much of whatever this is, or had I simply poisoned myself by drinking the tea too quickly? I call out for help, then curl myself into a ball and pray for death. Maybe living isn't all it's cracked up to be after all—at least not if it comes with this.

"Hey, Xandra, what's wrong?" Rachael asks from her spot near the door. Though she normally doesn't have much use for me, her most prominent power *is* healing. My illness must have called to her, overcoming her usual lack of interest.

"Tea," is all I manage to say, but it's enough. She rushes into the room and lays a cool hand on my forehead.

"Mom's crazy," she tells me. "I swear, your latency has pushed her completely around the bend."

"What did she give me?"

She looks at my pupils, shakes her head. "Best guess?" she asks grimly. "Belladonna."

I shudder at the confirmation of my worst fear. Guaranteed to bring out even the most latent magic—or so the herbal practitioners promise—belladonna has been a staple in witch gardens for centuries. I know my mom grows it, but I thought she burned it to get to its essence. Never in a million years did it occur to me that she would actually go so far as to feed me the toxic plant. Especially since, so far, the only thing it's brought out in me is my breakfast—an experience I really could have done without.

"What do I do?" I ask between cramps, forcing the words out from between my clenched jaws.

"I'm not sure. I need to look it up, and talk to her, find out how much she gave you. Probably no more than a berry or two, which isn't enough to kill you when brewed in a tea—it'll just make you really uncomfortable."

Another pain hits and I pull my legs even tighter against my stomach. "I think . . . uncomfortable . . . is an understatement," I gasp.

"I know, sweetie." She heads into my bathroom and comes out a few seconds later with a damp washcloth, which she lays across my forehead. "I'll be back in a little while, hopefully with an antidote to make this all go away."

"Pilocarpine," I tell her, because while I'm no good with actually wielding magic, I'm still up on all the plants and other ingredients that witches deal with—a leftover from when I was trying to be super-witch.

"I know. I'm just not sure if I can get my hands on any. I wouldn't put it past Mom to have gotten rid of all of it before you got here. You might have to suffer through this without it."

Terrific. I grit my teeth against another influx of pain and swear to myself that I am never coming back here again. I don't care about command performances anymore, don't care how much my mother pleads with me to return for special occasions. She's crossed so far over the line this time that there is no way I'll be able to overlook it. Winter Solstice or not, I am out of here the second I feel better.

If I ever do feel better, which seems doubtful right now. The pain is increasing as the belladonna works its way through my system, and I try not to think about what's coming next. Blurred vision, dizziness, hallucinations, convulsions. Already, I can see the edges of the walls bending, curving in on me. I tell myself it isn't real, that it's just another side effect of the belladonna, but the truth is I don't know what's real anymore and what's illusion.

It turns out my mother has indeed gotten rid of the pilocarpine and the potion my sister makes up to ease my pain barely touches the other symptoms. The next few hours pass in a blur as hallucination after hallucination works its way into my brain. Sometimes it's like the wall, when I can tell myself that it isn't really happening, but other times my imaginings feel so real that I can't help but get swept up in them.

Sweating, aching, trying desperately not to get sick again, I roll over and suddenly he's here, right in front of me. Declan. Like the last eight years have never taken place. Like he hadn't shown up, rocked my world and then abandoned me when I was at my most frightened and vulnerable.

Words of hate and fury burn inside of me, and I start to tell him what a bastard he is. But when I reach out to touch him he disappears, only to reappear next to the doorway. "Come with me," he whispers and somehow I feel his warm breath against my ear, though he is all the way across the room.

I glare at him, say that I'll never go anywhere with him again. He shakes his head sadly but it doesn't matter because then we're at the lake and he's kissing me like it's the last thing he'll ever do. I want to resist, to push him away, but it's been so long and he feels so good that I end up wrapping myself around him, pressing my body flush against his and kissing him with all the emotion I've locked deep inside myself.

That's when he disappears a second time and I'm left alone, stumbling barefoot through the rain-slicked forest in the middle of the night. It's like a replay of the night I first met him. I'm barefoot and frightened, and a part of me knows that I need to turn back. Need to find help. But I can't stop. There's this compulsion pulling me forward, this current deep inside of me that won't let me stray a foot off the given path.

My bare feet make a squishing sound as they sink into the waterlogged earth of the forest, followed by a loud, sucking noise as I wrestle them back out and take another step forward. Squish, suck, squish, suck ... I concentrate on the noise in an effort to keep myself sane. To keep my attention focused on something besides what's waiting for me at the end of this ill-advised trip through the woods.

I'm wrong, I tell myself desperately, even as I continue to put one foot in front of the other. This isn't the same. It can't be. It just can't be, because if it is, I'm afraid I'll start screaming and never stop.

It's been nearly eight years since the last time—the first time—and I—I squash the rest of the thought like I would a particularly disgusting bug. I'm not ready to go there yet, just can't acknowledge that that is what this late-night foray into the patchy wilderness around Ipswitch is all about. But even as I refuse to give the thought purchase, even as I lie to myself, the truth niggles through.

Somehow, it always does.

The wind picks up, turning the heavy rain into whips that lash against me. It stings the bare skin of my arms and legs and not for the first time I wish I had taken the extra five minutes to change out of my ridiculous party dress. While the hot pink silk was perfect for my birthday party, it leaves much to be desired when tromping through a wet, snarly forest at close to dawn.

Or whatever time it is—I can't be sure. Time is a nebulous thing for me at the best of occasions and now—out here—it's anyone's guess how many minutes have passed since I started on this journey.

In an effort to get my bearings, I glance behind me, hoping that I am still close enough to see the merry sparkle of the town lights in the distance. But, like the smooth, rich sound of Declan's voice in my ear, they have faded into oblivion.

I am on my own.

But then, these days, I almost always am. It's the curse of my gift. Or the gift of my curse—I haven't yet figured out which arrangement of words is most accurate. In the end, I suppose it doesn't really matter. I'm latent, powerless, undesirable in the world of magic. All of which I'm normally fine with—I swear I am—but that doesn't explain what I'm doing out here, stumbling around in the dark looking for God only knows what.

It's not the same as last time, I tell myself again firmly. I'm in a different part of the forest and I'm not nineteen anymore. Nothing is going to happen out here. To me or anyone else.

The storm is crazy loud now, thunder booming and rain falling in torrents. Every once in a while lightning scrolls across the sky, illuminating the world I have walked so blindly into. More than once, between flashes, I have stumbled over shallow roots. More than once I have plowed straight into the thick trunk of a tree.

I put my hand to my head, where it still stings from my last close encounter with a branch. I wonder if I am bleeding—assume that I probably am—but the rain is coming down so hard and I am so wet that it makes it impossible to tell.

I'm not normally so careless, but this compulsion is making me clumsy. Making me slow and more than a little crazy. Or maybe that's the belladonna?

I trip again, bang my shoulder hard against a tree. Pain shoots through my back and down my arm, and I tell myself to turn around. To go back. Whatever is out here can wait until the morning, wait until I'm not risking life and limb with every step I take deeper into the dark obsidian of the forest.

The thought makes perfect sense, and still I don't turn around. I can't. No matter how I try to convince myself otherwise, I know that tonight I don't have a hope of moving my feet in any direction but forward. I am a slave to the sensation that has wrapped itself around me—much more frenetic, much more terrible, than it was that time eight years ago—until there isn't an inch of my body that isn't on fire as I stumble around out here in the middle of hell.

I want to go back, but I can't. It's like someone has

wrapped a wire pulsing with electricity all around my torso, has burrowed the end of that wire straight inside of my stomach so that every molecule of my being feels like it's being lit up by thousands of watts of electricity. With each breath I take, with each moment I resist, the flame grows hotter. And then it's like someone starts to tug on that line, to reel it in—to reel me in—yanking me closer and closer to destruction, to devastation, with each step that I take.

The more I struggle, the harder they pull—which only makes me struggle more. It's a vicious circle, one I have no hope of escaping.

Suddenly the burn ratchets up a thousand volts, jangling every nerve ending I have. It sears my skin, my lungs, every organ in my body and for long seconds I wonder if I'm in the middle of being struck by lightning once again.

It isn't lightning that's ripping through me, though. It's the knowledge that I am close to the discarded.

Close to the raped, murdered, mutilated, burned, destroyed.

Close to the forgotten.

Even as I wonder who she is, images of her last moments tear through my brain with the power of a jackhammer.

She fought hard, this one, kicking and screaming and struggling, while he raped her. She clawed his face, pulled his hair, bit at him until he slammed her headfirst into the wall. Then she didn't fight anymore, even as he nearly ripped her apart.

For a second my own thoughts go even more cloudy, more confused. There's a ringing in my ears and a sickness in my belly that have nothing to do with my own situation and everything to do with hers.

This is what she felt like in those last few moments—disoriented, confused, in pain. So much pain.

I try to shake it off, to concentrate on the here and now, but it's impossible. Her agony is all-consuming and it hits me like a runaway semi, rips me right off my feet and sends me tumbling into the muck.

I gasp for breath, start to scramble back to my feet, but that invisible force has me pinned to the earth. Fear rips through me, and as I feel his hands closing around my throat, I tell myself desperately that it isn't real. That it isn't happening—not now. Not anymore. I am not this poor girl and he, the monster who did this, is far away from this desolate dumping ground.

It almost works.

At least until lightning splits through the sky, so bright and omnipresent that it illuminates everything around me for one heart-stopping second.

The trees, with their long, leafless branches.

The large rocks strewn along the side of the makeshift path I have been wandering.

The huge mound of newly disturbed dirt that I am standing only inches from.

In that split second, as light fills up the world all around me, scorching my retinas and making me slam my hands against my eyes in a futile bid for protection, I know that I have found her.

I drop to my knees and begin to dig.

I'm not at it very long before I touch something that isn't dirt. Though it's still dark outside, I know right away that the cold, stiff thing I have found is human. The knowledge is deep inside of me.

The second my fingers close around the slender appendage—I'm guessing it's an arm—images slam through me, more powerful and real than any that have come before. Her long black hair is covering her face and she's screaming, her fingers curled into claws as she tries for his face. But he keeps his head turned away from her so that her sad, weak defenses bounce harm-lessly off his shoulders and the back of his skull.

I feel her pain, her terror, as if it is my own and the still lucid part of my brain screams at me to let go of her, to scramble backward, to run far and fast in the opposite direction.

I can't move, can't step away. Can't do anything but kneel here, holding on to her and reliving every second of her last minutes on earth.

A cry splits the air and it takes me a second to realize that it is me. That I am the one making the high, keening noise that falls somewhere between a scream and a whimper. And then suddenly Declan is here again, hold-ing me, burying my face against his chest as he moves us away from the body. Away from what is left of that poor, poor girl.

The second his arms come around me, the pain less-ens, as if he is somehow muffling the connection between me and the dead girl.

"What's going on?" I demand, sobs wracking my body. "What's happening to me?"

"You really don't know?" He pulls back to look at me with those mysterious, onyx eyes of his and the noise inside my head gets bad again.

"No!" My fingers tangle in the wet fabric of his shirt, claw at the firm, resilient flesh beneath as I struggle to get closer to him. Struggle to make it stop. When he's touching me, nothing seems quite as bad as it really is.

He curses softly, strokes a not quite steady hand down the back of my head, over my short black hair. "Sssh," he whispers to me. "It's going to be okay, Xandra. I promise, it's going to be okay."

"How?" The word is pulled from deep inside of me. "I felt her die, Declan, felt everything that bastard did to her deep inside of me, like it was happening to me. And it won't stop. It just keeps playing in my head, over and over again. I feel like I'm losing my mind and I can't make it stop."

He stiffens against me, his whole body going rigid with a fury I can't begin to understand. Long seconds pass before he finally says, "I can make it stop."

He speaks with such conviction that it's easy to believe him, especially when the dead girl's voice stops speaking to me inside my head. "How?" I whisper. "Please, tell me what to do."

He doesn't answer and before I can press him, help arrives in the form of the Ipswitch police department and my parents. I'm hugged and coddled by my mother, by my father, by the police chief who is also my godfather, and long minutes go by before I realize that I can no longer feel Declan.

I look around desperately, hoping to catch a glimpse of him, but he isn't here. The buzzing in my head is back even worse than before, her pleas articulating themselves inside me—one after the other—now that Declan is no longer here to keep them at bay.

They rise up, overwhelm me, and that's when I start to scream. This time I don't know if I'll ever be able to stop.

Three

Rachael's hand crashes against my cheek. "Come on, Xandra! Snap out of it."

"What's wrong with her?" my mother demands hoarsely. "What's she doing out here in the rain?"

"She's hallucinating, Mom. Thanks to you and your bright ideas."

"I didn't know—" My mom stops speaking abruptly and I wish I could do the same. Could just close my mouth and stop the god-awful racket spilling out of me in all directions.

But it's impossible. I'm lost inside the hallucination, inside the dream that's actually a memory but feels like something else. Something more.

Rachael slaps me again and this time I slap back. She seems to take this as an encouraging sign, because the shaking stops even as her voice grows louder. "Come on, Xandra. Come back to us."

It takes a little while, but eventually I do just that, locking the screams deep inside myself.

"She's dead." They are the first lucid words I can form.

"Who's dead?" my mother asks, her eyes filled with concern even as she tries to wrap her arms around me.

I stay stiff, not yet willing to forgive her for the torture of the last few hours.

"It's just a dream," Rachael says. "She's drugged. Remember?"

She's talking to my mother, but I nod anyway. I know she's right. Even at its most terrible, what I'd just experienced had simply been a dream. A memory of my nineteenth birthday, that long ago night, come back to haunt me. That's assuming it had ever really left.

Still, something feels weird, off, and I wrack my brain trying to figure out what it is. Pulling away from my mom and sister, I stumble to my feet.

For the first time since I came around, I realize that it wasn't *all* a dream. I'm outside, wind and rain licking at my face and dormant peach trees all around me. My feet are buried in mud.

The urge to scream wells up with the memories, but this time I'm the one who slaps it back. Belladonna or not, I'm stronger than this. Yanking my feet free, I start to stagger back down the path toward home.

"Where are you going now?" my mother asks, her voice rife with concern.

I don't bother answering as I shuffle down the path to the house. With every step, I'm conscious of Rachael and my mom behind me and the memories all around me. I ignore them all as I stumble up the stairs to the back door and then down the hall into the bathroom, figuring my destination is self-explanatory. Besides, after the crazy, mixed-up acid trip of the last few hours, I don't trust myself to say anything nice to my mother.

I force myself into the shower, let the steaming water parboil me for a while as I try to make sense of my jumbled thoughts. It was just a dream, I remind myself again. It couldn't be anything else. After all, Declan was there, as was Uncle Mike, my godfather, and he'd died nearly five years ago. Because of the drug, I was open, vulnerable, and the memories I've suppressed for so long had come rushing back. That's all there is to it. There is no other girl lost in the woods waiting for me to find her.

So why do I feel so out of sorts then? Like my entire

world is about to come crashing down on me? One belladonna poisoning and it's as if the whole existence I've built for myself away from here doesn't exist. Which is crazy. I'm a successful business owner in Austin, have friends and a life that have nothing to do with the person I once was. One day, no matter how crazy, can't erase all that.

And still the hallucination niggles at me. I climb out of the shower, dry myself off. Do everything in my power not to think about Declan. I've only ever seen him in person that one time, right after my party, though he's haunted my dreams ever since.

I thought, after I went away from here, got an education and a job, dated a few men, that the memories of him would fade away. But they haven't. I'm stuck with them the same way I'm stuck with the stupid Seba in the middle of my palm. Not because I'm pining for him—goddess forbid—but because something about his magic reaches out to me, connects us. If I could identify it, if I could figure out what it was, I would sever it completely.

But I can't figure it out, so I'm stuck with him creeping into my dreams when I'm at my most tired and unguarded. Once, when I first got to Austin, I poured the whole story out to a shrink—minus the magic parts, of course. He told me it was normal for me to dream of Declan, considering how he's so tied into the worst night of my life.

And yet, today excluded, very little of what I dream about him feels like a nightmare.

That night by the lake, the night of my nineteenth birthday, we'd talked for hours. Had kissed and touched until I'd felt more connected to him than any other human being ever. He'd bowled me over and after a few hours I'd been seriously thinking about taking the next step. About giving up my virginity to Declan. He hadn't allowed things to go that far, though, had refused to let anything get out of hand.

I'd thought it was because he was beginning to fall for me as I was falling for him, but in the end, it was the exact opposite. He'd walked away like I was nothing and, except for his continued appearances in my dreams, I haven't seen him since.

Which is exactly how I like it. Stupid, one-night crushes aside, my new life is exactly the way I want it.

Feeling better than I have since I got to Ipswitch, I reach for a towel to dry my hair, and that's when I get my first real glimpse of myself in the mirror. I look like hell—again to be expected after the morning I've had— though everything is the same as it's always been. Same purple eyes. Same too-full lips. Same pale skin and freckles across my nose. Same black hair—

I freeze then, staring in dismay at my short, razor-edged cut. It's the same cut that was in the dream/hallucination/whatever the hell I'd just had and it's the same cut I've worn for the last four years. It isn't, however, the same hairstyle I'd had back when I'd known Declan.

And yet, in the dream, it had been so clear. He'd held me, had run his hand over my cropped hair even though, when he'd known me, my hair had skimmed my waist.

Another trick of my doped up mind? I wonder. Or something more?

For the first time since I walked away from that forest so many years ago, I strain to remember the details. Hot pink dress, pouring rain, Declan holding me. All of those memories check out. It's just the hair that's out of place. Just the hair that doesn't fit. My hair . . . and Lucy's.

Horror swamps me as I remember what I had once forced myself to forget. Lucy had short blond curls streaked with blue. I'd seen them in her struggle with her killer, then seen them again as they exhumed her body.

The woman in my hallucination today hadn't had those cute, multicolored curls. No, her hair had been long and black and straight.

My knees buckle at the thought and I catch myself against the vanity, then hold on for dear life as the truth finally sinks in.

Either I'm losing my mind and giving in to drug-induced paranoia, or there's another girl out there in the forest, just waiting to be discovered.

What does it say about me that I'm suddenly not sure which is worse?

"I have a surprise for you!"

Heedless of the closed door, my mother rushes into my room, a large, gift-wrapped box clutched in her arms. I glance at her, glance at the box, but don't say anything. Not that there's anything to say—the fact that I'm packing even though it's only Friday afternoon is pretty self-explanatory. If I'm lucky, I can be back in Austin by nightfall. After this morning, spending the Solstice and Christmas alone doesn't seem so bad.

"What are you doing?" she gasps, dropping the box on the antique desk in the corner and rushing across the room to me. "Where are you going?"

Again, answering seems redundant. But the barely hidden tears in her voice give me pause, make me feel guilty despite myself. Dropping my favorite pair of jeans onto the bed, I turn to her. "I can't do this, Mom. I can't be who you want me to be."

"That's not true. I don't you to be anyone but who you are."

"Which is why you nearly killed me from belladonna poisoning today?"

She turns bright red, looks at everything in the room *but* me. "That was an accident. I promise, it will never happen again."

Yeah, right. I point at the pretty pink and white polka dot box in the corner, a color scheme that is about as far away from who I am as that hot pink Dolce & Gabbana from my coming-out party was. "What's in the box?"

If possible, she looks even guiltier—which just confirms my suspicions. "Oh, that. It's nothing. Just a present for your sister."

"Oh, yeah? Which one?" I stroll over to the box, carefully take off the bow. She hadn't been all excited about giving this to one of my sisters when she'd come into the room. She'd wanted to give it to me.

"Umm, Hannah."

"Really?" I rip the paper off the box, and it's exactly as I suspect. A brand new pair of purple cowboy boots, size eleven. "Hannah wears a size eight, Mom."

"Oh, right. My mistake. Sometimes I get confused between all you girls." She stumbles over the lie—my mother is the sharpest queen our coven has ever had and she's never been confused a day in her life. Suddenly her face brightens. "Well, since they are the wrong size, maybe you would like them? It would save me the hassle of having to take them back to the store."

Raising an eyebrow, I just stare at her, waiting for her to crack. But she's not royalty for nothing and now that she's found her story, she's sticking to it. "Come on, Xandra. Try them on. Hannah probably won't like them anyway, since they're not red." She smiles encouragingly.

"I don't do cowboy boots, Mom." Not since my nineteenth birthday anyway. "You know that."

"Yes, but these aren't just any cowboy boots. They're Luccheses." She says the last with more reverence than she's ever shown me.

"I don't care. I don't want them."

"Please, Xandra. They'll be good for you."

"No. You mean they'll be good for you. If I wear them, you can pretend—for a little while anyway—that there's still a chance that I'm not latent. But that's not true, Mom. It doesn't matter how many pairs of boots you buy me or how many different ways you can find to poison me. I'm never going to be the witch you want me to be."

"That's not true!" For a second I think she's going to break form and tell me that she loves me, that I'm already exactly who I need to be. But then reality comes crashing in. This is my mother, after all. She proves I'm right when she continues, "We just need to try some new things . . ."

And then she's off and running, leaving me far behind as she paints a picture of the glorious future I'll have as soon as I stop being so stubborn and figure out how to beat this latency thing. She talks about it like it's a disease to be cured. Or a mountain to be conquered.

But after a minute or so, I can't take any more. It's the same old thing I've heard a million times before, which just proves that I'm an even bigger sucker than I think I am. Not this time, though. This time I'm standing my ground, no matter what my mother says.

I turn my back on her. Start packing again. Tune her out completely as I focus on folding my underwear and jeans with the most perfect of creases. The sooner I get this done, the sooner I can leave.

"Please, Xandra, won't you stay?" my mom asks, laying a tentative hand on my shoulder. "I know I made a mistake with the belladonna. It's not one I'll make again."

Her voice wavers, just a little, and I can feel myself weakening. But I can't do it, can't go there. It will only make me crazy.

Though I'm not done with my clothes, I cross to the bathroom and start packing up my toiletries. I'm going for distance, but my mom follows me. I try to ignore her, but when I reach for my moisturizer I get a glimpse of her in the mirror. She's watching me, her amethyst eyes filled with tears. One spills out, tracks its way down her cheek and I know, belladonna poisoning or not, I'm not going anywhere. At least not before Christmas.

Damn it.

"Do you promise you'll lay off the witch thing?" I ask her sternly. "No more potions, no more cowboy boots, no more magical charms?"

"I promise." The tears disappear as she claps her hands in childlike excitement before throwing her arms around me. "No spells, no tarot cards, no shells, no stars. I'll cancel everything."

My stomach churns a little at her list. What exactly had she planned to do to me this weekend?

"How exactly do you cancel the stars, Mom?" I stand stiff in her exuberant hug, wishing I'd done a better job of holding out against her. "I kind of thought they were a nightly occurrence."

She laughs a little nervously. "Don't be silly, Xandra. You take everything so literally."

It's hard not to when I spent my morning recovering from being poisoned. I don't say that, though. My mom already looks like she's been kicked. Anything else would be total overkill.

Before I can poke around anymore about what is obviously a very elaborate plan for my weekend at home, there's a knock on the door.

"Come in," I shout as my mother busies herself pulling out everything that I had just put into my suitcase.

My brother, Donovan, sticks his head in the door. He's the oldest of all my siblings and the only boy—both of which means he will one day take over the throne. He's been raised with that understanding and while he spent a number of years running wild, he's settled down in the last decade or so. His once wild black hair has been cut into a style even my father would approve of and these days his blue eyes are more compassionate than turbulent.

At the moment, he's focusing that compassion exclusively on me, and I have to admit it's making me twitchy. Like there's something I'm missing. But when he speaks, it's to our mother and not me.

"Hey, there's a woman at the door. Says her name is Salima and that you're expecting her?" Though there's nothing in his face or voice to give him away, the twitchiness morphs into uneasiness. Something is up, and as usual, I'm the last to know.

"Oh, of course." My mother flutters her hands ineffectually—something she does only when she's trying to act harmless—and the uneasiness becomes out-and-out dread. "I'd forgotten Salima was coming to dinner."

She turns to me. "I can't wait for you to meet her. She's fantastic. You'll love her." She heads for the door. "Why don't you wear your black dress to dinner? It'll go great with your new boots."

"What black dress?"

"That one." She's out the door before I can think of a response—my mother knows how to make an exit—and I'm left, staring at my bed. The black dress in question is spread out on the comforter, complete with bra, panties and socks to go under the boots. The kicker is I didn't bring it from home. In fact, I've never seen it before in my life. It certainly wasn't there five minutes ago.

"Go ahead and wear the dress," Donovan says as he slings an arm over my shoulder. "It'll give her a thrill. She's really missed you."

"Yeah, well, she has a funny way of showing it."

He snorts. "Belladonna's nothing. You should have seen me after she poisoned me with mandrake. She was a little overenthusiastic and I couldn't get out of bed for three days."

"When did she do that?" I couldn't keep the surprise

from my voice. "Why would she do that? You're not latent."

"She did it long before you were even born. I was fifteen or sixteen and my magic was pretty weak. I think she was afraid that I was doomed to a life of pulling rabbits out of hats—which wasn't exactly an optimum career choice for the crown prince. So she did what queens have done for centuries—took matters into her own hands."

"Did it work?"

"Not even a little bit. For which you should be grateful or this morning would have been a whole lot worse."

"Believe me. I am. The belladonna was more than bad enough." But I'm also curious. "So when *did* your powers kick in? It's not like anyone could exactly call your magic weak now."

"It was a gradual thing. By the time I was eighteen, it was better, but a lot of what I've got going on has been building for thirty years or so, Xan." He pauses, then sits on the bed—making sure not to crumple my new dress. "It could still happen for you, you know."

"I doubt it. And what no one seems to understand is that I don't want it to happen for me. I like my life, just the way it is."

"Oh, yeah? Is that why you spend so much time running away from here? Because you're happy with the way things are going for you?"

"I'm not running away. I just don't come to visit very often because when I do, I get poisoned."

"Hey, that's an argument you can use the next time you come home, but it doesn't explain your absence this time. She's never poisoned you before."

"How do you know? I did have a bad case of the flu when I came home for Christmas last year."

He laughs, as I intended, but soon turns serious. "You know, I don't like to give advice . . ."

"Who are you trying to kid? You live to give advice."

"Only when I'm right. And I know I'm right on this."

"You always think you're right."

He grabs my hand, holds tight. Nerves flutter deep inside me, but I beat them back. You learn early in the Morgan house that showing fear is a very bad idea. "Don't spend so much time running from who you don't want to be that you forget who you are."

He pauses, like he's just delivered the wisdom of the ages and this time, I'm the one who laughs. "Seriously? That's the best you've got? You sound like a bad self-help book. Or a fortune cookie."

"Xandra—"

"I'm fine, Donovan. Totally happy. And barring any-more run-ins with poisonous plants, I plan to stay that way. I don't need magic in my life. I don't want it."

He doesn't say anything for a minute, just keeps my eyes pinned with his. One of his gifts is truth-reading, but he has to be looking into your eyes when he does it. So I keep mine steady and ignore the little voice deep inside of me that warns me to look away. It's the same voice that's been screaming danger at me since I drove into town last night.

For long seconds, my brother doesn't say anything. But I can feel him searching for the truth and it makes me a little sick. Not because I don't believe what I'm say-ing, but because I need so badly for him to believe it too. I'm tired of being poor Xandra, the one everyone in the family—in the coven—feels sorry for. That's why I like Austin so much. No one there expects me to be anything more than what I am.

"If that's really the way you feel," he finally says with a wry grin, "you might want to stay away from a couple of Mom's dinner guests."

The dread grows until my entire stomach feels en-cased in ice. "What has she done now?"

"Well, first off, she invited Micah to the pre-Solstice dinner and celebration."

"Micah?" The dress suddenly makes perfect sense—especially its low neckline and high leg slit. "Why would she invite *Micah*?"

"Well, he is a witch doctor," he answers, tongue completely in cheek. "I'm sure she thinks he can fix you."

I flip him off. "I'm not broken. And if I was, there's no way I'd let him get his fingers or his magic anywhere near me. Been there, done that."

"Baby, there's no way *I'd* let him get anywhere near you again. Doctor or not, the guy's a scumbag."

Scumbag is an understatement, but I don't tell my brother that. The last thing I need is for him to turn Micah into a braying jackass at the kickoff of the biggest event of the year. Not that Micah doesn't totally deserve it, but it's been five years and I figure it's time to grow up and let bygones be bygones. As long as I don't actually have to break bread with the jerk while my mom does her best to lead us toward a happily never after.

"Why doesn't she ever ask *me* before doing stuff like this?"

"Because she knows you'll tell her not to."

"She just promised me she wouldn't do this anymore." Then again, this had probably been put into motion a long time ago. I can't hold it against her when she'd promised only ten minutes ago to call everything off.

"This is Mom. She'll be pulling stuff like this until she's six feet under. She can't help it—the queen is used to getting her way."

"Yeah, well, she needs to get unused to it." My eyes narrow as I go over the last few minutes of conversation in my head. "Besides, I'm not worried about Micah. But you said there were two dinner guests I had to be concerned about. Who's the other one?"

"The witch whisperer."

"The witch what?"

"Whisperer," he says with a grin. "You know, like those guys on TV. Horse whisperers, dog whisperers, cat whisperers . . ."

My eyes go wide. "Are you talking about those people who claim they can talk to animals and find out what's wrong with them?"

"Pretty much."

"But I'm not an animal. I am perfectly capable of communicating what's going on inside of me—I don't need someone to interpret that."

"Hey, you're preaching to the choir. I think Mom's nuts to hire some woman to woo-woo her way inside of you and figure out why your powers are locked up."

"Really? Woo-woo? Is that the technical term for what she does?" I know the sarcasm isn't helping anything, but my irritation is escalating with each new revelation. Still, I try to calm down. "Besides, there's nothing to worry about. Mom said she's going to cancel all the weird things she has planned for me."

He snorts. "You don't actually believe her, do you?"

Well, I had when she'd promised. Now I'm not so sure. "You don't think she's really going to sic a witch whisperer on me, do you?"

"Oh, I think she already has. Salima got here twenty minutes ago—long before the party is scheduled to start. And since Mom's outside right now, tinkering with your car, I think it's a pretty good bet that she hasn't called anything off."

"My car? What's she doing to my car?"

"You don't want to know."

"Actually, I do. I have to get back to Austin next week and I'm going to need my car to do it."

He has the grace to look sheepish. "It'll be fine. I'm sure she'll fix it tomorrow—*after* the Solstice."

I snort. "Well, that makes one of us." My mother has

been known to hold a grudge—especially when things don't go her way. And tonight is definitely not going to go the way she wants it to, not after she stood here and lied to my face.

"You worry too much." He pulls his keys out of his pocket, shakes them at me. "You can take my car if you want. Go get some dinner in town. Catch a movie. They can't stay here all night. I'll even go with you, if you want company."

Again, he's the only one of us who believes that Mom won't have Micah, Salima and a cast of thousands camping out in the family room waiting for me to return. But, poisoned at fifteen or not, he doesn't know her like I do. I stare at those keys and think about how easy it would be to grab them and run. Maybe all the way back to Austin—I'm sure Donovan wouldn't mind the three-hour drive tomorrow. Yes, I'd promised my mother I would stay, but that was before she broke all the rules and started taking my car apart.

I actually reach out for the keys before my pride—and my temper—kick in. "I'm not running away."

Donovan's face goes slack with surprise. "What do you mean?"

"I mean, I'm not doing it. I'm twenty-seven years old. I have to stop running at some point."

"This is true, but I'm not sure tonight is the night you should make your big stand."

"I can handle Micah. And the witch whisperer."

The more I think about it, the more pissed off I get. Not that that's a surprise. Since I was sixteen, being at home has been an exercise in anger management. What does surprise me, though, is the layer of shame right under the fury.

Is having me for a daughter really that bad? Am I really such an embarrassment to her that she has to revert to not only dragging old ex-boyfriends back into my life, but also to hiring any and all other nut-jobs who apply for the job of "curing" me? Part of me wonders if the witch whisperer, or whatever she is, is the one who suggested the belladonna that nearly killed me this morning.

Not that it matters. My mom's the one who did it. The one who did *all* of this.

"Hey? You okay?" Donovan pulls me into a hug, but I can't take the comfort he's offering. I hate that he can see the hurt deep inside of me when I've worked so hard to keep it hidden—even from myself.

"Look, don't let her get to you, Xan. She's just being Mom. You know how she is when she sets her mind to something."

I do. And that's what I'm afraid of. This has been a problem since I was a teenager and it's going to continue to be a problem—unless I end it, once and for all. Talking to her doesn't work so it's time for something more. Something drastic.

Donovan obviously doesn't know where my thoughts are going, though, because he presses his keys into my hands. "Don't let pride get in your way," he tells me. "I'll cover for you. I'll even call you when the coast is clear."

"Do you really think my not being there will change anything? What do you think she'll do if I don't show up at dinner—or the Solstice ceremony planned for afterward?"

"Make us suffer through Micah's impersonation of a guy with a stick up his ass? Tell us to sit back and let the witch whisperer have a crack at the rest of the family?"

I laugh, as Donovan intended. It's not as hard to do as I thought it would be—witch whisperer really is the worst description ever. "Well, yeah, but when that's over, she's just going to come up with a new plan to unleash my magic. And then another one and another one and another one after that. I've had enough. This has to stop, and I'm going to stop it. Tonight."

"Oh, yeah?" My brother eyes me curiously. "And how exactly are you planning to do that?"

I turn and stare at the black dress. I may not have magic but I have more than my fair share of ingenuity. "Watch and learn, Donovan Morgan. Watch and learn."

Four

When I walk into my mother's parlor—an old-fashioned word for an old-fashioned room—thirty minutes later, all eyes shift to me. And not because I'm fashionably late.

With the help of Willow, the sister who's closest to me in age, I've made a few adjustments to the dress my mother left for me. I've also made a few adjustments to the rest of my appearance . . . and from the look on my mom's face as she heads straight for me, they are adjustments she does not like. Which, of course, is exactly what I was going for.

"What do you think you're doing?" she hisses at me. Her left hand wraps around my upper arm and she tries to tug me from the room, but I'm not budging. She's the one who led us to this showdown and I'm not going to be the one who flinches first.

"You wanted a witch, so I gave you one." I smile at her out of a face turned lime green from the judicious use of my sister's underbase.

With her free hand she reaches for the broomstick I'm carrying. I refuse to let go—this time I am not backing down. "Are you insane?" she demands. "Get that hat off of your head!"

"What's the matter, Mom? Too pointy?"

"You look like a crazy person."

"And you act like one, so I think we're even."

She glances around, realizes the eyes of her most important advisors are on us and fakes a laugh. "Silly, Xandra, this isn't a costume party," she trills in the voice she reserves for recalcitrant subjects. A few seconds later, she ruins the benevolent affect by getting right in my face and whisper-yelling, "Don't push me on this, Xandra."

A few years ago that tone would have been enough to have me falling into line. But I'm not a teenager anymore and tonight it feels like I'm fighting for both my freedom and my sanity. "Why not? You keep pushing me. You're just upset because I finally decided to push back."

"I'm trying to help you and this is the thanks I get? You dressing up like a caricature on the most important night of the year?" She keeps tugging at me until finally I give in and let her lead me into the foyer and away from the hundreds of prying eyes.

"I want you to accept me for what I am, to stop doing ridiculous things to try to force something that just isn't there. I don't think that's too much to ask."

"No offense, Xandra, but I'm not the one being ridiculous right now. Not to mention completely demeaning our entire culture."

Touché. And as tears of anger and humiliation tremble on her lashes, I could almost be sorry for dressing up like the Wicked Witch of the West. Almost. "A witch whisperer, Mom? Really?"

Her eyes narrow dangerously. "Who snitched?"

"So many people know that you can't figure out who it was that told me? And you think I'm demeaning?"

"You need to trust me on this, Xandra. You'll be so much happier once we find a way around your disability and your powers are unlocked."

My disability? Is she kidding me with this? I stare at

her, openmouthed, and wait for her to take back what she's said. But she just stares at me, mouth grim and eyes enraged. "There are no powers to unlock, Mom. When are you going to get that through your head?"

"Of course there are." She waves a dismissive hand that does more to make my blood boil than anything else that has happened today.

I start to let her have it once and for all—so angry that I am not at all interested in pulling my punches— when a soft but clear voice comes from right behind me. "Pardon me, Your Majesty?"

We turn as one at the interruption, my mother's eyes laser bright as she focuses on the woman who dared to interrupt our conversation. I don't recognize her—and believe me, I'd remember her if I'd ever seen her before. She's short and rotund, and her bright orange hair is swept into a beehive of epic proportions. Even worse, she's dressed in a bloodred cocktail dress that clashes with her hair and does nothing to flatter her figure. But the pièce de résistance, the train wreck I just can't take my eyes off, is the pair of bright yellow cowboy boots with turquoise piping that are peeking out from under the gown's jagged hem.

Who in their right mind wears bright yellow boots? With a red dress? To the biggest social event of the year?

Tonight is the most important holiday celebrated by our coven and the house is filled with my parents' friends and most trusted advisors, all of whom have come to make merry before the solemn ceremony begins at midnight. I can't imagine this woman falling into either of those categories, especially considering the way my mother is looking at her at the moment—like she's a particularly disgusting specimen of fungus.

"This is *not* a good time." My mom is speaking between clenched teeth now, a surefire sign that she's furious. Which makes no impact on me, because I'm just as angry. Maybe more. How can she not see that she needs to get off the crazy-wheel? *My disability? Really?* It's not like I'm not a successful, functioning member of society. So what if I can't make fire out of thin air? We have matches and lighters for that.

Surprisingly, the scowl on my mom's face makes no impact on the woman standing in front of us, either. "Forgive me for saying so, Your Highness, but I think this might be the perfect time." She lays one hand on my mother's back and another on mine and gently pushes— as if she expects us to actually allow her to lead us across the foyer to someplace more private.

Neither my mother nor I budge. We may be acting like a couple of recalcitrant toddlers, but there's no way we're going to let anyone treat us as such.

"Salima, not now."

My eyes widen. Salima? *This* is the witch whisperer? This woman who is more clown than clairvoyant? *This* is who my mother expects to save me from myself?

Now I'm more insulted than angry.

"But, Your Majesty, if you look beyond the obvious, you will see that this"—she waves a hand up and down to encompass me—"costume is a step in the right direction. While it is a rather unschooled attempt, I admit, Xandra is obviously trying to engage in a dialogue with you about her feelings. I know she has not chosen to take a conventional route, but this might be even better than that. If she really feels that being a witch makes her into some kind of caricature, then that could be why she is latent. Her powers simply can't function when her ideal of herself is so incredibly skewed. In fact—"

"Seriously?" I interrupt, unable to take the bullshit any longer. I turn to my mother. "This is who you hired to fix me?"

Her eyes narrow and in those moments she is every

inch the queen. "Which should tell you just how broken I think you are."

It's a direct hit but I'll be damned if I let her see it. I turn to Salima, force a smile that I am far from feeling. Especially when it becomes obvious that my mother is actually considering her idiotic words. "Thank you so much for your remarkable insight into my neuroses, Salima. I can't tell you how much I appreciate it. But, if you'll excuse me, I need to mingle."

She nods, knowingly. "Bitterness is understandable. No one likes to be confronted by their own weaknesses—"

A strangled scream escapes from my throat—I can't help it—and for a few precious seconds I imagine what it would feel like to wrap my hands around Salima's throat. And squeeze.

The cold slap of my mother's voice banishes the fantasy. "The only place you're going is back to your room to change. I will not be made a fool of in front of my entire coven."

"But you have no problem casting me as the fool, right?"

For a second her eyes soften and I think we're making progress, but then Salima ruins it. "Am I to understand you think being a witch makes you a fool, Xandra?"

"It's neither me nor your legacy that makes you foolish, daughter." My mother's gaze sweeps over me, all traces of compassion gone. "You do that all yourself."

It's another direct hit, but that makes me only more determined not to back down.

"In that case, let me get on with it." I wrench my elbow from her grasp. "I'd hate to deprive anyone of their entertainment."

"Xandra, I forbid you to go back in that room until you've changed."

Amusement wells up—I can't help it. "I hate to be the

one to break the news to you, Mom, but you aren't in the position to forbid anything. I'm no longer a lost sixteen-year-old kid who will do anything for your approval."

"Xandra!" She all but stomps her foot with impatience and at another time I might have been amused to see the queen engage in such a mundane display of emotion. But with her one step away from breathing fire and my father bearing down on us like a ship that has set an immovable course, I figure this might be a great time to dive into the center of the crowd. So I do, hightailing it across the lobby as fast as my old-fashioned lace-up boots can carry me.

After all, the wicked witch thing might be a tad bit of overkill, but that doesn't mean I don't still have a point. And I'm determined to make it. I'll be damned if I spend the next ten years of my life waiting for her to give up on the belladonna and go a more poisonous route. I'm latent and that's never going to change. The sooner she and the rest of my family accept that, the better off we'll all be.

Determined to make the best of the evening—despite its inauspicious beginning—I head to the bar. But I've barely got my first mojito in hand when darkness creeps over me, blinding me for a second to all but the agonized screams in my head. For long seconds I am bound and bleeding, my head bowed and long dark hair waving in the wind. And there is pain, terrible pain that rises up like a tsunami and all but engulfs me.

My knees tremble and I'm shaking so badly that I slosh my drink over the rim of the highball glass. It's the cold wet on my hand that brings me back. I glance around to see if anyone noticed—after all, I'm not exactly inconspicuous in this getup. But everyone seems to be doing their studious best to ignore me, as usual, and for once, I'm grateful for the anonymity.

Still, as I slam my drink back in one long swallow, I can't help but wonder. *What the hell was that?*

After dodging Micah for the third time in as many hours, I duck out of the house and into my mother's garden. She and my father are already out here, preparing for the most important celebration of the year, and while I'm not keen on running into either one of them I figure being outside is a million times better than staying in the house and trying to avoid Micah, Salima and anything else my mother has cooked up for me.

I cut through the garden to the fence, and as I walk along it, I'm overwhelmed by the peacefulness of the night. The storm from earlier passed by a couple of hours ago, leaving the sky clear and the night glistening with the residue of leftover raindrops. Standing out here, surrounded by this tranquility as I watch the final preparations for the Solstice, I can almost pretend those terrifying moments earlier in the parlor never happened. After all, with my track record, it's hard to imagine they could mean anything—except that being at home completely stresses me out.

It's the only explanation, unless, of course, that belladonna my mother slipped me actually did the impossible. Which it didn't. I lock the thought away as soon as it comes to me. Of all the places I've been—or want to go in my life—that is definitely not on the destination list.

I glance over at where my family is setting the altar. Normally, I'd be in the middle of the preparations, helping my family and our advisors with any nonmagical tasks, but right now it seems wiser to keep the length of the garden between us. Especially with the fulminating looks my father keeps giving me. So, instead of joining the others, I content myself with watching from behind the rows upon rows of plants. Besides being queen, my mother is one of the great potion-makers of our time, and there are few natural ingredients she doesn't grow somewhere on the property.

Here, in her garden, it's all flowering bushes, vines,

and a few trees, along with a variety of stand-alone flowers that she harvests whenever she needs them.

Bright and happy marigolds to cleanse and foretell.

Soft and sweet peonies for protection and prosperity.

Wide-open primrose for truth-telling.

Delicate and lacy rue for healing.

Daisies for lust. Laurel for love. Lilies and mugwort and patchouli for fertility and row upon row of hydrangea for fidelity.

People are nothing if not predictable in what they want.

I turn to the right, watch as my mother clips some clover and dragon's blood. She'll use the clover for cleansing her tools while the dragon's blood will amp up the power of her spells. Not that her magic needs any help, but there are a lot of people here and the magic she generates will need to touch them all.

Just beyond the garden, a crowd has gathered. Though many of our coven will do their own Solstice ritual later, gathering here at my house—sharing this holiday with my family and so many others—is a tradition few who live in Ipswitch choose to ignore. Anticipation lights up the air around me, their excitement and exuberance nearly tangible as the clock creeps a little closer to midnight. It's hard not to get caught up in it, even for someone who has no power. Especially since tonight is perfect for the Solstice *Seshaw*, or prayer ritual.

The air is crisp but not too cold, while the fence and the forest shield us from the shadowy presence of the wind that moans through the wild, untamed forest that lies a few hundred feet beyond the boundaries of the garden.

Stars twinkle against the ebony backdrop of the sky above and a full, vanilla moon hangs invitingly in the center of the display. For a moment, just one moment, I wish for a tiny drop of the power that pulses all around me. I would love to draw down the moon, just for a moment. It's a simple spell and one I've seen performed hundreds of times, but it's one of my mother's least favorites so I know it will not be cast tonight. Which is a shame because I can almost feel the energy boost now.

In the center of the garden, my father and siblings have joined my mother to finish preparations for the ritual. Spells are murmured as they place nine candles to mark the boundaries of the circle.

One for each of the shares of magic that fell to Egypt over four thousand years ago.

One for each member of my family—except for me.

It's not a deliberate oversight, simply the way things have always been. Which is fine by me—especially as I don't have the magic necessary to hold what would be my part of the circle if they ever decided to give me the chance anyway.

Besides, I'm not exactly dressed for it. Every one of my family members wears a long emerald robe that skims the ground. My mother and sisters are also draped in charms and amulets meant to both honor and release the ancient magic, while Donovan and my dad each wear a crystal pendant big as a baby's fist.

They are the protectors, and the enforcers, of the circle. My mother is the caster, my sisters the binders. And I, along with the rest of the coven who have turned out for the ceremony, am the observer.

But not yet. It is not quite midnight and there is still work to be done, traditions to be observed.

My mother walks to the altar set up in the center of the circle. On it she places the Rw, a heavily embossed book with covers made of pure Egyptian gold and pages of the most fragile papyrus. It has been passed down to my mother from the women in her family—mother, grandmother, great-grandmother—for well over a thousand years and it contains the most sacred texts and spells of Heka. Though it is my mother's, she won't touch it again until the ceremony is over. First and foremost because it contains the energy of ages, energy that can bleed into and color her own *Seshaw*, and secondly, because she doesn't have to. She has the entire book, and all of its spells, memorized.

As do I. Not that I'll ever have a chance to use that knowledge. But the girl I once was—the girl who had hoped to be a different kind of woman—had spent months and years memorizing every spell so that one day she'd be ready to take her mother's place. Ready to be a conduit between the sacred and the mundane.

I feel someone watching me and suddenly I'm as disgusted by the costume I'm wearing as my mother is. Not because I'm ashamed of my lack of power—as she is—but because I've made something special into something profane. I can blame my mother if I like, but if I'm honest, the onus for this is all on me. Lacking power or not, I can't stand before the goddess in this mockery of ceremonial dress.

I glance at my watch. I have ten minutes before the ritual starts.

I slip into my room, clean the green gunk off my face and get dressed in the outfit I had planned to wear all along—a flowing emerald green skirt and jacket made of the softest velvet. It's not a robe, and I don't want it to be, but it's a beautiful outfit, one that even my mother can't find fault with.

I make it back to the garden just as the ceremony is starting.

My mother stands in the middle of the circle, next to a tall, gold-colored candle. Positioned equidistant around her are my father and siblings.

Rachael, the healer, stands due North, a green candle in her hand and chains with the sacred Eye of Horus around her neck. Bold, determined, protective, she is Earth.

Next to her, halfway between North and East is my father, a purple candle in one hand and a sacred ceremonial athame in the other. He is strength and unparalleled knowledge.

To the East is Nadia. Ankhs make up each loop of the gold chain-link belt that rests low on her hips. A yellow candle floats directly in front of her. Compassionate and kind, she is Air.

Beside her, holding the position of Southeast, is Donovan. His candle is black, his tool a long and wickedly curved sword. He is the silent and omnipresent eternity.

South is Noora. With a crimson candle in her hand, the knot of Isis decorating her robe and her red hair dancing in the wind, she is Fire. Bright, inviting and too often explosive.

To her left is Willow. Her candle is silver, her tool a wand made of cedar. She wears amulets of the lotus flower to signify transformation. She is strong, unbending will.

Standing due West is Hannah. She holds a half-full chalice in her right hand, a blue candle in her left. She is Water, cool and indispensable.

And finally, completing the circle is my favorite sister, Sophia. She wears a headdress with the sacred symbol of Djed. Her candle is orange and she is wild, unpredictable, determined action.

My mother lights her candle with a flick of her wrist and a prayer in the ancient Egyptian tongue. Then she lifts her arms and fire sizzles along her fingertips before leaping straight to Noora. Noora's candle alights followed by the other eight and then, urged on by my mother, flames race around the sacred circle growing higher and higher until they nearly eclipse my view of my family.

My sisters' voices join my mother's and an ancient prayer of thanksgiving fills the air around us all. It is burned into the earth by the fire, carried to the heavens on the curls of smoke that rise and rise and rise.

As the prayer ends, Hannah reaches into her chalice and flicks water from her fingertips onto the surrounding fire. It spits and hisses, grows even taller for one breath-taking moment and then dies in an instant.

The circle has been cast.

Though the crowd all around me is silent, energy throbs between us. It's always like this at the Winter Solstice when, on the longest night of the year, we celebrate the rebirth of the sun.

I know this ceremony by heart, have witnessed it twenty-six times now, and still the prayer and the power of it take my breath away. Inside the circle, my mother starts a new fire—a living symbol of the bonfire of old—and above us the moon burns bloodred.

Another prayer and seven stars shoot across the sky just as my mother reaches for the dragon's blood she cut earlier. She casts it into the flame and my father follows suit with mint and myrrh. The smoke mingles, curls, begins to drift outside the circle and into the crowd.

I have no magic, no power, and yet as the smoke reaches me I feel something quicken deep inside of me. It's happened to me before, when I'm in the presence of spectacular magic but never to this degree. Never this strongly.

I know it's the herbs, understand that they are used to strengthen the pull of the ancient Heka, but it doesn't matter. The blood in my veins starts to thrum, to vibrate, electricity sparking along every nerve ending. It scares me a little, has me pulling back as Willow approaches the fire and, with a few murmured words that I have no hope of hearing, casts her own plant into the flames.

The smoke swirls and seethes, spiraling up, up, up to the sky. She has tossed in her namesake, willow, for help in divining the stars.

Then it's Donovan's turn. He approaches the fire with arms full of bayberry and cedar—always the protector.

But before he can do more than invoke the favor of Sekhmet, a scream rends the air.

It's followed by a second scream and then a third one, and my nerves catch fire. By the time a fourth shriek rips through the empty field behind me, I'm running straight for the forest and the unmistakable sound of distress.

Five

Others follow me. I can hear their footsteps pounding along the ground behind me. But I'm quick and agile—as the eighth child, I had to be if I had any hope of getting out of my elementary school years alive—and I keep the lead.

I know Donovan will yell at me later about running off when he couldn't protect me—you can't break a circle like the one my family formed without observing certain rituals—but it sounds like someone is dying. Every second could count.

Panicked, I remember the vision from earlier, the one I've tried so hard to convince myself was a dream. I hit the forest at a dead run, dodging around trees and jumping over roots by memory alone. Thank goddess I ditched the boots along with the witch costume.

The people behind me slow down as they try to find their way in the darkness, but this is my forest. I know every inch of it.

Even so, I pull my cell phone out of my pocket, hit the flash light app so I have a better chance of finding the person who's screaming. She's still yelling, so I'm following that sound, but the last thing I want to do is plow right into her because I couldn't see her.

As I run, I try to figure out what's wrong. She sounds like a young girl, and I'm hoping she's just lost. Maybe she got bored at the ceremony and wandered off, then lost her way. Or maybe her flashlight went out. There are a million different reasons for her to be this upset — it doesn't have to be the one my mind automatically goes to. The one I faced when I was barely more than a girl myself.

Within a couple of minutes, Micah, who knows these woods almost as well as I do, catches up to me via his own flashlight app — who knew there'd be a circumstance when I'm actually glad to see him — and we run side by side until we stumble upon her about five hundred yards into the forest. A young girl about sixteen or seventeen, she is kneeling at the foot of a huge oak tree and trembling uncontrollably.

"Are you all right?" I ask, crouching next to her. "What's happened?"

"I . . . she . . . can't — " She says more, but she's crying so hard that those are the only words I can make out.

"It's okay, sweetheart." Micah speaks soothingly as he, too, squats down beside her. He takes her hand in his, strokes it softly even as he uses his index and middle finger to take her pulse. "Let's take a couple of deep breaths together and then you can tell me what has you so upset."

I pull back a little, let Micah do his thing. Though he was a lousy boyfriend, he's a hell of a doctor and within three minutes he has the girl significantly more calm. He's also checked her over well enough to ascertain that she's not the one who's hurt and learned that her name is Brenda and that she's nineteen years old.

I try not to let the coincidence remind me of my own hysterical flight through this forest when I was her age.

When it seems like she's got the freaking out down to a minimum, I once again ask, "What's happened, Brenda? Why are you so upset?"

She doesn't answer at first, but then — in a voice so low I have to strain to hear it over the soft whispers of the wind — she finally murmurs, "Someone's over there." She reaches out a shaking hand and points down a path to the left of where we are.

"Someone?" Micah asks. "Did he or she try to hurt you?"

She shakes her head, whispers, "I think she's dead."

Micah and I lock eyes over her head and he looks as alarmed as I feel. "Why do you say that?" I demand.

"I was taking a shortcut through the forest, hoping to make it to the Solstice ceremony before it got too late, and I tripped over her. She's next to the big, lightning-struck tree and at first, I thought she was just drunk, but"—she shudders—"she isn't moving and there's a lot of blood."

I leap to my feet, head for the path—and the tree—she's indicated, but Micah gets there first. He blocks me with his body. "You can't go down there," he tells me.

"We need to see if whoever she found needs help." I shove at him a little. We can't just leave the poor girl out here, bleeding, in the middle of the forest.

He doesn't budge. "It doesn't sound like she's simply hurt, Xandra. You know that as well as I do and the last thing the police need is us tromping around a crime scene. And I'm sorry to say it, but it's the last thing you need as well."

I know the words are coming before he says them, even think that I'm prepared for them—at least until they hit me with all the finesse of a two-by-four. He's right. I know that. I had nightmares for years after I found poor Lucy. Hell, I still have nightmares. What makes me think this will be any different?

And still, "We have to check. What if she's just unconscious?"

By now a group of half a dozen other witches has stumbled onto the scene. Among them is Detective Moira Montgomery, one of my least favorite people in the world. From the snarl curling her upper lip when she looks at me, it's obvious the feeling is more than mutual. I guess now that her father, my beloved Uncle Mike, is dead, she feels like there's no reason for us to hide our animosity anymore.

"What did you do now, feeb?" she demands in a querulous voice.

"It's called running. You should lay off the doughnuts and try it some time." It's a childish retort, and once it's out, I'm sorry I said it. But it was a knee-jerk, gut-level response to being called a feeb. As in feeble. It's a derogatory term for a witch without power and Moira has always thrown it around way too easily. Especially in reference to me.

"And maybe you should stay out of police business."

"I'm not in police business. This is private property, in case you've forgotten."

"I haven't forgotten anything. It belongs to the king and queen, of which you are neither, and as such is protected by the Ipswitch Police Department. But if you'd like, I can run you into the station and we can sort this all out down there. Including whatever part you've played in disturbing the peace."

"Whatever part I've played? All I've done is help calm the kid down." I speak through clenched teeth, even as I gesture to Amy, who is still huddled against the tree. I can't believe Moira's threatening me when all I've done is try to help. Not that I'm afraid of her—she may talk a good game, but there's no way she'd haul a member of our coven's royal family into the station house without a damn good reason.

But that's not the point. Finding the girl, the body, Amy tripped over is.

"So, that's the statement you're sticking with?" she asks, reaching into her back pocket for goddess only knows what.

"Seriously?" I demand. "You really want to do this

now? A girl is either dead or dying and you want to have a pissing contest with me?"

She barely glances at Amy. "She looks okay to me."

I roll my eyes, but before I can say anything else—like call her a moron—Micah jumps into the fray, explaining what we know so far.

Moira listens to him as she would never listen to me, then asks Amy to take her to the body. When the girl balks, not wanting to go anywhere near it again, I volunteer to lead the way. Though it's the last thing I want to do either, I know exactly what tree she's referring to. As a child, I climbed it a million times and as a teenager, I let Micah carve our initials into its warped and bumpy trunk before I knew better.

I glance at him out of the corner of my eye and from the way he's watching me, I know he remembers all the things we did at that tree as well as I do. Which is a shame, because some memories are better off forgotten.

"How do *you* know where the body is?" Moira asks as I skirt Micah. Her eyes are narrowed suspiciously.

"These are my woods." It's a simple answer but it's also the truth.

I weave around a clump of trees in the center of the path and start booking it. That poor girl shouldn't be out here any longer than absolutely necessary. But I've made it only a few yards down the path when I slam straight into the obscene. The whole area stinks of violence and black magic.

From the way both Moira and Micah stop, I know they feel it too. Every instinct I have screams at me to run in the other direction, but I can't do that. Not when some poor girl went through hell out here. Might still be going through hell.

I push forward, down a small hill and around a curve, aware as I do so that the tree in question is only a few feet in front of me. As soon as I clear the curve, I start sweeping the ground with my flashlight. It isn't long before I find her.

I see her feet first, encased in a pair of decorative brown cowboy boots. So she's a witch then, one of our coven—or at the very least a cowgirl who wandered across the path of the wrong dark warlock. She's face-down in the mud, wearing tattered blue jeans and a ripped University of Texas hoodie in burnt orange. The hood has been pulled up until it completely obscures her head.

Micah rushes past me, starts to roll her over, but Moira stops him. "No fingerprints," she barks, slipping a pair of latex gloves out of her pocket.

"She might not be dead," I object, though deep inside, I know better.

Moira focuses her own large flashlight—the reason it took her so long to catch up to Micah and me—on the body, and the huge pool of blood it's lying in. "She's dead."

But she tosses Micah a pair of gloves anyway.

Micah nods in confirmation, even as he slips on the gloves. He feels around her throat for a pulse, pulls back a hand covered in blood. "I think her throat is slit," he says weakly.

Moira nods, then pulls out the walkie-talkie she wears at her waist, orders a perimeter to be set up and a comprehensive sweep done of the forest. The look on her face says she knows she isn't going to find anything, but I know that doesn't mean it shouldn't be done. The warlock may be gone, but he might have left something behind.

The next hour passes in a blur. My mom and dad arrive with Donovan, and all three of them try to talk me into going home, but some invisible force keeps me pinned right here, watching as this new nightmare unfolds. I don't know why it matters so much, but I need to know who this girl is. Need to know what happened to her. Maybe because, standing here looking at her, I can't help but remember the last body I'd found.

That girl, Lucy Douglas, had been a college student at UT. She'd come to Ipswitch for what she thought was a romantic weekend with her new boyfriend and had ended up mutilated and strangled. It's been over eight years and I haven't forgotten anything about that night. Something deep inside warns me that forgetting tonight won't be any easier.

Donovan and my parents choose to stay with me and just like last time, no one—not even the new chief of police—can get them to move. Sometimes being royalty has its perks. I just wish we could use them for something other than viewing death.

Witchcraft Investigations shows up along with the more traditional CSI team and together they work the murder, taking pictures and measuring the magical signature that still hangs in the air all around us. It is dark and oppressive and stinks of blood magic at its most vile. It's not familiar to them, doesn't fit any of the signatures they currently have on record. Not that I would expect it to— warlocks of this caliber know how to disguise themselves.

After CSI finishes taking pictures in situ, Moira crouches down and rolls the girl over. As she does, the girl's hoodie falls off and there's a collective gasp from the small crowd gathered here, along with a muttered curse from both Donovan and my father. I don't make a sound. I can't. The first glimpse I get of her black hair throws me right back to my hallucination-that-was-really-a-memory-and-now-might-actually-be-called-a-prophecy from this morning. It immobilizes me, has my blood freezing in my veins. The girl in my dreams, the one who had lain battered and broken and bleeding in my parents' forest, had had the same exact hair.

Had I seen this coming? This morning, if I hadn't been so busy trying to bury the images, could I have somehow prevented this? Or is it all just a horrible coincidence?

"Do you recognize her?" I ask the group as a whole.

No one answers, and I finally move a few halting steps forward. Moira is so arrested by what she sees that she doesn't even bother to reprimand me. But she doesn't know about the hair, doesn't know about what I saw, and I can't help wondering what holds her and the others spellbound.

With effort, I yank my attention from her blood-matted hair and instantly wish I hadn't. One look at her vacant eyes and the gaping tear in her throat makes my stomach churn. No one should ever have to die like this.

"Does anybody know who she is?" I ask again.

Ipswitch is a relatively small town, made up mostly of witches and a few other creatures that go bump in the night. I haven't lived here in years, so it's not unusual that she doesn't look familiar to me. But Moira should recognize her. Part of the role of the small police department in this very low-crime town is to know the citizenry, simply because you can never tell when some kind of weird magic or otherworldly thing is going to happen. And if she doesn't, Mom, Dad and Donovan should certainly have some idea of the girl's identity.

When once again no one answers, I creep a little closer until I'm standing on the front line with my parents, Donovan and Micah, none of whom have said anything since the body was rolled over. And now that I'm this close, now that I'm staring at her from this angle, I finally realize what they're all looking at. Not the wound in her throat or the bruises all over her body. And certainly not her bloodstained hair. No, they are all staring at the large, black mark that covers her entire left cheek, a mark I've never seen on anyone else in my entire life.

At my first sight of it, I stumble backward, trip on a tree root and hit the ground, hard. I barely feel the fall. I'm too busy trying to wrap my mind around what I'm seeing. That girl, that poor girl who I'm becoming more and more convinced I really did see in a vision this morning, has been branded with a circlet of *Isis*.

She's been branded with *my* mark.

"You know, the whole purpose of sitting on that thing is to sway back and forth."

I'm curled up under a blanket on my mom's antique patio swing when Donovan finds me hours later. It isn't moving because I'm too shell-shocked to push, too shell-shocked to do much of anything but sit here and stare out into the garden I usually take such comfort from.

This morning, that's nearly impossible, especially with the ritual ring cast by my family still sitting front and center. Normally, it vanishes at the end of a ceremony as mystically as it appears, but the Solstice rites weren't completed last night and so it remains, a dark and lonely reminder of everything I would rather forget.

"You doing okay?" Donovan asks as he settles down next to me.

"Just peachy."

He snorts. "Yeah, that's what I figured." He doesn't say anything else for a while, just sits with me, swinging us back and forth in a slow, easy rhythm that makes me want to cry even as it relaxes me.

I ignore the prickles behind my eyes—crying won't do me any good—and instead let the warmth of everything Donovan isn't saying simply soak into me. I don't tell him, but I'm glad he came out here. Sometimes being alone isn't everything it's cracked up to be.

"They think I did it," I finally say, nearly choking on the words.

"*Moira* wants to believe you did it but she's not exactly objective. She's so blinded by hatred she'd arrest you for every crime that crosses her desk if she could."

"What's with that, anyway?" I demand. "I've never done anything to her."

He shrugs. "I think she's just always wanted to be you."

"Yeah, because being me is so great. I'm sure she'll change her mind once I go to prison for a murder I didn't commit."

"You're a princess, Xan. The one thing I can assure you with absolute conviction is that you are not going to prison."

"They think I did it," I repeat.

"No." He scoots over, hugs me to his side. I put my head on his shoulder despite my resolve to stay strong. "They don't know *who* did it so they're casting around, trying to figure out who in the community is strong enough to hide from them after doing something so terrible."

"Which should be reason enough for them not to bother looking at me at all. Yet here we are."

"Here we are." He starts to say something else, then stops himself and I'm left wondering what he's not telling me. From the look on his face, whatever it is is pretty serious stuff.

"Do you know?" I sit up straight, my hands clutching at his shirt. "Have you seen what happened to that poor girl?"

"You know clairvoyance is my weakest gift."

"I also know you didn't answer the question," I say with a glare.

He grins. "There's my Xandra. I knew my hard-ass sister was in there somewhere." He holds up a hand, his smile fading away. "And before you ask again, no. I have no idea who killed that girl. I just know that neither the chief of police nor any of the investigators—besides Moira—believe you had anything to do with it."

I should be relieved, but instead I'm just . . . numb. I slump against the back of the swing with a sigh, use my foot to rock it back and forth as I try to figure out what it is I want to say—and how I want to say it. Finally, I just burst out with, "Do you think it's possible that belladonna poisoning actually works?"

Donovan turns, eyes me sharply. "What happened?"

"Nothing."

"Xandra."

"Seriously, Donovan. Nothing happened. I was just wondering. You said the mandrake didn't work, but has Mom used belladonna on anyone besides me?"

"I don't think so."

"So none of the others had any trouble with their powers? Mom didn't have to do anything to kind of jump-start them—"

"No. Why are you asking?"

"I don't know. I had this weird hallucination thing when I was under its influence. I thought it was a memory, from before. But now I'm wondering if, maybe—"

"Don't go there, Xan. The whole thing's ridiculous. There's no way the belladonna did anything except confuse you about what's real and what isn't." He stands abruptly and in those brief moments he is every inch the future king, the usual indulgence he reserves for me buried under layers of royal detachment.

It only lasts a few seconds before he jogs across the porch and down the steps into the garden. "Are you coming?" he calls over his shoulder. The distance is gone and he's my big brother again. But I can't help being freaked out by the transformation. I've seen my mom and dad do it plenty of times, but not Donovan. Never Donovan, never with me.

"Where are you going?" I demand, wary of him in a way I never have been before.

"Mom needs some fresh clippings, since the Solstice

was ruined last night. She's planning a kind of makeup ceremony for tonight. One all of us will be involved in."

"All of us?" I repeat, a sick feeling starting in my stomach. I'm not very good with the whole ritual thing—I don't have much experience as anything but an observer. Add in the lack of magic and it's a recipe for disaster.

"Yep. You too." He pauses, holds out his right hand to me even as he grabs one of the pruning baskets Mom keeps at the bottom of the stairs with his left. "If you ask me, you should have been involved last night, too. Then you wouldn't have ended up out there in the middle of everything."

"You mean I'd have an alibi."

"You already have an alibi. The whole party saw you dressed like a character from the *Wizard of Oz*. You weren't exactly inconspicuous last night."

"And aren't you glad I wasn't?" I catch up to him, but instead of taking his hand, I pick up a basket of my own. "Where are we going to start?"

"With the bittersweet."

I stop dead, eye him with suspicion. "Seriously?"

"What? It's on the list." He waves a sheet of my mom's private stationery in my face, then shoves it back into his pocket before I can get a good look at it.

"I bet."

He just smiles, like he doesn't know as well as I do that bittersweet is rarely burned in rituals. Instead, it's placed in satchels and then charmed to encourage truth-telling.

We don't speak as Donovan clips several shoots of the bittersweet, complete with berries, but when he moves on to the basil—another odd choice for a ritual—he comments, "I love herbs. They're so much heartier than flowers."

"Not all flowers are weak."

"True enough," he agrees, even as he snaps a few basil flowers off the plant and drops them into my mom's compost bin. "But they are often unnecessary."

He clips a few large sprigs of basil and drops them into my basket. "Unlike the actual plant, which can be used a million different ways. Strange, isn't it, how we're taught to admire the bloom when it's so often the most dispensable part?"

"Not always." But two can play his game. I walk to the east side of the garden. It's the wettest area, and where my mother grows cattails. I clip a few, then return to Donovan and add them to his basket.

He looks down at the oblong spikes. "Feeling unsettled, little sister?"

"I thought you might be. What with all your talk of what's necessary and what isn't."

He just nods as he snaps a few more flowers from the basil plant. When he continues speaking, his voice is carefully modulated, like a professor in front of a class. I might even buy the act, except his eyes are a turbulent violet.

"Sometimes you have to pinch a bush back so that it can grow and you can get the most benefit from it," he instructs.

"Yeah, but what about the plant itself? It's kind of sad, isn't it, to think of it never flowering—never becoming what it could be—simply because it's of better use to someone if it never realizes its full potential?"

"Do you really believe that?" Suddenly he is focused exclusively on me.

Actually, I was just being contrary. But his intensity surprises me, makes me wonder what I'm missing. I decide to play along, and with a shrug I reach out and clip the last of the basil flowers from the bush. When I'm done, I raise one of the blossoms to my nose and inhale its rich, earthy scent. "I like flowers."

"Of course you do." He crosses to the back of the garden, to the fence lined with white oleander and pink bougainvillea. He picks a few of the oleander blooms and presents them to me with a flourish. His way of warning me to be careful.

I respond with a few angelica flowers and a sprig or two of thyme. Magic and bravery.

He laughs, then counters with a handful of chamomile and a small cactus blossom from the dry side of the garden.

"What exactly is it I have to patiently endure?" I ask even as I cut a huge bunch of parsley and drop it in his basket. I'm sick of feeling like I'm the last to know anything.

Donovan must have finally gotten sick of communicating with flowers, because he stops in the center of the aisle and refuses to let me go around him. "Having power isn't all it's cracked up to be, Xandra."

"I'm aware of that, Donovan. It's why I'm perfectly okay without it."

"Are you really?"

I exhale a long, frustrated breath. "I thought we covered this yesterday."

"So did I. But you're the one asking about belladonna again today." He pauses, like he's searching for the right words. Finally, he says, "You're going to have to trust me on this. Some things are better left unexplored."

"Tell that to Mom."

"I did. This morning."

"Oh, yeah? How'd she take it?"

He grimaces. "About like you'd expect."

"And yet, you're still here warning me."

"You're my baby sister. It's my job to take care of you."

I groan, completely exasperated. "I'm twenty-seven. It's my job to take care of myself. Besides, why the big change of heart?" It's my turn to watch him as he walks over to my mother's prize irises, then crouches down and strokes their violet petals. "Yesterday you told me not to give up, that my powers could still kick in, whether I want them to or not. Today you're full of all kinds of admonitions."

He doesn't answer and warning bells go off deep inside of me. "What did you see?"

His hand clenches involuntarily on the iris, crumpling the fragile bloom and snapping it off the stem.

"Donovan?" I squat down next to him, look him in the eyes and repeat, "What. Did. You. See?"

"Not enough." He pulls me into a huge bear hug and kisses the top of my head. "Not nearly enough."

Then he strides out of the garden like the hounds of hell are on his heels.

I stare after him for a long time, feeling like I'm riding a Tilt-A-Whirl. Like the whole world is standing still but I'm twirling by so fast I can't see anything but a blur of colors.

I'm missing something, but I don't know what. I wait for hours for Donovan to come back and explain things to me, until long after it becomes apparent that that isn't going to happen, even though he's left his basket of plants in the middle of the garden for me to deal with.

I mutter to myself as I gather up all the foliage and take it to my mother, who looks at me like I'm crazy. She has plenty of greenery left over from last night, she assures me. Though she does thank me for the thought.

I just nod and head back to my room as the feeling of unreality grows worse. As soon as I open my door, I'm overwhelmed with the lush, heavy fragrance of flowers. I glance around, try to figure out where the scent is coming from. And that's when I see them—bunches upon bunches of begonias covering my entire bed.

Okay, Donovan, I think as I walk over and lift one of the fragile pink blooms to my nose. *Message received. I need to beware.*

But of what? And more importantly, why?

Six

"I'll take a large latte with an extra shot of espresso."
I'm in the back room, mixing up dough for my world-famous (okay, Austin-famous) chocolate chip cookies when I hear the order—and the deep voice delivering it. It's been six days since I've heard that voice and I've missed it, and the man it belongs to. So, after checking to make sure my dough is in good shape—all it's missing are the chocolate chips—I switch off my purple commercial-grade mixer and scramble toward the front counter without bothering to take off my flour-coated apron or even smooth down my hair.

"I've got this, Jenn," I tell the teenage girl working the cash register.

"Sure, Xandra." Her voice is perfectly normal, but when she turns around, she's wearing a huge grin. I ignore it—and the fact that I know she's going to have something to say about my sudden reappearing act the second Nate, and his latte, exit my coffeehouse.

"I was hoping you'd be back today," Nate tells me as he reaches into his back pocket for his wallet.

"I was hoping you'd be in today. I thought I missed you in the morning rush."

"I was across town, on a case, for most of the day."

"I'm sorry to hear that." Nate's a homicide detective with the Austin Police Department, and though we're a relatively quiet town for our size, there's still more than enough work to keep him busy. After the better part of the week I just spent in Ipswitch, I've got a new appreciation for what he does—and what he goes through to do it. "How'd it go?"

"As well as can be expected actually. The perp is currently cooling his heels as a guest of the city and I am on my way home. It's the first night in two weeks that I'll be home before midnight and I plan on kicking back and actually watching the Stars game instead of catching the recap three hours after it's over. I'm still on call, but if there is any justice in the world, it will be a quiet night."

"You've been working late every night?" I ask as I take the ten-dollar bill he hands me and make change. "Did Austin have a run of homicides over Christmas that I don't know about?"

"My partner and I've been picking up the slack for everyone who's been out for the holidays."

"You didn't take *any* time off?" I want to kick myself the second the words come out of my mouth. I sound like I'm fishing. Which I'm not. At all.

"Part of Christmas. But holidays aren't much fun when you're alone, so I'd just as soon work."

I snort before I can stop myself. "You only say that because you've never met my family."

"Oh, yeah? Rough time at home?"

"You have no idea."

While there'd been no more bodies discovered—and I'd had no more weird effects from the belladonna—the rest of my days at home hadn't gone much more smoothly than the first two. Despite direct orders from the chief of police, Moira had insisted on hounding me whenever I left the house, and Salima, the crazed witch whisperer, had insisted on doing the same whenever I was at home. Needless to say, by the time I climbed into my hastily repaired Honda, I was chomping at the bit to get back to Austin, where things are normal—or at least as normal as they can be in a city whose official motto is "Keep Austin Weird."

"I swore to myself it will be longer than six months before I go home again," I tell Nate, who looks both sympathetic and curious. Not that I have any plans to satisfy that curiosity. One homicide detective on my ass at a time is more than enough.

The thought makes me nervous all over again and I wait for Nate to say something else or to at least give me a little wave good-bye before he heads out, but he makes no move to leave. And that's when I finally remember— I haven't made his coffee yet. The lapse makes me feel like an idiot, a feeling that's reinforced when I turn around and find Jenn staring at me from the kitchen, a hand clamped over her mouth to keep a laugh from escaping.

Real smooth, Xandra, I snarl at myself. *Real smooth.*

I go for the French roast, though Nate didn't ask for it specifically. But then he doesn't have to ask—he's been coming here long enough that I've got his order memorized. Our Costa Rican house blend in the morning with two extra shots, French roast in the evening with one extra shot.

"You know," I comment, glancing over my shoulder at him, "I probably shouldn't say this, since we're talking about my livelihood and all, but you might want to ease off on the caffeine a little."

His green eyes crinkle at the corners as he smiles. "You worried about me, Xandra?"

It takes me a few seconds to answer him—to be honest, I'm a little blinded by the grin. It lights up his whole face and showcases the dimple he has in his right cheek. I love that dimple, and am embarrassed to admit I've wasted more than a few minutes in the six months since he first darkened the café's doorstep thinking up one-liners that might have a chance of bringing it out.

He's never asked me out, and with his blond hair and boy-next-door smile, he's a far cry from my usual type. Still, there's just something about him that gives me a little buzz. Nothing major—not yet, anyway, but there's enough chemistry between us that if he asked me out, I'd probably say yes just to see what happens.

But this time, though he's laughing, I'm not trying to be funny. "More like worried you'll drop dead on the floor of my café," I say, sliding his coffee in front of him, sans lid. "Man cannot live by espresso alone."

His grin widens farther when he sees the skull and crossbones I've drawn in the foam. "You poisoning me, Xandra?"

I think of my mom and the belladonna—not to mention everything else that took place in the five days I was home—and feel my own smile droop a little. And now here I am, flirting with a homicide detective of all people. What does it say about me that death seems to be around every corner in my life?

"Not planning on it." The words come out more curt than I expected.

To apologize, and because Nate is such a good guy, I walk over to the baked goods display and pull out a giant sugar cookie—his favorite treat—and slide it across the counter to him. "To balance out all that caffeine," I tell him.

"Yeah, because loading up on huge quantities of sugar and butter is better for me," he complains, right before he takes a big bite of the cookie.

"Hey, you've gotta pick your poison."

"Can't you tell?" he asks as he slides the five dollar bill I handed him as change into the tip jar on the counter. "I already have."

Then, with a wink and another one of those killer smiles, he's gone, slipping out into the twilight stillness of the streets.

"Oh my God!" Jenn says, rushing back to the cash register the second Nate is out of sight. "Did you see the way he looked at you? He was totally imagining doing you right up against the espresso machine!"

"Jenn!" Heat creeps up my cheeks until I feel like my whole face is on fire.

"Don't even try to act innocent. He is *so* into you." She shoots me an arch look. "And judging from the way you ran in here when you heard his voice, I'm guessing the feeling is mutual. You don't abandon your cookie dough for much."

"I did not abandon my dough," I tell her. "And it most certainly is *not* mutual. Not that there's anything to be mutual. I mean, I like him. Of course I do. He's one of our best customers and he's nice. Why wouldn't I be personable to him?"

"Personable? Is that what you old people call it? Let me tell you, I wouldn't mind being *personable* with that either."

"Okay!" I fight the urge to clap my hands over my ears. "That's enough. We have work to do."

"What work are you talking about?" she demands. "I brewed the coffee while you were flirting with Mr. Wonderful. I also wiped the tables down, restocked the pastry display and got more napkins and go cups from the back. Barring the sudden onset of the apocalypse, I think we're set."

The front door picks that moment to chime, which is probably a good thing because I don't think I can come up with an answer to all that. Four teenage guys walk in and it's all I can do not to throw myself at their feet and thank them for being my salvation.

"That work," I tell Jenn, nodding to the group with a superior smirk. "I'll be in the back if you need me."

I escape to the kitchen, and my unfinished cookie dough. Jenn's set to work the rest of the evening and

Dara and Toby should be here any minute to help with the evening rush of students and couples on dates. Which means that as soon as I get the cookies done for tomorrow, I'm out of here. Considering I've been here since four this morning, I'm more than ready to head home and get some sleep—something else I missed out on when I was in Ipswitch.

It takes me only a couple of minutes to finish up the chocolate chip cookies and get them in the oven, and then I start on my secret recipe—the red velvet cookies that have made Beanz the busiest coffeehouse in the city.

My best friend and current roommate, Lily, thinks it's crazy that I walked away from being a princess to run this place, but that's because she doesn't understand that my favorite thing about this job—the baking and coffee making—reminds me a lot of what I used to do at home. From the time I was little, my mom drummed potion making into me—the importance of it as well as the excitement of creating something from a random sample of ingredients.

Unfortunately, I can't make a simple luck potion to save my life—let alone any of the more complex ones that Mom deals with every day. But what I can do, what I am good at, is mixing up coffee and bakery confections that literally fly out the door. It's a kind of potion making, I tell my mom every time she complains that I'm wasting my education or that I'm not trying hard enough to overcome my handicaps.

Just not the right kind, she tells me with a roll of her eyes. Not that I care. After the week I just had, my mother's approval is not something I plan on worrying about ever again.

Getting into the zone, I mix the batter up quickly and from memory. The dry ingredients—flour, cocoa powder, salt, baking powder and baking soda—go in one bowl. Then I cream together the butter and sugar before adding in the rest of the wet ingredients, including the secret to my award-winning cookies—vinegar and buttermilk.

In my opinion, most red velvet cakes and cookies have a cloying sweetness to them, which I definitely don't like. But I am in the South and velvet cake so red it looks like congealed blood is a way of life down here, so I use the vinegar to cut that sweetness and the buttermilk to give the dough just a little kick. It might sound strange, but don't knock it 'til you've tried it. I've got customers beating down my door every day trying to get their hands on them. God help us all if we ever run out— which is why I'm staying late to make eight dozen of the saucer-sized cookies.

Forty-five minutes later, I pull the last batches out of my huge double ovens. I know I should stay an extra hour, make the double chocolate muffins and sugar cookies for the morning rush, but I'm beat. I'll come in an hour early tomorrow to work on them.

After getting everything washed up and the cookies stored in the fridge, I wave good-bye to my evening crew and start the fifteen minute walk back to the house I share with Lily. I'm about halfway there when I get a text from her demanding to know where I am.

I dash off an answer, then shove my phone deep into my jeans pocket and just enjoy the rest of my walk. It's the first really cold day here in Austin—the temperature hovering in the mid-thirties—and I pull my scarf a little closer around my neck and chin. A lot of my customers came in complaining about it, but I love the chill in the air and the bite of the wind as it whistles through the branches. Six months of the year it's so hot here that my walk home is a misery, so this is a nice change of pace. One I'm definitely not going to complain about.

As I wind my way through the complicated maze of downtown, leaves crunch beneath my boots. Yes, in most places in the country, if leaves are going to hit the ground, they do it in October. But it was a hundred and three degrees here in October, so the trees have just now gotten around to shedding their leaves. I go out of my way to step on them as I walk—I love the happy sound they make.

Deciding the last thing I want to worry about doing tonight is making dinner, I stop at Whole Foods and pick up a couple of salads and some crusty bread. They'll go nicely with the sack of cookies I tucked into my purse for Lily. Then I turn the corner and duck into my favorite little boutique and pick up a new blackberry-scented candle. Its scent will blend well with the new bath oil Rachael made me for Christmas—and that I hope to try out as soon as I get home. If things go as planned, languishing in the bathtub will be the most strenuous thing I do tonight.

But the second I open the door to the spacious, two-bedroom house I share with Lily, I can tell that my evening isn't going to go quite the way I planned. My roommate is sitting cross-legged on the couch in the family room, her blond hair twisted into hundreds of elaborate braids and her green eyes focused intently on the front door. In her hands are her beloved tarot cards, though she's laid out a small spread on the coffee table in front of her.

Though the look in her eye warns me I'm in trouble, it's the tarot cards that really tip me off. She's chosen to lay the cards out in her own personal looking-for-love spread, a surefire clue that she's got a date with a new guy. I'm not certain where I fit into that equation, but I know that I do.

Sure enough, the second the door closes behind me, she pounces.

"There you are! I've been waiting for you to get home for hours!"

"Sorry. We had a run at the coffeehouse today, probably because of the cold. I had to make a few extra batches of cookies—"

She waves off my explanation, the fifty or so bracelets she wears clinking on her wrists as she starts dragging me toward the couch. "You'll never guess what happened to me today!"

"You met a new guy?"

"Even better! *Brandon* asked me on a date."

I drop the Whole Foods bag on the coffee table, but keep the cookies. Something tells me I'll need them before too much longer. "Which one is Brandon again?"

"Seriously? How can you not know? I've only been lusting after him for a year."

"Oh, right. He's the Rasta guy."

"No."

"The singer?"

"No. That was Braden. And he was a narcissistic moron, remember? We went out around Thanksgiving."

I don't actually remember—living with Lily means putting up with a never-ending parade of hot, but very often vacuous men. She's a Ph.D. candidate in Egyptian history at the University of Texas and one of the smartest witches I know, but her number one weakness is guys with smoking hot bodies and IQs lower than my bra size. Which is saying something since I'm not exactly gifted in that area.

"Is Brandon the swimmer?"

She rolls her eyes. "No. That's Brad."

"Okay, then. I give up. I have no idea who Brandon is."

"Yes, you do. He's the wizard. The one I met in my Egyptian symbology class last year. He's getting his doctorate in religious iconography. I told you all about him. Remember? He's the one with the dreamy blue eyes—"

"And the smooth pickup line." She's right. I do remember him, largely because she spent most of summer semester rhapsodizing about him. "He's the one who told you he liked the way you laughed, isn't he?"

"He is!" She bounces a little in her seat.

"I thought you'd given up on him when he started dating the med student last semester."

"It turns out that was just a big misunderstanding. They were only friends."

"Really?" Since it seems that I've misread the situation—since she's obviously going out, my plans for the evening are in absolutely no danger—I settle down on the couch and pull out a cookie.

Her tarot spread looks pretty good. The lovers in the first spot is promising, as is the magician and the ace of cups in the last two spots. Maybe she's finally found a keeper. Good for her. I lift the cookie to my mouth, but before I can take a bite, Lily slaps it out of my hand. I watch in astonishment as it careens halfway across the room, lands on the edge of the entertainment center and spins like a top for at least fifteen seconds.

"What the hell was that?" I demand. "Since when do you have something against chocolate chips?"

"You know very well that I have nothing against chocolate chips. I do, however, have something against you stuffing your face with a thousand calories right before our date tonight."

"*Our* date? I thought you said *you* were going out with Brandon."

"I am. But his brother's in town—"

"No."

"Come on, Xandra. It will be fun."

"No way." I reach into the bag, pull out another cookie and take a very defiant bite out of it. "I am *not* getting all dressed up just to watch you make goo-goo eyes at some Craft nerd all night."

"He's not a Craft nerd—he's just interested in the history of Heka, like I am. Besides, you'll really like Kyle. He's cool."

"Yeah, I bet. That's why he needs his brother to get a date for him." I shove half the cookie in my mouth, just to annoy her. Childish, yes? But the absolute last thing I want to do tonight is make awkward conversation with some strange guy on a blind date.

"It's not like that. He was with Brandon when I ran into him today and we just got to talking. They have tickets to a show tonight and the couple they were supposed to go with had to cancel, so they thought it'd be fun if we went with them. And it will be. Brandon's amazing, so I'm sure Kyle's pretty cool too. I know he's smart and cute *and* he's spent the last three years working in Europe for the ACW, so you totally have that in common."

"He works for the Council?" I ask, intrigued despite myself.

It's not very often that you meet someone who works for the Arcadian Council of Witches, Wizards and Warlocks. It's even more rare to find someone who actually admits to it. A group of twelve magical beings, they're the governing body that rules all of the covens—including mine.

In fact, they're the only people my mom and dad actually have to answer to. Usually, a member of our family sits on the Council, but when my uncle died ten years ago, my dad turned down appointment to the Council because he wasn't happy with their politics. My brother tried to convince him that that was the best reason to take a seat on the Council—so he could have some influence over the way things were going—but my dad wasn't interested. Doing his duty by taking care of his people is one thing, but playing witch politics is another thing altogether—and someplace he just won't go.

"He does. For seven years now. Pretty cool, right?"

"Or pretty scary. With the Council, you never really

know which until it's too late. What's he do for them anyway?"

"I don't know." She shrugs, then reaches for a cookie herself. Although she has a lot more self-control than I do, since she breaks off only a small piece to nibble on. "Something research related—he says it's not very exciting, but still. I think it sounds fascinating."

She picks up the cards again, starts to shuffle them. "Come on, Xandra. It'll be fun. Dinner, a show at the Paramount, drinks on Sixth Street afterward. What's not to like?"

"The fact that we probably won't get home before two in the morning? I have to be at Beanz by four, and after the week I had at home, I'm really looking forward to a little downtime."

"Downtime?" she asks incredulously. "What are you, ninety? Come on, live a little. We're only young once." She holds the tarot cards out, waits for me to cut them.

"I don't know, Lily. I don't think I'll be very good company—"

"You don't have to be good company. I'll dress you, do your makeup. He'll be blinded by your dazzling looks all through dinner and by the time that wears off, we'll be at the show and then you won't have to talk anyway."

"What show is it?"

"I don't know. Some illusionist or something. Come on. It'll be fun to watch some mortal play around at magic for a night."

It doesn't sound like much fun to me, but maybe that's my own background and bias coming out. Lily is a high-functioning psychic, so while she commiserates with me over the whole latent thing, she doesn't really understand it. Which is fine, most of the time. But every once in a while—like after I've spent a week taking crap from my family on all fronts—it'd be nice to have a friend who just gets it.

"Lily, I just don't think—"

"Please, Xan. Please. I'll do anything you want. I'll do your laundry for a month. Two months. And I swear I won't ask you for anything else for a long, long time. But I really like Brandon and I don't want to blow this with him. It might be my only chance."

I want to say no, but it's not like I can after a speech like that. Besides, the truth is she'd do it for me in a heartbeat. The fact that I'd never ask is totally beside the point. "Okay, I'll go," I finally agree. "But we have to be home by one o'clock."

"Sure, of course." She's all but bouncing up and down in excitement.

"I mean it, Lily."

"I know." She draws her finger across her heart in the shape of an X. "Cross my heart. We'll skip the drinks and come home right after the show, okay?"

"Yeah. That sounds fine."

"Awesome." She holds the tarot cards out again. "Now cut them. I want to prove to you how awesome tonight is going to be."

Unwilling to rain on her parade, I reach out and do as she says.

It turns out, we both should have quit while we were ahead.

Seven

"I think we should redo the cards," Lily says for the fifth time in as many minutes.

"It'll be fine," I tell her. "No big deal."

She looks at me dubiously. "It kind of feels like a big deal."

"So the cards are a little . . . off. So what? It's not the first time that's ever happened to me." I sneak another look at them, try not to be nervous. I'm telling the truth, after all. Tarot cards have never been particularly fond of me. But still—

"These are bad, Xandra. These are really, really bad. Like I'm a little terrified for you bad."

So am I, but no good will come from admitting that to Lily. Or from dwelling on the cards. If I've learned one thing from being latent, it's that some things you can change and some things you can't. Worrying about the ones you can't doesn't get you anywhere.

"They're probably just picking up on all the junk that happened at home," I tell her. "My feelings for my mom, that poor girl we found, the witch whisperer. It was a bad week."

"Right. That must be what it is." Except she doesn't look any more convinced than I am. After all, there's no feminine energy on the cards at all, which rules my mom and Salima right out of the equation.

"Maybe we should rethink this double date?" I suggest. "Because if this symbolizes Kyle, I think I'm in serious trouble."

"Actually, I'd be happy if I thought these cards were talking about Kyle. In the grand scheme of things, one bad date is no big deal. But I didn't ask about him. I asked about your future, because I knew you wouldn't. Plus, I've been having flashes . . . anyway, what the cards seem to hint at . . ."

She trails off, I'm sure because she doesn't want to give voice to what she's thinking. Which is fine by me, because I really don't want to hear it. Still, it's like we're watching a train wreck—neither of us wants to see it but we can't quite step away either. As one, we look back down at the simple five-card spread she's done for me.

The first card, which lies at the center of the spread and symbolizes the present, is the magician. In and of itself it isn't a bad card at all—it represents power, good and bad. It also represents making a decision, taking control, making life what you want it to be. Which is all good—except when it's combined with the other four cards on the table.

My second card, past influence, is the nine of swords—one of the worst cards to see in a tarot reading because it symbolizes deep emotional pain and prolonged suffering. When looked at with the other cards on the table, it also means that a dark point in my life is about to make a resurgence.

My future card, the third to be laid on the table, is the Devil. Again, not a necessarily bad card on its own, but in this combination, it isn't good either. It promises I'll be attacked from both within and without by forces I have no hope of controlling.

None of which sounds like a good time to me.

Even worse, the fourth card is the seven of swords. It's the thief's card, and is all about trickery, deception and vigilantism. It calls into question my entire belief system, at least in reference to the awful situation that seems to be brewing, and in the fourth position also signifies something deliberately put in my path by someone who wants to hurt me.

And finally, in the last position—which is all about possibilities—I've got the five of swords. It's pretty much the worst card in the entire tarot deck, particularly in this spot because it basically says that no matter what I do, I'm going to be defeated. I'm just not strong enough to stand up to the malignant outside forces that are bent on my destruction.

So, all in all, I'm feeling pretty screwed right about now. If only I knew how and why.

I know I could just say, so what? They're just tarot cards and I'm pretty sure, in the end, that's what I'm going to wind up doing anyway. But these aren't just any tarot cards picked up at the local bookstore and read by any charlatan.

Lily's deck is amazing. It's been passed down in her family for five generations, has been handled and blessed by some of the most powerful clairvoyants ever born. Plus, Lily herself is incredibly talented. The fact that she's as nervous as she is by the way these cards turned up means there's a lot she isn't telling me.

Normally I'd demand to know what she's hiding, but I'm kind of at the end of my rope today. I'm not saying I'll never ask, but tomorrow over breakfast is more than soon enough. Especially if I'm supposed to go out on a date tonight and not act like a raving lunatic.

Speaking of which . . . I glance at the clock. It's six thirty. "What time are Brandon and Kyle coming to pick us up?" I ask.

"Oh, shit!" Lily scoops the cards up and puts them back in the deck before making a mad dash for her room. "They'll be here in half an hour!"

Thirty minutes is plenty of time for me to get ready—after all, I'm going for presentable instead of knock-his-socks-off. After that reading, it's not like I'm anxious for Kyle to hang around. Lily may swear that the cards aren't about him, but when it comes to guys, I'm more of the better-safe-than-sorry ilk. Declan taught me that a long time ago.

Still, I meander back to my room, figuring it can't hurt to put on a little lipstick and mascara. But before I even make it to my bathroom, Lily comes in like a whirling dervish. She has a makeup bag in one hand and what looks like a silver thong in the other.

"Come on," she says, shoving me down onto the bed and all but straddling me. "We don't have much time to get you ready."

"Get *me* ready? Shouldn't we be focusing on you?"

She shoots me an incredulous look and I have to give it to her. Lily is one of those naturally beautiful women, inside and out. She looks good in just about anything and a dab of lip gloss goes a lot farther on her than it does on me.

Still, I can't help being nervous when she empties the contents of the makeup bag on my bed. "That's not all going on my face, is it?"

She sighs hugely. "No. More's the pity. But I'm smart enough to know I've only got about ten minutes before you lose patience."

"More like seven. And the clock started the second you climbed on top of me."

"Then shut up and let me get started."

True to her word, Lily's done with my face in six and a half minutes and even I have to admit I look pretty good. "Is that purple eyeliner?" I ask as I look in the mirror she handed to me.

"It is. I picked it up for you at the MAC counter the other day because I knew it'd look sizzling hot on you.

And I was right. It really makes those crazy eyes of yours pop."

"You make me sound like a piece of bacon."

"Whatever. You look good and you know it." She finishes gathering up her makeup and reaches for the silver thong.

"I've got my own underwear, thanks." Sometimes it pays to head Lily off at the pass.

"Well, I hope so. What does that have to do with anything?"

"Nothing. I just thought you were going to make me wear that." I nod to the thing in her hand.

She bursts out laughing. "I am. But it's not underwear, it's a halter top."

"Well, then, I'm definitely not wearing it. It's thirty degrees out and that thing looks like it belongs on a beach in the Bahamas."

"Don't worry about it. Kyle will keep you warm."

"I'll keep myself warm, thank you very much." I cross to my closet and pull out my favorite black cashmere sweater. It's soft and warm and just clingy enough to be interesting.

"Oh, God. Not the sweater. Not again." She throws herself down on the bed, hand dramatically covering her eyes.

"There is nothing wrong with this sweater."

"There's not much right with it either—at least not for a first date."

We bicker back and forth for a little while until finally we reach a compromise. I get to wear the sweater as long as I also wear the super-tight skinny jeans Lily finds at the back of my closet (of course, they're at the back of my closet for a reason) and a pair of fuck-me red, five-inch Jimmy Choos that are her current pride and joy.

When she dashes back to her room to get her own clothes on, I check myself out in the mirror and admit the compromise actually worked out pretty well. The shoes are gorgeous, the sweater looks good with my hair and if I could just take a full breath, I'd probably be more fond of the jeans as well.

All in all, it's better than I expected when Lily came marching through my bedroom door. And at least I'm not wearing a thong for a shirt.

Brandon and Kyle are right on time and the date starts out smoothly enough. Both guys are attractive, though I don't think Brandon is quite the golden god I remember Lily describing him to be. He's got a good sense of humor, though, and keeps us laughing the whole ride over to Haddington's, which is awesome.

Kyle's a little more reserved, but he's got a great smile and he seems really nice. Which is a good thing because we haven't been seated more than five minutes before Lily and Brandon end up deep in discussion about the historical significance of a set of religious artifacts recently found in Chile.

It's an interesting enough conversation for a while, but after listening to them debate it ad nauseam, I'm considering choking on a toast point just to break up the monotony.

Kyle catches my eye and grins. "Is she always like this?" he asks.

"Are you kidding? She's just getting warmed up."

"Him, too. Maybe we should get our own table."

It's obvious he's kidding, so I glance around the crowded restaurant to play along. "Nah, too much trouble."

"Guess we'll have to make the best of it, then. Can I get you another drink?" He nods to my empty glass.

I think about saying no, but I'm not driving and a second glass of wine just might smooth the last of the edges out and help me relax. Something I could really use right about now. Not that Kyle is doing anything to make me uncomfortable—he's not—but I can't quite get over the tarot cards from earlier.

On the plus side, there's zero chemistry between the two of us, which is more than okay by me. Especially since Kyle seems to recognize it, too. With the pressure off, I end up having a pretty good time just talking and joking around with him.

We're working our way through dessert—sharing a sticky toffee pudding—when I finally get up the nerve to ask him about the ACW. My parents and Donovan haven't had a good thing to say about them in years and I'm curious about the opinion of someone on the other side.

"So, what's your favorite part of working for the Council?" I ask, after we spend some time talking about the places they've sent him. "All the travel?"

He doesn't answer at first, just looks thoughtfully at me across the table. "You sound like you don't think I could have a favorite part."

"No, that's not it at all," I assure him, though I guess that is what a small part of me believes. "I've just heard that they can be difficult to work with sometimes."

He shrugs. "Yeah, well, that can be true of anyone, right?"

The waiter chooses that moment to stop by with the check and Kyle takes care of it before the rest of us can offer. But his movements are slow, deliberate, and I get the impression that he's using it to buy himself some time to think. I just don't know why—unless he doesn't like the direction the Council is going in any more than the rest of us do.

When he finally does answer, his voice is deliberate, like he's being very careful to weigh his words. "The Council is made up of twelve indomitable personalities, all of whom are convinced they are right one hundred percent of the time. Which can be . . . challenging when they're at different ends of the spectrum and I'm stuck in the middle, trying to figure out whose orders I'm supposed to follow."

"So you actually work closely with the Council members?" I ask, surprised. Lily had given me the impression that he was on the outskirts of the organization, though now that I think about it, she never actually said that.

"As close as it gets. I'm head of public relations for the entire Council, which means I'm in charge of getting their message out to the media—and everyone else—in a manner that can be easily understood and digested. Sometimes they make that easy on me and sometimes they don't."

"You're a spin doctor." The words pop out before I know I'm going to say them.

He flushes a little. "Not exactly."

I back off—I don't want to interrogate him, or make him feel uncomfortable, but still, I'm fascinated. "But you are in charge of their image? Making them look good?"

"Well, yes, but I'm not the only one. I head up the group of PR people who take care of all manner of publicity for them."

"I find that so strange."

"Why?" Now he does look a little offended. "I don't look like your typical PR guy?"

"No, no, of course you do—"

"Ouch. I think that was an insult."

He makes a face at me and I laugh. "No, it wasn't, and you know it. It's just, I always thought of the ACW as this untouchable group of witches and wizards who don't actually care what people think of them since they're appointed to the Council for life. It's strange to imagine that they actually employ a whole department to make them look good."

"Yeah, well, their image isn't exactly Mary Poppins right now. Imagine what it would be like if we didn't exist?"

It's a good point, one I'd like to explore more. Donovan is always complaining that the Council has taken a dark turn, that it's skirting Heka laws for itself even as it enforces them for everyone else. No one around here gets too upset about it though—including me. They're in Europe, we're here, and as long as we don't do anything too heinous, they pretty much leave us alone.

And as I have no power to abuse, anyway, it's not something I've ever spent much time thinking about. But now that I am thinking about it, I'm curious.

"What kind of stuff do you cover up for them?" I ask. "Or is that too off-limits?"

"Well, I can't give you specifics or anything . . ."

"Oh, right. Of course not. I was just talking generally."

"Mostly it's just things that would make the individual members look bad if they got out—for example, one member of the Council having an affair with a much younger witch even though they're both married, another one unwittingly invested money backing a Ponzi scheme. Stuff like that."

"What about things that affect the witch community as a whole? New laws that have passed—"

"That's not my area. They have a separate department for that."

I start to ask why that is—after all, how much spin does one group of people need?—when Brandon looks up from his conversation with Lily for the first time since we ordered. "We should probably get going," he suggests. "The show starts in fifteen minutes."

I'm a little surprised that so much time has passed. I may not be attracted to Kyle, but he's a great conversationalist. Once we started talking, I didn't even feel the time pass.

The theater is only about a half mile walk from the restaurant, and parking down here is a bitch, so we decide to hoof it. But we're only on the street a few seconds before I start to feel sick. Really sick.

My stomach is churning, my legs feel shaky and I'm having a hard time catching my breath—and this time it has nothing to do with the jeans. Plus I'm breaking out in a cold sweat despite the fact that that temperature has dipped down to the high twenties.

Food poisoning? I wonder. But I didn't eat any meat or seafood, so that seems unlikely.

The flu? God, I hope not. After taking last week off, I can't afford to be away from Beanz any more than I have to be.

I keep walking, up Nueces to Sixth Street, but I'm getting shakier by the second. Something is wrong. Something is very, very wrong. The smell of alcohol and crush of bodies on Austin's famed party street only makes things worse.

I figure I'm doing a pretty good job of covering because we're at Guadalupe before Lily notices. She breaks away from Brandon and wraps an arm around my waist. "You doing okay?" she murmurs.

I force a smile I'm far from feeling. "Something at dinner must not have agreed with me."

"Do you want to go home?"

The offer's sincere—she's that kind of friend—but I know she'll be crushed if I end the date early, so I just shake my head. "I'll be fine once we get inside and I can sit down."

"You sure?"

No. Not at all. "Yeah, absolutely."

By the time we make a left onto Congress, the nausea has died down a little, but the shakiness is worse. My legs feel like they can't support me and suddenly, the Jimmy Choos don't seem like such a good idea. Not that there's anything I can do about it now—Lily's shoes are even higher and more precarious than mine.

We stop outside the Paramount and Brandon and Kyle walk up to will call to get our tickets. Normally, I love this place. It's an old-time movie palace in the tradition of Hollywood's Golden Era. One big theater with sweeping arches, rounded ceilings and elaborate gold paint, it's one of the most popular places to perform in Austin. When they don't have comedians or musicians booked into it, they have movie marathons that run the gamut from B movie thrillers to Golden Era romances like *Casablanca* and *Gone with the Wind*.

I can't begin to list the number of happy times I've had here, curled up in the huge, red seats drinking beer and eating popcorn while B movie villains plotted to take over the world. But today I don't want to go in. A feeling of dread overwhelmed me the second we stopped in front of the box office and it's only grown worse the longer we stand here.

Brandon and Kyle still have a few people in front of them at the window when I glance up at the marquee to check who we're seeing. I'm not a big fan of illusionists, but there are a few I wouldn't mind . . .

The world stops. Literally stops. Or at least my small section of it does, my entire being freezing where I stand. Except my heart—that starts pounding so fast that for a moment I fear it will explode right out of my chest.

He's here. Right here. In Austin. Even though he's supposed to be eight thousand miles and half a world away. Not that I've been keeping track or anything.

I look again, just to make sure. Just to be certain. And there it is in huge black letters that can't be ignored. THE WORLD FAMOUS DECLAN CHUMOMISTO, IN TOWN FOR THREE NIGHTS ONLY. MAGICAL ENCORE TO THE DARK ILLUSIONS WORLD TOUR.

Eight

The sick feeling I've been having for the past ten minutes intensifies into a full-blown panic attack and suddenly it's not just about being unable to take a deep breath. It's about not being able to breathe at all. I turn away from the theater so I won't have to see his name and noisily try to suck air into a windpipe that has narrowed to the size of a pinhole.

He can't be here. He just . . . can't be here. Not here, in Austin, where I am. Not when I need him to be anywhere but here.

"Hey, Xandra, are you getting worse?" Lily's moved so that she's right in front of me, her concerned face inches from mine. "You look like you're going to throw up."

I feel like I'm going to throw up. The nausea from earlier is back triple-fold and all the weird feelings, the not-quite-feeling-like-myself awkwardness oozes through me. I glance back at the marquee, one more time—just to prove to myself that I'm not imagining this. Imagining him.

I'm not. Lily is waiting for an answer, the look on her face both impatient and concerned. I want to point, to show her what it is that has me so uneasy, but she doesn't know. I never told her about my one night with Declan. I probably should have, but as a princess of Ipswitch, so much of my life is for public consumption that it felt good to have this one little secret. This one thing that no one else knows about. Even if it ended up not meaning anything—to him anyway. As for me, it was the final proof that I'd never fit into the life my coven expected me to lead. Which is a good thing—I should be shaking his hand for the lesson instead of feeling like I'm about to shake apart.

The thought steadies me and I finally suck in one breath, two. I can do this, I tell myself. Seeing Declan again is nothing. I'm part of the audience in a sold-out show—he'll never know I'm here. Not that he probably remembers me anyway, but still. It's not as if I have to worry about running into him in the lobby.

My throat relaxes a little more and slowly, surely, my breathing returns to normal. As it does, the nausea subsides. I don't feel normal yet—there's still a strange uneasiness inside me, like my body knows there's something wrong but it just can't quite figure out what it is.

Part of me wants to plead sickness, to just go home, but I know Lily will insist on coming with me and I don't want to ruin her night. Or Kyle and Brandon's, especially now that I know we're seeing Declan's show. He's world famous, the best illusionist in the business (because he actually possesses magic, I'm sure) and I know tickets for his shows regularly go for upward of two hundred dollars. If I insist on walking away, Kyle and Brandon will be out close to a thousand dollars and weird, churning sickness in my stomach or not, I can't bring myself to do that to them.

"I'll be fine once we get in there and sit down," I tell Lily. "I'm just a little dizzy. I probably shouldn't have had that third glass of wine."

She doesn't look convinced, but the guys choose that minute to come up to us, and faced with a grinning Brandon, Lily chooses to let the subject drop. Which is exactly what I was counting on.

It'll be fine, I assure myself as we walk through the lobby. I'll go in there, find a way to sit through the next two hours and then get Kyle and Brandon to take me home. No harm, no foul. Lily will have gotten her uninterrupted first date and no one will ever know about those stolen moments with Declan.

It's a good plan and it should have worked. But the longer we sit waiting for Declan to come onstage, the worse the uneasiness gets until I can't even sit still. An electric current is working its way through me, and my body is no longer under my control as it shakes and twitches.

There's a low-grade itchiness right below my skin that I have no hope of scratching and it's getting worse every second, until I'm so miserable that I want to die. Even worse, I'm afraid of these sensations. Surely seeing Declan again isn't enough to do this to me? Something else must be wrong, but I have no idea what it is. I know only that I need it to stop.

In desperation, I focus on the elaborate angel painted above the stage. Done in shades of gold and pink and ivory, she's ornate and beautiful and completely over the top. She's also perfect for this place that is both too much and just enough.

The shaking gets worse and I concentrate on counting every curl on her head. It calms me down, makes it easier to breathe—at least until the lights go out.

There's a collective gasp from the audience and Lily reaches over and squeezes my hand. I don't blame them—everyone here is thrilled at the chance to see Declan. His world tour had sold out in every venue, no matter how big (again, not like I'm keeping track), and was supposed to have wound up two weeks ago at Madison Square Garden. I'm not sure why he's here in Austin now, let alone performing at the Paramount instead of at the UT center, which is so much bigger. Not that it really matters. He's here for three days and then he's gone and I'll never have to see him again.

The music starts, low and eerie and a little mystical, and all around me I can feel people shifting in anticipation. A spotlight illuminates center stage, where a wisp of smoke winds its way across the open expanse. It's soon joined by another curl, then another and another and another.

I can feel its power calling to a place deep inside of me—this is elemental fire magic at its most basic, though I'm sure most of the audience believes it's just the clever use of a smoke machine. As I watch the stage slowly fill, the itchiness inside me eases just a little. I breathe a sigh of relief, until I realize it's been replaced by a low-grade hum—a vibration—that has taken over every cell in my body.

I shift a little, lean forward, until I realize that—like everyone else in the theater—I'm on the edge of my seat, waiting for Declan's entrance.

I immediately sit back, feeling like an idiot, but it doesn't really matter. The theater itself seems to be holding its breath as everyone looks around, trying to figure out where Declan will come from. The reviews of the show say he bursts from a new place every time and I brace myself for my first glimpse of him.

But no amount of preparation could have readied me for what happens next. With a crash of music and a flash of lights, the smoke on the stage—not thick, not condensed, still just wispy tendrils of gray—seems to explode and Declan is standing center stage, dressed in black pants and a simple, V-neck black sweater.

I try to wrap my mind around what I just saw. Had he really turned himself into smoke and then, in the blink of an eye, turned back to human form? It's impossible magic, takes immeasurable power and skill to do such a thing and I can't imagine how he did it. Beside me, Lily,

Brandon and Kyle all look at each other and I know, they too, are wondering if we really just saw what we thought we did.

The rumors in the Hekan community about his power deteriorating are obviously no more true now than they were eight years ago.

He doesn't speak, doesn't bow, barely acknowledges the audience's wild applause at all. Instead, he moves seamlessly into his next "illusion," a demonstration that has him levitating twelve feet above the ground. Arms lifted above his head, he starts to spin faster and faster until he bursts into flames.

He burns and burns and burns, until gasps of surprise become cries of dismay and the audience begins to glance uneasily at one another. Even knowing it's magic not illusion, even knowing how talented he is, I start to get nervous too. Especially when I notice a few stage-hands stepping forward, fire extinguishers in hand and looks of fear on their faces.

Has something gone wrong? Is he burning too long? My stomach clenches and the strange vibration inside of me becomes something more, something all-encompassing. A fire of my own, licking along my nerve endings and burning me to a crisp from the inside out.

And then the fire extinguishes as quickly as it began, ash falling through the air to the stage below. Everything is silent, everyone looking around for where Declan went. Suddenly, someone screams at the back of the theater—in the opera boxes—and the spotlight rushes to find the woman who screamed. And there he is, sitting on the edge of one of the opera boxes, tossing back a bottle of water like he hadn't just self-immolated.

The theater fills with relieved laughs and people finally relax. All around me I can feel them settling in for what promises to be a kick-ass show. Too bad I can't do the same.

Lily leans over and whispers, "Who can do that? I mean, if that's real and not illusion, what wizard is strong enough to do all that?"

I don't have an answer for her, except the obvious. Declan Chumomisto can do all this and more. "He's not a wizard," I finally tell her. "He's a warlock."

"Still. It's crazy. Even dark magic can't do that."

I shrug because she's right and yet, obviously, it can be done.

Declan finishes the bottle of water and tosses it behind him. Then he stands, balancing precariously on the narrow edge of the box. Once again, the music builds. As it crescendoes, he steps off the ledge and begins walking calmly toward the stage. The fact that he is fifteen feet in the air when he does it, balanced on nothing but empty space, doesn't faze him at all.

It fazes me, though, especially since I can't take my eyes off of him. I want to look away—from him and the spectacle he's creating—but like the night of my nineteenth birthday, he's all that I can see.

He reaches the stage safely, and once he does, he acknowledges the audience for the first time since the show began. A couple of arm waves, an obvious thanks for the applause, and then a scan of the crowd with those midnight eyes of his.

I know he can't see past the stage lights, but I duck a little in my chair anyway. Again, not because I think he'll remember me, but because—

His eyes brush past me, then return, lock with mine. I gasp at the power I see in their swirling depths. It's so immense that it startles, then frightens, me. It's too much. No one should have that much magic inside them. It's dangerous, for everyone.

Beside me, Lily gasps. "He's looking at you," she hisses.

Like I haven't already figured that out? I try to turn

my head, to look anywhere but into those eyes that have already caused me too much grief, but it's like his fingers are on my chin, holding my head in place, my eyes locked to his.

I don't like it, not the feeling of my body being out of my control and not the presumption he makes that he should be the one to control me.

"Do something," Lily hisses, and I know she means for me to smile or wave. The spotlight has picked us up because Declan isn't moving, isn't speaking, isn't getting on with the show, and I wonder if this is a nightly thing. And if so, am I supposed to pander to the crowd?

Inside me, the vibration grows a million times worse until I'm sure that I will shake apart any second. I gasp, press a hand to my stomach, and watch as Declan's eyes flair with satisfaction.

Before I can react, a powerful wind sweeps through the theater. It ruffles my hair, has Lily's scarf slapping against her cheeks, before surrounding Declan with a cyclonic force. I expect him to stumble under it—it might be his, but it's still power gone rogue, too strong to control. He doesn't even flinch. Instead, he just stands there, legs spread and braced, and takes it without any reaction at all.

And his eyes never leave mine.

Using every ounce of strength I have, I jerk my gaze from his. As the connection shatters, sparks fly, literally, lighting up the dark theater for a few brief seconds.

It's all I need, the proof that he is not invincible. That I am strong enough to stand against him.

I struggle to my feet, throwing off the hands that feel like they're pressing me into the chair. I feel it then, a command deep inside my head, telling me to stay. To sit back down.

I ignore it—and him. Turning away from the spectacle

he is making of us both, I make my way drunkenly down the aisle. For long seconds the walls around me seethe with rage, until fire explodes along the edge where they meet the ceiling. The flames race around the circle until the whole ceiling is ablaze.

And then, just that suddenly, it's all gone. The anger, the fire, the connection between us—everything locked down tight. On the stage, Declan starts up an easy dialogue with the audience and before I even reach the door, he's onto another trick, one that has the audience oohing and aahing with glee. I don't turn back to see what it is.

Once in the lobby, I make my way to the restroom on legs gone shaky. Double date or not, best friend or not, there is no way I'm going back in that theater. No way I'll allow Declan to assume that kind of control over me again. Oh, I managed to fight it, but that's not good enough for me. The fact that he did it to begin with—and that I hadn't able to stop him—is enough to tell me that I need to steer clear of him. All the way clear of him. As if that night eight years ago hadn't already proved that.

Leaning down, I splash some water on my face, not caring if it ruins Lily's amazing makeup job. I feel like I'm suffocating, and though I have no actual power, I still have enough Heka in my veins to feel connected to an element. For me, that element is water. Nothing revives me more, nothing feels better, than the touch of water against my skin.

Which is funny, really, when you consider that Declan's element is obviously fire. Because there haven't been enough signs that we should have nothing to do with each other, the universe obviously felt like it needed to rub my face in one more.

Despite the drought, I leave the water running. I thrust my hands under the faucet, reveling in the feel of the cool liquid dribbling over my wrist, down my palm, between my fingers. It grounds me, fights back the nausea and dizziness once and for all.

Eventually, I shut off the tap and dry my hands. The low-grade vibration I felt earlier, sitting in the theater, has almost disappeared, and I'd be lying if I said I wasn't grateful. And yet, my body isn't at peace. Yes, I'm a million times better than I was, but something still feels off.

And that itchiness, that fire along my nerve endings— it's back and worse than ever.

I step out of the bathroom, figuring I'll sit on a bench in the lobby and wait until intermission. Then I'll either make an excuse to Lily and Kyle and find a cab to take me home or I'll try another round in the theater. No promises about how that's going to turn out, but now that I'm prepared for Declan and the force he exudes, it should be a lot easier.

Except, when I turn, it isn't toward the empty bench near the inside doors. It's to the right, toward the street.

I walk outside and it's raining a little now, the low temperature turning the water icy and painful as it slaps against my face and hands. I should go back in, get off the dark street and out of the rain. Austin is a pretty safe place, but it's getting late and I'm smart enough to know I shouldn't be wandering around on my own in the dark.

But even as I think this, even as my brain tells my body to go back into the Paramount, I turn to the south and start walking down North Congress. I don't know where I'm going, don't know why I'm going anywhere, but I can't stop. That strange, invisible wire is back, pulsing with electricity as it pulls me farther and farther away from my friends. From what I know.

I walk about half a mile, hunched inside my jacket. The wind has kicked up so that the rain hits me with stinging force. I don't know where I'm going, but when I get to Cesar Chavez, something tugs me to the left.

I turn, keep walking. A cab drives by, its FOR HIRE sign lit up, and I tell myself to hail it. To climb in and let it speed me home. It's the smart thing to do, the safe thing, as both the rain and the wind are picking up. And yet I can't bring myself to do it. The same electricity that made it impossible for me to sit still in the theater makes it impossible now for me to do anything but keep walking.

Lightning splits the sky, lighting up the desolate street and scaring the crap out of me. I don't know how a street can look worse when it's illuminated by lightning than it does in the eerie glow of a very few streetlights, but somehow this one does. It doesn't help that Cesar Chavez, while bustling during the day, is all but deserted at this time of night—the occasional car my only company.

I start to run, which is really more of an awkward shuffle in Lily's high heels. Part of me is terrified that I'll slide on the slippery street and plunge headfirst into the path of one of those few cars, but I'm even more terrified of the lightning that is exploding all around me while thunder rumbles nonstop in the background.

I know I need to get out of the rain, know this kind of lightning could be deadly. But somehow all the logical parts of my brain—the parts that should be in control of my decision making process—are shorting out at once. Instead, I can't do anything but continue walking, following the inexorable pull down this street toward goddess only knows what.

I cross side street after side street, huddling against buildings and under awnings when I can get the shelter. More than once a cab slows as if to pick me up, but I wave it on. I don't understand how I know this, but where I'm going no cab can take me.

Finally the compulsion drags me to the right. I cross the street and start up Pleasant Valley toward the lake.

And just that suddenly I know where it is I'm heading. To Town Lake.

I just wish I knew why.

I see it, up ahead, and I know I'm right. Especially when my entire body starts to pulse with the need to hurry, the need to be there now.

Strangely, it's the urgency that sets me off, that makes me remember. When I do, the true fear sets in, a living breathing nightmare inside of me that feeds on the knowledge and chokes the very air from my lungs.

And still I don't stop.

I'm almost to the lake now and I stumble off the sidewalk, head for the grassy knoll that sits a few feet from the water. The ground is soaked from the storm and my heels immediately sink into the earth until every step is a challenge. I wince at the sucking sound that comes every time I pull my foot out of the earth, then cringe more every time I put it back down and the earth draws it under.

Like it isn't bad enough I walked out of the Paramount with no explanation to Lily, no text, nothing. When she finds out I ruined her Jimmy Choos, she's going to kill me. Slowly and with great relish.

But even that can't make me turn back. Nothing can. The water is calling to me and there's nowhere to go but forward.

I try to stay on the balls of my feet to protect the shoes as best I can, but the grass is too slick and the heels too high. Besides, they're the only things that give me purchase as I stumble off the grass and onto the running path that goes around the lake.

I'm under the bridge now, trying to take what little shelter it provides. The rain is slashing in at an angle, slamming against me despite the coverage. Still, it's better than being out in the full force of the storm—and at least I'm less likely to be struck by lightning.

I pause, take a second to brush my drenched hair back from my forehead and rub a palm down my face to squeegee the rain from my eyes. I expect to feel a wave of relief, but the chest-clenching drive to get to the water doesn't let up. This isn't where I'm meant to stop. Hiding here under the bridge isn't enough. I take a step closer to the lake. And then another.

As I do, the wind caterwauls through the place, stirring up the sickly cloying smell of guano. Though the bats haven't migrated back from Mexico yet, years and years of the stuff layers the area, creating a stench that not even the storm can chase away. Usually the scent makes me ill, but tonight it doesn't repel me the way that it should. Though I'm having trouble breathing through my nose, I have no urge to flee. Instead, I want to go closer.

I *need* to go closer.

Grabbing on to a tree branch, I use it to steady myself as I creep down the slope to the water's edge. The fear is bigger now, nearly all-consuming. Not for myself, not about what will happen to me, but for what's drawing me in. For what I might find down here under this bridge. I don't know what I'm doing down here, don't know what spell I'm under that has brought me here. But something has and somehow I don't think it's for the midwinter view.

Unable to bear the suspense any longer, I drop to my knees by the edge of the water. Muck squishes under my jeans, causing me to slide a little as I bend forward to peer into the lake. I don't see anything, despite the lights stationed every few yards on the running path, and I fumble for the flashlight on my key chain.

I shine the small beam at the water, then jump when I see my reflection on the surface. For a second, I'm surprised that it's bright enough to see anything shining off the rippling water, even if the reflection is little more than a pale oval and tangled fan of short, black hair. Except the longer I look at it, the more I realize the mirror image is all wrong. It's upside down and her eyes are closed. No, not a mirror image I realize as the water smooths out. Not a reflection at all. The face I see in the lake belongs to someone else entirely.

Nine

Confused, unsure, I reach a hand out to touch her. But the moment my fingers break the icy surface of the water, understanding hits me and I instinctively recoil, falling ass over teakettle as I do. My brain screams at me to get away, to run as fast and as far from here as I possibly can. But in the end, I don't go anywhere. I can't.

She's trapped, tangled in the plants that edge the lake, and I can't just leave her there alone, in the dark. I can't just—

I force myself to scoot forward once more, to drop my keys—and the flashlight—onto the ground beside me and reach into the lake, though it's the absolute last thing I want to do. The water is cold and a little slimy, and so is she when I brush against her shoulder. That's when I know, when I'm certain, but I've started down this path now and have to see it through.

I reach for her again and images bombard me.

A dark room.

A knife, slicing cleanly across flesh.

Pain.

Fists raining down on bare skin.

A hand thrusting between legs stubbornly clamped shut.

More pain, excruciating pain.

Cold steel around wrists, ankles.

A heavy body thrusting between open legs.

A silent scream.

Pain, unimaginable and never ending.

I rip my hands away as her pain wells up inside me. I'm not touching her anymore but it's too late for me to escape her torment. It surrounds me, tears through me with each shuddering breath I take, until I'm completely sucked under. Overwhelmed. Held in thrall to her anguish and distress.

I try to pull away but a conduit's been opened between her final hours and my brain and I can't do anything but absorb the images that run through my head like a snuff film on high speed. It goes on and on and on, every flicker of pain, every cry of emotion, rolling through me. Desperate to stop the agony, I pull my knees up to my chest. Wrap my arms around them and curl myself into a ball as I pray for it to end.

It does, finally, with a powerful blow to the head that has my ears ringing and me seeing double when I finally work up the nerve to open my eyes. I'm afraid to move, almost afraid to breathe for fear of triggering the nightmare all over again. But when minutes pass and nothing else happens, I force myself to my hands and knees. Then I crawl to the lake's edge and bracing myself for goddess only knows what, I slide my hands under her armpits and—as quickly as I can—pull her halfway onto the shore.

There's no pain now, just a yawning emptiness that is somehow worse.

My first real glimpse of her face cements the knowledge that I'm too late. Her cheeks are pale white, her lips tinged with blue. I feel for a pulse, but of course, there is none.

What she does have are hundreds upon hundreds of shallow cuts—up her arms, across her bare breasts, down her stomach, over her thighs. I don't need to see them to know that they are there—I felt each one as it was made.

Long before some sick bastard shoved her in the water to dispose of her, he made her suffer.

For a moment, just a moment, I get an impression of cold deliberation. Of determination not sickness. Like she was just a small stumbling block in his path, barely a bleep on his radar.

Somehow that makes all of this so much worse.

I can't stand touching her any longer. Her pain was bad enough, but feeling what he felt—it's horrific. I try to stand, but she's partly draped over my leg. Not that I'm sure my legs will support me anyway. In the end, I scuttle backward through the mud like a crab. I want to say I'm gentle with her abused body, but the truth is, I don't think I am. There's a red haze in front of my eyes and all I can think about is getting her off me, and getting away.

As I scramble out from under her, her head falls to the right and I get my first glimpse of the elaborate circlet of Isis that has been carved into her left shoulder. Just like the body in my parents' forest, she has been branded with the mark of Isis.

Though hers is easily three times as large as the one I bear on my neck and collarbone, it is very obviously my mark.

For long seconds I can't process what I'm seeing, can't do anything but sit here in the muck as, inside, I scream and scream and scream. Then I'm turning over and crawling up the embankment, my hands slipping off the wet vegetation as I slip and slide through the rain and the mud. I make it a few feet before the shock and pain get me and I collapse.

I don't know how long I sit here, the horror—and implications—of what I've just seen reverberating through me.

Long enough for the world around me to grow fuzzy, and then clear again.

Long enough for bone-rattling shivers to set in.

More than long enough to figure out that this is no accident. I am meant to be here. No matter what I try to tell myself, no matter what I want to believe. Two dead bodies in eight years is a bad coincidence. Two dead bodies in less than eight days is something else entirely. Especially when they both carry my mark.

Goddamn that belladonna. If I find out that it actually worked, that my mother somehow opened me up to this, I will never forgive her. Because next to this, the humiliation of being latent feels like one big party.

But whatever it is that got me here—belladonna, malicious spell, bad luck of epic proportions—I can't walk away now. Not when that poor girl lies here, unclaimed and unprotected.

I fumble in my pocket for my cell phone, dial 911. Report the body. The operator on the other end assures me that the police are on the way. She asks that I stay at the scene, offers to stay on the line with me until the first patrol car rolls up.

But I can already hear the sirens, and they aren't that far away. They'll be here any minute and I still haven't come up with a reason for why I'm down here. I'd say I was jogging, but the five-inch Jimmy Choos on my feet would mark me as a liar.

The sirens are getting closer and, after hanging up with the operator, I hike my way back up the hill to flag the officers down. It's still raining and Town Lake isn't that small—it'll be easy for them to miss the spot if I'm not there to direct them.

I get to the top just as a car screams around the corner, red and blue lights gleaming in the rain-slicked darkness. Moments later, a second car pulls up and then a third and a fourth. This is Austin, after all. A body in Town Lake is huge enough that everyone wants in on it.

Everyone but me, that is.

The first officer makes his way down the waterlogged hill, his shoes doing a much better job on the slick grass than mine are. "Are you Xandra Morgan?" he asks me, eyes narrowed and voice gruff.

"Yes."

"Can you show me where the body is?"

I nod, before turning back toward the bridge with a notable lack of enthusiasm. As we walk, we're joined by two of the other officers. I glance behind me, trying to figure out where the fourth cop is. He's still at the top of the hill, rolling out yellow crime scene tape.

Somehow the sight of that yellow tape makes all this so much more real. I don't know why. It's not like I didn't realize she was dead before. But that tape . . . there's just something about it.

It takes us only a couple of minutes to get to the body, to get to *her*. It seems so impersonal and awful to refer to her as "the body," even if that's what she's become.

The second the officers see her, they start firing questions at me.

Did I move her?

How far did I move her?

Do I know her?

What was I doing down here in the middle of a storm?

When did I find her?

Did I have a problem with the victim?

The first two officers seem to believe me when I say I have no idea who the victim is, but the third is a lot more suspicious—as evinced by the questions he fires at me. I do my best to tell the truth, except of course for the whole strange compulsion thing that got me down here to begin with. Instead I tell them I'd been out with friends and had gotten sick, had decided to walk home instead of cutting the evening short for the others. That was, of course, before the thunderstorm hit.

They want the names and numbers of my friends, but

all I have is Lily's number so I give it to them. I don't even know Brandon and Kyle's last name, but surely she does. I feel awful about bringing police questioning down on any of their heads, but I don't know what else to do but cooperate. Besides, the sooner they rule me out as the one who killed this girl, the sooner they'll start looking for the real culprit.

Within a few minutes, Town Lake is crawling with cops. Some are securing crime scene boundaries while others are setting up lights and starting to comb the area for I don't know what. Evidence? Clues? The murderer?

After a few more questions, I'm shuffled aside. Told to go wait by the police cars for the detectives to show up, in case they have more questions for me. The rain is starting to let up, thank God, so at least I can see where I'm going when I make my way up the hill to the main road for the second time tonight.

I slip a couple of times on my way up as my heels get stuck in the mud and refuse to come out again. The third time I'm poised to go down hard. As my knee twists beneath me, I'm saved by a hand on my elbow. Whoever it is bears my weight, keeps me upright, and saves me a nasty fall.

I turn to say thank you and find myself staring into Nate's startled eyes. Earlier, I'd wished that I had his phone number, or at least that I knew what precinct he worked for. The fact that I didn't, and that somehow he's ended up here anyway, feels an awful lot like fate. Or magical interference. I really hope it's the first, but everything inside me screams that it's the latter. I just wish I knew who or why.

"Xandra! What are you doing out here?"

"I'm the one who found her."

"You're the witness?" He sounds incredulous, and more than a little wary. I guess he's not a big believer in fate either.

"Yeah." I try a smile, but I know it's lopsided. Still, it's the best I can do with everything that's happened tonight. "Sorry to pull you away from the basketball game."

He shrugs. "The Mavericks were losing anyway." He glances down at my feet, the back half of which are currently sunk in the mud. "Can I help you up to the street?"

Maybe I should say no, let him get to work, but the longer I stand here, the more I'm beginning to doubt my ability to get back up to the street. If Nate wants to help me, who am I to brush him off?

"That'd be great," I say, holding an arm out to him. He ignores it, wraps his arm around my waist and pulls me flush against his body. Then he all but carries me up the hill.

I have no idea how he makes the muddy climb look so easy, but he does and I appreciate it. He waves off my thanks, tells me I can go wait in his car for a while and then he'll give me a ride home. This is the most gruesome murder they've seen in years and he knows none of the beat cops are going to want to leave the scene for something as mundane as dropping me at home.

I should probably decline the invitation and just head home on my own, but there are a few problems with that scenario. One, I can't see a cab actually stopping to pick me up when I'm covered in mud and grime. Two, the compulsion still isn't gone. It's weakened, enough so that I can walk away from the body, but not so weak that I can leave the area yet. I don't know what's holding me here, but whatever the spell is, it isn't ready to let me walk. And I'm not ready to fight it—after that last little experience in torture, I really don't need any more pain. And three, I don't want to go home. I don't want to be alone, not when I see that girl's face—and her mark—every time I close my eyes.

In the end, I take Nate up on his offer. He lays a sweatshirt out on the front seat of his car so I don't mess it up too badly, then hands me a blanket from the trunk. I climb in, let him close the door, and then I just sit there, trying not to think, as the minutes pass.

It's harder than it sounds. Especially when I'm smart enough to know that this—that she—is somehow meant for me. But why? Who is doing this and what are they hoping to get out of it? It must be pretty horrific if they're willing to kill two innocent women to accomplish it.

And what is happening to me? What spell am I dealing with that let me feel that poor woman, that brought me to this place? And that is keeping me here although I've already done everything I can for her?

I don't know enough magic to determine the spell— or even if what I'm experiencing is something a normal witch can engender. Not that I think a normal witch is behind this—from what I saw and what I felt, I can't imagine anything about the person who did this is normal.

For one brief moment, my mind flashes on Declan. I'm not stupid. I recognize that the only constants between the first girl I found, eight and a half years ago, and this one are Declan and me. And while I don't have the ability or the desire to cast a magical spell to find dead bodies—just the thought creeps me out—I can't say the same about Declan. But why would he do this to me? What's in it for him?

Nothing that I can see—

Nate opens the door without warning and I jump, strangling a scream before it can escape.

"Whoa, Xandra." He holds his hands up in surrender. "Everything's okay. I'm sorry I scared you, but I just wanted to check and make sure you're doing okay?"

Okay seems like a bit of an overstatement, but I'm not going to argue with him. "Yeah. I'm fine."

He studies me in the dim light afforded by the car's interior lamp. "Did you fall?" he asks.

"What do you mean?"

He points to my cheekbone. "You have a cut and some bruising right under your eye."

My hand flies to my face and I feel a line of dried blood inches from my eye. For a second, I feel it again, his fist slamming into my face, his ring cutting me. Her, I remind myself viciously. Cutting her. But then why do I bear the mark?

"I tripped a couple times, down near the lake," I whisper. "When I was trying to get her out." Again it's not a lie, but it's not the whole truth either.

I must be convincing, though, because Nate just nods. "I've got a few more minutes here, but not long. Between the rain and the dark, we can't see much, so we'll have to come back tomorrow during the day. Most of the trace evidence has already been destroyed."

Because of me or the rain? I think of how I was slipping and sliding all over the embankment and my cheeks burn with embarrassment. I definitely played a part in destroying evidence, but I don't know what else I could have done. Left her there, in the water? The compulsion wouldn't have let me. Besides, something tells me that the wizard or warlock responsible for this didn't leave any evidence anyway. He was far too deliberate to do something that stupid.

Still, I should say something. "I'm sorry about that."

"I would have done the same thing. Besides, the rain doesn't leave us with much to work with anyway." Someone calls his name and he repeats, "Just a few more minutes," before slamming the door shut.

Sickness—and a new worry—churn inside of me. The need to stay right here with the victim is deep inside of me. Just the thought of driving away from here, from her, is barbed wire in my gut. What am I going to do when Nate actually tries to leave? Throw myself out of the car?

The rational side of my brain says that will never happen, but it isn't exactly in control here. Obviously. If it was, I never would have left the Paramount, or if I had, I would have taken a cab straight home instead of wandering downtown Austin in search of a mutilated woman.

As Nate walks away a second time, I slide my feet out of Lily's prize—and now ruined—shoes and consider making a run for it. But where would I go when I can't leave this damn lake?

A few minutes later I'm still debating what to do when I see people dressed in clothes labeled TRAVIS COUNTY MEDICAL EXAMINER walk by, carrying an obviously full body bag. I try to look away—I don't want to see—but the barbs prick at me until I turn back to follow their progress down the sidewalk to the big white van on the corner.

They open the back doors, slide her in, before closing the van back up.

And that's when it happens. The second the doors close behind her, the spell turns off and the compulsion that has been riding me for the last two hours disappears. I am free to go.

As the realization sets in, it takes every ounce of self-control I have not to run screaming down the street and away from this hellhole. And even that probably wouldn't have been enough to keep me here—I'm actually reaching for the door handle when Nate once again opens up the driver's-side door.

This time, though, he slides into the car beside me. Despite his raincoat, he's now as soaked and muddy as I am.

"How are you doing?" he asks as he starts up the car and pulls away from the curb.

I want to ask him how the hell he thinks I'm doing, but antagonizing the homicide detective doesn't seem like a good idea. Besides, he's just being nice, just trying to be my friend. I can't blame him for that, even if what I really want right now is just to be left alone.

In the end, I say, "Fine," and he leaves it at that. At least for a few minutes. But when he starts to make the turn onto the major street that will lead him to the house I share with Lily, I freak out. I know she won't be there yet and I can't stomach the idea of being alone, even for a little while.

"Can you take me to the station?" The words are out of my mouth before I even know I'm going to say them.

Nate glances at me dubiously. "Don't you want to go home and take a shower?"

I know I must sound like a nut-job, but I don't care. "I can't go sit in my empty house right now. I see her every time I close my eyes and I just—"

Nate reaches over and pats my knee. His hands are clean, at least until they touch my jeans, and I wonder how he managed to keep them from getting dirty in all that mess. Then it hits me. Gloves. "It's okay," he murmurs, his voice low and soothing. "You don't have to be alone." The soft rumble of his tone calms me on a visceral level and I wonder if they teach classes in this stuff at the academy or if Nate is just really good at dealing with hysterical women. Maybe it's a little bit of both.

"Is there someone I can call? Someplace else I can take you?"

"My roommate will probably be home in an hour or so."

He sighs, runs his still-clean hand through his hair in a what-the-fuck gesture that's hard to miss. "You want to come to the station with me? I have some preliminary paperwork to get done. By the time I finish, your roommate should be home."

"Thanks."

He nods, keeps driving. "You know, pulling the girl

out of the lake tonight was really brave, trying to see if she was still alive. I'm proud of you."

"Yeah, because I'm so brave. I won't even go home to the completely nonthreatening house I've lived in for the past four years."

"Hey, don't beat yourself up. The first time anyone sees a body—especially one that got that way through violence—is difficult. It's nothing to be ashamed of."

I don't correct him, though the other two bodies are burning brightly in my head—and my conscience.

The rest of the ride passes quickly as Nate asks me questions about what I was doing down on Town Lake in the first place. I dance around the inquiries, knowing this is an interrogation of sorts, but Nate doesn't seem to mind the way I leap around. Or maybe he just doesn't recognize it as such. Either way, I must do a good job, because he seems satisfied when we finally pull up in front of the precinct.

I follow Nate inside, through the main lobby and up the stairs to where he works. There are a lot of people still in the precinct—police officers and civilians—and I'm a little shocked at all the hustle and bustle at this time of night. Not that I have anything to compare it with. The only other police station I've ever been in is Ipswitch's and since very little criminal activity happens in my hometown, I don't think that counts.

"The bathroom is over there," he says, pointing to the back of the room. "In case you want to clean up."

"I do. Thanks."

He just nods, yanking off his mud-encrusted coat and dropping it on the floor near his desk.

I hurry to the bathroom and one look in the mirror assures me—freaked out or not—I should have let Nate drop me at home where I could spend the next year of my life in the shower trying to get clean. Standing here, with nothing but a faucet and some paper towels, I'm not sure that anything I do will make a dent in the disaster.

Still, I can't spend the night looking like the Creature that escaped from Town Lake, so I gingerly make my way over to the sink. I start by doing the same thing Nate did, dropping my jacket on the floor next to me. Then I wash my hands and face. I don't think there's anything to be done to salvage my clothes—the sweater I'm upset about, the jeans not so much—but I try anyway. Which seems incredibly shallow, even as I'm doing it. How can I care about a sweater when that woman is dead?

Twenty minutes later I decided I've done the best that I can with what I've got. I've pulled my hair back from my face with a butterfly clip I found in my purse. It's still filthy, but I draw the line at washing my hair with hand soap in a police bathroom. But at least the parts of my body I can see are all clean, as is the cut under my eye. It's a doozy and I'm afraid it will scar, but I don't let myself dwell on it. The last thing I want is to feel that fist hit my face yet again.

I even managed to get most of the mud off of Lily's shoes. They still need to be professionally cleaned, but at least I can walk without leaving a trail of mud in my wake.

All in all, I'm feeling about as human as I can get when I walk out of the bathroom. At least until I glance toward Nate's desk and realize that things have just gotten a million times more complicated. Because it isn't Nate's gaze I meet as I start across the room. It's Declan's. And he does not look happy.

Ten

Not that I care if Declan is happy or not, I remind myself determinedly. My first glimpse of him sitting over there like he owns the chair, Nate and this entire police station have rage shooting through me. If he's somehow responsible for this mess—for what's happening to me and what happened to that poor woman—I swear I'm going to find a way to make him pay.

Before I can think better of it—or think at all for that matter—I'm storming across the room, fury a volcano inside of me just begging to erupt. "What are you doing here?"

Nate looks at me curiously. "You *know* Declan Chumomisto?" I can see him processing the fact that I didn't mention this earlier and I feel like an idiot for pulling the whole diva act. The last thing I need is to make the police more suspicious—the existence of witches with real, magical power isn't exactly well known and I do not want to be the one to bring our coven out into the open.

"We've met," I finally tell him. "Briefly."

Declan raises a sardonic brow at my clipped answer, but he doesn't contradict me. Instead, he smiles and says, "It's good to see you again, Xandra. Though I'm sorry my performance earlier wasn't to your liking."

"I wasn't feeling well. My leaving had nothing to do with you." I refuse to admit how he affects me, to him or anyone else. He might already know, but if he doesn't . . .

I'm not going to give him any ideas about picking up where we left off.

"I'm sorry to hear that you were unwell. Are you feeling better now?"

Yeah, because fishing from Town Lake the tortured, mutilated body of a woman who looks remarkably like me was just a barrel of laughs.

"I'm just dandy," I tell him. "Can't you tell?"

Something flashes across his face—amusement, remorse, anger—it happens so fast I can't tell which emotion it is. "I've seen you look better."

"Actually, I don't think you have. Whenever you're around, I seem to be at my worst."

This time there's more than a flicker of emotion on his face, and I grind my teeth when I finally peg it as amusement.

I *hate* the idea that he's laughing at me. Or worse, indulging me, like an adult with a cranky child.

The anger ratchets up a notch to full-fledged fury, puts me on the offensive when that's the last thing I want to do. I'm not a coward, but going head to head with Declan takes more guts than I currently have—at least in a very public police station.

"Why don't you just leave? I don't need or want anything from you."

He holds out his hands in the age-old signal for surrender, which might be believable if his jaw wasn't locked and his eyes weren't swirling with power. "What makes you think I'm here for you?"

It's a reasonable question. I flew off the handle when I saw him, leaped to conclusions that really don't make any sense. Why would he be here for me? For that matter, why is he here at all? I start to ask, but am suddenly afraid of the answer.

Especially when Nate clears his throat, sits straighter. Up until this point, his head has been bouncing back and forth between Declan and me like he's following the ball at a Ping-Pong match.

And even now that the match has stopped, I can all but see his cagey detective's mind trying to figure out how Declan and I fit together. Too bad for him that there's no answer to that puzzle. No matter how you twist and turn us, Declan and I *don't* fit and we never have. Him showing up here after I find a dead body isn't going to change that.

Nate clears his throat. "He's here to see me, Xandra."

Now I'm really confused. It must show on my face because Declan clarifies, "The woman you found tonight was one of my crew." He doesn't sound lazily amused anymore. Instead, there's a thread of his own rage running through the words.

"You've identified her already?" I ask Nate, but he's staring at Declan with narrowed eyes.

"Her purse was found a few yards farther down the lake," Nate tells me before turning to Declan and demanding, "How do you know she's the one who found the body?"

Declan raises a brow, then points at me with a languid finger he shakes up and down, as if to say, *Just look at her*. He has a point. It's not like my bathroom cleanup did much to disguise the fact that I've been rolling around in the mud tonight.

"She could have been mugged," Nate answers.

"Which is why she's hanging out with a homicide detective?"

"We're friends."

This time it's Declan's eyes that narrow. "Not such good friends that it precludes her from coming to my show with another man." The air around us crackles with . . . I don't know what. Something unpleasant.

"Stop baiting Nate," I tell Declan, but my teeth are chattering so hard that I'm not sure he understands me.

Though the police station has the heat turned up, I'm still shivering in my wet clothes. The longer I stand here, the worse it gets.

"But it's so much fun," Declan answers as he stands. Without asking permission, he crosses the room to the ancient coffee machine against the wall. Pours a cup, doctors it, then heads back toward us. As he walks, I notice every eye in the place is on him. The two other women in the room watch his every move with a sensual interest they don't try to hide, while the men very obviously see him as a threat. More than one cop's hand moves to rest on his gun while Declan passes.

Then he's back, standing in front of me and thrusting the cup of coffee into my trembling hands. I take a grateful sip, then nearly spew it back out. No wonder Nate hits Beanz at least once a day. This stuff is horrific. But I'm in no position to complain—it's hot and sweet and exactly what I need to keep the shock at bay.

"Where is Lina?" Declan asks Nate without sitting back down.

"At the morgue. But it's closed right now. I'll set up a time for you to identify her body tomorrow."

Declan nods. "That will be fine." He turns to me. "Come on, Xandra, you need to get home before you catch pneumonia."

Nate stands up. "I'm taking her home." He gestures to the redheaded man who is sitting at the next desk, and who I also saw at the crime scene. "My partner has a few questions for you—"

"Which can wait until tomorrow. Xandra's coming down from an adrenaline rush and when she crashes, she's going to need to be at home."

He wraps an arm around my waist and pulls me into his side, completely disregarding the fine cashmere coat he's wearing. I try to pull away—the last thing I want is Declan Chumomisto manhandling me—but the adrenaline crash he's talking about must be setting in because I have almost no strength. In fact, I feel like my legs are going to go out from under me any second.

"Actually, the questions can't wait." Nate bites out the words from between clenched teeth. "And again, I brought Xandra to the station and I will be the one to escort her home."

Declan smirks, actually smirks. "You're welcome to try."

Shocked and a little uncomfortable, I try to shrug him off as Nate moves out from behind his desk. But Declan holds firm even as Nate gets in his face. "You don't get to decide whether or not you answer these questions."

"I didn't say I wouldn't answer them. I just said I wouldn't answer them now." He starts to walk toward the door, the arm he has around my waist propelling me along with him.

Nate's redheaded partner is there before we take more than a couple of steps and I find myself caught in the middle of three very pissed off men. Oh, Declan is holding it together better than the other two, but it's obvious that he is just as angry. Or at least it's obvious to me—his body is rigid against mine, his jaw so tense that I'm amazed he hasn't yet cracked a tooth.

"You want to sit back down for me, buddy?" Nate's partner asks.

"I don't actually."

"That wasn't a request."

"Really?" Declan tilts his head, looks the guy up and down. "It sounded like one. It probably should be one, unless I'm under arrest. Am I?"

"Not yet," Nate answers him. "Would you like to be?"

"Not particularly. Especially since the last time I saw Lina she was alive, and on stage with me, putting my set together for tonight's show." His smile is full of insult. "But arresting me is the only way you're going to keep me from walking out the door with Xandra, so do what you have to do, officers."

It's a deliberate—and petty—insult, one that busts both Nate and his partner down at least one rank. I see it register on them both, watch as Nate's stance becomes significantly more threatening.

Not that Declan looks threatened. But then again, he's a three-hundred-year-old warlock who also happens to be a fire element. I can't imagine that much frightens him.

Suddenly, I've had enough of all three of them. Using every ounce of strength I have left—which isn't much, I admit—I shove against Declan. Since he's focused on Nate, it works, his hold slackening just enough for me to slip away.

As soon as I'm free, I head for the door as fast as Lily's Jimmy Choos can carry me. "Don't worry about me, gentlemen," I toss over my shoulder. "I'll catch a cab."

My annoyance carries me down the stairs and through the lobby, but the last little burst of adrenaline runs out once I'm at the precinct door. I'm tired, so tired and all I really want to do is curl up into a little ball and hide from the whole world. At least for a little while.

And it totally sucks that Nate got so wrapped up in his little dominance display with Declan that he completely forgot about me. Because I've been around enough men to know that that little match upstairs was about a lot more than who was going to take me home.

And who the hell do Declan and Nate think they are, laying claim to my welfare when neither one of them has any right to make any decision for me, anyway?

I stumble down the stairs to the street on legs like spaghetti. Look up and down the street for a cab, but the abundance of earlier has obviously dried up. Which means I'm walking. Thank God the rain and wind have died down—I don't have the strength left to fight them.

Hell, I don't even have the strength left to fight the shoes. Bending down, I slip them off and then walk barefoot toward the corner, ignoring the chills that wrack my body. I've gone only a couple of steps when a sleek, black Porsche pulls up beside me. I'm not sure what it says about either of us that I'm not even surprised when I see Declan behind the wheel.

"Get in, Xandra. I'll take you home."

Part of me wants to fight him on general principle, but the truth is, I don't have any fight left in me. I'll take the ride home and worry about telling him off later.

When I open the door and slide into the car, Declan's relief is almost palpable. Which is strange—I can't imagine why my going along with him would matter one way or the other.

He doesn't say anything as I fumble my seat belt on, just hands me a Snickers bar before flipping the heat to high and pulling smoothly away from the curb. He turns at Red River, then again at Eleventh Street without any prompting. It freaks me out.

"How do you know where I live?"

"Don't confuse me with that bumbling detective," he tells me. His voice is smoother now that we're alone, and I can hear the power in it. Not just the strength, which he had no problem showing Nate and his partner, but the magic he somehow managed to keep under wraps.

"Have you been spying on me?"

The look he gives me says very clearly that he considers my question beneath him. It might have shut me up when I was nineteen, but now all it does is make me mad. "Declan, it's been almost nine years since we've seen each other. Frankly, the fact that you know where I live smacks of stalkerdom."

"Eight years."

"What?"

"It's been eight years, five months and three weeks since

I last saw you. Not nine years. And why should it upset you if I know where you live? Have I ever bothered you?"

"You're bothering me now."

He makes the turn onto Guadalupe smoothly. "No, I'm taking care of you. I thought the difference between the two was obvious."

"I don't need you to take care of me."

"No offense, Xandra, but I don't think you know what you need." He pulls to the curb in front of my house but I'm so outraged that all I can do is stare at him with my mouth open and teeth bared.

He smiles—a smug, infuriating grin that makes me want to scream—then bops me on the nose like a child. I gasp, a million different insults rushing to my head at the same time, so many that I can't wrap my tongue around any particular one of them. Before I can get over being tongue-tied, he's out of the car and opening my door for me with an old-fashioned flourish.

"I can open my own doors," I tell him stiffly as I climb out.

"Just like you can do your own spells."

"You *asshole*." I lash out before I think it through, my closed fist connecting with his mouth and snapping his head back.

I stare, fascinated, as blood leaks from a cut on his upper lip. He wipes it away with a careless flick of his hand, but the look in his eyes is anything but careless. I should probably apologize—for self-preservation, if nothing else—but I can't bring myself to do it. It's nice to know he's got one human vulnerability. Besides . . .

"You had that coming," I tell him.

"You're right. I did. I apologize." He steps closer and I realize that weird electric current is back. Or, more accurately, it's been back for a while, humming right under the surface, just beneath my skin. But now that Declan is so close, it's intensifying until I can barely think.

Until all I can do is feel.

That's dangerous, though, so I fight against the feelings. Do my best to ignore them. Which is nearly impossible, especially when Declan reaches out a hand and strokes my cheek.

"What happened to your face?" he asks.

I don't know how to explain when I'm not sure I understand it myself. "I fell."

"At the lake?" His fingers probe the wound gingerly.

I jerk my head away. "It was slippery."

"I bet." He pauses for a second. "Thank you for finding her."

As if I had a choice. I start to snap at him, but his words seem sincere, as does the sudden sadness on his face. "Were you ... together?"

"Not for years. But she was a good friend."

I hate the relief sweeping through me at that news. "I'm sorry. For Lina, I mean."

"Yeah, me too. But that's life, isn't it?"

He sounds callous, but only if you don't read between the lines. Declan looks ... weary, and I'm reminded of just how long he's been alive. I think of what I've seen in my twenty-seven years on Earth and wonder how the hell he even gets up in the morning. I have a feeling he's seen more death and destruction than any person should have to.

I lean forward, give him a brief hug because he looks like he needs one, though I refuse to examine the need I have to soothe him.

"Thank you." He smiles as he strokes the backs of his fingers down my cheek. "It's nearly time," he murmurs.

"For what?"

He doesn't answer as his fingers toy with my lower lip for one second, two. I can barely breathe. My diaphragm feels frozen even as every nerve ending I have is lit up like Times Square.

"Declan . . ." I don't know what I want to say, don't know what I'm asking. Only that now isn't the time for this—whatever *this* is. Not when I still stink of death and not when I can actually see flames flickering in his eyes. He's on edge and I'm tapped out. It's not a good combination for anything, even conversation. Especially conversation when I know that I need all my wits about me if I have any hope of holding my own with Declan. Already, something he said is niggling at me, but I'm not lucid enough to figure out what it is.

He pulls away abruptly. "I'll walk you to your door."

"It's a safe neighborhood. I think I'll be okay."

"When are you going to figure it out?" he asks, escorting me onto my front porch. He holds his hands out for my keys and for some reason I give them to him.

"Figure what out?" I ask as he inserts the correct key into the lock without asking.

"It's not the threat you can see that you have to worry about." I start to ask him what he meant by that, but he distracts me when he continues. "Are you going to be able to sleep?"

I look at him like he's crazy as he opens the door, then hands the key back to me. "Oh, yeah. Because I want to relive tonight over and over again."

"I can help you sleep, if you'd like."

"No, thanks." I know he means a spell, and while it's tempting to let him do that for me, the truth is, I just don't trust him enough. This is the man who left me alone on the worst night of my life. The fact that he's here now, seeing me home when I don't need him, doesn't make up for the fact that he skipped out when he did. "While I . . . appreciate the offer, I'm pretty sure I can take it from here."

He takes a step back. "I guess this is good night, then. I'll see you soon."

"I don't think so."

"That's okay. I do." He looks almost tormented by the thought, which only reinforces all the reasons I shouldn't be standing here talking to him. "I'm going to go in now."

He nods. "Eat your Snickers. It will help with the shakiness." Then he touches me, a brief brush of his hand against my shoulder. I feel the tension slowly leak from my shoulders. "Good night, Xandra."

"What did you do?" I demand as he turns and walks away without answering. "Damn it, Declan!" I start down the steps after him, intent on telling him off for messing with me when I expressly told him not to. Except I'm talking to myself, because Declan is already in his car and pulling away from the curb.

Which should be impossible, when one second ago he was standing in front of me. But my brain has been blown enough tonight without me having to worry about the laws of physics and how easily Declan breaks them.

Exhausted, annoyed, frustrated—with both Declan and myself—I turn and walk back onto the porch. I desperately want a shower and then, after that, I'm not sure what I'm going to do. I know I should go to sleep—I've got to be at Beanz by four thirty and it is already well after midnight. I so should have finished up that cookie dough this afternoon. I could have had an extra hour in the morning.

Not that I could have known the night would end up like this. Hell, I've been living it for the past few hours and I still can't believe it.

I shut the door behind me, lock both locks and put the chain on—something neither Lily nor I usually bother with. But after what I saw tonight, I have a feeling I'm going to be walking around jumping at shadows for quite a while.

"So, you're not dead."

Lily's voice comes from the corner and I realize she's

been sitting here in the dark, waiting for me for goddess only knows how long.

"You want to tell me what your disappearing act this evening was all about? And why you've forgotten how to answer a text—or your phone?"

I laugh at her tone, at how much she sounds like an annoyed mother whose daughter has just missed curfew. I laugh and laugh and laugh, the sound tinged with hysteria that I can do nothing about.

"Xandra." Her voice filled with concern now, Lily stands up and snaps on a nearby light. "Holy shit! What happened to you?"

"It's been a long night." I head to the shower, conscious as I do that I'm probably dropping mud all over Lily's clean hardwood floors. She's not OCD about much, but the floors are kind of her thing. If they're dirty, she freaks out.

Nothing I can do about that now. I'll just have to mop when I get home from work.

Lily follows me toward my room, and the fact that she doesn't say anything about the mess I'm making is a definite indicator of her level of concern. Though she does pause along the way to grab a trash bag.

"Tell me," she says, gesturing with the trash bag so that I know to drop my clothes straight into it instead of on the floor. I spend a second mourning my favorite sweater, but in the grand scheme of things, a ruined sweater doesn't seem so bad. Especially since I'm not sure I'd ever be able to wear it again anyway. Memories from tonight are not ones I particularly want to hang on to. Hell, I'm not sure I even want to tell Lily what happened. Not because I want to keep it a secret, but because I don't want to bring the ugliness into our home.

Still, I owe her an explanation, so I begin the story with halting breaths and choppy sentences. As I talk, I begin to strip. First the shoes. "I'm sorry. I'll buy you a new pair," I tell Lily as I hand her the beloved, and now ruined, Jimmy Choos.

It's a mark of what a good friend she is that she barely hesitates as she tosses them into the trash bag. "They're just shoes," she tells me.

She must have been more worried about me than I thought.

I strip my sweater off just as Lily clicks my bedroom light on. She screams and drops the trash bag before I can launch the ruined garment into it.

I whirl around, visions of an attacker tearing in my head. "What's wrong?" I demand when I don't see any kind of threat.

But she's just staring at me with horrified eyes, both hands clasped over her mouth.

"Lily? Are you okay?"

"What happened to you, Xandra?" She crosses the room, puts tentative fingers on my arm.

I glance down, try to figure out what has her so startled and nearly scream myself. My entire upper body is covered with bruises. My arms, my breasts, my stomach — and judging from the way Lily is tracing crisscrossing lines across my shoulders, so is my back.

"What the hell happened to you?" Her voice is shaky now and there are tears in her eyes.

"I don't know." But then I think back to those agonizing minutes when I relived everything Lina went through. "Are there any cuts?" I demand, craning my neck to get a look at my back.

"No. Just bruises. But these look like whip marks. And I swear this is the imprint of a fist." She swallows audibly. "Were you attacked, Xandra? Were you—"

"No! I swear, none of this happened to me." I rush to tell her what happened and as I do, her eyes grow wider and wider.

"Dear goddess, dear goddess, dear goddess." She repeats the words over and over again as I strip off my jeans and stand before her in my wet bra and panties. Then she looks me over, writing down every injury she finds. Most are bruises, like the whip marks across my back but every once in a while there's a cut like the one on my face.

I have a shallow slice on my left thigh, a welt on my right hip. There are some scrapes on my breasts and ribs that I know I got from the tree branches near the lake, but all the other injuries seem to be shallow imitations of Lina's.

"Psychic echoes," Lily breathes, running her hand lightly over the array of bruises that decorate my ribs.

"Watch it!" I yelp when she presses a little too hard.

"With physical manifestations. I've never heard of anything like this before," she whispers. "It's definitely not white magic doing this."

Like I need to be a Heka scholar to figure that out? If she'd been there, if she'd seen and felt what that monster had done to Lina, then it wouldn't even have occurred to her that it could be anything but the darkest magic that did this.

I shudder at the thought. I don't like that it was this close to me, that it got the chance to mark me like this. "What does it mean?" I ask, forcing my voice steady by will alone.

"I have no idea."

"Is it inside of me? I thought magic like this could only touch you if you open yourself to it. If you let it inside."

Lily must hear the rising panic in my voice, because she grabs both my arms with gentle hands—enough to get my attention but not to hurt. "Xandra, you're one of the best people I know. Whoever did this, however he did it, his magic isn't inside you. You don't have to worry about that."

"How do you know?"

"Because I know what dark power feels like and what I feel coming from you is nothing like that."

I'm abruptly ashamed. I'm so caught up in freaking out that for a moment I forgot Lily had lost her only brother to the lure of dark magic. "I'm sorry," I tell her.

She shakes her head. "You have every right to be concerned—there's nothing to apologize for."

"None of this should be happening at all. I'm latent!"

"You were latent. Now I don't know *what* you are. But you're definitely packing some kind of power."

"The belladonna—"

"I don't think so." She shakes her head. "I mean, I'll do the research, but that's pretty much an old witch's tale. Your mom got suckered."

"Then what's going on?"

"I have no idea." She gestures to the bathroom. "Go take a shower and while you're in there, start at the beginning. You need to tell me everything. I have two weeks before I head back to school—I'm going to run this to ground before then, or die trying."

What Lily doesn't say but what hangs in the room is that if we don't figure out what's happening, she won't be the one who dies. After all, how many times can I go through what happened to me tonight?

I start the shower and she turns her back while I strip off my muddy bra and panties, dropping them in the garbage bag with the rest of my clothes. Then I step into the shower and let the boiling hot water wash away the dirt and the blood and the tension. If only it could wipe away the memories as easily.

But they're still there, pouring out in fits and starts as I wash my hair and scrub my body again and again and again. Lily doesn't say much, just listens. But when I reach for my bottle of Amber Romance shower gel for the fourth time, she quietly says, "Enough, Xandra. You're clean."

"I don't feel clean."

"I know. But you are. You have to trust me on this or you'll peel your skin right off your body."

That doesn't sound so bad. Maybe then I'll finally stop feeling her cold, clammy body under my fingers. Against my legs.

"Besides, that can't feel good against those bruises."

Funny, but I barely notice them. It's not that they don't hurt—because they do—but they're nothing compared to the anguish that threatens to rip me apart every time I think of Lina and the girl back home in the forest. I try to block the pain, to focus on the rhyme and reason of this whole situation, but it isn't easy. Not when I keep thinking I'm to blame for their deaths.

The way I see it, either there's some strange connection between the killer and me, which allows me to feel things about the murders, or those poor women were just pawns, a way for him to strike at me without actually going after a member of the Ipswitch royal family. I really hope it's the former, no matter how scary and twisted that is. Because the alternative—that I'm responsible for the brutal deaths of two young women who look an awful lot like me—I don't know how I'll live with.

At Lily's continued urging, I finally flip the shower off. When I turn back around, Lily's arm has crept around the edge of the shower curtain and she's holding one of the big, fluffy red towels I love.

"I'll make some tea," she says.

"You don't have to do that. I know you're tired."

She snorts. "Don't be a martyr. Besides, I want to do your tarot again."

"I'm not being a martyr. And there's no way you're doing my tarot, ever again." I climb out of the shower wrapped in the towel, then turn to get my hairbrush off the sink.

Lily gasps. I'm about to tell her to knock it off—I

know the bruises are bad and don't need to be constantly reminded of them—when she says, "When did you get a new tattoo?"

A sick feeling starts in the pit of my stomach, separate from the knot that's already there. "What are you talking about?"

She doesn't answer. Instead, she lays her fingers gently on my left shoulder blade and traces a star into my skin.

And not just any star. A Seba.

"I swear these weren't there before your shower," she murmurs. "But I suppose they could have just been covered by mud."

Completely freaked out now, I rip off the towel, disregarding modesty as I whirl to look at my back in the mirror. Sure enough, on my left shoulder blade—underneath a colorful array of bruises—is a silver Seba. And then, about an inch over, arching like it wants to follow the curve of my upper back, is a second one. They are identical to each other, and more importantly, to the one I already have in the middle of my palm.

The one I got from Declan eight years ago.

Eleven

I don't sleep. Though I escape from Lily's coddling, and slightly claustrophobia-inducing clutches, sometime around two thirty, I don't bother trying to sleep. One, because I have to be up at four to get to work and two, because I'm terrified that if I close my eyes I'll be bombarded by images of that poor woman. Of Lina. Or worse. I'll get sucked into a world where I'm fascinated, instead of repelled, by Declan Chumomisto.

Instead, I sit in the center of my bed, iPod blasting old Aerosmith and Metallica songs, while I play game after game of Mah-Jongg. If I work at it, if I play fast enough, then I can't think. Can't feel.

Except, every once in a while I'll click on a tile and it will remind me of something. The trees down at Town Lake. The bridge. The number seven, which started this whole mess twenty-seven years ago.

Every time they creep up, I push the thoughts away. I concentrate harder on the game, on the music and the lyrics pouring through my earbuds. It almost works. Except I know I can't run forever. Sooner or later, I'm going to have to decide what to do. Who to trust and who to run from, because the more I don't think about this, the more I become convinced that I am in really deep trouble. Trouble that pleading ignorance isn't going to get me out of.

Finally, the longest hour and a half of my life draws to

a close and I spring out of bed. I've never been so relieved to get to go to work in my life. I dress quickly, in a clean pair of jeans and a bright red turtleneck sweater. I can use the pick-me-up from the color today, plus both garments do a decent job of covering my bruises.

Except for a little cover-up on the cut under my eye, I don't bother with makeup. Just brush my teeth and run a quick brush through my hair. I look like hell, but I didn't expect anything else. Combine everything that happened yesterday with a night of no sleep and I figure I'm doing good not to look like a flesh-eating zombie. Although, now that I think about it, my eyes are awfully glazed . . .

Shrugging it off, I slip into a pair of comfortable red flats and head for the door, picking up my backpack on the way out. Normally, I walk to and from work every day—it's only about a mile and it saves a parking spot for customers in Beanz's small lot—but after last night's horrific stumble through downtown, I find myself craving the safety of my car.

Besides, it's raining again and I have no desire to ever walk in the rain again.

I'm at work in less than five minutes—there's no traffic at this time of the morning—and it's not until I'm locked in the shop, music blasting and baking ingredients spread out in front of me, that I finally relax.

I have a little more than an hour before Beanz opens and plenty to do to keep me busy. I mix up a big batch of pumpkin muffins and get them in the oven before starting on the blueberry streusel ones. I pop them in the second oven, then work on a huge batch of chocolate cookies.

Normally, I love to make cookies. I love the mixing of the dry ingredients, the mixing of the wet ingredients and then the combining of the two to make something wonderful. Maybe it's because it reminds me of potion-making with my mother, which was my favorite activity when I was young. She always mixes different parts of her potions in different containers before combining them at the end. She swears they're more powerful that way, and having been the recipient of more than one through the years, I tend to agree with her.

Cooking, especially baking, isn't much different from making a powerful potion, really. You have a recipe to follow—a little of this, a lot of that—all combined in perfect, preset proportions. But at the end, when the main dough, or potion, is set . . . that's when you get to experiment. Add a different kind of nut or some butterscotch chips or maybe a few ground-up toffee bars for the cookies. Play with the herbs and flowers and magical binders for the potion. And suddenly, depending on the talent of the cook, you have something amazing. Something just a little bit better than the competition.

My ability to turn experiments into something wonderful is what's made Beanz the most popular coffeehouse in Austin and it's that same ability that has made my mother the most revered potion-maker in our coven and several others. Though I know it won't get me anywhere, I often wonder if I wasn't latent, if I actually did have power, would I have followed in my mother's footsteps?

Not that it matters, I suppose. It's just interesting to think about. Especially when Lily's voice echoes in my head, telling me that while she might not know what is going on with me, she does know that I'm no longer latent. I'm not sure that I believe her, but I could just be burying my head in the sand. It's a popular pastime of mine, after all.

I relax as I cook, fall into a familiar rhythm where the motions are so second nature to me that I don't have to think. I can just be. Normally, I love that rhythm, but today it's dangerous. I've barely gotten the wet ingredients into the mixer when a picture of Declan flashes into my mind. Only it's not the Declan I know, dressed all in sophisticated and expensive black. Instead, he's draped in the red robes and golden crown of the Magician, the infinity sign on his pointy hat with a wand in one hand and a crystal ball in the other.

I blank the image away, focus instead on how the sugar and eggs and butter and vanilla blend together. But when I start to add the dry ingredients, Lina's body flashes into my mind's eye, only with my face in place of hers. I blink a few times, shake my head—as if it's that easy to get the image out. It's just a daymare, I tell myself, a daydream gone horribly wrong. And I might actually believe it if that damn five of swords didn't float right at the edges of my consciousness. Taunting me with my inescapable future defeat.

Again, I don't set much store in tarot by itself, but Lily is a powerful seer. When she reads tarot, you can't help but pay attention. It's why she was so nervous last night before the show and why I'm nervous still, even after everything that's happened. A sick feeling in the pit of my stomach tells me that all this is only the beginning.

The buzzer at the back door of the café goes off, and I glance at the clock. It's five fifteen already and I forgot to unlock the door for Meg and Travis, the two UT students who help me handle morning rush every Monday through Friday. I rush to the door, let them in, then hurry to get the muffins out of the ovens and the cookies into them.

"Big night?" Travis asks, as he slips into an apron and starts brewing coffee in the four large carafes we always keep fresh during open hours.

"Why? What have you heard?"

As soon as the words are out of my mouth, I know I've said the wrong thing. His eyes gleam with interest as he fills one of the carafes. "Nothing yet. But please, do tell."

"Nothing interesting, I swear."

"Why do I doubt that?"

"Doubt what?" asks Meg, sticking her head through the doorway from the front of the house, where she's getting milk ready to steam and checking to be sure that everything's stocked for the morning rush.

"Boss lady's holding out on us." Travis winks at me. "She had a scorching hot date last night and refuses to share the details."

"Sorry to disappoint you," I say, slipping the muffins from the tins and onto a platter for the front display cabinet. "But there was no hot date."

"Really? So he fizzled out?" Travis asks.

"Who?"

"The guy Lily was setting you up with. She called yesterday when you were with a customer and we discussed whether you would be, let's just say, *amenable* to the idea. I would never have voted yes if I'd known he was a dud."

"Ugh. Duds are the worst," Meg pipes in. "Especially when they're blind dates."

"Don't let ole Kyle get you down," Travis says as he slides the platter of muffins from my hands and carries them to the front.

"You know his name?" I demand, pulling the first batch of cookies from the oven.

"Honey, I know his shoe size. You don't actually think Lily and I would send you on a date with some guy if we didn't know almost everything there was to know about him, do you? The world's a dangerous place."

"Don't I know it." I slide another batch of cookies into the top oven and finally slip the blueberry streusel muffins from the bottom.

"So, what's the flavor of the day?" Meg asks, as she

pulls out the cookies I baked yesterday and starts arranging them on another tray.

I try to remember which holiday flavors we'd brewed lately, but it doesn't take long before I give up. My brain is fried. "You and Travis decide."

"Peppermint," they both say at the same time.

"Again?" I ask. "Wasn't that yesterday's flavor, too?"

"It's always the first carafe to empty. Besides, New Year's is just three days away. We won't be able to serve it after that, so I say let's go for it." Travis is already pouring the peppermint flavored beans into the grinder.

"We open in five," Meg warns, transferring a few of the snickerdoodles from the warm cookie tray onto the serving platter.

"We're ready," I say as I put the last of the muffins in the display case. I walk around the front to make sure everything looks good, just as Travis flips the sign on the door to OPEN.

Within ten minutes, customers start trickling in at a fairly steady rate. Doctors and nurses heading into the nearby hospitals for a six o'clock shift change, cops and paramedics doing the same, construction workers getting ready to start before the sun finishes coming up.

By seven o'clock we're slammed, even without the college business, and I don't have time to think much before eleven when the last of the late-morning rush finally eases off. But the lunch crowd is just around the corner, and while it's lighter than the coffee hounds, we still do a pretty brisk business.

Behind me, I hear Sarah and Meg chattering away as they prep the vegetables for the various sandwiches we offer. Travis, who works only enough hours to keep himself in beauty products, shrugs out of his apron and blows me a kiss. "See you tomorrow, Xandra."

I wave good-bye, then turn to deliver the cinnamon

latte I've just made to a waiting customer. As I do, I catch sight of the tall, lean, dark-haired man walking through the café's doors. It's been years since I've seen him, but I recognize him right away. Ryder Chumomisto, Declan's younger but still powerful brother.

The latte slips from my suddenly nerveless fingers, hits the ground and explodes. I'm drenched in hot coffee that I barely feel.

"Shit." Though I'm the one getting burned, Travis is the one who reacts first. Grabbing a couple of towels from under the counter, he rubs them down my legs in an effort to collect as much of the coffee as possible.

"I'm sorry," I tell the customer whose drink I'm now wearing. "Travis will make you a new one."

"Right away," he says, handing me the towels so I can finish drying myself off. But before he heads for the espresso machine, he sneaks a quick glance at Ryder. "Tell me that wasn't the dud?" he says under his breath as he moves past me.

"No."

"Thank God. Maybe there is justice in the world after all."

Within two minutes, I've cleaned up the mess and he's sliding a fresh latte across the counter to the woman, who seems as blinded by Ryder's good looks as Travis is. He actually has to nudge her along to make room for Ryder at the counter.

When she finally takes the hint and leaves—or at least, retires to a corner table where she can continue gawking at Ryder in peace—Travis turns the full wattage of his on-the-prowl grin at Ryder. "What can I get *you*?" he purrs, leaning across the counter in that way he does when he wants to show off his ab definition.

I know some straight guys, especially in Texas, would be offended, but Ryder takes Travis's interest in stride.

Then again, when you look like Ryder, I guess you have to get used to people tripping all over themselves to get your attention.

"Ummm . . ." He skims the menu for a second, then says, "I'll just take a cup of coffee."

"Coffee, it is." Travis pulls a large cup from the stack and hands it to him. "Have you been here before?"

"No."

"We're a little different than some coffeehouses. All our regular coffee is free refill, and you can help yourself over there." He points to our coffee stand. "Cream and sugar is against the wall, and, since we love to see new faces in here, the cookie is on the house." He reaches into the display case and pulls out one of my secret recipe chocolate chip cookies and slides it into a pastry bag. "I hope you enjoy."

Ryder grins and I swear I can see Travis melt right there, which is a rare occurrence. Travis, as he likes to remind me regularly, has been around the block a few times. It usually takes more than a pretty face to turn him into a puddle of goo.

"That'll be two fifty," he tells Ryder after ringing up the coffee only.

"Actually, his whole order's on the house." I figure I'd better step in or Travis will have Ryder naked before he knows what's hit him.

Ryder's smile grows wider. "Xandra."

"Ryder. Long time no see."

"It sure has been. I've missed you."

"Of course you have."

"Do you have a few minutes?" He holds up the cup Travis gave him. "Time for coffee?"

"I can make time, if Travis doesn't mind staying a few minutes longer." I turn to Travis with a raised brow.

He's facing me now, and sulking over the fact that he

lost his new toy. "Whatever," he mumbles to me, complete with eye roll.

"Thanks, Travis. I owe you."

"Huge," he answers. "You owe me huge."

"Gigantic."

As Travis starts working his way down the small line that's formed behind Ryder, I grab an empty cup and head around the counter toward my unexpected guest.

"So, what brings you into my humble shop?" I ask after we're both seated at a corner table, our coffees on the table between us. My jeans are wet and sticky and they feel gross against my legs.

"Declan mentioned he ran into you last night. I wanted to stop by and say hello. Check out the most happening coffeehouse in Austin." He looks around. "You did good, kid."

"Thanks."

I preen a little bit at the compliment. And if things hadn't gone down the way they had last night, I might even have believed him. After all, Ryder and I have known each other for years—he and my sister Hannah were a serious item for a long time when I was young. We'd all thought they'd end up getting married, but something happened right after my nineteenth birthday and he left town in a hurry—*after* breaking my sister's heart.

It's a trait that must run in the Chumomisto family.

"So, what are you actually doing here?" I ask. "Not that I don't appreciate the bullshit, but the lunch rush is about to hit and I'm covered in designer coffee. I've got things to do."

He laughs then, a low, delighted sound that lights up the air around us. I find myself laughing with him, this man who always had time for Hannah's little sister, even when Hannah didn't.

I've seen him only a couple of times in the last eight years, but he hasn't changed a bit. Same mischievous green eyes, same long dark hair tied in a small ponytail at the nape of his neck. Same gorgeous face and wicked smile. He looks a lot like Declan, actually, with different-colored eyes and without the dangerous aura that surrounds his brother wherever he goes.

"That's my Xandra," he says. "Always the straight shooter."

"Which is more than I can say about you or your brother."

"I hear Declan really blew it with you last night."

"Did you? And here I didn't think he'd noticed."

"Oh, he noticed. He sent me here to wave the white flag. I think he hoped you'd be blinded by affection for me and forget what a dumbass he was."

"That's a lot of affection."

"Which is what I told him. But he's tied up this morning with those tiresome homicide detectives and he insisted I come and invite you to dinner." I feel a little nudge around the edges of my mind, but it's so light it barely registers. I don't pay any attention to it.

"I don't think so," I tell him with a shake of my head. "Last night was pretty rough and all I want to do is get through work today. Then I'm going home and going straight to bed."

"We can make it a late dinner. You can take a nap and then we'll pick you up whatever time you'd like." The nudge grows a little stronger, into a full-fledged push, and I realize it's Ryder at the same time I slam down an instinctive barrier between us.

I don't know why I didn't register what he was doing before. It's not like I don't know what Ryder's powers are. He's a powerful telepath and a very strong influencer — he can get inside almost anyone's mind, usually without them knowing he's there, and sway them in whatever direction he'd like. It's a useful talent, and a frightening one. He's never used it on me before, and now that he has, I find myself pretty damn annoyed.

"What are you doing?" I demand.

He just smiles enigmatically. "You really are all grown up, aren't you, Xandra?"

"Did you expect differently?"

"I'm not sure what I expected."

"Me neither. But I can tell you, it wasn't a trick like that from someone I consider an old friend."

He has the grace to look ashamed. "I'm sorry. That was uncool."

"It was extremely uncool." I shove back from the table, stand up. "I think it's probably time for you to go now."

He stands as well. "No second chance?"

I gesture to the table. "This was your second chance. You hurt Hannah."

For a second, regret flashes in his eyes. "I really am sorry about how that whole thing turned out."

This time I don't say anything, just fold my arms over my chest and wait for him to leave.

"You sure I can't convince you to see Declan tonight?" This time the fingers creeping around my brain are a lot lighter, nearly nonexistent. "He'd very much like the chance to talk to you."

If I was thinking straight, I'd probably say yes. After everything that happened last night, there are things I need to know and Declan might be just the warlock to tell them to me. But I'm so offended that he and Ryder thought to crawl inside my brain like this that I'm not interested—at all.

This time when I shove Ryder out, I'm not nice about it. I watch in satisfaction as he winces, presses a hand to his forehead.

"I guess that's a no."

"That's a hell no."

We stare at each other a moment and I feel it there, between us. The question of how a latent witch like I am has the power to even notice Ryder picking through my mind, let alone shove him the hell out of it. On the heels of that question is the realization that Ryder has probably picked his way through my mind numerous times before, only I was too stupid or blind to notice.

So what's different now? What is going on that all of these strange things are happening and I seem to be squarely in the middle of them? Again, I think about accepting Declan's invitation, but at this point I don't know if that thought came from me or if Ryder has found a way back into my head, one I don't notice this time.

Until I know for sure, I'm not agreeing to anything he suggests. I'm paranoid like that.

Before I can kick him out of my shop as well as my brain, the bell at the door jangles and I turn to greet the new customer with a forced smile on my face. Except it's not a customer, it's Nate, and he looks about like I feel. If I added on twelve hours of actively trying to track down a murderer, that is.

He spots me right away, and I can tell from the annoyed look on his face that he knows who Ryder is—and he is not pleased to find him here with me. The two men glare at each other for a second, then Ryder pulls a card out of his pocket and presses it into my hand. "In case you change your mind," he whispers, bending down to kiss my cheek. That I know he does it just to infuriate Nate pisses me off even more.

For a second I fantasize about kicking him in the balls. But that would probably get Nate all riled up, not to mention the rest of my customers, so I satisfy myself with a tight smile. "Don't count on it."

"You're the one I am counting on, Xandra." And with that cheesy line, he makes his exit.

I want to watch him, to see if he actually walks away or if he disappears like Declan somehow manages to every time I see him. But Nate's here and from the look on his face, he is out of patience. It's definitely time for some damage control.

"You want the usual?" I ask him as I head toward the front counter.

He grabs my wrist, pulls me to a stop. "I'm pretty sure you know I'm not here for coffee."

At the counter, Travis's eyes widen and I can only imagine what he's thinking. I turn to Nate. "This is my place of business. I'm working."

"That didn't stop you from taking time out to talk to Ryder Chumomisto." There's a hint of accusation in his voice that he doesn't even try to hide.

I don't owe him any explanations and at the moment I'm annoyed enough to want to not give him any. But that smacks of cutting off my nose to spite my face, so I finally tell him, "He's an old family friend. He used to date my sister."

Nate's eyes narrow, like he's recalculating some equation I don't even know about. "And what about Declan Chumomisto? Did he used to date your sister too?"

My whole body recoils at the thought of that, a little voice deep inside me screaming, No! The knee-jerk reaction, and the possession that seems inherent in it, stresses me out, but now isn't exactly the time to deal with it. Still, it takes every ounce of composure I have to grind out the word, "No."

"So, how do you know him?"

This time it's my eyes that narrow. "Is this an interrogation, Nate?"

"It doesn't have to be."

"That sounds like it already is. Should I call a lawyer?"

I'm baiting him, I admit it, but the last thing I expect is for him to answer, "Do you think you need one?"

"What? No!" I turn to walk away, and that's when I realize he's still holding my wrist. I wrench it away, disregarding the pain the sudden movement sends shooting through my already abused body. "I don't think I want to talk to you anymore right now."

He sighs, runs a hand through his hair in that gesture of his I usually like so much because it means I've caught him off guard, and that he's thinking about me. At the moment, though, it just pisses me off since I'm afraid what he's thinking about is how to trap me into confessing to a murder I did not commit.

"Come on, Xandra. Let's not do this the hard way. I have some questions—hopefully you have some answers." He sighs. "I thought we were friends."

"So did I, but I'm not in the habit of letting my friends manhandle me."

"You didn't seem to have a problem when Chumomisto did it last night."

There's a hard edge to his voice that was never there before, and I realize I'm dealing with more than just a suspicious cop. "I never said he was my friend."

Silence, taut as a high wire, stretches between us. Nate breaks first. "I know you didn't kill that girl, Xandra. So can I please take you to lunch and ask you some follow-up questions about last night?"

My anger drains out of me at the reasonable request, and all I'm left with is exhaustion. Between Ryder and Nate, they've pushed me right up against my personal wall and I can feel myself drooping. It's not the best time to talk to a cop, but then I don't have anything to hide. Except, of course, for the fact that I'm a witch. And Declan's a warlock. And the killer probably is one too. And I'm covered in inexplicable wounds and bruises inflicted by magic. Oh, and Ryder can get inside people's minds.

Scratch that, I have a lot to hide.

"Grab a table," I tell Nate. "I'll get us something from the back."

"Can you stay an extra half an hour?" I ask Travis as I pass the counter. "I'll pay overtime."

"I'll stay for regular pay, as long as I get the scoop."

"There is no scoop." I start making a triple espresso for myself and a coffee with steamed milk for Nate.

Travis snorts. "Xandra, honey, two of the hottest men I have ever seen just snarled over you like two dogs that want the same bone. There is definitely a scoop here."

"You misunderstood."

"Baby girl, there's a lot of things I misunderstand. Two men getting territorial is not one of them."

"Ryder's like my brother. In fact, he was almost my brother-in-law." I pop the drinks on a tray along with a couple of cookies, then head to the back where Meg and Jenn are filling orders.

"Can I take these?" I ask, gesturing to a couple of grilled veggie sandwiches they've just assembled.

Meg nods, wide-eyed, which means Travis has been keeping them apprised of all the action that's gone on in the last half hour. Terrific. Nothing like working years to establish myself as a serious business owner only to have two alpha males tear the whole thing to pieces in less than an hour. I can only imagine what will happen if Declan ever shows up here.

Tray loaded with food, I storm out of the kitchen and back to Nate. Ryder may be out of my reach, but Nate's still here and he has a very short time to clean up his act or I'm going to kick him to the curb too. Loudly and publicly.

"What do you want to know?" I ask as I slam the tray down onto the table.

"Thanks for the food," Nate says, accepting the plate I hand him. "It looks great."

"I only have a few minutes," I tell him. "If you really want to spend that time complimenting a sandwich . . ."

"Okay, fine." He takes a sip of his coffee before sitting back in his chair and just looking at me.

His stare freaks me out a little bit. I haven't done anything wrong, but just sitting here, knowing he's thinking I might have had something to do with that poor woman's death, makes me nervous.

Trying to look cool, I fumble my own coffee cup to my lips and nearly drop it in the process. Because nothing says cool like dropping two cups of coffee on yourself in under an hour.

Nate smiles at my nerves, but that's about all he does to disabuse me of them. Instead, he sits there and watches me squirm. I know he's waiting for me to break the silence, to blurt something out that he can run with, but I keep my mouth shut. I haven't done anything wrong and he has no right to treat me as if I have.

I pick up my sandwich, take a bite. I already told him I have only a few minutes. If he wants to waste those minutes in a glorified staring contest, then that's his problem, not mine.

I've eaten about a quarter of my sandwich when he finally breaks the silence. In my head, I make another tally mark in my column. Something tells me I'm going to need all the points I can get in this interview. "Tell me about Declan Chumomisto."

I swallow the red pepper I've just popped in my mouth. "I don't know if I'm the right person to tell you about him. I don't know him very well."

"When did you meet?"

"At my nineteenth birthday party. It was a big deal, kind of like a coming-out party. My parents invited hundreds of people and he was one of them."

He pauses, like that isn't the answer he was expecting. "You had a coming-out party?"

"It's a big deal where I'm from."

"And where is that?"

Damn. The last thing I want is him digging around my hometown. Still, flat-out lying to Nate seems like a very bad idea. "Ipswitch," I tell him.

He writes it down. Double damn. "When was the next time you saw him?"

"Saw him? Last night, on stage. Talked to him? Afterward, at the police station."

He frowns. "You're telling me that you only met him once before last night?"

"Yes."

"It didn't feel like that. It felt like you two knew each other pretty well."

"We did a lot of talking the night of my party. When it was over, he disappeared and I never heard from him again."

"Even though you knew his brother."

It's not a question, but I answer anyway. "Even though."

"When you were down at the lake last night, did you see anyone?"

"No."

"Not Declan or Ryder or anyone else?"

"Declan would have still been on stage when I first got to the lake. And I called for help not long after I got there, so your police officers know everyone who was down there as well as I do. Besides, it was raining. It wasn't exactly a popular place to be last night."

"And yet you were down there."

"Yes." I know I sound wary now, but it's not like he's being subtle about the trap he's laying.

"Why were you down there again?"

"I told you last night. I wasn't feeling good, but I didn't want to interrupt anyone else. The tickets for Declan's show are expensive."

"Declan didn't give you those tickets?"

"No. I told you, I haven't spoken to him in over eight years. Kyle and Brandon had the tickets and they invited us to go."

"And you said yes."

"More like my friend, Lily, roped me into going on a blind date with Kyle so she could go out with Brandon, but if that's how you want to look at it, then yes. I agreed to go out with them."

"And then you left in the middle of what I've heard was a one-in-a-million kind of show because you didn't feel well?"

"I was nauseous, afraid I was going to throw up."

"But you didn't throw up."

"No."

"So, can you tell me how you ended up down at Town Lake when you live in the other direction? You could have been home in ten minutes after leaving the Paramount last night, yet you deliberately turned in the wrong direction."

I cringe a little, but only inside where no one else can see. It's the question—and the explanation—that I'd been dreading ever since I called the police last night. "I made a couple wrong turns. It was dark. I didn't feel well. I got disoriented. I made a mistake."

"That's a two-mile mistake, in the pouring rain."

"Yes."

Nate doesn't answer for a minute, just concentrates on eating half of his sandwich in three efficient bites. The quiet, after all those questions, is somehow worse than the interrogation.

And when he does speak again, the question he asks is so unexpected that I stumble over it from sheer shock. "Xandra, why are you wearing a turtleneck today? I don't think in all the months I've been coming to Beanz that I have ever seen you in one."

My hand goes instinctively to the collar in question. "It's been hot. Only recently has it cooled down enough for me to pull it out and wear it."

"That's it? No other reason?"

"What other reason could there be?" A drop of sweat rolls down my back. Nate will flip if he sees the bruises.

He doesn't answer immediately, just stares at me with eyes that burn with a verdant, unquenchable fire. Then he says, "I've seen it, Xandra. Numerous times." He reaches out and taps my neck.

"My circlet of Isis? So what if you've seen it? I don't exactly keep it a secret." But I know what he's getting at and I have no idea what I'm going to tell him.

"I'm not going to play this game with you. It's an unusual tattoo, one I've never seen anywhere but on you. What do you think the odds are that you're the one who just happens to find a body that has that same symbol carved into it?"

Pretty damn low, actually, which is one of the many reasons I didn't sleep last night. But I don't tell him that, I can't. Not without explaining to him that there are a lot of forces at work here that neither one of us has any hope of understanding. Especially him.

At the same time, I'm not going to just roll over either. "I didn't kill her, Nate."

"I don't think that you did. At the estimated time of death, you were at dinner with three other people, all of whom swore you were eating a vegetarian entrée and drinking a glass of Pinot Noir."

"You checked my alibi."

"Of course I did. I had to rule you out." He reaches across the table and grabs on to my hand. "Listen, I know you, Xandra. I know you and I know you didn't do this. But I still had to make sure, because for people who don't know you, you're a pretty damn viable suspect."

"But I didn't do it."

"No. But that doesn't mean someone doesn't want us to think you did it."

"By someone, you mean the killer."

"Yes. I think he might very well be setting you up to take the fall for all of this. I want to make damn sure that doesn't happen."

Twelve

Nate's words make an awful kind of sense, especially if I factor in the weird compulsion from last night that I am desperately afraid was some kind of spell. All this time I've been wondering if this is happening because someone wants to kill me. But what if that's not it at all? What if they want to frame me instead?

If they're trying to use me to get to my family, it's a good way to do it.

This time, I'm the one who is quiet—and the one who finally breaks the silence. "Who would do something like that?" I whisper. I'm asking myself as much as Nate. I've kept a low profile in the Heka community for years—at least as much of a low profile as a member of Ipswitch's royal family can. If Nate's right, my profile hasn't been low enough. Or maybe it's been too low and whoever this is figures I'm the weak link in my family chain.

Which is true, no doubt about it. But there's no way I'm going to let anyone turn me into a weapon to be used against my parents. My mom may drive me nuts, but I love her and my father fiercely. If what Nate is surmising is true, I must find a way to protect them. To protect all of them.

"Finding out who's doing this is going to hinge largely on what the motive is," Nate says in answer to my question. "I have to figure out which part of the equation is the payoff for the killer. Either someone killed Lina because she was the intended victim and framing you is just an attempt to cover up his guilt or someone is after you specifically and killed Lina as a means to get to you."

His thoughts are very close to mine from earlier, which reinforces both my logic and my guilt. Of course, they also scare the hell out of me. "How do we stop this from happening?"

"I have to figure out who's really doing this. Right now, I'm looking for someone who has a connection to both you and the victim. And after preliminary runs, only two people fit that bill."

"Declan and Ryder."

"The Chumomistos, yes." He uses their last name like he can't bear the familiarity of the first names. Which I guess I understand if he actually thinks one of them is a killer.

"They wouldn't do that. I know Ryder and Declan. They couldn't do what was done to that poor girl. They don't have that kind of violence in them."

"You just got through telling me that you don't know Declan very well. Or Ryder, really. Now you think you know whether or not they're capable of murder?"

"I think everyone is capable of murder under the right circumstances, Nate, but that doesn't mean these are those circumstances for either of the Chumomistos."

"It doesn't mean that these aren't those circumstances either. You don't know what's in either of their minds. Are you aware that Declan was sleeping with Lina?"

He's just thrown a sucker punch to my gut and he knows it, but I struggle not to let anything show. "They were over a long time ago."

"Is that what he told you?" His phone rings and he stops, glances down at it, then silences the ring. "Look, I'm not saying I think they're guilty. I shouldn't be talking about the case with you anyway—I only did because I'm worried about your safety. I'm just saying that you need to be careful, because one way or another, I'm afraid someone has you in their crosshairs and I don't think they're going to let up until they have what they want."

"Which is?"

"You dead or in prison for a crime you didn't commit." He stands. "Look, thanks for lunch. I appreciate it. But I want you to promise me you'll be careful. No more wandering the city on foot alone after dark. At least not until we have a better handle on what's going on here."

I nod, because really, what else am I going to do? I walk Nate to the door, watch him stroll away, as if he doesn't have a care in the world, when I know he does. I wonder if the walk is part of the persona he cultivates as a homicide detective. And if it is, what else about him is simply part of that persona?

Still pondering that question, I head back to the counter. The lunch rush is starting to pick up and poor Travis has been handling it like a trouper. But he always works mornings—the lunch menu is somewhat of a mystery to him and it's past time I send him on his way.

But when I slide behind the counter and murmur to Travis that he can go, he looks at me like I'm crazy. Then turns to take the next order, while I get the drinks and start delivering the food to the table. That frees up Meg to help with the assembling and plating of food, which in turn has orders coming out faster.

The whole lunch service runs like a well-oiled machine, though we're hit with a steady crowd for nearly two hours. At least my professional life is going well, I tell myself, considering my private life has gone to hell in a handbasket in the last few days.

I can tell Travis knows something's wrong from the concerned looks he keeps shooting my way. I attempt to look as carefree as possible while we work, but I know I'm not doing a very good job of it. How can I when it feels like my whole life is hanging in the balance? One wrong move and nothing will ever be the same again.

I think back on what Nate told me, about how he thinks someone is trying to frame me for murder. He came to that conclusion based on one body. On Lina. But what would he think if he knew about the woman back home? I know the state has a database where they can plug crimes in to see if anything similar pops up, but I don't know if the Ipswitch PD actually enters their data in it. Somehow, I doubt it, especially when it comes to the murder of a witch or wizard. It doesn't happen very often, but when it does IPD, the ACW and my parents have a tendency to want to keep things as quiet as possible.

Would the knowledge of that girl in the forest simply reinforce his belief that I'm being set up? Or would it move me to the top of the suspect list?

I wish life came with a user's manual, a set of unbendable dos or don'ts. Maybe then, I'd know what to do. Part of me thinks I should tell Nate everything so that he has the best shot of catching whoever is doing this. But if I do that, it's bound to open up a whole bunch of questions I'm not sure I want to answer. Questions I don't think I can answer, at least not without breaking the confidentiality my coven—and the entire ACW—lives by.

Another part worries that if he knows everything, any shot I have of staying free will completely dissolve. Friendship can only get me so far before he starts wondering if I'm playing him. And once that happens, I am completely screwed.

And there's a final part of me that is, quite simply, terrified for Nate. If he digs far enough and finds out that witches, wizards and warlocks really exist, what's going to happen to him? There are a lot of people who would do anything necessary to keep that knowledge quiet and

I don't want Nate caught in their crosshairs. Nor do I want him caught in the crosshairs of a sociopathic warlock intent on committing murder.

At the same time, what if knowing about the murder in Ipswitch helps Nate solve this murder? I'm in a Catch-22, and whatever way I turn I end up screwed.

God, what a mess this is. Part of me wants to crawl into bed and pull the covers over my head until all this goes away. Not that I actually think I'll be allowed to stay there for long—if Lily doesn't drag me out, I have a feeling this strange compulsion will. Though the idea makes me sick, I really don't think this is the end of it. Why would it be, when so far, whoever's doing this has been untouchable?

Dear goddess, I wish I had even a glimmer of an idea about what to do to fix things. I can only hope that Lily has found something in her research today that will help me figure out a little bit of what's going on here; because I may not have a clue how to do it yet, but the one thing I do know is that I can't sit by and watch more women die.

I have to find a way to stop this.

The line behind the cash register is getting longer again—probably because I'm standing here lost in my own little world—so I step over to take the next customer's order while Travis makes change. As I do, I find myself face to face with Salima, my mother's personal witch whisperer. Today, she's dressed in a wild gypsy skirt in varying shades of purple and a matching peasant blouse that don't suit her shape at all. In fact, she looks like a giant eggplant, especially considering the fact that her beehive is leaning a little to the side, just like an eggplant stem.

"What are you doing here?" I demand, furious that she's invaded my space. I do my best to keep my life in Austin separate from my life in Ipswitch, and while it doesn't always work—last night being a perfect case in point—the last thing I want are the complications of home encroaching on the peace I've found at Beanz.

Travis gawks at me—I don't think he's ever seen me be rude to anyone before—but Salima just smiles sweetly. "Ordering a bowl of French onion soup. I hear yours is the best in town."

"It's not actually that good."

Travis steps on my foot even as he hip bumps me out of the way. "Don't listen to her. She's strangely crabby today. The soup is delicious, as are all of our desserts. Can I get you a cookie or brownie, on the house?"

As she agrees, and wanders over to the display case to pick something out, I want to protest. To tell him that he has no right to be nice to her. Only the fact that there are other customers in line and they all appear to be listening keeps me silent. I can't afford to look like I've gone around the bend—not when I've worked so hard to make Beanz a success.

Still, when it's time for me to get her drink—a large, gingerbread latte—I can't help wishing for some hemlock. Or at least a little arsenic. At the moment, prison seems a small price to pay to be rid of Salima forever.

Especially since, according to Nate, it looks like I might be headed there anyway.

I thrust the drink into her hand and start to turn away, but she stops me with a hand on my arm. "Do you have a few minutes to talk? I have some really exciting news to share with you."

I can all but feel Travis brace himself to be abandoned behind the counter again. But this time I'm not going anywhere. "I'm sorry, Salima. As you can see, it's lunchtime and we're busy—"

"That's okay. I brought plenty of work to occupy me." She pats the bright orange tote bag hanging over her arm, though I would swear it wasn't there two minutes ago. "I'll grab a table and whenever you have a few minutes, we can chat."

"I don't think that's a good idea—" I break off in midsentence because she's already walking away, latte in one hand and cookie in the other.

I try not to think about her while we serve the other customers, but I can't help it. The rhythm Travis and I set earlier is broken and I keep making amateur mistakes. Damn it. Isn't it enough that my mom tries to take over every second I spend at home? Does she really have to send her craziness into Austin after me, as well?

"Go talk to her," Travis tells me after I hand a third customer the wrong cup of coffee. "Otherwise we're going to have a riot on our hands."

"I don't want to." I'm a little shocked by the whine in my voice and I can tell from the way his eyes widen that Travis is too.

"Are you kidding me? You took on Nate and that other guy without blinking an eye, but one little old lady sends you running for the hills?"

"Trust me, she's the scariest of the three."

He just looks at me.

"I'm serious. She is."

"Somehow I doubt that."

"Only because you don't know her like I do." Still, Travis is right. I can't put the confrontation off forever, especially since all I'm doing behind the counter right now is making his job harder. With a sigh, I take my apron off—again—and loop it over the open door that leads into the kitchen.

"I've got five minutes," I tell Salima, whose face lights up the second she sees me walking toward her.

"Only five? I was hoping for—"

"Take it or leave it." It's my turn to cut her off. And how childish is it that I'm hoping, really hoping, that she'll leave it?

"Then I'll take it." She reaches into her tote bag and pulls out a ridiculous pink and lime green polka-dotted binder. "I've made you something."

Aren't I lucky? The words tremble on my tongue, but I don't actually say them. So far, Salima has been nothing but nice to me and I can't bring myself to be any more obnoxious to her. After all, she's just trying to do her job. It's not her fault my mother hired her to do the impossible.

In the end, I settle for, "You really didn't have to do that."

"Of course I did. We're going to get this latency problem of yours taken care of in no time flat."

"What if I don't want my latency taken care of?"

"Oh, sugar, you're only saying that because you're afraid to hope. But don't worry. I promise, we're going to be successful. I have just the thing to break through whatever barriers are keeping your magic in check."

I think about telling her that I like my barriers—particularly after what happened last night—but the words would fall on deaf ears. She might be a softer, rounder, more fashion-challenged version of my mother, but they are definitely two peas in a pod.

"Look, I'm sorry, but I have to get back to work."

"Our five minutes aren't up yet! Give me two minutes—I can be quick." She slides the binder across the table to me. "I've spent the last four days making a workout plan for you. It's very specific and has to be followed exactly, but I promise, it will yield great results."

Workout plan? Is she insane? I step back from the table. "I already have a gym membership, thanks."

She giggles, which sounds odd coming from a woman who is so obviously ancient. "It's not that kind of workout. It's to get your magic in shape."

"I don't have any magic."

She pats the hideous, polka-dotted binder. "Follow the exercises I outline for you and you will. I guarantee it."

I start to argue some more, but then decide, what the hell. If it will get her out of my hair I'll take the stupid plan and promise to do the exercises. She'll never know the difference.

"All right," I tell her. "I'll try it."

"Wonderful!" She claps her be-ringed hands, then reaches back into her tote bag and pulls out the cowboy boots my mother had tried to give me for the Solstice. "Your mom wanted me to bring these to you," she tells me. "She said you'd forgotten them when you packed all your other presents from the Solstice. Now, you have to make sure you wear them when you do the exercises I laid out. They're specially made and charmed and will make everything so much easier for you."

I stare at the boots that have become the bane of my existence—and the symbol of the battle between my mother and me. I want to tell Salima to take them back to Ipswitch and suggest my mother shove them somewhere very uncomfortable, but years of royal training keep me silent. Mom and I may be at war, but in public it's all about presenting a united front. Besides, our ongoing fight over cowboy boots has nothing to do with Salima. She probably thought she was doing me a favor bringing them here.

I force a smile I am far from feeling. "Great. Thanks."

"No problem. I figured you'd be missing them." She reaches back into her bag and pulls out a tall glass container. I stare from it to her purse, wondering how the hell she managed to fit all of this in the bag. Part of me wants to stick around, just to see what else she has in there.

"I almost forgot the best part. These are some herbs, picked and charmed by me. Mix two spoonfuls into a glass of lukewarm water and drink it about an hour before you begin the exercises. You'll be astonished at how much it opens you up. You'll see things in a whole new light."

Yeah, only if the herbs are really just a blend of magic 'shrooms . . . which, now that I think about it, I wouldn't put past either Salima or my mother if they thought it might help. I reach for the jar gingerly.

"You can open it up," Salima tells me. "Get a feel for the herbs. Maybe even take a spoon now if you'd like."

"That's a great idea, but I still have to work for a while. I'd hate for my magic to burst out while I'm making someone's coffee."

She nods wisely. "That's a very good point. And such a good attitude. Optimism really helps with problems like yours."

The bell on the door jangles and I look up warily. At this point, I wouldn't be surprised if the entire ACW decided to pay Beanz a visit this afternoon. Goddess knows, everyone else has.

Instead, it's just a large group of high schoolers. I nearly weep in relief. Gathering up all of Salima's gifts, I comment, "Well, that's my cue to get back to work. Thanks for everything, Salima."

"Oh, no problem, sugar. No problem at all." She reaches into her bag one last time and pulls out two books, which she hands to me. At this point, it's all I can do not to roll my eyes. I mean, seriously. Does she have an entire store in there? "The first book is some common spells used in Heka. I didn't know if you had your own spell book so I brought it along. The second one has some special spells and incantations that I put together to help get you in the mood to practice magic. Say a few every day before you start your workout—"

"Before or after the herbs?" I deadpan, tongue firmly in cheek.

She doesn't seem to notice. Instead, she stands and this time pats my cheek instead of one of her inanimate objects. "It doesn't matter, sugar. Whatever feels best to you. And remember, while you go through the workout, to conjure up a picture of your mark and hold it in your mind's eye the whole time. Magic is a very personal thing and the more you have on or around you that is unique to you, the more successful you'll be."

My magic, or lack thereof, doesn't exactly feel personal right now, but I'm not going to go there. Not while I'm still holding out hope to get her out of my coffeehouse sometime today.

"Good luck," she tells me as she gathers the papers she's been working on. "I'll stop by in a few days, just to check on you. See how you're doing."

"Oh, right. Of course. I can hardly wait."

She comes around the table and pulls me into a hug—which feels a little ridiculous to me since I tower over her by about a foot. Still, submitting to her patchouli-scented embrace is easier than fighting it.

Finally she lets go. "I don't know what your mother was so worried about. You are just delightful."

"That's what I keep telling her." She starts out, but I don't turn away until I've made sure that she is actually on the sidewalk, walking away from Beanz as fast as her Technicolored cowboy boots can take her. Then I head back to the counter—and Travis, who is currently surrounded by flirty, giggling high school girls who haven't quite figured out yet that they're barking up the wrong tree.

As I round the corner, I toss Salima's gifts—binder, boots, books and most especially herbs—into the closest trash can. Salima might be nice, but that doesn't mean I trust her, or my mother, any farther than I can throw them. Magical workout be damned. I'll stick with the gym.

*   *   *

Travis finally gets to go home, after asking a number of pointed questions about what's going on with me. I fill him in on the basics—only because I figure he has the right to know after the way he's come through for me today—and he turns unexpectedly serious, asks if there's anything he can do to help.

I tell him I have things under control, but when I make my way out of the café at four o'clock, I find him leaning negligently against the building in the back.

"What are you doing here?" I demand. "I thought you had a hot date for this afternoon?"

"I postponed it a couple of hours." He follows me to my car, climbs in the passenger seat before I can even get my door open.

"What are you doing?" I repeat, incredulously.

"Making sure you get home safely."

My heart melts just a little over the fact that this twenty-year-old kid cares enough to look after me like this. But still, it's unnecessary. "I'm fine, Travis. I don't think anyone is going to hurt me between here and my house."

The look he gives me is filled with annoyance. "Yeah, and you thought your little walk by the lake last night wouldn't be a problem either." He shakes his head at my stupidity. "I'm not asking you to bear my children, Xandra. Just to let me ride home with you."

I don't argue with him after that, though I do offer to drop him at his apartment—he lives a couple of miles closer to UT—but he ignores me. Instead, he waits for me to park, then walks me to my front door.

Once I have it unlocked and open, I tell him, "I think I've got it from here."

He just nods, wraps an arm around my shoulder and pulls me in for a very un-Travis-like hug. "Be careful, okay?" he whispers. "An awful lot of trouble came looking for you today and I kind of like you in one piece."

He calls that trouble? I wonder what he'd say if he ever saw Declan? Probably tell me to run for the hills while he distracts him—with his body, if possible.

"Thanks, Travis." I hug him back and he pulls awkwardly away. For all of his sassiness and teasing, Travis isn't big on displays of affection, public or otherwise.

The last thing I see before I close the front door is Travis walking down the block, his skinny shoulders hunched against the wind.

Though I think I put on a pretty good face at the coffeehouse, I'm dragging. Exhaustion hit about two hours ago and just getting down the hall to my room seems to take more effort than I've got right now. I tell myself what I really want is a shower and twelve uninterrupted hours of sleep, but the truth is I'm terrified of going to bed. Terrified of the nightmares I'll have when I close my eyes and terrified of what will happen to my life in those hours of downtime.

I think back over what Nate said, about how he believes Declan is responsible for Lina's murder. I tried to tell him that wasn't the case, but I know he didn't believe me. I know he's the homicide detective and that he's supposed to know best, but I just don't buy it. Yes, I know that in ninety percent of cases when a woman turns up dead it's the boyfriend or husband, but that means in ten percent of cases it *isn't* the boyfriend—I studiously avoid feeling anything when I think about Declan sleeping with Lina, now or before. It's not my business after all. Especially since I have a hard time imagining a warlock as powerful as Declan resorting to killing in such an ugly manner.

Do I think Declan is capable of murder? Under the right circumstances, absolutely. He isn't a dark warlock for nothing.

Do I think he would do murder like that? No. I really don't. Especially not someone he cares about. And especially not when I consider the malicious feelings that emanated from the body, the sadistic pleasure that turned my stomach even more than feeling what the killer had done to Lina. To put it simply, that evil didn't feel like the man who had kissed and comforted me so tenderly all those years ago.

Could I be wrong? Maybe.

Do I think I'm wrong? No, I really don't.

Which means Nate is partially right. The killer might be doing all this in order to set someone else up, though I personally think he takes too much pleasure in the deaths for it to be just that. Nate thinks the person being set up is me, but I can't help wondering if it's Declan instead. The thought makes me sick. Especially since I'm somehow involved. I've spent years dreaming of telling Declan off for what happened in the forest that night, but the idea that I'm being used to hurt him is more awful than I can stand.

Still, I don't know what to do about it. And even if I did, it would have to wait a few hours. I need a nap, desperately.

But when I open my front door, it's to find Lily sitting on the sofa with Brandon, while Kyle lounges on my favorite chair. The big black trunk that functions as a coffee table as well as storage for my unused pairs of cowboy boots holds a wine bottle, three wineglasses and what looks to be a hastily put together fruit and cheese tray.

I can't help it. I look at Lily like she's crazy. Does she really think, after everything that happened last night, that this is what I need? To entertain the guy I inadvertently ditched? So much for being psychic.

"Hey, Xandra," Kyle says, shoving to his feet. "Are you feeling any better?"

Do I look like I'm feeling better? I don't say it, but I come close—which is yet another clue that this little get-together is a bad idea. I mean, I haven't glanced in a mirror lately but I've got a pretty good idea about what I look like and better is definitely not it.

"Not really," I tell him. "We were slammed at work today and last night was . . . difficult."

"We heard." Brandon speaks up from where he's cuddled on the couch with Lily. "A homicide detective got in contact with us this morning, to verify your alibi. I have to admit it freaked me out a little, especially when we turned on the news and saw the murder at Town Lake. The newscaster mentioned that the body was found by an unidentified woman and we put two and two together."

"You did?" I can't keep the horror from my voice. The last thing I need is to add being hounded by reporters to this mess.

"Oh, don't worry. We won't tell anyone." Kyle places a comforting hand on my lower back. Or at least, I think it's meant to be comforting but all it really does is piss me off. It's a pretty personal move, and one date or not, I don't like Kyle assuming that he has the right to touch me like that. I take a couple of steps away, until I'm just out of reach.

"They wouldn't do that." Lily pipes in for the first time. "Kyle and Brandon were worried, so they stopped by to check on you. Make sure you were doing okay. To be sick and then have to deal with what you did"—she shudders—"is awful."

It is awful, and I can't help wondering how much Lily has told them. Normally she's very closemouthed, but she's crazy about Brandon and I'm afraid confiding in him wouldn't feel like a betrayal of me. But the last thing I need is for a bunch of wizards to find out what's going on here—especially one who works for the ACW. If things get worse, as those damn tarot cards say that they will, I don't want to have a bunch of people privy to the inner workings of the case. Especially Council members. It will just make it that much harder to ensure Nate, Declan and I all escape this with our lives.

Which is just one more reason why I want to lie down for a while instead of making small talk with two guys who don't interest me at all.

I start to excuse myself—surely, after the night I had they can't take offense if I back out of whatever plans are brewing—but I glance over at Lily and she looks so happy snuggled up next to Brandon that I just don't have the heart to do it.

So instead of showering and falling face-first into bed as I had originally planned, I end up sitting on the floor next to Kyle, eating grapes and talking about sports, Austin, Ipswitch and the ACW. None of those topics interest me particularly, but they keep Kyle talking happily, which means all I have to do is pretend to listen while I zone and remember to make an appropriate noise every once in a while.

Still, when he starts talking about the Council members like he knows them, I get interested despite myself. As a group, they're notoriously reclusive and while my parents have met them all at one time or another— usually when their policies clashed with the Council's wishes—I've met only three Council members in my whole life, two of whom have since died.

"What exactly do you do for the ACW?" I ask when Kyle stops to take a drink. "I thought you headed up their PR team?"

"I do. But I'm also an enforcer of sorts," he tells me with a grin that I find a little creepy under the circumstances. "It's all tied together."

"An enforcer? Of what?"

"Council laws, mostly. Your coven is one of the best, but some of the others aren't so good about following Council dictates and sometimes even the basic rules of

Heka. I travel around, making sure all is going well in those covens. And, of course, I also help the Council deal with other magical creatures. The cats and fairies are particularly troublesome," he says with a grin.

I'm intrigued, despite myself. "Really? What kind of trouble do they get into?"

"The leopards think everything's a game and they hate following rules—any rules. I spend most of my time reminding them of the agreements that exist between all the different magical groups and convincing them to play along. As for the Fey"—he shakes his head ruefully—"they just don't want to listen to anyone and it infuriates them that the Council thinks they have the right to tell anyone who isn't a witch what to do."

I kind of agree with them. The ACW is made up exclusively of witches, wizards and warlocks—so obviously, that is where their loyalties lie. How can anyone expect the other groups—the shifters, the Fey, the water creatures, the blood mages—to live under our rules then, especially when they don't have vested representation in the Council that sets the rules?

My parents and I have had this discussion numerous times, and while they always come down on the side of the ACW, I've noticed that lately, even they are beginning to see that such uneven representation can only lead to problems.

But when I say as much to Kyle, he shuts me down pretty quickly. "You're not old enough to remember what it was like before the Council seized control," he tells me.

"And you are? They seized control from the others over seventy years ago."

He smiles. "I'm older than I look."

"Obviously."

We move on to other topics, but I never really get over what Kyle said. I know his paychecks come from the

ACW, but still, his blind allegiance to a group that I find both power hungry and narrow-minded disturbs me.

As for the fact that he's so much older than I am ... that kind of bugs me too. It shouldn't, especially considering the fact that Declan's age has never bothered me and he is obviously older than Kyle.

But Kyle isn't Declan, a little voice whispers in the back of my head and I have to agree. Declan might be dark and mysterious and I might not be able to count on him, but he isn't corrupt like the Council is. Or, at least, he wasn't eight years ago when we talked, and while I don't know much about Declan, I remember his vehemence on the subject and doubt anything has changed in less than a decade.

Suddenly, I've had enough. I'm tired, miserable, stressed out and more worried than I can ever remember being in my life. Sitting here making small talk with a guy who seems very nice but who is obviously not going to knock my socks off anytime soon, seems like a waste of time.

I stand up abruptly, not even bothering to wait for Kyle to finish the story he's telling about his beloved Lakers. "I'm sorry," I say when he pauses and everyone looks at me. "I didn't sleep at all last night and I'm still not feeling very well. I think I need to get to bed."

"Oh, of course." Brandon climbs to his feet. "We'll get out of your hair, let you get some sleep."

"Right." Kyle rises more slowly and there's a look in his eyes that I'm not sure I like. I can't place it, exactly, but I think I've offended him. I try to feel bad, but frankly I'm too exhausted to care. Not to mention pretty damn offended myself. He and Brandon have to know I'm running on fumes and it didn't matter to them at all that they were making me uncomfortable by staying. Which means that my removing myself from the situation shouldn't bother them either.

As they head to the door, they say a bunch of things that I'm too tired to listen to, so I just nod and try not to scream at them to get the hell out. In the end, after checking to make sure I'm really okay, Lily decides to go with them—for which I am eternally grateful. The last thing I want is to listen to her dissect her entire conversation with Brandon, sentence by sentence. Usually, her effusiveness about a new guy doesn't bother me, but I haven't slept in close to forty hours and I'm done. Nightmares or not, I'm getting some sleep.

I lock the door behind Lily and the guys, then stumble into my bedroom. Sitting neatly on my dresser are the binder, books, jar of herbs and cowboy boots that I shoved into the trash at Beanz hours ago. I stare blearily at them for a few seconds, trying to figure out how Salima managed it. But it's too complicated and I'm too tired, so in the end I just turn away and fall face-first onto my bed. Spitting out a feather from my pillow is the last thing I remember before oblivion hits.

Thirteen

I wake up some time later, heart racing, my own breath harsh in my ears. Something's wrong, though I'm not sure if that's true in reality or just in my dreams.

For long seconds, I lie here in the dark, half-asleep, half-awake, trying to figure out why I'm so alarmed.

Did I hear something?

Am I not feeling well?

Do I have to pee?

There's nothing distressing in the answers—everything sounds and feels fine. So why am I awake?

I'm still on my stomach, face half buried in my favorite pillow, and I start to roll over to find a more comfortable spot. Except I can't.

I can't move.

Can't sit up.

Can't swing my legs off the bed or move my limbs at all.

Can't do anything but turn my head and wiggle my hips a little.

I have one more moment of confusion, of noncomprehension, then panic grabs on to my stomach and squeezes before zinging outward like an electric shock. I yank at my arms, my legs, try to twist and turn, even buck against what feels an awful lot like restraints, but nothing happens. I'm stuck, tied spread-eagle and facedown to my bed.

And I have no idea how it happened.

By now my heart is pumping so hard and fast that my whole chest hurts. I try to catch my breath, but I can't—every inhalation is a jagged saw cutting through my lungs and the perceived safety of my dark and quiet room.

I'm suffocating, drowning in my own fear and there's nothing I can do to stop it. There's a tiny part of me that's still in control, that tries to tell me to calm down, to think. To reason this out.

But the words aren't getting through. I'm too busy screaming and yanking, wrenching and trembling to pay attention to anything else. Even myself.

I jerk against the restraints until my legs cramp up and my wrists burn. Something thick and warm rolls down my palms to my fingers and I realize that all my struggling has drawn blood. The knowledge brings on another freak out, and still the restraints don't budge an inch. Neither does the panic.

"Is anyone there?" I scream. "Lily? Kyle? Brandon?" There's no answer.

"What's going on? What do you want?"

Still no answer.

Images of Lina and Amy are running through my head and all I can think is that I don't want to end up like them. Please, Isis, don't let me end up raped and mutilated, my body dumped for some other unsuspecting woman to find.

"Hello?" I call out one more time. My voice is hoarse from all the screaming and now my throat hurts too.

No one answers, and finally it gets through to me. Either there's no one here or whoever it is is playing with me and won't answer anyway. So unless I can calm down and think, I'm pretty much screwed either way.

Exhausted, terrified, *furious*, I rest my cheek on the bed and for the first time since I realized I was tied down, I try to think past the terrified buzzing in my head.

Experimenting, I wiggle my right wrist. It burns and more blood leaks onto my hand, but I ignore the pain. Instead, I try to concentrate on what the binding feels like. I can't really tell though—the broken skin and throbbing make it impossible to isolate the feel of the bonds.

I focus on my feet instead. They're sore, but I don't think I've bloodied them yet.

I twist my ankle in a circle, feeling the hard wood of my bedpost against the bottom of my foot. I try to focus on the bonds, to figure out if they're rope or cloth or metal, but I can't actually feel anything. I know I'm being held down—I can feel the pressure, the inability to lift my foot—but when I actually try to concentrate on texture, it's like there's nothing there. Nothing soft or hard or cold or hot or silky or rough. It's the strangest thing.

I turn my head to the left again—that wrist isn't bleeding as badly as the right, plus it's closest to the faint light leaking in through the sliver in my curtains. I wiggle my fingers, just to check if I can see them move. I can, barely, but it gives me a point of reference. I look about four inches south and find my wrist, slickly shining.

If I look closely I can see the width of my wrist along with the line of blood encircling it. But if I can see that, it means there's nothing there to block my view. No rope or handcuffs or fabric. Nothing tangible at all.

Which means I'm being held, tied across my bed, by nothing but a spell.

It's a hell of a time for me to realize that I should have listened to my mother and her damn witch whisperer. A little magic would go a long way right about now.

I close my eyes for a second, do my best to think through the adrenaline still racing along my every nerve ending. I don't know what to do, how to get myself out of this, but I have to do something. I don't know when—or even if, Lily will be back tonight—and I'll be damned if I'll lie here trapped for the next however many hours. I can't take the vulnerability, especially not when everywhere I turn, women who look like me are being murdered.

When I'm calm enough, I think back over the spells I learned when I was still trying to be über-witch. There were a lot of them, but I don't think any of them covered how to tie a person down using magic—or how to free them. And even if they had, it wouldn't have been this spell. Now that I've been able to work through the panic, I can smell the stench of black magic all around me. It freaks me out, makes me even more determined to get free.

But how?

I pull against the restraints one more time, just to test them, but of course the bindings don't loosen at all. In fact, I'd swear they were tighter, but they could just feel that way because of the rawness of my hands and feet. I decide to go with that, simply because I won't be able to function if I lie here imagining the restraints getting tighter and tighter and tighter.

I clear my mind, try to think of what Salima told me at Beanz today. I was supposed to take the herbs and conjure up an image of my mark deep inside my mind, to use it as a talisman. It's too late for the herbs, but my mark is never far from my mind, especially lately, so that shouldn't be too difficult.

I take a deep breath, build a picture in my head of the Heka tattoo I carry embedded in my skin. Round, empty circle topped by a semicircle with points on the end. The circlet of Isis.

I concentrate, focus on it to the exclusion of all else, and mutter the words for a simple necessity spell. At first, nothing happens. And then, miraculously, I feel my restraints start to move. Thank the goddess. I have no idea how I did it and at this moment, I don't care—all that matters to me is that I'm almost free.

I start to murmur a quick prayer of thanksgiving, but stop before I get to the end of the first line—my bindings aren't loosening at all. Instead, they're getting longer, slithering around my arms and legs until the lower half of each limb is completely engulfed by the restraints. Terrific. The first bit of magic I've ever been able to perform and it has made everything worse.

Part of me isn't even surprised. I'd known from the second I first met her that Salima was a quack.

So, what am I supposed to do now? I can actually move less after trying to escape than I could when this whole thing started.

Quickly, I run through the list of the spells I actually remember—which aren't that many. Oh, I know bits and pieces of hundreds of spells, but to be certain that I know them word for word, in their entirety, is altogether different. After all, I thought I knew the necessity spell and look where that got me.

The spells I do know are from my childhood, incantations that were impressed on me in school and at home before I even knew my times tables. It's hard to forget those. But none of them are going to help me out of this predicament.

If I ever find out who did this to me, I swear I'm going to kick his ass. At the moment, I'm more than mad enough to do it, even sans magic. Unable to hold it in anymore, I scream in fury, one long, loud shriek that releases a bunch of tension and ratchets up my anger.

I'm glad of that, glad I've moved beyond fear into something more constructive. And though it didn't work the first time, I pull up my mark a second time. Concentrate. And go for the first spell I learned—an entreaty to Isis to imbue me with the power to perform my most desired spell.

It's a long shot and I know it—after all, I'm asking for the magic to do a spell I don't actually know. But the second I murmur the final words of the spell, I feel Isis's power sweep over me ... right before the carpet on the far side of my room bursts into flames.

Oh, shit. Oh, shit. OH. SHIT. I guess I should have been more clear about which spell I wanted above all else at this particular moment. Because now I've gone from being tied down to being tied down in a room that is on *fire*. How the hell am I supposed to get away from this?

The panic is back, as thick and overwhelming as the smoke that is even now beginning to fill my room.

I stare at the flames, which are licking at the ends of my curtains and starting up my wall even as they spread across the carpet, getting ominously closer to my bed with each second that passes. Terror beats at me from every side, and I struggle to think through it. I know I need a water spell but I'm too frightened to grasp anything but a couple of words here or there. I have to calm down, but I can't. How can I when I'm about to burn to death?

In the middle of my panic and the encroaching flames, my cell phone starts to ring. Of course, it's across the room—next to the binder and books Salima gave me—and is absolutely no use to me at the moment. I try to will it over to me, but telekinesis is a gift that few witches have and while I'm spouting all kinds of weird magic tonight, moving objects with my mind is obviously not one of the things I can do.

The ringing stops abruptly and I'm left alone with the fire and my fear. Okay, I can do this, I tell myself even as doubt is a huge, empty cavern inside of me. I *have* to do this. Either a water spell or something to loose these bindings—I don't actually care which. But I need something now, because the fire has made it to the posts of my bed. I can feel the heat of it on the bottoms of my feet.

The smoke is heavier now and I'm coughing constantly, my lungs spasming with every breath I try to suck into my lungs. Freedom, I think, focusing on my mark one last time. *I need to be free. I need to escape. I need these bindings to cease to be.*

Except it isn't only my mark I see in my mind's eye anymore—Declan's is there, as well. Seba, the ancient Egyptian star glowing and spinning around my mark until the circlet of Isis is all but swallowed by the star.

At the same time the restraints jerk a little, loosen, and I repeat the spell I've just made up even as I yank and pull against the imaginary straps. It's a silly spell, childish and immature and completely ridiculous, but if it's working—even a little bit—I'm going to go with it.

My phone starts to ring again and at the same time I hear a loud pounding coming from outside of my room. Someone's knocking on the front door and calling out. The words are muffled, but whoever it is must know I'm in trouble because the tone is frantic.

I scream then. "Help me! Help me! Fire! Help!"

The phone cuts off again and I mutter the freedom spell one more time as Declan's mark intertwines with mine until I can't tell where one begins and the other ends. And in that moment, when the symbol of his power is merged completely with mine, the restraints break. I scramble off the bed, make a mad dash for the front door just as it is ripped off its hinges and crashes inward.

It flies across my living room, slams across the back wall and Declan strides in. I'm as shocked by his sudden appearance as I am by the agitation that all but pours off of him. His eyes are wide and anxious as he grabs me and shoves me the last few steps to the front door even as he dashes through the living room to my bedroom.

Fresh air hits my aching lungs and I collapse, sinking to my knees on the front porch as I suck in the life-giving oxygen. Over the coughs that wrack my entire body, I hear the roar of the flames as they devour my room. I can't see them or Declan, but the sound of his voice drifts to me on the wind. I don't know what he's saying, can't make out the words, but the moment he stops chanting, the crackling of the flames dies as well.

He's used magic to put out the fire.

Seconds later he's on the porch again, crouching next to me and pressing me down so that I'm lying flat on my back on the rough boards. "Xandra?" His voice is low and urgent. "Are you okay?"

I'm coughing too hard to answer him.

He lays a hand on my chest and though he doesn't speak, I know he's done something there too because I can breathe again. My lungs still ache, my throat still burns, but it's bearable now.

"Xandra?"

I push at his hand—now that I know I'm not going to suffocate on my front porch, it's way too close to my breasts for comfort. "I'm fine." But when I try to sit up, the night spins around me.

"Yeah, I can tell." Firm pressure on my chest has me lying back down, and this time, I stay down. At least until I watch Declan turn around and stroll back into my house.

"Where are you going?"

"To make sure the fire's out. Unless you'd like to explain to the fire marshal how you lost your whole house to an inexplicable wall of flames."

He's inside for a few minutes, long enough for me to get my body back under control and start feeling stupid about being draped across my front porch like a Victorian lady on a fainting couch. I sit up, push slowly to my feet so that when Declan finally comes back, I'm standing, ready to face him. Why is it that he always seems to be here for the most awful moments of my life?

It's maddening.

Still, he did save me. I'm working on the words to

thank him when he leans against one of the posts on my front porch and asks, "So, what happened? You didn't have enough going on with bodies popping up left and right? You felt like you needed more of a challenge?" There's a sardonic twist to his lips and his eyes are filled with annoyance.

That's all it takes to get my back up, the words of gratitude flying right out of my head. "What are you doing here anyway? Nobody asked you to come."

He raises one perfectly sculpted brow. "Well, there's appreciation for you. Next time I'll leave you to your . . . barbecue."

"I was going to thank you before you opened your mouth and ruined everything. And that's not an answer."

"Because the answer is self-explanatory. I came to save your ass."

I think of his star and the way it had swallowed up my own mark. "You freed me?"

"No." His face was grim now. "I couldn't tell what was wrong, only that something was. You saved yourself."

"I don't believe you. Not when it's obvious that I'm a complete and total screwup when it comes to magic."

He sighs, then walks back inside my living room and opens the front windows. "Screwup seems a little harsh."

"No. It doesn't. For twenty-seven years I haven't been able to do any magic at all and now that I can, I nearly *barbecue* myself as you so eloquently put it." I keep my voice low with an effort. The entire neighborhood doesn't need to know I'm a witch. Or half of one.

"You're doing fine, Xandra." At first it looks like he's going to say more, but then he just shakes his head. Walks through to the kitchen. I follow him, watch as he slides the window open in there as well. "You should go back to the porch. You need fresh air."

"What I need is to know what the hell is going on. I feel like I've been dropped into an episode of *The*

Twilight Zone where everyone knows the answers but me."

"Not everyone."

"Damn it, Declan, you owe me."

"Really? And here I thought it was the other way around?"

"Why?" I scoff. "Because you put out the fire? I am capable of calling 911, you know."

He stalks toward me and I have to force myself not to take a step back in retreat. But there's this look in his eye, like there's a whole world between us that I can't even begin to grasp and it alarms me even as it intrigues me.

"You're messing with things you don't understand." He reaches a hand out, tucks a wayward strand of hair behind my ear.

His fingers don't brush my skin and yet it's enough to send shivers down my spine. Suddenly that long ago night is right here. It's been years, but that doesn't seem to matter as electricity arcs between us.

His eyes darken and I know he remembers too. It's enough, more than enough, to have my body reacting to him in a way I swore would never happen again. Even worse, it's obvious he feels my response. It's in the way his own body stiffens, in the way his jaw flexes and his hands clench.

I do retreat then, one slow step at a time. He matches me move for move, until my back is against the wall and his body is a scant few inches from my own. His lips are curled in a sardonic smile I don't remember from that night so long ago, and he looks like he's waiting for something. Me to call mercy, probably, but that's not going to happen.

"You said dead bodies. There's only been one." There's no reason for him to know about Amy. Except the look he gives me is almost pitying. Almost.

"You really think lying to me is a good idea?" he asks, his arms coming to rest on the wall on either side of me so that I feel caged. Not frightened, not threatened ... yet. Just restrained. But after the way I've spent the last half hour of my life, it's not a feeling I care for.

"Who says I'm lying?" I shove at him but he doesn't move.

"I do. Lina wasn't the first." There's an echo of something in his voice—pain, maybe?

I forgot he'd been involved with her. I shouldn't care, but for some reason the recollection makes me feel strange. A little off. Even so, I say, "I'm sorry. Nate told me you two were ... together."

"I told you last night. It wasn't like that between us for a while." He glances down at my wrists. "We need to get you cleaned up."

He places a finger gently on my wrist, traces the jagged edges of the wounds I inflicted on myself in my desperation to escape. I wince at the first movement of his hand, expecting there to be pain. Just the touch of the air against the rawness has had me in agony since it happened.

But there is no pain. There's nothing but a subtle warmth that resonates through me—which is somehow worse. I don't want to feel anything for Declan, don't want to remember those hours by the lake where I poured out my heart to him and thought he'd done the same for me. I don't want there to be any electricity or warmth, don't want there to be any connection at all. And yet there is. I felt it at the police station last night and I feel it now as his fingers circle my wounds.

When he pulls his hand away, there is no blood, no jagged tears. Oh, the rawness is still there but the open wounds are gone and so is a good deal of the pain.

"I didn't know you were a healer."

He shakes his head. "I'm not normally."

I hold up my hand, incontrovertible proof to the contrary.

He just shrugs. "There's a lot of excess power bouncing around inside of me right now. I just focused it on your wrists."

"Like you're coming down from an adrenaline rush."

"Something like that. I was afraid you were going to die before I could get here." He shudders as he guides me to a kitchen chair, presses gently on my shoulders until I sit.

"You knew about the fire."

"No. But I felt—" He breaks off, his face darkening at the reminder. "I had no idea you'd managed to practically set yourself on fire."

"I don't know how it happened," I confess before I think better of it. "I've never been able to do it before."

"I have a feeling that's going to be happening a lot more in the next few weeks," he comments cryptically. But before I can demand an explanation, he asks, "Do you have a bowl around here somewhere?"

I'm not willing to let him off the hook so easily. "What does that mean?"

"It means I need a bowl."

I glare at him. "You know that's not what I'm talking about." I start to get up, but a gentle hand on my shoulder presses me back into the seat. "What do you need a bowl for anyway?"

"To clean you up." He points to my hands, where blood has leaked down my fingers. "And a first aid kit wouldn't hurt either."

Again I start to get up and again he stops me with a hand. "Just point me in the right direction and I'll get it all together."

I direct him to the proper cabinets, even as I wonder what I'm doing. I take care of myself and have for years. I don't need anyone to do it for me, let alone Declan, whom I'm smart enough not to trust this time around. And yet here he is, in my kitchen. With me. Alone.

He finds the bowl, fills it with water and then grabs a clean dish towel from the hook at the end of the cabinets. He also snags the first aid kit before kneeling down beside my chair.

Shock ricochets through me as he lifts my right leg and places it on his thigh before rolling up my jeans to midcalf. I realize for the first time that my ankle is bloody—I guess in my last frantic attempt to get away from the fire, I managed to tear it to pieces too.

He does the same thing there that he did to my wrist, spreading a healing warmth through the wounds as he traces them with his fingers. It feels different, though, to have him touching my ankles, my calves. More intimate. It's a dangerous feeling, one that has me shaking a little even before he lingers at the nasty bruises I have on my shins. He caresses them, soothes them, and I feel the ache slowly dissolve under his careful ministrations.

When the pain and the bruises are both nearly gone, he dips the dish towel in the bowl and begins to clean my feet.

His hands are tender, his long, elegant fingers both efficient and gentle as he slowly, carefully, rinses the blood from me. He takes his time, doesn't miss a spot as the towel glides over my lower calves, my heels, the bottoms of my feet, my toes and finally back around to the tops of my feet. I'm trembling full out now, and I know he notices even though he doesn't say anything.

I comfort myself with the explanation that it's just another adrenaline crash—nearly being burned to death would shake up even the most stalwart of people. But even as I'm thinking it, I'm not sure it's the truth. After all, I didn't start quaking until he touched me.

When I'm clean, not even a drop of blood left to remind me of my ordeal, he smooths Neosporin over my still raw ankles and wraps them in gauze. Then he repeats the process on my hands, cleaning the blood before bandaging the wounds.

I don't know what to say to him, don't know what I *want* to say. He takes the problem out of my hands by standing up and carrying the bowl to the sink, where he rinses it out. Now that he's no longer touching me—or looking at me—my brain synapses start firing again. It's time to push for an answer to the question he dodged earlier.

"What did you mean, about my powers? What do you know that I don't?"

He turns slowly, drying his hands on another dish towel. "Nothing. You're the one who said your magic was behaving strangely."

"I don't have any magic. That was established once and for all eight and a half years ago."

"Yet you managed to set your room on fire and get yourself free from a madman's shackles. You must have something going for you."

"That's what I'm trying to say. Something weird is going on and I don't understand it. But I think it's tied to you and I think you know what it is."

"That's a lot of assumptions on your part." His lips twist in that smirk I once found so charming but now only annoys me.

"No more than on yours. How do you know it was a madman who had me restrained on that bed?"

"Did it feel like the mark of a sane person to you? You know, while you were trapped and about to die a fiery death?"

He has a point, but I'm not about to go there. Not yet. I narrow my eyes at him. "What's your angle?"

"Excuse me?" The smirk is gone now, replaced by a dark scowl. I know he means it to scare me, but all it does is piss me off. I'm not nineteen anymore and I don't frighten that easily.

"I don't get it. I haven't seen you in eight and a half years and now suddenly you're with me two nights in a row—and neither one of them has been exactly pleasant. It doesn't make sense—unless there's something you're not telling me about how you'll benefit from all this."

"Solving Lina's murder isn't enough motivation?"

For a second, I feel petty, pushing him like this when he's lost a woman he obviously cares for. But then I realize that's what he wants me to feel—he's manipulating me in an effort to make me back off. That knowledge only makes me angrier and I steel myself for a showdown I'm in no shape for and can't win. But I don't care. I'm not backing down. Not here. Not over this.

"Of course it is, but that still doesn't explain what it has to do with me. Again, unless you know something you're not telling me."

"The fact that you found her isn't enough?"

"No. While I feel bad and hope her murderer gets caught, this isn't my fight. I'll help the police any way I can, but there's nothing else I can do. It's just a case of me being in the wrong place at the wrong time." I don't believe that for a second, but I want to see what he says about it.

"Was it the same way with Amy back in Ipswitch?" he asks, his voice harsh against the silent backdrop of my kitchen. I swear even the refrigerator has stopped humming. "You were just in the wrong place?"

"Half the town was there."

"Yet you found her first. You really think that was a coincidence?"

"I didn't find her first. A young girl did. And how do you even know about Amy? Nate doesn't."

"That cop doesn't know much."

"He knows enough to be suspicious of you. He came to Beanz to talk to me earlier, and to warn me to be careful around you. You need to watch your step here, Declan."

"You worried about me, Xandra?"

"More like worried about me. You've got an agenda and I don't know what it is."

"I already told you. I want to find Lina's killer."

"What does that have to do with me?"

"You think it's a coincidence that you just happen to find bodies? It's a gift."

More like a curse. "I've only found two in my entire life."

The sardonic twist of his lips is back, but his eyes are deadly serious—and concerned—when he looks at me. "I have a feeling that's about to change."

Fear slithers down my spine, different from what I felt when I was tied up in the bedroom, but no less debilitating. But before I can say anything, his cell phone pings. He pulls it out of his pocket, glances at the text. "I need to go."

I move to block his way. "You still haven't told me anything."

"What exactly do you want me to tell you?" he demands. "Do you think if I knew who was killing witches— witches that look a hell of a lot like you, by the way—that I wouldn't be saying something to you or that damn cop? I'm flying blind here."

He sounds earnest, frustrated, but I don't believe him. He knows more than he's letting on. If not about the murders, then about me and the weird power surges I've been having. I don't know how I know, but I do.

"You're going to have to tell me eventually." I inject as much hard-ass into my voice as I can, but I know I fall woefully short—at least compared to Declan.

"Eventually, I won't have to tell you anything. You'll already know." He brushes past me and I grab his arm. I'm not done with him yet.

He whirls on me, and then I'm right back where I was a few minutes ago, back against the wall and Declan an immovable barricade in front of me. Only this time he *is* touching me, his chest and hips pressing me against the wall as his hand comes up to cup my cheek.

My heart goes crazy, beats way too fast and hard. I lift my hands to his chest, try to shove him away. But he's not budging and no matter what my brain tells me about keeping him as far away from me as possible, my body has no problem with the proximity.

I register all this in the split second before he lowers his mouth and his lips find mine—hot, elemental, possessive as hell. It's as different from the kisses he gave me back by the lake all those years ago as I am from that girl who was so desperate for her parents' approval.

And yet, some things are exactly the same.

He still smells like sandalwood, still tastes like lemon and cinnamon and my early-morning latte. His lips are still firm, his body still hot and hard against mine. And I still melt the second he runs his tongue along the indention in my upper lip.

My hands come up and clutch at his too-long, silky hair, holding him in place even as he holds me. His response—a quick nip of my lower lip—has me gasping and pressing my body against his.

He takes instant advantage of my open lips, his tongue sneaking inside to slide over my own before exploring the rest of my mouth with lazy strokes that make me forget everything but the heat flaring to life deep inside of me.

He strokes the roof of my mouth, the sensitive skin between my upper lip and my gums, and then the spot right behind my front teeth that always makes me crazy. I shudder, press myself more tightly against him as I pull the flavor, the essence of him, deep inside me. It's his turn to inhale sharply and then his tongue is thrusting against mine in a powerful in and out motion that has me trembling and crying out. Then he's brushing his thumb

over my cheek in a caress that is both tender and exciting.

It freaks me out a little—not the excitement, but the
sudden tenderness, because it speaks of more than this
one passionate moment of time. It takes me back, really
back, to those hours by the lake when he held and kissed
me like he was never going to let me go.

Except he did.

And when he shifts, moving his hand from my cheek
to the back of my neck in a hold so blatantly possessive
that it makes me squirm, I pull away. After eight and a
half years without so much as a postcard, he has no right
to touch me like this. I have no right to let him.

We're both breathing hard and Declan's body feels
like it's carved of stone wherever it's touching mine.
Something tickles my cheek and I reach up to brush it
away just as Declan does the same. At that moment, as
our fingers intertwine, we both recognize that I'm crying,
tears running silently down my face.

Declan curses at the first touch of wetness, yanks himself back. And then he's gone, striding through my house
and out into the night without a backward glance.
Though the front door does slam behind him, meaning
he fixed it on his way out.

This time, I don't even think of following. After all, I
should have seen it coming.

Fourteen

The slam of the door behind Declan echoes through my empty house and I let out a breath I wasn't even aware that I'd been holding. I wipe the last remnants of tears off my cheeks and walk over to the fridge, open it up. I haven't eaten since the half sandwich I'd had for lunch during Nate's inquisition and hunger is beating at me, turning my legs shaky and my breathing uneven.

Yes, I tell myself as I pull out some lettuce and sliced turkey. It's lack of food that's making me shaky, not the fact that Declan just kissed me senseless. And I let him.

For a moment I want to lay my head down on the counter and just bawl. But I'm not a child anymore and I've never been much of a crier anyway, no matter that Declan brings it out in me. I can't believe I let him kiss me, can't believe I let myself be sucked in all over again. Hadn't he hurt me enough eight years ago, when he'd left me in the middle of the forest after spending most of the night making me feel like I mattered? Like I was important to him?

Am I really willing to just forget all that?

To open myself up to that kind of pain and rejection all over again even with everything else going on in my life right now?

It's not like I can ignore the fact that I've found two bodies in my entire life—both times under a strange compulsion and both times after I'd come into contact with Declan. I don't count Amy because, while I was there soon after she was found, I wasn't the one who stumbled across her. Thank God. But Declan knows about her anyway, even though the IPD kept it quiet and her death didn't make any of the papers.

I don't know why, but a picture of my bed back home flashes in my mind—covered in bunches and bunches of begonias. A warning from my brother to be careful, and yet that interpretation suddenly doesn't feel right anymore. Declan? I wonder, as I assemble my sandwich. Or am I just being paranoid?

There's no evidence that points to him being in Ipswitch at all, and yet I can't shake the idea that he was there the entire time. Especially when I remember those terrible moments in the parlor when I felt such overwhelming pain or in the garden when I was certain I was being watched. At the time, I'd put it down to the ridiculous costume I was wearing, but now I'm not so sure.

Some people, most people, would probably say that a lot of this is just a case of horrible coincidence, but then, I'm not most people. I accepted many years ago that all things happen for a reason. I had to believe that or I would have gone bat-shit crazy trying to figure out a solution to my latency—maybe even as crazy as my mother and Salima.

The thought of them makes me cringe as I put the sandwich fixings back in the refrigerator. They're both crazy enough that they'd be thrilled to find out I made fire—even if that fire nearly killed me. Somehow, I think they'd both view it as progress.

And maybe, in a messed-up way, it is. It's not like I've ever been able to do anything like that before. But why now? That's the million-dollar question, and one I don't have even a semblance of an answer to. Except that I'm pretty sure it has something to do with Declan.

I think back to those moments on the bed when I was

finally able to free myself from my bonds. Again, Declan hadn't been there, but he'd been aware I was in trouble. He'd called twice, and then shown up at my door, like he'd known exactly where I was.

I don't know how he figured it out, any more than I know why his star, his mark, had spun through my head in those final moments before the fire would have engulfed me. Just like I have no idea why that mark is even now engraved in the skin of my back—not once, like my own, but twice.

I start to sit at the kitchen table, but my curiosity overwhelms me so I grab my sandwich and head to the back bedroom to eat it. It's hard to forget those moments, lying stranded on the bed and thinking that maybe I should have tried harder. Maybe I should have listened more to my mother and Salima. While I don't think the stuff the witch whisperer gave me will make any difference in my ability, or lack thereof, to do magic, I figure reading it is worth a shot. Especially if there's anything in there that talks about bizarre moments of magical clarity.

I know they exist, have heard witches and wizards— even warlocks—talking about them my entire life. Those moments when everything comes together and the magic you do is pure, perfect, easier than anything you've ever done. Heka has always been impossible for me but I'm wondering if the fire, and the release of the restraints, were my own moments of clarity. Except nothing about those moments had felt pure or easy.

I pause in the middle of the hall, one step away from the spot where I can see into my bedroom door. I admit to myself that I'm a little afraid of going in. I don't know how much work it's going to take to get it back together and I just don't know if I'm ready to see, really see, just how close I came to dying.

But I can't stand in the hall forever, clutching a half-eaten sandwich and cowering like a little girl in the dark. So I take a deep breath, steel myself, and walk into my bedroom.

It's nowhere near as bad as I expected it to be. Declan must have done a lot of work in those few minutes when he went to ensure the fire was out. The wall opposite my bed is still scorched, but it's nothing a coat of paint won't be able to take care of. There are no holes in the wall, nothing to show that flames spent long minutes eating away at it.

The carpet is gone, yanked out and rolled up in the corner, waiting to be disposed of. I'm walking on a bare cement floor. My bed is fine, the iron gleaming like it had never been touched—I'm not sure how he managed that—though my sheets and comforter are ruined. Declan has stripped the bed and folded the bedding into a neat pile on the floor near the trash can. The mattress is untouched.

I don't know how he did what he did, have no idea why he could repair things like the wall and bed, but not the carpet or bedding. Instinctively, I know that if he could have fixed everything, he would have. I can sense his anger, his impatience, when I look at the ruthlessly folded sheets. It's hovering in the room, all but tangible to me. Though I try to deny it, I know his feelings come from the same place the deep-rooted horror I'm feeling comes from—looking at the burned comforter reminds me of just how close I came to being set on fire myself.

Worry blooms inside me, along with a healthy dose of self-pity, but I push them away—just like I push away the little voice deep inside of me that says this would never have happened to a real witch. Whining over the obvious isn't going to change anything.

I walk into my bathroom, grab a spare set of sheets and a heavy blanket from the linen closet and smooth them over the bed. The blanket will have to do until I can get to the mall and pick up a new comforter. It's not very warm—especially against the open windows that are clearing out the last of the lingering fire smell—but I can't see myself doing much sleeping for the rest of the night anyway. Not when the memory of how I almost became flame-broiled is still vivid in my head.

Then, because I can't not do it, I pick up the books Salima gave me. There's no way I'm taking the herbs—been there and nearly died doing that—but it can't hurt to at least look through the book. If there's something in there about this weird pull I seem to have to Declan, then I want to see what it is.

Climbing onto my bed, I open the spell book randomly, letting it fall open to whatever page it chooses. I may not be much of a witch, but I've been in the community my whole life and I know not to discount the power of the universe to do what needs to be done—or to tell me what I need to know.

The book falls open to a binding ritual, one that is meant to tie two people together with powerful bonds. It's the closest Heka has to a marriage ritual.

Since Declan and I are very obviously not bound in that way, I flip past it a few pages and somehow land on another binding ritual. This one is meant to tie a person to his or her wandering soul.

I've never heard of such a thing and I read the ingredients and words of the ritual carefully. At the bottom of the page is a list of characteristics for a person with a wandering soul and I have none of them, yet these pages are oddly compelling to me. I read them again and again until I have the strange ritual memorized. Then I flip over yet another section of pages, and land on a binding ritual yet again.

The goddess is definitely trying to tell me something. I just wish I knew what it was.

This spell is the most complicated of the three I've

looked at, and its purpose is to bind powers of great strength and magnitude, to prevent the magical being from being able to access his or her magic. For some reason Declan pops into my head while I'm reading the spell, his face hovering on the page in front of me no matter how many times I blink to clear the image from in front of my eyes.

The whole idea that this spell was used on Declan is ridiculous—I've never seen a more powerful warlock. Or wizard or witch, for that matter. And if the universe is suggesting that I try to do this spell on Declan, maybe as a way to jump-start my own powers, then it is out of luck. Because there is no way I would do this to anyone, let alone the man who sets every nerve ending I have aflame.

I have no plans to let Declan get close enough to kiss me again, but at the same time I don't want to harm him. Not when he's never done anything to hurt me and in fact tonight did everything he could to save me. I deliberately ignore the pain of his desertion all those years ago. That pain is nothing compared to what this spell is suggesting—part of me can't even believe it's in a book of regular Hekan magic. Especially when I read over the spell and realize just how dark it really is.

This is black magic, the kind no smart witch dabbles in. Because while it may deliver power more potent than any other, it also demands a steep, steep price for whatever it gifts. That's just the nature of the beast.

I slam the book closed, drop it on the floor. What kind of witch is Salima, that she has a book like this in her collection? Though I know it's foolish, I have an almost overwhelming urge to go into the bathroom and wash my hands. I wish I could scrub my brain out as easily— that's how dirty that spell has made me feel.

And yet I can't stop thinking about it—or the other binding spells I just looked over. Maybe it's because I so obviously just escaped being bound myself. None of those spells had dealt with being physically restrained, but I'm not certain it matters. Tying up someone in any way is abhorrent to me.

At the thought, a sudden chill sweeps through me, turns my calm to panic in the blink of an eye. Maybe I know what the universe is trying to tell me after all. I grab my phone, dial, before I can think better of it. Declan had asked who I'd pissed off and I hadn't been able to answer him. Since then, I'd been so wrapped up in the weird stuff going on between Declan and me that I had completely forgotten to focus on the most important question of all—who had bound me to my bed like that, and why?

I wouldn't put it past Salima or my mother in yet another effort to wake up my latent powers, but it seems extreme—especially considering what had almost happened. Not that extreme isn't my mother's middle name, so maybe I'm giving her too much credit here.

But when she answers the phone, she sounds surprised to hear from me. Not fake surprised, like she's trying too hard, but actual surprise. Surely, if she'd had anything to do with that little nightmare from earlier, she would have been expecting my call.

"Xandra, how are you, sweetie?"

"I've been better."

The delight fades from her voice. "What's wrong?"

Part of me wants to just come right out and ask her if she bound my physical body to my bed, but if she didn't, she'll freak out and then I'll have a houseguest or two tonight that I didn't plan on. Especially since I can't see my quiet but overprotective father staying home after news like that.

"Mom, do you know anything about binding spells?"

There's a long silence on the other end of the phone. "Xandra, are you practicing your magic?"

I think of the fire I started and don't know quite what to say to that. "Yeah, I am. A little, anyway."

"That's wonderful, sweetheart. But don't mess with binding rituals. They're so dangerous and they backfire so easily. Not to mention that any of the really effective ones are also very dark."

"So you don't do them?" I want to clarify this, to be certain.

"Absolutely not. Not for well over a hundred and fifty years." She pauses, and when she continues she sounds sober and more than a little reticent. "When I was young I had a group of friends who were into the dark arts and I dabbled with some spells then that I wish I hadn't. They demanded a lot—more than I had to give. It was a very bad idea.

"But if you want some simple spells to practice, I can e-mail you some. They'll help train your magic, make you more open to accepting the energy of the goddess deep inside you."

That's the last thing I want, but now that I've gone down this road with her, I'm not sure I have a choice. "Okay, Mom. E-mail me two or three, but don't expect miracles."

"Of course not! I know these things are slow going. Are you wearing the boots I sent with Salima?"

I glance at the dresser where the boots are resting drunkenly, having been knocked over in all the commotion from earlier. Not in a million years am I putting those things on my feet. Been there, done that, and it really didn't work out that well for me.

But sometimes saying less is better with my mother. "I'm not now, no."

"I know you have an irrational phobia of cowboy boots—"

"It's not a phobia, Mom. It's not like I run away at the sight of them."

"Okay, not a phobia. A little fear, then."

"Dislike, Mother. The word you're looking for is dislike. I don't like boots."

"Fear, dislike, whatever. What I'm trying to say is that they'll help you. My magic is much stronger when I'm wearing a pair of Luccheses."

"Okay, Mom. I'll remember that. I need to go now."

"Already? We've barely talked—"

"I know, but I've got a lot still to do tonight. Work, you know?" I refuse to feel bad about fibbing. I recognize the signs—if I don't get off now, I'll be stuck here for hours.

She sniffs a little, her normal reaction to the mention of my work. "I'll send you those spells, Xandra. You'll probably remember them from when you were younger, but they're really good starter spells. Oh, sweetie, I'm so pleased you're doing this."

I can't help feeling a little guilty at the excitement in her voice, at least until she continues, "Salima deserves every penny I'm paying her! I can't wait to tell her about your progress—she'll be as happy as I am. And I'm sure she'll be calling you with some suggestions as well."

"Fantastic. I can't wait."

Either my mom doesn't notice or she chooses to ignore the singular lack of enthusiasm in my voice. "I have a good feeling about this, Xandra. I'll come up next weekend and we'll have a girls' day. Get facials, work on potions. It'll be so much fun."

I want to argue, but it won't do any good. Once my mother has her mind set on something it doesn't change easily. Besides, nearly burning to death tonight made me realize something. "I love you, Mom."

There's a startled little silence and then she says, "Oh, Xandra, I love you, too."

I hang up before things go from mushy to maudlin. I debate for a few seconds, but my questions are nowhere near answered and I need someone who will give it to me straight. My mom would freak out, Declan dances around the subject, and spells are not Lily's area of expertise. Which means I need to call Donovan. My brother never lies to me.

He picks up on the third ring. "Hey, Sis. What's up in the big city?"

I laugh, like he intends me to. "I have a couple questions if you've got time to answer them."

"Sure, why not? The Spurs are losing anyway." I hear him turn a TV down, then a sleepy feminine voice murmuring in the background.

"I didn't realize you had company," I tell him. "I can call back later."

"Lisa's not company," he says, mentioning his fiancée. "Besides, she's dozing on the couch. Now what can I do for you?"

"What do you know about binding spells?"

Again, there's that long silence. Coming from him, it makes me even more uncomfortable. "What the hell are you involved in, Xandra?"

I start to tell him that I'm just curious, that I'm exploring Heka and ran across some binding rituals, but this is Donovan. If I trust no one else in the world, I trust him. "I don't know," I finally say.

I hear a door shut firmly on his side of the phone and then he says, "Tell me everything."

So I do. I start with Declan's reappearance in my life and the body in Town Lake and end with what happened tonight. By the time I'm done, Donovan is cursing viciously. "I'll be there in three hours."

"You don't need to come, Donovan. I told you, I'm fine."

"Shut up, Xandra. And do me a favor. Check your body out and see if anything's different."

I look down at my bandaged wrists and ankles. "Different how?"

"Do you have any new tattoos? Has your mark changed colors? Anything like that."

I think immediately of the two Sebas on my back. But I don't know what else has joined them since the last time I looked. "It's going to take me a couple minutes to check," I say, climbing to my feet. "Do you want me to call you back?"

"No. I'll hold. I need to get dressed anyway."

"You're not coming."

He ignores me and I can hear him murmuring to Lisa, though I can't make out the words. I know her voice sounds a lot more alarmed than it did earlier.

"What if there is something?" I ask Donovan. "What does it mean?"

"Did you find something?" he asks sharply.

"I haven't even looked yet."

"Damn it, Xandra!"

"Tell me what it means first."

"That depends what you find. Hopefully, there will be nothing."

I get up, walk carefully into the bathroom. My heart is beating too fast and my hands are shaking. Donovan is making me nervous with his doom-and-gloom voice and determination to be in Austin tonight. He's my older brother and I know he considers it his job to look after me, but sometimes all I need is information. If he'd just tell me what's going on, I could stop imagining the worst.

I shed my top, then look in the mirror. After wincing at the sight of the bruises—somehow they look worse today than yesterday—I focus on searching the skin beneath them. There's nothing new on my chest, stomach or neck, and my mark—the one I got on the day I was born—looks the same as it always does. But I wasn't really worried about the front of my body, anyway.

I take a deep breath, and turn so that my back faces the mirror and I'm craning my neck to look behind me.

On my shoulders, the two silver Sebas are still there. I breathe a sigh of relief when I realize nothing else has joined them across my shoulders.

Though they belong to Declan—or maybe because of it—I know instinctively that they aren't malicious. That they aren't what Donovan is concerned about. It could be wishful thinking, but I doubt it. I can still see the panic in Declan's eyes when he crashed through my front door. I can't believe—won't believe—that he's the one who put me in that position.

I tell Donovan that I haven't found anything and he breathes a sigh of relief. "You've checked your whole body?" he demands. "There's nothing anywhere?"

"I checked my upper body—" I start, but he cuts me off.

"This isn't like getting a mark from the goddess, Xandra. Dark magic can scar you anywhere."

"You're being ridiculous," I tell him. "I'm fine." But I unbutton my jeans anyway, just so I can tell him I've checked. I pull them off, and right there on my inner thigh is a circlet of Isis—only instead of being gold, like mine, it's black and looks like it's been branded into my skin.

It looks, I realize with a detached kind of horror, exactly like the markings we found on Amy and Lina.

Fifteen

D onovan makes it to Austin in a little more than two hours. Since it's usually a three and a half hour drive, I decide not to ask him how fast he was going. Not that he gives me much of a chance to ask him anything—he hits the door shouting questions so fast that I feel like I'm dodging a firing squad. All I need is a blindfold and a cigarette to make the scenario complete.

After answering every other question or so for what feels like forever but is probably more like thirty minutes, I hold up my hands in the universal time-out symbol. "Whoa, Donovan, I'm not sure you've breathed since you walked in the door. Let me make you a cup of tea and then we'll keep talking." What I'm really saying is that I need a break, but he doesn't appear to be listening.

"I don't want a damn cup of tea." He bites the words out like bullets and as I look at him I'm reminded what a formidable wizard he is in his own right. Sure, being the heir to the Ipswitch throne gives him a little extra oomph, but even without it, he's packing a lot of power. Power that he has very much on display as he prowls down the hallway to my bedroom. I follow him, noting as I do that he's wearing his ass-kicking boots. Usually he runs around in a pair of plain well-worn brown boots that he's had for years and just gets resoled when they need it.

But this pair, black and fancy and more formal than

any other pair he owns, tells me he means business. Because these are his ceremonial boots, the ones he wears on the Solstice and other big holidays when he has to channel a lot of power to a lot of people. If possible, my tension ratchets up a notch.

"Jesus," he says when he sees my room. "Were you trying to kill yourself?"

"I was, yes. How did you know?"

He ignores me. "Take your pants off."

"Excuse me?"

"I want to see the mark."

I walk over to my dresser, pull out a pair of short pajama bottoms that I usually wear in summer. "I already told you, it's not a mark. It's more like a brand. Which is better, right? Because it means whoever does it isn't strong enough magically to tattoo the mark." Without thinking, I stroke my fingers across the Seba on my palm, the mark that showed up all those years ago when I was with Declan by the lake.

My brother shoots me a look of disgust. "I think you'd remember some guy coming in here and branding your thigh."

"I don't remember anyone coming in and casting a spell to tie me to my bed either, but that obviously happened."

It wasn't a prudent thing to say, as my brother growls low in his throat. He actually growls. It's a noise I've never heard Donovan make before, one I know I never want to hear him make again.

I close the door and hastily change from my jeans to my pj's. A quick glance in the mirror tells me the bruises on my legs aren't too bad—especially after Declan healed the ones on my shins and calves. Which is a good thing—telling him I experienced what Lina went through is one thing. Him seeing physical evidence is quite another. After all, my brother isn't exactly loaded with patience right now. Not to mention the fact that I think he's about one more disaster away from dragging me back to Ipswitch and handcuffing me to Mom.

With that in mind, I'm back out in under a minute and still Donovan scowls at me. The scowl only darkens when he sees the silver dollar–sized brand on my inner thigh. He squats down in front of me and places two fingers on it.

Agony, white-hot and overwhelming, shoots through me and instinctively I jerk away. The pain's bad enough that I stumble and nearly land on my ass, probably would have except Donovan reaches out and catches me. If possible, he looks even more grim than before.

"Do you know how to get in touch with Declan Chumomisto?" he demands.

"Yes." Dread pools in my stomach. After that kiss, I'm not ready to talk to Declan yet. Especially since, if he'd just been a little more forthcoming I could have asked him all the questions I've been asking Donovan and spared all of us the trauma that comes with getting him involved. "Do you want me to call him?"

"I don't know yet. Now that I'm here, take me through everything that happened again."

I do, and am just about at the part where I free myself when he reaches out and touches the brand again. This time I do fall down from the pain, my eyes rolling back in my head as I fight to stay conscious.

"Stop doing that!" I yell at him, punching him in the arm when I can finally breathe again. "What the hell is wrong with you?"

"Does it hurt when you touch it?"

"It stings a little, but nothing like when you do it."

If possible, he looks even more grim. "Damn it, Xandra, what the hell have you gotten yourself into?"

"You tell me. You're the one freaking out."

He points at the brand. "That brand is a product of the blackest Heka there is."

"Well, that's a big surprise. I thought it was a white wizard who tortured and raped those poor women before branding them."

"You're not hearing me." He holds up a hand at about eye level. "This is where regular practitioners of Heka are. Down here"—he holds his other hand at neck level—"is where your average sociopath or practitioner of dark magic is." He moves his first hand down to waist level. "Someone who can make those kinds of brands is practicing dark magic way down here—at a level so far removed from the Heka you and I know that it's a perversion to even refer to it by the same name."

His words make me nervous. I can't pretend otherwise. But even more than that, they get me curious. "Where would a warlock fall, Donovan? Someone with Declan Chumomisto's capabilities?"

My brother's violet eyes darken until they're almost black. Then he holds a hand far to the left of where he'd held any of the others. "Declan Chumomisto operates on an entirely different plane from where the rest of us are," he tells me with a grimace. "He is not someone you want to mess with."

Me messing with him is not something I'm worried about. Him messing with me, however? Of that, I am absolutely terrified. Especially when I can still taste him.

"Hey, Xan, you look like you could use these."

I glance up from the order sheets to find Travis standing at the door to my office, holding a cup of coffee in one hand and a bottle of Advil in the other.

"Bless you," I tell him, disregarding the directions and pouring three Advil onto my palm. "How did you know?"

"You mean besides the fact that your very fine brother has spent the entire day sitting in the corner of the café and glowering at anyone he deems suspicious—

which is our entire clientele, by the way. He even gave poor Mrs. Rodriguez the evil eye and she's got to be eighty."

"Eighty-four last September," I correct him, downing the pills with a big gulp of coffee. I burn my mouth in the process, but I don't even care. I'll do anything to stop the headache currently pounding away at the muscles at the top of my spine.

"Right. Or, it could be the fact that Officer MacCutie stuck around way too long today—and there was absolutely no flirting. You didn't even make a design on his coffee."

Damn straight. I'm not exactly thrilled with Nate right now—especially with the way he kept staring at my brother and the way he keeps sniffing around, trying to dig up information about Declan. And me. Of course, he wasn't feeling very flirtatious either—I guess my being a murder suspect puts a damper on that whole thing.

"Or"—Travis pauses dramatically—"it could be the fact that it's the afternoon of New Year's Eve and you're hiding back here working on orders that you won't send in for two weeks when you could be in the front wishing all the customers a Happy New Year."

"Okay, okay, I get it. I'm being antisocial." I lean my head down and rub a hand over my aching eyes. "I'll be out in a couple of minutes."

"No rush. I just wanted to make sure you were alive." But he doesn't leave. Instead, he comes up behind me and starts rubbing my neck, exactly where the blinding tension is gathered.

I all but melt into a puddle right there at my desk.

"Why are you so good at that?" I ask, laying my head on my desk to give him better access.

"Remember masseuse Jack? He taught me everything he knew."

"Remind me again why you broke up with him?"

Travis shudders. "He was the worst snorer ever. I couldn't sleep, like, ever. Remember? After a few weeks, I was a zombie."

I do remember, but still—"For back rubs like this, I'd put up with a hell of a lot of snoring."

"And yet, you have me, so you don't have to." He finishes up, then gives me a quick hug. "Happy New Year's, gorgeous! Meg just came in and I am out of here—I've got to go home and get ready for a big night out on the town."

"Be careful," I tell him, feeling more like his mother than his employer and friend. "Don't do anything stupid."

He laughs. "I'm young and hot. Of course I'm going to do something stupid. A lot of somethings, if I'm lucky." He pauses, grows serious. "But before I go, I just want to make sure that your gorgeous, glowering brother will be seeing you home. You don't need me to stick around?"

My heart melts as quickly as my muscles did. "I'm pretty sure Donovan won't let me out of his sight, like, ever," I assure him.

"Yeah, that's kind of what I thought. More power to him."

If only he knew just how much power Donovan already had. "Have a great time, tonight. Kiss a few hotties for me."

He snorts. "I think you have enough trouble on your hands between Officer MacCutie and tall, dark and adorable from yesterday. Any guys I kiss tonight will be all for me."

He disappears from the doorway and I stand up to stretch. If Travis is off, then it means it's close to five o'clock—which in turn means I've been hiding back here for close to two hours. It's a miracle Donovan hasn't poked his head in just to make sure I haven't made a run for it. He's been über-protective since he saw the dark Heka mark on my thigh yesterday. While he hasn't called

Mom and Dad yet, he did put in a call to the Council—one they'll return because he's the heir to the Ipswitch throne—to get their take on the whole warlock/serial killer situation. Plus, Travis wasn't exaggerating when he said Donovan hadn't moved from his spot in the corner of Beanz. Except to introduce himself to Nate and glower at the masses a little, that is.

I spend about ten minutes more straightening up my office—no one wants to start the new year with their desk completely covered—before making my way out to the front. But when I get out to the front counter it's to find Donovan nowhere in sight. A little frisson of alarm works its way down my spine and I start to ask Meg where he went just as a couple of college kids mosey in. I help Meg fill their orders—even going so far as to draw party hats in the foam at the top of their coffee—but the whole time I'm freaking out.

The second the kids wander away from the front counter I turn to ask about Donovan, but she's way ahead of me. "Your brother, who is super-hot by the way, left a couple of minutes ago. He asked me to tell you that he has a meeting with the AWC, but he'll be back in one hour to pick you up."

"The ACW?" I ask.

"Yeah, something like that. Oh, and a crazy-hot guy came in looking for you right before your brother left. I don't know what he wanted, but whatever it is Donovan took care of it. They left together."

When she says crazy-hot, my mind goes immediately to Declan. Not that it's been far from him all day, but still. "The guy. What did he look like?"

She smiles a Cheshire cat kind of grin. "He was dark, really dark. Not just his hair but the whole package, you know what I mean? He just gave off this dangerous vibe that had every woman in the place giving him a third or fourth look. You know what I'm talking about."

Did I ever. "Did he have a tattoo right here?" I gesture to where my own mark is.

"Yeah, he did. Except it was kind of like a starfish. You know, like the one on your palm, only black."

I nod, a feeling of disbelief moving through me. So Declan stopped by and he and my older brother—who fewer than twenty-four hours ago warned me to stay as far away from him as I can get—have taken off for parts unknown? It doesn't make sense. My brother barely knows Declan.

"Do you know where they went?" I ask.

"No idea." She rolls her eyes. "You know men—they're not exactly forthcoming. But I will say, they both looked pissed as hell when they left."

"Pissed as hell? At each other or someone else?"

"Oh, each other, definitely." She lowers her voice. "Whatever that guy said, your brother didn't like it and vice versa."

I close my eyes and try to ignore the fact that the tension headache I've had most of the afternoon is now working its way around my temples to the spot right behind my eyes, so that now my whole head feels like it's being squeezed in a vise.

Before I can say anything else, the bells Travis tied to the front door for the holidays jingle. I look up in time to see Salima entering my coffeehouse, her bag of doom over her right arm.

"Shit." I duck into the kitchen before she can see me. "Tell her I'm not here."

But somehow I have a feeling that isn't good enough— I'm terrified she has radar where I'm concerned. Determined not to get trapped in another discussion about how I can flex my magic muscles, I grab my cell phone, shove it in my pocket and duck out the back door.

I'm totally aware of how ridiculous it is that I'm running from a little old lady with a beehive and atrocious fashion sense but I can only imagine the discussion she and my mother had about me this morning. I'd rather freeze to death out here than go back in my shop until I know she's gone.

While I'm standing here, I pull out my cell phone and call Donovan. If he's already had a chance to meet with the ACW rep for our coven, he might have some answers for me. And to be honest, I could really use some of those. As well as some advice on how to deal with it.

He doesn't pick up his phone.

Which means he's either in the middle of the meeting or Declan and he have beaten the hell out of each other and he's lying in a ditch somewhere. In my head, I see how easily things between Declan and Donovan can go south, and while I love and admire my brother and his magic, deep inside I know he's no match for Declan. Of course, from what I've seen, nothing short of a nuclear bomb really is.

I fire off a quick text to Donovan asking him how everything is going with the Council.

Uneasiness is growing in me, razor blades of anxiety rocketing along my nerve endings and I pace up the block a little to relieve the tension, then turn to return to Beanz. Except I can't go back.

It's like I've run into a giant wall right here in the middle of the sidewalk. I can't see it, can't touch it, but it's there all the same, preventing me from moving forward.

And then it starts. The compulsion that wants me to walk and the pain that comes from trying to resist it. There's something inside me pushing, pulling, *dragging* me up the street, making me walk faster and faster. Part of me wants to grab on to a passing light post and just hold on for dear life, but somehow I don't think that will work. Plus, it will make me look completely insane. And while this is Austin, a place where most people respect others' rights to be completely nuts at any given time, it's probably better to keep a low profile. That way I have at least a chance of staying out of jail tonight.

As I stumble up the street, I try Donovan's number again. No answer. Damn it.

The compulsion is getting heavier, but I'm still thinking this time and I'm smart enough to know I don't want to do this alone. Not after what happened last time. Not ever again.

I call Lily, no answer. Shit, if I end up having to call the witch whisperer to get me out of this, I will never forgive myself. Or my mother.

I'd call Declan, but I left the card from Ryder at home. He might not be my first choice to get me out of this mess, but I know if anyone can help me, he can. Suddenly I remember those phone calls from him last night when I was tied to the bed. Maybe I don't need his card after all.

Freaking out now because the compulsion is building— the electric current deep inside me getting more and more painful—I fumble through my phone to the call log and hit the most recent unknown number on it. According to the log, the call came in at seven eighteen last night.

"Hello?"

As soon as he picks up, I open my mouth to pour out the details of where I am and what's happening to me. After all, I don't know how long I'll have before this thing takes me completely over. Except, right before I start babbling, it registers on me. The voice that answers isn't Declan's. It's vaguely familiar and I know I've heard it before, but I can't place it—especially since whoever is on the other end is either whispering or very hoarse.

Not that I'm at my best right now, anyway. I can barely think, barely breathe through the electricity rocketing through me.

"Who is this?" I demand. Not the most polite greeting I've ever given, but a whole new set of alarm bells just started shrieking in the back of my head.

"You don't know? You're the one who called me, sweetheart."

"Sorry. I guess I have the wrong number."

I know I don't—this is the number that called me last night—but instincts I didn't even know I had are warning me that something is very wrong about this guy. I know that he can't hurt me, that he has no idea where I am right now, but that doesn't matter. My whole body feels bruised and achy again, like every word this guy has said is somehow a physical weapon, striking out at me, battering me. Even worse, there's an electricity deep inside me that shouldn't be there. I don't understand it, but it's making me frantic.

Is this how he got me in my own home? How he chained me to my bed with only a spell—this electric connection we seem to have despite my best intentions?

Or am I just imagining things? Seeing the boogeyman around every corner because I'm freaking out over everything that's happened.

Either way, I'm done with this guy. "I'm hanging up," I tell him, pulling the phone away from my ear as I turn the corner onto South Congress.

"Xandra, wait."

I freeze. Not a wrong number after all. I put the phone back up to my ear, but not before I press record. Everything inside me screams that this is it, this is him.

"Who is this?" I repeat. I'm running now, straight down Seventeenth Street without any understanding of what I'm doing or why I'm doing it. The streets are almost empty everyone's gone home to prepare for tonight, so there's no one to look at me strangely as I sprint down the street in the platform heels I wore to celebrate

New Year's. I'm not looking for Donovan or Declan any-more. I'm just following the invisible string that's pulling me along.

"Are you almost there?"

"Almost where?"

"I think you'll know when you see it."

When I see *what*? I make the left turn onto Congress on the fly. I'm running flat out now, slowing only when I slip or slide on a puddle left over from last night's rain. It will be a miracle if I don't kill myself out here—or at the least, break an ankle.

"Are you the one who did that to me last night?" I demand.

"I have to admit, I was a little disappointed. I was sure you'd have freed yourself by the time I called. Such a disappointment you're turning out to be."

I laugh, though it isn't a pleasant sound. "If you're try-ing to get in my head, it's going to take more than calling me a disappointment to do it, you sick fuck."

"Now, now." His voice is little more than a hiss now. "There's no reason to get testy."

"You nearly killed me."

"You nearly killed yourself. You were perfectly safe until you set the room on fire." He clucks his tongue. "What a mess you made."

Chills run down my spine. How does he know that? How does he know that? He wasn't there—I would have sensed him. And if I didn't, surely Declan would have, right?

I skid to a stop at the end of Congress Avenue. I'm standing in front of the gates to the Texas State Capitol. It's a huge building modeled after the U.S. Capitol—with one exception. It's taller, because when they were build-ing it, the Texas State legislators were determined that it be bigger and grander than the building where the U.S.

Congress meets. It was totally egotistical and totally Texas, and of course, they succeeded. To this day, it's the tallest capitol building in the country.

And also one of the most heavily guarded.

Because the Capitol is closed to tours tonight, the heavy, decorative gates that block the driveway up to it are also closed. There's a police car in front of the gates and I know from experience—I tried to take a tour of the Capitol last year, just for fun—that there are a lot more security measures inside the fence.

Which is a problem, because I need to be in there.

Each second I'm standing here, the electricity is getting worse, the compulsion inside of me growing until I feel like I'm going to shatter into a million pieces if I can't get past this gate. If I can't get to where I need to go.

"You're there. Good girl," he croons from the other end of my phone.

How does he know? Is he watching me? I whirl around, scan the almost empty streets. I don't see anyone staring at me, but that doesn't mean he isn't here, sitting in one of the restaurants or other buildings, looking down on me. Or he could be skulking in the dusky shadows between the streetlights. Anything is possible.

I need to get out of here. I can feel it. Every brain cell I have is screaming at me to flee. It's not good that this maniac—this monster—knows where I am. It puts me in danger.

From him.

From the cop slowly climbing out of his car and heading toward me.

And maybe, most urgently, from the pressure building inside of me until I feel like I'm going to explode.

I try to leave, but the second I take a couple of steps away from the fence, sharp jolts of lightning rip through me. For long seconds, I can't think. Can't breathe. Can't do anything but feel the excruciating agony as it sizzles along my nerve endings. I force myself to take one more step, though all I can really manage is to slide my right foot two inches forward along the ground. It's enough to cause another shock to tear through me and this time, I can't take it. My body wigs out, my legs going out from under me so that I slam into the ground, knees and hands first.

As I fall, I lose my grip on my phone and it hits with a clatter. I sit there for long moments, trying to absorb the agony from the shocks. In the background I can hear the faint sounds of him laughing at me through the phone line.

"You don't actually think you'll be able to walk away, do you?"

I scramble for the phone as night closes in around me. "Are you doing this to me? Are you making me feel this?"

"I'm not doing anything, except enjoying the show. It's a good one."

The police officer chooses that moment to approach. "Ma'am, are you all right?"

Pain is still ricocheting inside of me, so severe that I'm afraid I'll vomit at any second. Still, I force myself to turn my head, to look at him. His body posture is aggressive, his hand on his gun, but his voice is concerned—like he can't quite decide if he's dealing with a drugged-out weirdo or a woman in the middle of a seizure.

Over the phone, I can hear him laughing again and I hit END CALL. Maybe I should have kept him on longer, tried to give my brother and Nate something to work with, but I have enough to deal with right now without keeping the bastard responsible for all of this in the mix.

"Ma'am?" The officer's voice is more insistent. "The Capitol building is closed. It's New Year's Eve."

I nod, force myself to my feet though every movement is an agony. I breathe through my mouth as I do it, long gulps of air that help combat the nausea from the pain. "I'm sorry. My heel bent and I fell." I force my left foot out, show him the high, skinny heels I've been running on.

He nods, relaxes a little. "Are you all right?"

"I'm fine." I brush my hands against my jeans, ignoring the sting on my palms. It's nothing compared to the pain that just whipped through me. "A little banged up, but okay."

"You can't be here. It's after hours. I'm not allowed to let anyone linger near the gates."

"Of course. I'm sorry. I was just hoping to get a picture of it all lit up at night. It's so beautiful." I hold up my camera phone. "I was here yesterday and did the tour, but it's so much prettier at night. I just want a photograph of it for my trip to Austin scrapbook."

He looks at me for a minute, duty warring with his need to give in to a request from an attractive woman. He's pretty young himself, probably midtwenties, and I'm sure he's bored sitting out here all night, especially since it's New Year's Eve. I force myself to smile flirtatiously and he responds with a slight grin of his own.

"I guess one or two pictures won't hurt."

"Thanks so much." I turn around, make a big deal of getting the perfect photo as I inch nearer to the entrance. The closer I get, the more the pain eases, until all that's left is the burning compulsion to get inside these gates.

"Will you take one of me?" I ask, plastering myself against the wrought iron and pasting on a smile I am far from feeling.

"Yeah, sure." He reaches for the phone and tells me, "Say 'cheese.'"

I do, and then pose and preen a little, cracking jokes so he'll take a few more pictures, which he does. I'm not sure what I'm doing, except buying myself more time—

and trying to get him to like me, so he won't shoot me when he finds me hopping the fence in a little while. Which I have absolutely no doubt that I'm going to do.

Because while I don't know much when it comes to the magic that surrounds this mess I'm involved in, I do know that I'm not going to be able to leave this place anytime soon—no matter how much I want to.

Part of me wants to just sit down in the middle of this driveway and cry because I know what's waiting for me when I finally make my way onto the Capital grounds. There's a body somewhere on the other side of this fence, a woman brutally murdered by the same psychopath who killed the other two. The same psychopath I was just talking to on the phone? I wonder. I think so, but I can't prove it. I can't prove anything, including the fact that some poor girl is inside here, just waiting to be discovered.

I think about calling Nate, telling him what I suspect. But what am I supposed to say to convince him? That I got a call from the killer telling me the girl was here? But I'm the one who called him. And I don't have any guarantee that there is a body in there, except for the pain I can't escape from.

I probably know just enough to indict me as an accomplice and nowhere near enough to convince Nate of my innocence. And if I tell him about the compulsions—about this weird magic unfurling inside of me—I can only imagine what will happen. I'll get stuck in a mental institution for violent offenders and this monster, whoever he is, will end up getting away with his agenda. Whatever it is.

The cop hands me back my camera and I thank him, before turning to take a couple more pictures. I can tell the excuse is wearing thin, though, and I have no idea what I'm going to do when the officer has had enough. Dive for the fence and pray to God he doesn't shoot me?

Surreptitiously, I dial Donovan's number as I continue to take pictures of the Capitol. It goes straight to voice mail. Damn it, what's the point of having all these people hassling me all the time, if none of them is around when I need them?

Because I'm out of time and choices, I take a few steps back from the gate and just as I suspected, the pain hits immediately. This time I'm prepared for it and it doesn't take me to my knees, though it does scramble my brain for a good thirty seconds.

When I can breathe again, I try out another smile on the officer. Of course, with the pain I'm in, it's probably more of a grimace. He smiles back a little uncertainly, and I figure the curve of my lips must be more frightening than seductive. Terrific. He probably thinks I'm deranged. Why the hell didn't Salima's book open to any seduction spells when I was flipping through it last night? Or mind-wiping spells, for that matter? I could use one of those right about now. Of course, with the way my luck's been going, I'd probably end up setting him on fire. Just the thought makes me shudder.

So no magic, then. No Donovan. No Declan. No Nate. I'm on my own. And considering I can't leave without literally frying every nerve ending in my body, the best bet I've got is for this guy to discover the body himself. Too bad I don't have a clue how to get that to happen, especially since I have no idea where the body is. She could be anywhere, including inside the Capitol building itself.

"Did you get enough photos?" the policeman asks.

"Oh, yes." I take a couple more steps back, refusing to acknowledge the pain and confusion that comes with overriding the compulsion.

I hold my hand out to him and pray he won't notice the way it's trembling. "I'm Xandra, by the way."

He takes my hand, shakes it. "I'm Brett."

"Thanks so much for helping me out with the pictures. I really appreciate it."

"No problem." There's a noise in the bushes and he steps back, hand once again on his gun. I tense, too, brace myself for goddess only knows what. Seconds later, a squirrel runs out of the bushes, a nut clutched between his little paws.

It breaks the ice between us and we both laugh, Brett harder than I, simply because he doesn't sense the danger lurking all around us.

"So, where are you from, Xandra?" he asks. He begins walking back toward the sidewalk, escorting me away from the gates, and I have no choice but to follow.

Each step is excruciating, but sheer will has me placing one foot in front of the other—while I formulate a believable lie at the same time. "I'm from New Mexico. Santa Fe."

"Wow, Santa Fe is beautiful."

"It really is. But Austin's got its own charm."

"That it does. Are you just here for vacation?"

"Kind of. My best friend from college just got a job at Dell. She starts on the second, so I took a couple of weeks off and came down to help her move in." I'm kind of shocked at the lies spewing forth from my lips. Who knew I had a talent for this sort of thing?

"That's nice of you."

I drop my phone a second time, use the "accident" to stop our forward momentum. I can't go any farther. My brain feels like it's being crushed inside my skull and every inch of my skin is stinging. Deep inside me, every nerve ending I have is aflame. Something wet seeps from my ear, and when I touch it, my fingers come away bloody.

I'm in trouble.

While Brett bends to get my phone, I wipe the blood away and then rub my fingers on my jeans to clean them.

He stands, hands the phone back to me with a frown. "The glass broke. I'm sorry about that."

"It's not your fault I'm so clumsy," I tell him. My voice is huskier than usual, my eyesight going dim. More physiological changes that I can't control. I look away, pretend shyness. "I guess talking to you makes me nervous."

He laughs, then reaches a hand out to pat my shoulder. "How long are you going to be in town?"

I shift my weight, inch myself a little bit up the driveway. The vise loosens just a smidge. "Just through tomorrow."

"That's a shame. I was kind of hoping to ask you out."

"I would have liked that." I glance back at the Capitol. "Are you working all night?"

He nods. "My shift just started."

"That's a bummer. Maybe I'll come find you next time I'm in town." I peek at him through my lashes, bat my eyes a little. "I guess I should let you get back to work."

I step away, not even having to feign my reluctance. After all, it's hard to be anything but concerned when I'm afraid my head is actually going to implode.

He glances over at his police car, and I watch, breathless, as he wages an internal debate. I'm beginning to believe that whether I live or die depends on his decision.

"I have to do my patrol of the grounds soon," he finally says. "You can come with me, if you'd like. It's not very exciting, but you could take some more pictures. And we could talk a little longer."

He sounds a little surprised, and uneasy, even as he makes the offer, but I'm not about to let him change his mind now that I've gotten exactly what I wanted all along.

"I would love to." I inject extra enthusiasm into my voice, even reach out and brush his shoulder with mine as I link our elbows. "Do you patrol the whole Capitol?"

He shakes his head. "Just the grounds. There's another officer stationed inside."

It's not perfect, but it'll have to do. At the very least, it should make the pain stop for a while. And right now, that's enough for me to follow him anywhere.

"I just have to get my flashlight out of the car," he says, guiding me back up the driveway. Thank God. When he stops at his car, I take my first deep breath in what feels like hours and just revel in the fact that the pain is almost completely gone. The compulsion—the throbbing pull deep inside my gut—is still there, but after the agony of the past ten minutes, it doesn't feel so bad.

Still, as Brett is getting his flashlight out of the trunk of his car, new thoughts creep into my head. Scary ones. Like could this all be a setup on Brett's part? Making me think I'm the one pulling the strings, when in actuality he's been doing it since the beginning? I think back on my fear from earlier, that the killer was watching me. Could it have been Brett all along? Has he been messing with me this whole time, laughing while I played right into his hands?

He hadn't been on the phone when he was walking toward me, and I don't remember his mouth moving, like he was talking on his Bluetooth. But at the same time, I'm the first to admit that I wasn't paying close attention to him. I was too busy dealing with everything else going on.

As he slams down the trunk, I'm struck with the crushing realization that I should have thought this out better. I should have made sure—somehow—that I wasn't about to jump from the frying pan into the fire.

Pasting on a smile I'm far from feeling—I'm getting really good at that, by the way—I say, "Do you mind if I text Lily real fast? Tell her I'm going to be a little late?"

His face falls. "If you need to go—"

"No. I want to stay. I just don't want her to worry." I roll my eyes, pretend indulgence. "She's one of those, you know?"

"I do. And that's fine. You should always let someone know where you are anyway. It's safer, especially if you're with some guy you don't know."

I find it a little odd that he's invited a strange woman into his security detail and now he's suddenly Officer Safety, but I'm not going to argue. I pop off a quick text to Donovan, telling him where I am, and then another to Lily—just in case. I haven't seen her since she left the house yesterday afternoon, but she texted me this morning to let me know she was spending the day with Brandon.

Then I follow Brett along the fence line until we come to a small gate—which, had I known about it to begin with—could have saved me a lot of pain and trouble. Hannah taught me to pick locks when we were kids, part of our campaign to torture and harass Donovan and Rachael.

I wait while Brett fumbles the right key into the lock. The pain is gone and in its place is that same humming I felt right before I found Lina. Whoever I'm meant to find is close. I can't help being relieved—I don't have to search for a way into the building, after all. The body must be outside, on the grounds somewhere.

My relief is followed closely by horror. How can I possibly be relieved at the thought of finding a body? Of another woman being dead?

Brett holds the gate open for me and we walk through. There's a trail that winds through the sprawling yard and connects our small gate with the main pathway that leads up and around the building. When we get there, Brett turns right. I start to follow him, but the second I step onto the walkway, the pain starts again. Not as overwhelming as before, but sharp enough to get my attention. To tell me that we're going in the wrong direction.

I wrack my brain, try to come up with something to get him to turn the other way, but I'm sure he's got his own routine worked out. He's already deviated from the program by bringing me back here—if I push him any more, he'll probably get suspicious. Especially if what I suspect is true and there's a dead body over there.

I grit my teeth and bear the pain that comes with each step I take in the wrong direction. If I could concentrate on it, just breathe through it, it might not be so bad. But Brett is talking—a lot, thank goddess—but still, I have to pay attention and respond.

We're halfway around the circle before the pain starts easing up, only to be replaced by that strange vibrating that makes me feel like I am on the verge of coming apart.

The pathway is lit, but Brett sweeps his flashlight over the lawn and bushes as we walk. We finally circle around, so that we're on the left side of the Capitol, near the huge grove of trees that fills up this part of the common area. The shaking is getting worse until my entire body seems to be throbbing to the time set by some invisible metronome.

We're close now, I know it with every cell of my being. I try to look under the trees, but it's too dark over there and Brett seems determined to concentrate his flashlight on the areas near the path. Which is pretty damn stupid in my opinion—not just him, but the fact that there aren't many lights out there in that huge, shaded area that is obviously a perfect body dump.

"What kind of trees are those?" I ask, a little bit desperate as I point toward the copse of trees. I'm terrified we're going to miss her and that poor woman will have to spend all night out here on the cold ground. Not that it will matter to her, I suppose, but it matters to me and

I don't want to see that happen. Plus, I have a feeling my entire body will go up in flames if I somehow manage to screw this up.

"The trees?" Brett asks, surprised. I guess I don't blame him as he was in the middle of a story about a couple of tourists that would have been really amusing if I wasn't so damn terrified.

"I saw them when I was here yesterday and they were so pretty I wanted to ask someone, but when I went inside and saw all that pink marble I totally forgot about it."

"They're mesquite trees," he tells me with an authority that's laughable, considering they're actually oaks. I don't mention to him that mesquite trees grow in West Texas and are ugly as hell.

"All of them?" I ask. "I thought there were a couple of different varieties."

"I'm not sure." Finally, finally, he sweeps his flashlight over the grove. It's so quick that I don't have a chance to see anything, and obviously neither does he.

Still, I have to do something or I will be completely screwed. "Did you see that!" I demand.

"What?" He looks at me like I'm crazy.

"There's something over there, near those trees." I point at a random grouping, making sure to keep things a little vague.

"Probably just another squirrel," he tells me with a laugh.

"Are you sure? It looked awfully big to be a squirrel." I clutch at his arm and bat my eyes hard enough to achieve liftoff.

"Maybe it was an armadillo. Have you ever seen one up close?"

"No! I don't think I have." Bat, bat, bat. I think I'm giving myself another headache.

"They're pretty cool. It's the Texas state mammal."

He sweeps his flashlight over the trees a second time. This time, something really does move. "Hey, you want to go check it out? See if we can spot you your very first armadillo?"

Thank goddess for the official Texas state mammal. "I would love to!" I tell him, squeezing a little closer to him for extra encouragement.

We're only a few steps off the path before my phone goes crazy. A couple of text messages followed by a phone call and then another text message. Donovan has obviously gotten out of his meeting.

Brett looks at me questioningly. "Do you need to get that?"

"It's probably just Lily calling to check in. I'll text her later. I really want to see that armadillo."

There's no way I'm stopping now—no way I could even if I wanted to. The live wire is back, tugging me forward, forward, forward until I'm practically running as I make a beeline across the lawn. My heels sink into the grass a couple of times, get stuck, and I swear to myself that I'm going to wear flats until this damn nightmare I'm involved in resolves itself.

The third time my heel gets caught, Brett snags my elbow and keeps me from falling for the second time tonight. "Careful," he tells me, wrapping an arm around my waist and pulling me flush against his side. "You're going to end up killing yourself out here."

I'm not the one I'm worried about. I don't say that to him, just keep walking—though at a more sedate pace. If I get hurt we'll never make it to those trees.

Brett has his flashlight on low and is sweeping the whole grounds with it, trying to catch some motion, which is why we stumble over the body before we see her. I trip on something solid, go flying and probably would have landed on her if Brett hadn't caught me. At first he doesn't realize anything is wrong, he just thinks

I've tripped again. But I know. I felt her, cold and a little clammy from the dew that's settled on the grass as the temperature drops.

"Brett. There's someone here!" I drop to my knees.

He whirls the flashlight around. "What are you talking about?"

But then he sees. We both do.

Sixteen

She's naked, lying facedown on the ground, her body covered with so many cuts and burns and bruises that there is almost no unmarred skin to see. Her long black hair is matted with blood and her left arm is angled oddly, the bone poking through the skin in a compound fracture I desperately hope happened postmortem.

"What the hell!" Brett says, squatting down to get a closer look at her. I don't think it's yet registered on him what he's seeing. When it does, he drops the flashlight and uses both hands to turn her over.

The large black circlet of Isis is branded into her left breast. It's about double the size of the one I have on my inner thigh, and somehow so much more intimidating on the flesh of the dead woman in front of me.

Dead girl, really. She doesn't look much more than eighteen—though she does look an awful lot like me.

"You shouldn't move her," I tell him, though this is the first time I haven't done the very same thing. The first time I haven't tried to save her. Because I've known all along that she was already gone.

Brett isn't listening to me, though. He's trying frantically to find a pulse—in her arm, her neck. I could tell him there isn't one to find, but then he'd know this isn't a coincidence.

"Brett." I crouch down next to him, pull him away. As

I do, my arm brushes against her and it starts—the thing I've been dreading all along.

Emotions rush at me, one after the other.

Terror, disbelief, sickness, pain, anger, hope, resignation, agony.

I jerk away, instantly, but it's too late. Her feelings are followed closely by images of what she went through. They bombard me, flashing through my brain at high speed. A knife cutting her skin, a fist slamming against her face, a foot plowing into her midsection. I feel the blows as well as see them and I wrap my arms around myself, start to rock as the horror of the moment grows.

She's spread-eagle on a bed—like I was last night—only she's naked, and he's above her, his hands rough as they poke and prod at her already abused skin. I feel every pinch and slap he gives her and then he's between her thighs, raping her and I'm screaming in my head, my own hoarse shouts mingling with hers as I feel him over me, tearing me apart.

I try to pull away, to get out of the vision that is so much more than a vision, but I'm dug into it and can't make it stop. The pain, the fear, the humiliation—they go on and on and on—until everything ends abruptly, with a quick slice across my throat that has me gasping and clutching at it, expecting to feel blood flowing down my neck.

There's nothing there, though, and that's what brings me back. The realization that I'm still alive, that this didn't happen to me—no matter how much it currently feels like it did.

I'm still sitting on the grass, knees drawn up to my chest in an effort to ward off the pain. Brett's given up on finding a pulse, is instead puking his guts up in the grass next to me. She must be his first body.

I wonder abstractly how long I was out of it. It feels like forever, but it must not have been that long if Brett is only now pushing to his feet.

"She's dead," he tells me after he wipes his mouth, his voice hoarse from horror and throwing up.

I nod. After all, I can still feel the knife slicing across my jugular.

He looks at me strangely, like he expects me to scream or cry or freak out completely. But I already did that—even if it was just in the privacy of my own head. He doesn't get any more.

When I don't answer him, he gets in my face. "You okay?" he demands. His breath is puke-scented and it knocks me back.

I nod again. Now that the worst is over, I can't find it within me to form words. Even simple, reassuring ones.

Brett looks worried as he stands up and pulls me to my feet. "Xandra, you need to go," he says. "You need to get the hell out of here. I have to call this in and you can't be here when I do. I broke procedure inviting you inside the gates."

That's fine with me. More than fine, to be honest. He's worried about his job and I just want to get away—from her, from him, from *here*. Part of me—the part that is still able to function—is worried about Nate finding out I was here. After what happened the other night, the last thing I want is to be caught here in the middle of all this.

Nate may believe I'm innocent, but I don't want to push him. I didn't do this, but I can see how the police might doubt it if they realize I helped discover this body as well. And if they dig, if they find out about the one in Ipswitch? Friends or not, I'm pretty sure I'll find myself locked up before I can say cowboy boots.

The other part of me is too numb to think. Too empty and hollow to do anything but stand here and stare down at this girl who looks so much like me. This girl who could have been me. Maybe should have been me. I don't know.

"Xandra, go!" Brett's voice is harsh and it gets me moving—which is exactly what he intended, I'm sure.

I stumble away, every step a horror. It hurts—I hurt—and I don't know how I'm going to make it through the gate and down the long driveway to the sidewalk. I know I can't leave—not until she's taken away from here—but I don't know how I'm going to find the strength to stay. Not when I ache deep inside from what that bastard did to me.

Did to her, I remind myself viciously. Not me. Her. That poor girl whose only crime was to have a haircut like I used to have and skin like mine.

Behind me, I can hear Brett calling in the body—female, DOS, Capitol grounds. I've barely made it out of the small gate Brett brought me in through before I see someone running up the main driveway. He stops at the main gate, right under the streetlight, and I realize that it's Declan. He's come for me.

He doesn't see me, though, and as he raises his hands, I know Brett is about to get a show he may never recover from.

"Declan!" I call to him, my voice ragged from all the pain I've endured tonight and all the emotions I am holding in check. The numbness is wearing off and I want to yell and scream, to throw myself on the ground and rage at the goddess for letting yet another senseless death take place. But most of all, I want Declan to somehow make tonight's nightmare disappear. I know it's not fair, but that's what I want. "Declan, I'm here!"

I don't yell very loudly—I don't want Brett to get suspicious—but Declan hears me anyway. He turns, runs toward me and I just wait for him where I am. I hurt too much to move any farther.

The second he reaches me, he pulls me into his arms. Just yanks me against his chest and wraps himself around me. And I let him. Frankly, I need the comfort, and judging from the way he's trembling, so does he.

"I thought it was you," he tells me hoarsely, burying

his face in my hair. "I thought it was you lying there under that tree."

"How did you know?"

"I have no idea. I was getting ready for the show tonight and suddenly I knew you were in trouble. So I cast a seeking spell and it led me here." His arms tighten around me until he's all but crushing me. It hurts, especially since my body already aches from everything it's gone through tonight and the last few days. I don't pull away, though. The chill that has been with me since I walked out of Beanz over an hour ago is finally dissipating.

I press my face against his hard chest and simply breathe him in. He smells like he always does—of clove and lemon balm and rain—and though I've spent the last eight years telling myself that I hate him, I want to stay right here forever. I feel safe here, in a way I haven't felt since the night in the forest all those years ago.

Eventually he pulls away and I have to force myself not to cling to him. "Let's get you out of here," he tells me, wrapping an arm around my shoulders and pulling me against his body. "You're shivering."

"So are you."

"Yeah, well, there's a solution for that." He starts to propel me back the way he came, but at that moment two police cars show up, sirens blaring. He turns in the opposite direction.

I don't move. I can't, and probably won't be able to for hours—not until the morgue finally takes her away. Declan learns this the hard way as I make it to the edge of the fence and not one inch farther. He urges me along and I crumple in on myself, arms wrapped around my midsection as my legs refuse to cooperate any longer.

"What the hell?" Declan mutters, his arm sliding down to my waist to tug me along.

"I can't go. I have to stay here, until they take her body away."

"What are you talking about?" He looks incredulous.

"It's part of the spell. The compulsion doesn't ease until the woman's been seen to."

He doesn't say anything at first, just looks at me. Then he drops his arm from around me, steps back. Immediately I'm bereft—then I'm angry. How can he make me feel like this so easily?

"It's not a spell and you know it," he mutters, right before he lifts his arms and calls to the goddess.

"What are you doing?" I hiss at him as I look wildly around. We're on a public street for goddess's sake, where anyone can see.

"Getting rid of the compulsion."

He starts a chant—it's a simple one that I remember from childhood—but as he speaks, I feel the tangled webs that are wrapped around me start to ease. I relax, breathe a little easier though the pain engendered by the attack makes it difficult to actually enjoy the act of breathing. Still, it'd be nice to get out of here. If Declan can break the spell—I refuse to think of it as anything else—than maybe I can go back to my normal routine. My normal life.

The spell winds down and I feel the pulse of Declan's magic as it brushes over my skin. It's as powerful as the compulsion, maybe even more so, but when I try to take that one extra step, everything inside me clamors for me to stop.

"It didn't work," I tell him.

He looks almost comically shocked, like he can't imagine a world where his power doesn't take over everything. "You still can't leave?" he finally asks, demanding clarification.

"Nope."

Down the street, two more cars pull up—they're familiar to me as I've been here, done this before. Sure enough, Nate and his partner pile out and head straight for the main gate, which Brett has since opened for them. They don't spot Declan or me halfway down the block, lurking in the shadows, which is exactly how I want it.

I'm not sure how long it will last, but I'm going to go with it as long as I can. Besides, we're in the middle of downtown at the beginning of one of the busiest nights of the year. People are already starting to gather on the sidewalk as they try to see what's going on. With any luck, I'll be able to just stand here, unobserved, until the coroner takes her body away.

Declan pulls me deeper into the shadows and now that the adrenaline has worn off, it hurts to have his arm wrapped around my waist. He must have found a particularly bad bruise to rest against.

For a moment, her naked body flashes across my mind and I experience—again—what she did in those final moments. It's too much. I can't stand the oily feel of him against me, inside me. I punch out with a blast of power that blocks the sensory details. The images are still there, but this time I can't feel them. I don't know how I did it or where the magic came from, and to be honest, I don't care. All that matters is, for the moment, I'm free from what that monster wants to do to me.

Declan turns to look at me sharply—almost like he felt the surge of power I used—but before he can say anything, my phone starts ringing. I fumble it out of my pocket, check the number carefully. The last thing I want to do is stand here and listen to him gloat over his latest handiwork.

But it's just Donovan, and he is pissed. "Where the hell are you?" he demands the second I answer the phone.

"In front of the Capitol."

"Bullshit, because that's where I am and I don't see you at all."

"I'm down the street some, in the shadows."

"Okay, I'm coming. Don't move."

I bristle a little at the tone in his voice, like I'm some recalcitrant child who wandered away the second his back was turned. He's the one who left me and it's not exactly like I enjoy my little forays around the city after dark.

I see him emerge from the crowd down the block, cell phone to his ear, as he reads me the riot act. "What the hell are you doing out here, anyway? I told you to stay put."

"It doesn't work like that." I bite off the words, as annoyed now as he is.

"Where are you?" he asks again, though he's striding straight toward us.

"I'm right in front of you."

Declan murmurs something I can't hear, then steps out of the shadows. I go to follow him, but find I can't move. That's when I realize he's done something to hide us from police eyes. I'm grateful—I really don't want to explain this to Nate—but at the same time I'm livid that he's so easily holding me in place. Like there isn't enough of that going around right now?

Donovan spots him and jogs over at the same time I shove Declan in the back. He doesn't even stumble, though he does cast me an amused look over his shoulder. The bastard.

"What the hell are you doing here, Chumomisto?" Donovan is decidedly hostile as he takes up a position to the right of me.

"Watching out for Xandra." The answer is mild, but the implications aren't—and Donovan's eyes narrow at the veiled accusation.

"Well, I'm here now. She doesn't need you."

Except I do. I can practically taste the killer's malicious intentions in the air all around me. Down by the lake, they hammered me, even while I waited in Nate's car. Here, it was the same—at least until Declan showed up. Oh, he isn't stopping everything—he can't touch the compulsion or those flashes of memory that I have—but he is stopping the endless waves of misery and sadness that battered me the other night. Right now, it's enough.

"I think that's up to her, isn't it?" Declan raises a brow.

"Stop it," I snarl at them. "I'm fine. I was fine before you got here and I'll be fine if both of you leave—so stop with the cavemen routines." I turn to Donovan. "How did the meeting with the Council go?"

"You went to the ACW with this?" Declan demands.

Donovan bristles. "Damn right I did. There's a dark warlock killing women and putting my sister right in the middle of it. What I don't understand is why you didn't demand that she go to the Council last night, after she nearly burned to death?" His eyes narrow dangerously. "Unless you're somehow involved in this?"

"Trust a prince to see everything in black and white." When Declan sneers it, neither the word prince nor the term black and white sound like a compliment. "The Council is dangerous and I don't want them anywhere near your sister."

"Yeah, well, you don't get to make that decision, do you?" Donovan's hand clamps around my upper arm and I gasp from the pain. It's not his fault—he doesn't realize that he's squeezing one of the worst of my bruises.

But Declan doesn't wait for an explanation. He shoves me behind him even as he rips Donovan's hand off my arm. "Don't touch her."

"She's my sister."

"Yeah, well, this isn't the Middle Ages and that doesn't mean much these day, does it?" He deliberately uses Donovan's phrasing and I can see it pisses off my brother enough that I'm afraid he'll take a swing at Declan. Or worse, pull out some magic that can't be undone.

"That's it!" I hiss at them in a furious overtone. "Declan might be concealing us, but that doesn't mean either one of you gets to act like a moron." I turn to Declan. "Whether or not my brother chooses to go to the ACW is none of your business."

"You'd be surprised what's my business when it comes to you." He smirks at me, like I'm amusing him, and suddenly I realize why my brother wanted to punch him. It's a hard look to walk away from.

"And you." I turn to Donovan with a scowl. "Stop antagonizing him. You're just making this whole thing worse for me." I deliberately inject some of the shakiness I'm feeling into my voice and Donovan immediately melts.

"I'm sorry, darlin'. I went nuts when I got back to Beanz and couldn't find you." This time when he reaches for me, I let him hug me.

"Now that that's settled, why don't you enlighten us?" Declan drawls. "What did the wise and wonderful ACW decide in terms of our . . . situation?"

"They're going to look into it," Donovan tells him between clenched teeth. "There are only about twenty warlocks in the world capable of doing everything this one has done, so it shouldn't be too hard to find them." His eyes narrow. "I find it interesting that both yours and your brother's names are on that list."

"Along with eighteen others," Declan drawls.

"Yeah, but none of them are in Austin."

"One of them is." He gestures to where the CSI team has begun photographing the body and looking for evidence. "Or we wouldn't be here."

Just then, a black Mercedes roars around the corner and slams to a stop in front of us. Which makes me wonder how the driver can see us. Donovan tenses beside me, but Declan just sighs irritably. All of which makes sense when the passenger window rolls down and Ryder is there, leaning across the passenger seat.

"Come on, man," he tells Declan. "The show starts in ten minutes. We need to go."

I'd forgotten all about Declan's show. "Go!" I tell him, shoving him toward the car.

He doesn't move. "They can wait."

"They waited thirty minutes for you yesterday! Which is understandable," Ryder quickly backtracks when both Declan and my brother narrow their eyes. "It's not like we want Xandra to burn to death." He shoots me a grin I can't help but return—Ryder's amusement is too infectious to ignore. He's so much lighter than Declan that I've often wondered why he chose to become a warlock instead of a wizard. Following in his big brother's footsteps? If so, I can understand the appeal.

"But she's fine now. Right, Xandra?" He shoots me a questioning look.

Fine is a bit of an overstatement, but I'm not about to set Declan or Donovan off. "I'm good," I say, reaching over and squeezing Declan's hand. "Go do your show."

"Yeah," Ryder agrees. "Come do your show. I'm sure Donovan's got everything under control. And I have people from the event promoter's office crawling all over my ass after last night. I'd appreciate it if you would get in this car so I can shake them off."

"Do I look like I give a shit about the event promoter?" Declan asks. "I'm not leaving Xandra alone."

"I'm not alone. Donovan's here. And he's not going anywhere, right?"

There's a strange look in Donovan's eyes as he watches Declan, like he's seeing something he doesn't expect. "I've got her," he finally says. "No one will get near her."

"Including those assholes from the ACW," Declan growls.

Donovan looks set to argue, but I step on his foot. There's no way Declan's leaving unless he agrees, and I think we're all smart enough to know that.

"Fine, no Council. But you'd better have a damn good explanation for this."

"I do." He turns to me, grabs my hand in his own cold one. I realize it's the first time I've ever seen Declan affected by the weather. Even last night, when I was freezing, he was perfectly warm.

He leans forward, brushes his lips over my cheek in a soft caress that makes my stomach jump, even as he coasts up to my ear and murmurs, "Don't trust anyone but your brother. Do you understand?"

I don't, no. But again I'm smart enough not to say it. Instead, I just nod.

"I'll see you soon." He kisses my cheek again and then he's gone, sliding into the sleek, black car and speeding into the night.

Donovan and I watch him go and then my brother turns around and demands, "What the fuck is going on between you and Declan Chumomisto?"

If he'd asked me yesterday, I would have said that nothing was going on. That I despised Declan. Now, however, I don't have a clue what to say. Am I wary of Declan? Absolutely. Do I trust him not to leave me high and dry again? Not in the slightest. But now there's a different question, one I can't help asking myself. Do I trust him to help me through this? To keep me safe from a force I have yet to begin to understand? The answer, unbelievable though it is, is yes.

But I can't tell Donovan that, at least not without my brother flipping out completely. So I just shrug and say, "I have no idea." It's the truth, after all.

Seventeen

It's nearly two o'clock in the morning when the medical examiner's van slowly pulls away with the girl's body. Just like that, the compulsion lifts and I'm finally able to go home. Thank goddess. There's nothing quite like celebrating New Year's Eve standing outside a murder scene, praying that you aren't spotted. I can only hope this isn't a portent of things to come in the new year.

Donovan stays with me the entire time, and he doesn't say another word to me about leaving the safety of Beanz. I guess he's figured out just how real this compulsion is, and that I can't fight it—even when I'm desperate to.

Once we get home, I kiss Donovan on the cheek and send him to the guest room to sleep. Neither of us have had dinner, but we're both too soul-weary to eat, though I offer to make something for my brother. He just pats my head and goes down the hall to his room. He's got his cell phone in his hand and I know he wants to call his fiancée. Just one more thing I feel guilty about.

Lily's asleep on the couch, television on and a text on Hekan history dangling from her fingertips. I turn off the TV and cover her with a blanket before picking up the text with the intention of marking her spot. As I do, a little sizzle zings along my fingertips and I glance at the page, just to see what's up. The term "soulbound" jumps out at me. Lily has underlined it twice and written "curse?" in the margin of the book. Despite my exhaustive training when I was young, soulbound isn't a term I've ever heard of. I skim the page, looking for a definition, but it's only mentioned that once, a passing reference in a chapter devoted to an ancient priestess of Isis and her mystical lover.

Making a mental note to ask Lily about it in the morning, I prop the text on the coffee table before heading straight for my room. Though I have to admit I'm a little freaked out after what happened yesterday, I'm too tired to let it keep me up one more night. If I don't get some serious sleep soon, I'm going to be talking in tongues. Besides, Donovan and Lily are right down the hall if I need them.

I start stripping the second I hit my doorway. After everything that happened tonight I feel dirty—inside and out. I want to take the world's longest shower, to scrub away the grime I feel all over me. Too bad the dirt on the inside isn't as easy to get rid of.

Without bothering to hit the lights, I head for the bathroom. I'm not sure I want to look at myself in the mirror right now anyway.

"While I'm sure I'll appreciate the view once the lights are on, I figure I should warn you I'm here before you take anything else off." Declan's voice drifts through the darkness.

A strangled little cry emerges from my throat as I dive for the lights—just to ensure it really is Declan standing by the window in the front corner of my room. Too late I remember all I'm wearing from the waist up is the fuck-me red bra I put on when I got dressed this morning.

I clutch my turtleneck in front of me, but the damage is already done. The temperature in my room plummets toward frigid as the amusement on Declan's face turns to fury.

He's across the room in a second, his rage a malevolent force that presses in on me a little more with every breath he takes. "What the hell happened to you?" He bites the words out from between clenched teeth.

"I'm fine," I tell him as I start to jerk the turtleneck over my head.

He's faster than I am, and he rips it away from me, sends it flying across the room to land on my lamp. The light in the room grows a little dimmer, which I figure can only be a good thing. But he doesn't even notice.

Instead, he places a gentle finger on my chin, presses upward so that he can get a better look at my neck. I'm not sure what the bruises are like there, but judging from how I felt when I relived the killer slitting that girl's throat, I'm guessing it's not good.

"This is a long way from fine. Who hurt you?"

I don't know what to say to that. "No one."

"I don't believe you." He traces a finger over my neck to my collarbone, stopping just short of the upper swell of my breast. I look down, realize he's tracing one of a dozen or so bruises, just on my chest area. Between the bruises from two days ago and the ones from tonight, I'm a Technicolor mess. Red, black, blue, purple, green, yellow. Throw in some orange and I could pass for a rainbow.

I don't make that observation, though. Declan already looks more dangerous than I have ever seen him.

He steps back, starts to walk around me, and I try to plaster my back to the wall. I don't know what I'm more ashamed of—the bruises or the Sebas that so obviously reveal the tie I feel to him, even after all this time.

He wraps a hand around my shoulder, and though his grip is gentle—tender even—it is also inexorable. I know he won't be denied, not in this.

He curses when he sees my back, low and long and furious. "These are whip marks." He traces one with a soothing finger. I flinch anyway and he jerks his hand back. "Did I hurt you?"

I shake my head no, though it's not exactly the truth.

"Is it just your upper body? Or is there more?"

I flinch. His tone is so icy it feels almost like a blade sliding along my flesh. I scramble away from him, but there's nowhere to go.

He notices, pulls himself back. "I'm sorry," he tells me. "You have to know I'd never hurt you."

I do. At least, I think I do. "This isn't what you think."

"Tell me what it is then." He's prowling the room now, pacing the length of the back wall like a tiger in a cage.

I don't know what to say. To tell him that I'm connected to the victims this way makes me vulnerable and I can't stand to be that way—not to him. Not again.

Plus, though he might have viewed Lina's body yesterday, I doubt they shared with him the extent of the damage. If he doesn't already know everything that was done to her, I don't want him to see the evidence of it on my body. I have no problem fighting with him, but explaining this—showing him this—seems cruel.

"It's nothing," I repeat. "No big deal."

The temperature drops so fast and far that my teeth actually start chattering from the cold. He must hear them because he closes his eyes, takes a deep breath and after long moments, the room warms back up to its normal temperature.

"Thank you," I say when I can talk again.

"Tell me."

"I don't know. It's some weird psychic thing." Please, let him leave it at that.

"Tell me." He looks calm and controlled, but his eyes are wild. Dark. Bottomless. Seething.

"They just showed up—"

"Goddamn it, Xandra! Don't bullshit me. Who the fuck did this to you?" he roars, as the final, tenuous ribbons on his control snap free. Power surges through the room, shattering the lightbulb in one of my lamps and making the others flicker.

"I'm trying to tell you!" I snarl back, even as I wrack my brain for something that will make this whole thing sound less terrible than it is. But in the end, I've got nothing. After three days of hell, my brain is fuzzy and I'm coming up blank.

Besides, there's a little voice inside me whispering that if I can keep Declan from seeing the extent of the damage, maybe it won't be so bad to have him know. He's lived a long time, is more powerful than I can wrap my mind around. Maybe he'll have some idea of what's going on here.

I glance up at him, hoping for some reassurance that I'm doing the right thing, but one look into his face tells me I'm doing the *only* thing. There's no way he's letting this go, no way this is going to go any other direction than how Declan wants it. That chafes a little, but in the end, I know when I'm beat.

I cross the room, sink onto the bed. Gesture for Declan to do the same. He's seething with rage, but he does what I ask without a word of dissent. And then he just waits, immovable and impatient.

"I don't know how to explain," I finally start, holding up a hand when it looks like he's going to say something else. "But the first of these bruises showed up after I found Lina down by the lake. More showed up tonight."

"They just showed up?" He sounds skeptical. "For no reason?"

"Not exactly." I go on to tell him what happens to me when I find a body—and what Lily and I surmised the other night. I try to skim over the worst parts, not wanting him to figure out all the awful things that happened to Lina, but I can tell by the look on his face that Declan reads between the lines quite well.

When I'm done, silence reigns. He doesn't move, doesn't speak, barely breathes for long seconds, until I'm all but squirming in my seat, waiting for the other shoe to drop. He doesn't look angry anymore—doesn't look anything, really—but I can sense a volatile fury simmering just under the surface. Instead of calming him down, my explanation has made only him angrier.

Minutes pass and I'm just about to chalk this whole open communication thing down as a really bad idea when Declan finally speaks. "He's connected to you."

"That's what I think—"

"That wasn't a question. I was telling you what's going on. Somehow this bastard has figured out a way to link with you." His eyes skim over my body. "Are you marked?"

My hand flies to my collarbone, and the circlet of Isis that has been with me forever.

He sees the action, shakes his head impatiently. "By him. Have you been marked by him."

I nod reluctantly, knowing as I do that he's going to insist on seeing the brand on my thigh.

Sure enough, his eyes go to my lower half, the only part of my body he can't currently see. "Show me."

"It's on my thigh—" I start. Before I can finish my sentence, he's fumbling with my jeans. For one, brief second I flash back to that moment at the Capitol, when I felt *him* inside of me, and I freak out. I claw at Declan, shove him away.

He lets out a low hiss and at first it seems like he's going to force the issue—which I'm not sure I'll ever be able to forgive him for. I'm not thinking now as I push away from him, pressing myself into the corner in an effort to protect myself.

He gets it right away, which only makes things worse—for both of us. Though his entire face closes down so that I can't read any emotion in it, I can feel it seething in him. An overwhelming force he has only the most tenuous control over.

He swallows convulsively a time or two, so that when he speaks his voice is gentle. "Why don't you go take a shower, get cleaned up? Then you can put some shorts on and show me. Does that sound okay?"

I don't even bother to nod. I just grab a pair of pajamas and run for the bathroom. Which makes me feel like a coward and an idiot, but I can't do anything about either right now. I need some space, a chance to regain some perspective. And I need to be clean. I can't do any of those things in my bedroom, with Declan watching me.

I turn on the shower and strip out of my jeans and underwear. Then, as soon as the water is viciously hot, I step under it. Let it wash away all the filthy things inside me. Except it isn't working—I can still feel all the obscene and terrible things he did to those women.

I'm furious, horrified—at both him and myself. It didn't happen to me, he didn't actually touch me, and yet here I am whimpering in the shower. It's a disgrace, to me and to those women who suffered so wretchedly at his hands.

I've been in here long enough, too long really, and I tell myself to woman up. To get out of the shower and go face Declan—who is even now calling my name from the other side of the door. And yet I don't make any move to turn the shower off. I can't.

Instead, I reach for my puff and shower gel and I wash myself from head to toe, again and again. I pay no attention to the bruises, scrubbing so hard that they all begin to ache and twinge even when I'm not touching them. It doesn't matter. I want to be clean.

I'm okay—I hold it together—until I get to the bruises on my upper thigh. The ones where he held that poor girl while he—

That's when I break. I slide down to the shower floor and start to cry, harsh, wracking sobs that hurt my whole body. I want to stop, but I can't. I keep feeling him on top of me, ramming himself inside of me. Inside of her, I remind myself viciously. Not me. Her. She's the one who had to live through the violence—not me. All I experienced are the residual memories and I'm falling apart. It's ridiculous, demeaning, infuriating, and yet I can't get off the shower floor.

I don't know how long I sit there, arms wrapped around my knees as I fight against the memories and emotions bombarding me from all sides. Lina's experiences blend with this other girl's until I can't tell one apart from the other. Which is somehow worse, like who they are and what they suffered doesn't matter. And it does. It really does.

The water goes from hot to cold and still I sit there, rocking back and forth. In a corner of my mind, I hear Declan on the other side of the door, demanding to know if I'm okay. But his words don't register—nothing does but the pain and the filth. I reach for the shower gel.

Except Declan is suddenly there, opening the glass shower door and turning off the water. His face is white, his eyes livid with more emotions than I can hope to name. But his hands are tender as he squats next to me in the shower, shoes and all, and wraps a towel around me.

He murmurs to me as he dries me, soft nonsense words that make no sense but that somehow fill up that empty, aching space inside of me. When he's dried all the parts of me he can reach, he picks me up and carries me to my bed.

I tense when he lays me on it, but he just walks back into the bathroom for my pajamas. Then he turn his back and gazes out the bedroom window as I pull them on.

"Can you show me the mark now?" he asks hoarsely, and I nod before I realize he can't see me.

"Yes."

He nods and turns slowly, his hands hanging loosely at his side where I can see them. Part of me is horrified that he thinks I'm this fragile little flower, but another part is thankful for the treatment. Which just goes to show how messed up I really am right now.

I stand up and turn around, legs spread so that he can see the mark that curls from the back of my thigh to my inner thigh.

His breath hisses out at his first sight of it, and he sinks to his knees behind me. "Can I touch it?" he asks after studying the brand for long seconds.

I nod, bracing myself for the same excruciating pain I felt when Donovan touched me.

Eighteen

Except with Declan, there is no pain. Just the soft brush of his fingertips over my skin as touches the mark for the first time, and the softer sound of him murmuring ancient words of safekeeping.

He says the spell again and again, and I can feel heat blooming on my thigh wherever he touches. Not sexual heat, just a healing warmth that takes away pain from the mark that I barely even know I was feeling.

When he finally pulls away, I start to turn toward the mirror, to see what he has done. He stops me with a hand on my leg.

"I can take the bruises from you and the pain."

It's a question from a man used to doing exactly what he wants, and I know it's a concession based on my fragile state of mind. It makes me angry—not at him, but at myself for being so weak. For needing someone to take care of me.

And yet, at the same time, I want to take him up on the offer. I hate these bruises, hate what they stand for and what they remind me of every time I glimpse or think about one of them. If I could look in the mirror tomorrow morning and see again, maybe I could forget that there's a part of me that will never be the same again—no matter if I get rid of one bruise or all of them.

"Xandra?" he asks from where he's kneeling between my thighs.

I nod. "Please. I would appreciate it."

"Okay." He stands in one effortless movement, ushers me over to the bed. "Lie down. It's going to take a few minutes."

I'm nervous though I don't want to be. I tell myself it's stupid, that Declan is trying to help me. And while I know it's true, the memory of earlier is fresh in my head and I'm afraid. I don't want to hurt like that ever again.

I do what he says, stretching out across my bed with my eyes wide open. I wait for him to do something, to murmur a spell or touch me or something, but for long seconds he just stands there. Eventually, he sinks to his knees beside the bed.

"Is this okay?" he asks as he reaches for my foot and gently rubs his fingers over my heels and arches.

Surprisingly, it is. "Yes," I say, my body relaxing marginally.

"I'm going to try my best not to touch you," he tells me, "but there are going to be times I have to. Tell me if I do anything you don't like and I'll stop immediately."

I nod, and he lets go of my feet. Even so, I can feel him touching me, his hands skimming over my feet and shins and calves. A healing warmth flows through me and I swear I can feel the sore spots lessening a little more with each second that passes.

Eventually, he moves from my lower legs to my knees. Under his ministrations, the huge scrape on my left knee disappears, followed slowly by the bruise on my right. He moves up a little more, to my thighs, and I can't help myself. I tense, lock them together.

His magic disappears immediately, along with the heat that's been warming even the coldest spots inside of me. I'm instantly bereft and I turn my head so that our eyes meet, so that he can see I'm being truthful. "It's okay," I tell him. "I know it's you."

Declan nods, reaches for my hand where it's resting

on my stomach. "We can wait for those. Or, I can do everything but the bruises on your thighs. Whatever you're most comfortable with." He gently places my hand next to me on the bed.

And then the heat starts again, this time over my torn-up fingers and bruised wrists. He spends a lot of time on my scratched-up palms—especially the one that bears his mark—before moving up my forearms to my elbows and then my biceps.

I close my eyes as he works—it feels so good that I can't stop myself from relaxing. From giving myself over to the tenderness I can sense coming off of him in waves. I know we have a murky past and that he's the last person I should trust right now, but I do trust him. He came for me last night, then came for me again today. And now he's giving me this incredible gift, taking away the pain I won't let anyone but Lily see, let alone touch.

"Are you okay rolling over for me?" he asks softly, his mouth only a couple inches from my face. His exhalation tickles my ear and I shiver involuntarily. At the same time, the first sparks of something else—something more—kindle deep inside of me. After everything I went through tonight, they're unexpected but not necessarily unwanted. Something good and right to chase away the dark abuses I want desperately to forget.

"Xandra?" he asks, and I nod, rolling slowly onto my stomach.

"If I'm going to heal the marks, I need to pull your shirt up. See what I'm dealing with. If you don't want me to do that—"

"It's fine," I say. He is the one who got me out of the shower tonight, who dried my naked body without even thinking about making a move. I tug at my shirt, pull it over my head and then drop it onto the bed next to me.

He pauses for a second, like he's collecting himself, and I worry that I made a mistake. That he'll think I'm too forward. But then his hands are on me. Not just his magic, but his actual hands, his fingers skimming over the Sebas magically tattooed into my skin. Except, after he traces two, he continues on to a third one.

"Declan?" I ask hesitantly, not sure I want to know the answer.

"Yes, Xandra?"

"How many stars are there on my back?"

He traces that last one again. "Three."

"Last night there were only two."

He doesn't say anything for long seconds, just continues to stroke the same spot until the skin beneath his finger feels like it's about to catch fire.

Deep inside me, the sparks glow more brightly, until it becomes a sweet kind of pain for me to lie here on the bed while Declan touches me.

"Relax," he tells me soothingly, as he removes his fingers from my back. I arch a little in silent protest, and he whispers, "I promise I won't hurt you."

I'd forgotten that was even a concern. "I know," I whisper back.

I slide my hand along the bed until I find his, then tangle our fingers together. He squeezes me tightly and I swear I hear him murmur, "Thank you," before he lets me go.

But I should be the one thanking him. I start to tell him that, but he chooses that moment to start in on my back. His magic moves through my aching muscles and it feels so good that my eyes nearly roll back in my head. The heat winds along the old and new whip marks alike and I feel them dissolve under the strength of his healing, until all that's left is a pleasant warmth that turns me into a melted puddle of goo.

He skips back down to the backs of my thighs, and this time I don't even think about protesting. Even when his hands skim under my shorts, over my rear, I don't tense. Don't freak out. This is Declan. There's nothing to freak out about.

When the last of the marks fades away, he starts to ask, "Do you want—"

I don't give him a chance to finish, just flip over onto my back. My breasts are exposed, but then I kind of figured they'd have to be, though I hadn't let myself think about it. Much of the damage that was done was to them, after all.

Declan inhales sharply, and a quick look at his face tells me it's not a sexual thing—the look on his face as he examines my injuries is both fierce and sickened.

"I'm okay," I tell him. "It isn't as bad as it looks." Which is technically the truth, I suppose. Since it's worse.

"You can trust me, Xandra. You don't have to put up a front." He passes a hand over my hair and I have to turn my head away as tears burn my eyes. It's ridiculous that I'm so emotional tonight, but the intimacy between us right now is overwhelming. I feel cracked open. Like every part of me is on display. In the morning, I may kick myself for opening up to Declan like this. But for now it feels right. Good. Like this is how it's meant to be between us.

Declan starts at my abdomen, small little sweeps of heat that both ease the pain and fan the sparks inside of me, so that all I can feel is him. He skims up my rib cage, taking care of the bruising that has made it difficult to breathe these last three days before moving up to my breasts.

He's not touching me, though if I close my eyes I can almost imagine that he is. That the moist line of fire that follows the bruising, bruising that imitates the knife slices on both Lina and the girl I found tonight, is actually his finger. Or even his tongue.

The thought has me gasping, arching, as I search for the reassurance of his hands. It's ridiculous, and more than a little embarrassing, that I'm getting aroused by the way Declan is touching me. I was so anxious at first and he worked so hard to set me at ease, that it's hard to imagine that thirty minutes later I'm this needy.

He doesn't seem to notice as he continues to ease the aches, even as he creates new ones. By the time he's worked his way to my nipples, I'm all but panting for him. His magic slides over them and I gasp, tremble.

He pulls back immediately and I nearly moan in disappointment.

"I'll stop." His voice is hoarse, his breathing a little quicker than usual, and I realize he's reacting to the vibes I'm throwing out.

"You don't have to," I tell him, shocked at the low, gravelly sound of my own voice. And at my own audacity, when I grab his hand and place it on the front of my thigh—the last place on my body that still has bruises.

"Are you sure?" Part of me thinks he's asking about more than the healing, but that could just be wishful thinking.

"Yes."

He swallows, then I feel him stroking me here too, his hands resting on my thighs, his fingers stroking the cuts from branches near the lake before moving on to the bruises that decorate my inner thighs. Bruises that look an awful lot like fingers from where that bastard held her down—

I cut the thought off before I can complete it. It doesn't belong here, not now, not in this moment that is so pure and sweet and sexy. I want these moments with Declan, need them to finish wiping away the horror I saw—and felt—earlier tonight. When I think about my body, about sex, I don't want to think about the sick perversions of a monster. Instead I want to remember the tenderness and light that is Declan at these most intimate moments.

Declan freezes when he reaches those bruises and I feel his rage break through the light, through the gentleness that he's been showering me with. But I don't want to lose it—lose him—so I grab his hands in both of mine and hold him still, hold him there, as my thumbs stroke over the back of his palms.

"I'm fine," I repeat. "Don't bring him in here with us."

"He's already here." It's more of a growl than actual words and I know I'm losing him to the darkness.

"No, he's not." I move his hands up a little until they're only inches from the heart of me. "I need this from you," I tell him huskily. "I need you to make me forget."

Maybe it's not fair, but at this point I'm so over fair. All I care about is assuaging the need Declan has built deep inside of me—the need for comfort, for passion, for him.

Declan's not buying it though. He pulls away, scoots to the head of the bed until his face is mere inches from mine. Then he studies me, those midnight eyes of his probing at my own, prying open my every secret fear and desire.

I don't know how long we stay like that, but eventually he must find what he's looking for because he bends and presses soft kisses to my forehead and eyes before skimming his lips down my cheek and jaw.

"You have to tell me," he says, right before he claims my lips in the sweetest kiss I've ever experienced. "I won't take the chance of making a mistake with you."

"I want—" My voice freezes in my throat. Normally I'm not shy, but for some reason I have a hard time asking this bold, beautiful, brilliant man for what I want. What I need.

I arch against him, try to show him with my body what I'm having trouble putting into words and he leans over me again, his mouth a mere inch or so from mine. "Do you want me to give you an orgasm, Xandra?"

"Yes." Oh, goddess, yes. Please. I can't remember ever being this aroused.

Declan doesn't wait for a second invitation, instead he takes my mouth in a kiss that is a million times more potent than any we have ever shared before. He's restrained, careful even, as his tongue coasts over my upper lip, then my lower one, before running along the seam between them. And still it's too much.

I open to him as my body threatens to go into sensory overload. And then he's kissing me, claiming me, his tongue sliding over and around mine. At the same time, he's touching me with his mind, his hands—his magic— everywhere at once.

I feel his hands sliding over my legs—playing with the sensitive spots behind my knees at the same moment they tickle my toes and cup my rear. And his mouth, his wicked, wonderful mouth continues to torment my own, even as I can feel him licking at the hollow of my throat.

I arch and tremble against him, trying to get closer, trying to draw him over and inside me. But he isn't budging, except to glide his mouth over to my ear. His tongue traces the delicate lower lobe of my ear—I can feel the warmth and wetness of it there as I clutch his silky black hair between my fingers. At the same time, though, I would swear his mouth is on my right nipple, drawing on the bud strongly enough to curl my toes and have me begging for release. Begging for him.

In the back of my head, I know what he's doing. He's using his magic to replace the killer's, using his gifts to bring me pleasure instead of pain, so that I won't forever associate the use of power with brutality. And while I can understand, and even admire, what he's doing, there's a huge part of me that doesn't care. It's the same part that's going crazy at the scent and touch and taste of him.

"Declan, please." I'm not above begging if it will get me what I want.

He reaches for my hands, entwines our fingers. Then sends his magic deep inside of me. I climax at the first thrust of it, and the feelings are so intense—so out of control—that for long moments I'm lost. Exhilarated and terrified and ecstatic, all at the same time. The only thing keeping me grounded, keeping me from flying apart at the seams, is Declan's grip on my hands. His mouth at the hollow of my throat.

The reality of Declan keeps the fear in check, lets the joy soar through me unencumbered as my orgasm goes on and on and on. He keeps stoking it. Keeps pushing me higher and higher until I don't know where his soul ends and mine begins. For someone who's spent the last eight years going it alone, it's a disturbing feeling. And also a tempting one.

When it's over, when I finally come back down, I pull Declan onto the bed with me and try to give him just a little of what he's just given me.

He stills my hands with one of his own, even as he wraps an arm around me and pulls me close. "Sleep, Xandra," he murmurs, and I'm not even surprised to feel a blanket drifting slowly over us.

I want to disagree with him, to make love to him as he just did to me, but the last few days are catching up to me. Plus I'm cozy and warm and for the first time since this nightmare began, I feel safe. Really safe.

I drift off to sleep with Declan's heartbeat strong and steady beneath my ear.

Nineteen

I awake some time later to find Declan propped up beside me on an elbow. I'm on my stomach with my head turned toward him and my hand resting on his chest, like I need to be close to him, even in near unconsciousness. I'm not sure what that means, but I'd be lying if I said it didn't scare me.

Still, I smile sleepily at him. He doesn't return it. He's too busy tracing the thin white lines on the back of my thigh, going over the freshly healed scars that replaced the branded-on circlet of Isis.

"I'm sorry I couldn't remove it completely," he says huskily, when he realizes I'm watching him. "But this should minimize your exposure to . . . *him*."

"No. It's good. It's really good. Thank you."

"Don't thank me. Not for this." He sounds venomous now, so angry that I can't believe this is the same person who earlier touched me so gently. "Don't ever thank me for this. Not when it's my fault it's happening to you."

I start to placate him, to voice one or two of the meaningless platitudes that women keep on tap to make men feel better. But then what he said actually sinks in. "What do you mean? How can this be your fault?"

He sighs, shifting so he's sitting up in bed. I do the same, waiting for an explanation that I expect to be able to poke holes straight through. At least until he does something so unexpected, I can only gape. He rolls up his sleeve and shows me the inside of his forearm, where a perfect circlet of Isis is tattooed on his skin. It's identical in size and color to the one on my collarbone and I stare at it in shock for long seconds.

Then I open my hand, stare at the silver Seba that has rested there since Declan and I met on my nineteenth birthday.

He nods before taking my hand and stroking his thumb lightly over my palm. The Seba starts to glow, much like the sparks that created it on that long ago night.

I can't help myself. I do the same to him, running my fingers over Declan's forearm and watching in shock as his circlet of Isis lights up as well.

"How? What? I don't—" I know I'm babbling, but I can't seem to stop. None of this makes any sense.

"I'm not sure how to explain it to you," he says. "Except to say that our souls are connected."

I wait for more of an explanation, but nothing else is forthcoming. Finally, I ask, incredulous, "That's it? The best explanation you've got is a cheesy pickup line?"

"It's not a pickup line," he tells me with the first grin I've seen from him all night. For a second I forget what we're talking about—I'm that dazzled by his smile. I'm not sure I've ever seen it before, not like this, and it lights up his face. Makes him look a million times more approachable than usual.

"Well, it sure as hell isn't an explanation of magic. 'Our souls are connected?' How lame is that?"

"It might be lame, but it's also true. Your magic—"

"I have no magic."

"Your magic," he continues like I haven't even spoken, "is tied to mine. And vice versa."

"Well, then, you definitely got the better end of that deal. Because I'm latent."

"Not anymore. In case you haven't noticed, your

power has woken up with a vengeance." He runs a frustrated hand over his face. "And the longer we're in contact, the more magic you're going to get."

"What about you?"

"It's the same with me."

"But you already have a ton of power."

"It's only a drop in the bucket to what I used to have."

I think back to those long ago whispers. I'd chalked them down to sour grapes, but had they been right all along? Had Declan really lost most of the magic he once wielded?

"When? When did you lose it?"

"The night you were born. The same night you lost yours."

"I never had mine."

"Are you sure about that?"

I think back to the stories I've heard of that night—of the lightning and Isis and all the signs that pointed toward my having a copious amount of magic. It's enough to have me thinking that maybe—just maybe—he knows what he's talking about.

"How do you know all this?" I finally ask him. "I've never even heard of anything like this and you say it so calmly."

"I've had twenty-seven years to get used to it. It took me a while to figure out exactly what had occurred, but I knew something was different."

"'Something was different' is a long way from thinking our souls are connected. I mean, how do you know?"

He laughs, but it's a rusty sound. "I felt it."

"Yeah, but I don't feel anything. Maybe you have the wrong person."

"How do you know you don't feel it? You've lived with this every day of your life—you don't know any differently. I did. I spent over two hundred and fifty years without you."

His matter-of-fact assessment sends me reeling. Sends me searching inside myself for some kind of neon sign that tells me Declan is right. But there's nothing there, just this feeling of unease deep inside of me.

Declan must see it because he smooths a hand over my hair. "Don't freak out on me."

"How can I not freak out? How come *you're* not freaking out?"

"I've known about you, in the abstract, since the moment it happened. I just didn't know it was you, not for a long time."

"Why didn't you tell me when you figured it out?"

"You were young, too young to deal with this."

"I was nineteen."

He shakes his head. "You were twelve. I waited seven years before I came back for you."

The information sends me reeling all over again. "You knew when I was twelve? And you didn't say anything?"

"What was I supposed to say? What was I supposed to do? Just walk up to your parents and drop the news on them? Your father would have done his best to kill me."

"He wouldn't have succeeded."

He shakes his head in disbelief. "No, but I could have hurt him, even killed him. I didn't want to do that."

"So you went away until my Kas Djedet. When you came there that night, you wanted ... what?"

For the first time he looks away from me, tension making every one of his muscles taut. "I don't know what I wanted."

He's lying, but I don't push it. Not now. Instead, I think back to that night, to the way he'd seemed as wary of me as I was of him. I'd thought it was strange considering he held all the magic, but now I understand. Or at least think I do. If our souls are connected, then I have as much power over him as he does over me. I'm not sure how I feel about that, about any of this. I trust Declan more today than I ever have before, but that doesn't mean I want to give him access to my *soul*.

"So, what happens now?" I finally demand. "Say you're right and our souls are actually connected in some weird Heka thing? Now that we're in contact with one another? What happens?"

"That's the million-dollar question. I would guess that we both continue to get more powerful, but I figure there's a loophole. Beyond the obvious, I mean."

"What's the obvious?" I demand. "Maybe I'm an idiot, but from where I'm sitting nothing about this conversation is obvious."

Declan stares at me with deliberate calculation, like he's trying to decide what and how much he wants to say. It annoys me enough that I snap, "Spit it out, Chumomisto."

"Okay. To put it frankly, your magic sucks."

"I already told you that. I'm latent. You're the one who keeps insisting—"

"No, not that way. What I'm saying is, the powers that you do have—they're pretty terrible. Finding dead bodies, linking with sociopaths, feeling people die ... I wouldn't wish that on my enemy, let alone—" He breaks off abruptly.

Why is it suddenly so hard for me to breathe? "Let alone?"

"Let alone you, Xandra," he finally says, reaching up to brush a lock of hair out of my eye. "I hate that you're having to go through all of this. I hate that it's my fault."

I think about what he's saying for a few seconds, and then about what I'd already realized—that he's been around every time I've found a body.

So it really wasn't the belladonna after all. Salima and my mother are going to be so disappointed.

Something he said tickles at my brain, a thought not

quite formed that hovers around the periphery of my consciousness. I try to focus on it, but it flits away, leaving me confused and almost hyperaware of Declan.

"It's not actually your fault, right? I mean, if we weren't tied together like this then I'd have these powers all the time. Not just when you're close to me."

"I don't know. I'm not sure about that."

"Why not? If my powers awaken only when I'm with you—"

"Again I'm not sure that's the case. You were latent from birth because our powers had never come into contact with one another before your nineteenth birthday. But now that they have, who knows if you'll continue to be latent if I'm not around? Will you be as powerful away from me as you are near me? No, of course not. But will you continue being latent?" He shakes his head. "I doubt it."

"You're confusing me." It's my turn to pace the room a little.

"Welcome to my life."

"So, do me a favor and spell things out for me. I'm stuck with these powers now? Forever? Whether you're around or not?" Another thing I don't know how to feel about. Too much has happened tonight and I've dealt with too many emotions. I'm not sure I have any left to deal with this, too.

"I think so."

"You *think* so?"

"This isn't an exact science, Xandra. It's not like I look into my crystal ball and the answers just magically appear. I'm flying blind here, just like you."

"No," I tell him. "Not just like me. You've known about this for years." I pause, consider. "You have a crystal ball?"

He rolls his eyes. "Seriously?"

The question that's been haunting me since he began

talking slips out. "Why didn't you stay? You left after one night."

He looks uncomfortable, miserable even, and for some reason his obvious guilt has another piece of the puzzle sliding into place. "That's why you left. Eight years ago. Because my magic kicked in, right?"

He pushes to his feet, shoves an agitated hand through his hair. "You didn't see yourself. You were heartbroken, completely devastated—and in so much pain. How could I stay knowing it would only get worse for you?"

"So you didn't even bother to ask me? To talk to me about it? You just picked up and left?"

"I was trying to protect you."

"By keeping me ignorant?" I know I sound skeptical, but I can't help it. While I've finally made peace with a life without magic, it wasn't an easy road to get here. It took years, years of my life I could have spent learning my magic so I wouldn't be in this situation now—a sitting duck for a sadist with vengeance on his mind. "By leaving me latent?"

"Sometimes ignorance really is bliss."

"And sometimes it's hell. Either way, it wasn't your decision to make. But you made it. Just like you made the decision to finally come back and find me, right? Your being in Austin now is no coincidence." I pause, see the truth of my words on his face. "Did you know about the killer? Did you know he was going to do this?"

"If I had that kind of inside line, don't you think I would have stopped him before he'd killed one woman, let alone three? Before he tortured them—and you?"

I don't know what I think. This whole conversation is so confusing, especially when you consider I've gotten only about five hours of sleep in the last seventy-two. But still, I'm not ready to let this go. Not when Declan is being candid with me—or at least as candid as he's capable of being. I'm not stupid enough to think he's telling me everything. There's too much that just doesn't fit.

"So, you came back and it wasn't for him. Something must have brought you here—must have made you decide you no longer want to protect me."

For the first time since I met him, he looks torn. Not just like he doesn't know what to say, but like he doesn't know what to *do*. It's a strange look on him—and a strange feeling for him, I'd bet. Declan is the man with the plan, the one who always knows what's going on.

"Of course I still want to protect you," he finally says, sounding anguished. "I may not be doing a very good job of it, but I'm trying."

"So what are you doing here? Why did you come back?"

"Because I need my magic!"

It's a real kick in the ass to realize I was holding out hope that he would say he needed me. Which is ridiculous, of course. We barely know each other, no matter how it feels to the contrary.

"I need the power I once had," he continues, "and I can't get it any other way than being in contact with you."

"And if you didn't need the power?"

He looks away, doesn't answer, though his jaw moves convulsively.

"You never would have come back," I say with a calm I am far from feeling. "I would have been latent my whole life."

"Do you think I enjoy seeing you like this?" He gestures to me. "Bruised, emotionally battered, in danger? Do you think I like being the cause of it? Why wouldn't I try to keep you from this if I could?"

"Because it's not your decision to make! It's my magic, my life, that you've been playing games with for the last fifteen years."

"This isn't a game!"

"You sure about that? Because it's beginning to feel a whole hell of a lot like one to me. One where you hold all the cards." That's when it hits me, the knowledge that's been there all along just waiting for me to put the final puzzle piece together.

I don't want to believe it, though, so I cast around for another explanation. Any other explanation. None comes to me, and I finally ask, "How could you have left Ipswitch without explaining any of this to me?"

"It wasn't my job to explain it to you."

"Bullshit. Why were you at my Kas Djedet, if not to enlighten me?"

He doesn't look at me, doesn't say anything at all. And that's how I know I'm right.

"You were going to kill me." Even as I say the words, I'm desperate not to believe them. Desperate not to understand that the man I've spent the last eight years of my life pining over, no matter what lies I told myself, could be so unworthy. "You came to my nineteenth birthday party with the intention of killing me."

He looks tormented, but I can't work up any sympathy for him. "I couldn't do it. The second I saw you up on that stage, trying to create fire, I knew I'd never be able to harm you."

"But how did you even think you'd get away with it? I'm a princess of Ipswitch, for the goddess's sake! My parents, and the Council, would have hunted you to the ends of the earth."

He doesn't answer me for the longest time. And when he does, it's reluctantly. With no hint of arrogance at all, only rock-solid truth. "They wouldn't have been able to touch me, Xandra. Not with my magic fully restored."

I think of the moment by the lake when the tree caught on fire.

Of the moment on stage when Declan burned and burned and burned.

Of how he touched me earlier, so tenderly, and took away the brand my brother—one of the most powerful wizards in existence—couldn't do anything with.

And I realize he's probably right. He could have killed me without any kind of repercussions. That he didn't makes it better somehow, and also worse.

"Get out," I tell him.

"Not until you let me explain." He doesn't move from his spot by the window.

If he explains any more my brain is going to spontaneously combust. "Contrary to recent actions, I'm pretty good at figuring things out all on my own."

"You're not thinking straight right now. Which is understandable, but you need to let me take care of—"

A blast of magic—of overwhelming power—wells up inside of me, then slams across the room to strike the wall inches from where he's standing. He doesn't flinch, but the look in his eyes turns wary, like he's just now clueing in to what he's dealing with. "You may be older than I am. You may be stronger than I am. But you don't have the right to tell me how I'm thinking or what I'm thinking or if I'm clear or not. Not after everything that you've done."

I realize I'm speaking through clenched teeth and pause, force myself to take a few deep, calming breaths. "Now I would like you to go. I'm not angry. I'm not even that upset. I'm more than happy to talk with you more tomorrow or whenever you'd like, but I can't do any more tonight. I'm exhausted and I. Need. You. To. Leave."

At first it seems like he's going to argue with me. But as he looks me over with blank eyes, something shifts in his expression—and the room. He turns, walks toward my bedroom door. Then stops before he's halfway across the room. Without looking at me, he says, "I'm sorry. I never wanted to hurt you."

It's a heartfelt apology from a man who rarely, if ever, apologizes. But I'm not ready to accept it. "I have evidence to the contrary."

He does look at me then, his lips twisting into that half smirk I first saw all those years ago. "You're tougher than you look."

I lift my chin in blatant challenge, unwilling—unable—to give an inch. "I've had to be."

"No doubt. Good night, Xandra." Though he's halfway across the room, I feel his hand stroke my cheek, his fingers brush against my lips. And then, from one second to the next, he quite simply disappears.

For long seconds, my brain goggles at how he does that, but in the end, I let it go. Power is power is power, and I have more than enough to think about without worrying how Declan does what he does.

Instead, I focus on everything he told me—and everything he didn't. For all his talk of our souls being connected—which seems to fit even though it sounds like crazy talk at the same time—there seems to be a lot of death wrapped up in all of this. Not to mention the stink of black magic.

Not just from the warlock who is even now killing women who look like me, but from this whole thing. People aren't just born like this. Obviously, or Declan would have been connected to someone else long before I was ever conceived. And I don't believe I was born connected to Declan either.

My hand creeps up to play with my mark from Isis. She gave me this when I was born, as a symbol of the enormous power with which she had gifted me. Sometime after that, sometime after I was touched by the goddess, is when our souls were connected.

But how?
Why?
By whom?
And another question I am beginning to believe is the most important one of them all. Is whoever did this also somehow connected to the brutal deaths of Amy, Lina and the woman last night?

Twenty

"**I**'m not sure what happened last night, but keeping up with your social calendar is getting to be a little too challenging for me, Xandra. Not to mention seriously freaking me out. You need to get the hell up. Now."

I open bleary eyes to see Lily standing over my bed, her face concerned and more than a little exasperated. "Who's been calling?" I mumble as I rub my hands over my eyes. I swear, it feels like I just went to sleep.

"Who hasn't been calling? Your mom, Salima, Declan. Your brother wants me to tell you he has lunch with his fiancée's parents and that you are not to leave the house until he gets back. And"—she pauses, pretends to think for a second—"oh, yeah. A *cop* is here to see you. Says his name is Nate and that you'll know what he wants. What the hell happened last night, Xandra?"

I don't answer her as my stomach sinks down to somewhere around the vicinity of my knees. Either I wasn't as inconspicuous as I'd hoped to be at the Capitol or there's been some kind of break in the case that's led Nate straight to my doorstep. Either way, I'm pretty sure it's not a good thing that he's here at—I glance at my alarm clock—ten thirty in the morning on New Year's Day.

"Can you stall him?" I ask hoarsely. Not forever. Just until I get my head on straight. Which, come to think of it, might be forever after all.

"What do you think I've been doing?" Lily asks with a frown. "But he's getting impatient, so I suggest you brush your teeth at world-record-setting pace." With that, she flounces back out of the room.

For long seconds I don't move, just sit there trying to clear the last of the cobwebs from my brain. Considering I hadn't had so much as a glass of champagne last night, it's much harder than it should be.

Voices drift down the hall to me. Though I can't make out the words, I can hear the impatience in Nate's tone, the barely concealed panic in Lily's. That panic is what finally galvanizes me. I stumble out of bed and to the bathroom.

It isn't the world's fastest toothbrushing and grooming session, but in less than ten minutes I'm walking toward the living room on unsteady feet. Again, I didn't drink last night, but it sure feels like I did. I'm shaky, queasy. Not to mention having the mother of all headaches. I swear, if this nightmare doesn't end soon, I'm not going to be able to function.

Nate, who's been sitting on my couch—an untouched cup of coffee on the table in front of him—leaps to his feet at my appearance. He's across the room in seconds, his face concerned as he wraps an arm around me and guides me to the nearest chair.

Maybe I'm not under arrest after all.

"You look like hell," he bluntly tells me when we're both seated.

"I went to bed four hours ago. What do you expect?"

"What'd you do last night?" His eyes search mine. But Lily chooses that moment to bring me a cup of coffee—thank the goddess—and I use that as a chance to glance away. I'm a lousy liar on the best of days, and that's without looking straight into the guy's eyes while I do it.

"Oh, you know me. Party, party, party," I tell him blithely.

"I didn't think you'd be in much of a party mood after discovering Jacqueline French on the Capitol grounds." He takes a blasé sip of his own coffee as he drops the bombshell, but every muscle in his body is tensed for a fight. Or my flight, I'm not sure which.

But I'm not running from this, not this time. No matter how much I want to. "I don't know what you're talking about."

"There are cameras, Xandra. I saw you."

I close my eyes, barely resist the urge to bang my head against the table. Of course there were cameras! Why hadn't I thought of that? Not that there was much I could have done about that fact, but surely Declan or Donovan could have done something to—

Nate shifts forward in his seat, avidly cataloging each and every emotion flitting across my face. And that's when I know—I'm not sure how, but I do—that he's just fishing. Declan or my brother must have taken care of the cameras after all. "Saw me what?" I take a sip of my own coffee, try not to choke on it. But my throat is so tight that I can barely get the hot liquid down.

"Saw you on the grounds, with the body. And that cop, who had no business letting you through."

Okay, so maybe he's not fishing after all. Still, it's too late to do anything but brazen this out. "What cop?"

Nate sighs in exasperation. "Is this really how we're going to play it? I'm not here to arrest you, Xandra. I'm here to help you."

"I don't need help."

He snorts. "Baby, if I had to point to one person I've met in my entire career as a cop who was over her head in a situation that could get her killed, I would pick you. Now, I don't know why you're turning up at my murder scenes or why the victims are all marked with your very distinctive tattoo, but they are. Which says to me either you're involved—which my gut tells me you aren't—or there's a sociopath out there who wants you to be. And frankly, that scares the hell out of me."

His eyes are sincere when he leans forward and takes my hand. "I don't want to show up at one of these scenes and find you lying there Xandra. I'd never be able to forgive myself."

His concern touches me. It's different from Donovan's protectiveness or Declan's enraged determination, but it feels good nonetheless. Another homicide detective would probably have hauled me to jail already and the fact that Nate trusts me enough to look beyond the surface clues tells me he's a better friend than I ever imagined. And a better homicide detective. Because, no matter how good of friends we are, I know if he really believed I was guilty that nothing would stop him from taking me in. Surely I owe him some kind of explanation to justify his faith in me.

The fleeting thought that he's playing me runs through my mind, that this is just another interrogation technique, but at this point it doesn't really matter. I need to tell him some part of the truth—I just wish I knew how much or how little I could say.

"I don't know why this is happening." I start with absolute truth. "I don't know who is doing this or why he's branding women with my tattoo. I don't know if it's a coincidence that the victims look like me or—"

"It's not a coincidence."

"Okay. Then I don't know why he's choosing women who look like me."

"Do you have any old boyfriends that things ended badly with?" Nate asks, reaching into his pocket and pulling out a pen and a small pad of paper.

"No."

"Any old boyfriends who seemed a little bit weird or whose behavior was outside the norm?"

Immediately I think of Declan, but I don't think his "outside the norm" is quite what Nate is talking about.

I clear my throat. "No."

He raises a brow, like he knows there's something I'm not telling him. But he chooses not to pursue it, because his next question is "Any stalkers? Any man who threatened you, wanted more than you could give him?"

"No one." I shake my head. "Seriously, Nate, I can't imagine anyone wanting to hurt me the way those women have been hurt."

He doesn't answer, just moves on to the next question—which totally takes me by surprise. "How well do you know Ryder Chumomisto? I know you said he dated your sister, but how well did *you* know him?"

"Ryder?" I'm prepared for questions about Declan, but Ryder? "I don't know. We were friends, I guess. Or we were. Before the other day, I hadn't seen him since he and my sister broke up."

"Why did they break up?"

"The usual. They grew apart, wanted different things." Hannah is as white a witch as they come and Ryder, like Declan, always treaded a little too close to the darkness for her. I'm not sure what it says about me that Declan's darkness doesn't bother me the same way. My only problem with it is I know it hides a side of him he doesn't want me to see, a past hurt so great that it shifted his path forever.

"Ryder's a good guy. He wouldn't do this."

"I thought you didn't have any idea who the killer was."

"I don't. But Ryder?" I shake my head. I can't get my head around even the suggestion of it. "He's one of the good guys, who genuinely likes women. I never once even saw him raise his voice to my sister."

The sound Nate makes doesn't sound very convinced. "What about Declan Chumomisto?"

Immediately, a wall goes up between us. I don't know if he senses it, but I can feel it. My magic seeking to distance me — not just from Nate, but from the question itself. "It's not Declan."

Nate's eyes narrow, but his voice sounds the same as always when he says, "Why don't you let me worry about who it is or isn't?"

"Because you're wasting time, going in the wrong direction."

He ignores this. "How well do you know Declan? As well as you know his brother?"

I don't know how to answer that. I think of everything Declan did to me last night and want to tell Nate that I know him very well. But though he healed me — not to mention gave me the most intense orgasm of my life on the heels of one of the worst experiences of my life — I know very little about him that isn't common knowledge. Or common lore.

Twice he's come into my life and turned it upside down and still I know less about him than a common acquaintance would, while he seems to know nearly everything about me. It's just one more example of the power imbalance between us and it grates. Hard.

"I didn't realize that was a difficult question." Nate's wry tone jerks my attention back to him.

"It's not that. I just don't know how to answer. I met him eight years ago and we spent an evening together. But I hadn't seen or talked to him again until the other night."

"Yet you left the police station with him. Even knowing that someone had just killed a woman he is connected to, a woman who looks an awful lot like you, you walked away from certain safety and got into a car with him?"

Put like that, it sounds ridiculous. No wonder Nate is looking at me like I'm crazy — and like he doesn't believe a word I've just told him.

"It was a really intense night."

"For most people finding a dead body is."

"I meant the night eight years ago, when I first met him." The words are out before I register that I'm going to say them. I wonder what he would say if I told him I'd found a dead body that night too? Declan would probably find himself in jail before he could say "Hocus Pocus."

"What are you hiding?" Nate demands.

"About Declan? Nothing."

"About yourself. I've been doing this job for over a decade, Xandra. I know when a witness is lying to me."

"I haven't told you anything that isn't true."

"Yeah, but you haven't told me the real truth either, have you?" He tosses his pad and pen onto my coffee table, thrusts a hand through his hair in obvious frustration. "I'm trying to help you, Xandra. You need to get that through your thick head and start cooperating with me or . . ." He trails off.

"Or what?" My voice is too loud, my heart beating too fast.

He scoots closer to me on the couch, his hands wrapping around my upper arms in a grip that is firm but painless. The look in his eyes is wild but concerned and I know I'm not talking to the homicide cop anymore. I'm talking to Nate, the guy who came close to asking me out more times than either of us could count.

"Why were you at those murder scenes?" he demands. "You found the first body, and I'm guessing you were responsible for the second one being found as well. My gut tells me you don't have anything to do with those women dying, but I can listen to it for only so long—especially when my brain, and the evidence, is screaming something else entirely."

Panic crawls through me. This is it—do or die time. I need to decide how much to tell him, and fast. I can't reveal my coven or Heka or the power that winds itself through me at the most inopportune of times. It's part of my oath as a witch, and definitely part of my duty as a princess of Ipswitch. I am to safeguard the secrecy and the sanctity of my coven's magic—not reveal it to the first cop who ever presses me for answers. At the same time, I have to tell him something because it's fairly obvious he's not going to let himself be brushed off. Not this time.

In the end, I skate as close to the truth as I can manage. Which isn't very close, but maybe—just maybe—it will be enough to satisfy Nate.

"I'm psychic," I tell him baldly.

His face goes completely blank. "Excuse me?"

"See? This is why I don't tell people. You should see the way you're looking at me."

"Xandra, this is serious—"

"I am serious. I'm psychic," I say again, though it isn't exactly true. "I get ... flashes of knowledge, usually about nothing important. But the other night when I was sitting in the theater, I picked up on Lina's pain. On her death."

Nate doesn't say anything and I find myself biting my lip and jiggling my foot as I wait for him to answer. Does he believe me? Does he think I'm lying? Does he think I'm crazy? Not that I really care what he thinks about me, but being hauled to the hospital for a psych consult is not how I want to spend my day off. Especially with all this going on.

"You're psychic?" he finally says, repeating my words back to me.

"Yes."

"And you saw Lina?"

"Yes."

"What about Jacqueline? You saw her too?"

"Yes."

"So you talked your way into an after-hours tour of the Capitol grounds? Because you knew her body was there?"

I hesitate, not sure how much he knows. I don't want to get Brett in trouble—

"He caved, Xandra. Started talking about the beautiful girl with the short dark hair within seconds of me questioning him."

"That was me."

Nate gives me a no-shit look. "And you expect me to believe you knew about the body because you're psychic."

"Actually, I don't expect you to believe anything." Suddenly, I'm angry. At him, at Declan, at my family, at Salima, and most specifically at the bastard who is doing this, who is killing women in the most brutal manner possible simply because he can. "This isn't some trick I trot out at parties, Nate. I can't control what I see or when I see it. I didn't come to you because I know how crazy it sounds, but that doesn't make it any less true. Believe me, if I could make it all go away, I would."

I can't stand the inactivity of just sitting for one second longer, so I push myself off of the couch. The agonizing pain from last night is gone—Declan took it all away—but I'm still sore, like I've pushed my muscles just a little too far.

I walk to my front window, gaze out at the street in front of the house. It's another dreary day, dark and rainy and cold. It's a holiday, so almost no one is out in it. There's nothing to look at except for the rain itself, beating against the porch in windblown sheets of water.

"How much do you see?" Nate comes up behind me, and for a second I think he's talking about the view outside my window.

"Not much, really. Just glimpses."

"Do you see the killer?"

"No."

"How about where he lives? Or where he takes the women to kill them?"

"No."

"Do you see any landmarks or street names around where he does this?"

"No!" I'm beginning to feel useless, but then that's not exactly a new feeling for me.

"Can you help me out here, Xandra?" Nate asks, exasperated. "If you don't see any of that, what does happen?"

"I see them die, feel them die." Nate sucks a deep breath in through his teeth, but when he doesn't say anything, I continue. "And I don't know how, but I always know where the bodies are. That's it."

"That sucks."

"Believe me, I know. If I could have told you more, I would have found a way to come forward. I'm sorry I can't be of more help—"

"No. I mean, it sucks for you." He puts a hand on my arm, the friendly heat of him sinking through the thin cotton of my shirt. It warms me. His acceptance, his understanding, of me. "I'm sorry you have to go through that."

"So am I." I sag a little, so that my side is resting against his. He shifts, wraps an arm around my shoulder. There's nothing sexual here, none of the pain or confusion or heat that I feel when Declan touches me. No spark. But the connection, the friendship, is nice. So is the comfort.

"I wish I could be more help," I tell him after a few minutes. "But by the time I know about the body, it's too late. He's long gone."

"Not really." Nate pulls away. "The coroner put Jacqueline's time of death at only an hour or so before you and Brett found her. So if we'd gotten there sooner, if we'd known about her as soon as you knew about her—"

"Then maybe you could have caught him." I think back, try to figure out when the compulsion hit me. By the time I walked all the way to the Capitol and talked my way onto the grounds, it had probably been close to an hour.

"Do you believe me?" I ask Nate abruptly.

He shifts, runs an uncomfortable hand over his head. "I don't disbelieve you. How's that?"

I think about it. "Good enough." Especially since I'm telling him only a little bit of the truth. "The next time I feel something, I'll call you if I can."

"Not if you can. You *will* call me. You can't keep traipsing all over the murder scenes, Xandra. You're going to get hurt."

I think of the cuts and bruises Declan removed from me in the early hours of the new year, and nod. I will call Nate as soon as the compulsion hits me—if it lets me. Not that I think he'll be able to protect me from reliving the women's deaths, but if calling him sooner actually gives him a chance to catch this bastard, then I am all for it.

"Good." He glances at his watch. "I have to go—I'm doing a briefing in an hour."

I walk him to the door.

He steps onto the porch, then turns back toward me. "You need to be careful," he warns me. "I know you think that Declan and Ryder Chumomisto aren't involved in this, but my gut says differently. And my instincts are rarely wrong."

I don't know what to say to that and by the time I figure it out, he's halfway to his car.

"Nate!" I call after him.

He turns, an impatient look on his face. I know he expects me to plead Declan's case again, but what I want to say is the opposite really. But how do you tell a man like Nate that if Declan *is* involved, he won't stand a chance of stopping him? No one will.

In the end, I just shrug and lamely call, "You be careful, too."

He grins and I realize it's the first smile I've seen on his face in days. Not that there's been so much to smile about lately. "Call me, Xandra."

I nod, then watch as he pulls away. It's freezing out and I'm dressed in only a thin shirt and jeans, but I'm not ready to go back inside yet. The air feels fresh, less stifling. If I close my eyes and try not to think, I can pretend my life hasn't spiraled completely out of control. Can pretend that the walls aren't closing in and that I still have choices.

But then Lily steps onto the porch and even that illusion is shattered.

Twenty-one

"**Y**our mom just left a message on the answering machine. The witch whisperer is on her way over."

I can't help smiling at the way Lily's latched on to my name for Salima even as annoyance shoots through me. "What does she want from me now?" I wonder. "She already gave me enough crap to study for a month."

Lily smirks. "Maybe she wants to drop by some more of your mom's special tea?"

I flip Lily off as I contemplate my options. The polite option would be to just wait here for Salima, so that she can make good on whatever scheme she and my mother have cooked up now. I can reassure her that I'm working on the exercises she gave me and she can report back to my mom that everything is exactly on schedule. It's certainly the grown-up thing to do. The responsible thing. But then I think about the drama she'll bring—along with goddess only knows what kind of poison this time around—and I hightail it to my room for my coat.

"Want to go grab a burger?" I ask Lily as she follows me.

"I was thinking pizza." For the first time I realize her jacket is already in her hand. Just one of the many, many reasons she's my best friend.

I start to grab my UGGs out of my closet—I can use the comfort of them today—but then I see the purple cowboy boots. They're still sitting on the dresser where Salima put them, though the right one is now resting drunkenly against the left.

For the first time since I was a kid, I want to slide my feet into a pair of boots. At first I resist the urge, but then decide, what the hell? A little extra help sure wouldn't hurt right about now.

When I step into the living room a couple of minutes later, Lily notices the boots right away—it's kind of hard to miss them, after all. But she doesn't say anything, just smirks at me. That's when I realize she's wearing her old, broken-in boots as well.

Great minds obviously think alike.

We head around the block to my favorite Italian restaurant, and as we do, my conscience niggles a little. Not because I'm ditching my mom and Salima—that's just self-preservation—but I know Donovan will worry about me if my mom tells him I'm not home. But surely even he recognizes the folly of me hanging around the house waiting for Salima to show up.

I text him a quick message, let him know where I'm going to be. And then do my best to enjoy the brisk walk through the cold, my arm linked with Lily's. This feels so normal, so right, after the nightmare of the last few days and I want to absorb every second of it.

But we're barely seated at our favorite corner table before Lily says, "I think I found something." She looks stressed, more stressed than I've ever seen her and I immediately tense up.

"About the killer?" I demand even as I wonder how that's possible. Maybe her cards—

She shakes her head. "About you and Declan." Her voice breaks a little.

I think back to Declan's and my painful conversation last night, about how he'd been prepared to kill me in order to escape the magic that binds us together. Then I think of what I read in that book of Lily's last night. I'd wanted to ask him about it, but had gotten sidetracked by the knowledge of just how close to death I'd come eight years ago. I won't be sidetracked today, not when it feels like everything hangs on the answer to this one question. "Does it have anything to do with being soulbound?"

She looks at me, surprised. There's something else in her eyes, too, something I can't quite identify, though it looks an awful lot like fear. "You already know?"

"I saw the book you were reading last night. You fell asleep with it open to a page that mentions it."

"Oh, right." She relaxes, then smiles at the waiter who approaches to take our order.

I'm on tenterhooks the whole time, now that I know the answers to my questions are just within reach. The second the waiter walks away, I grab Lily's hand and demand, "Tell me."

She clears her throat, shoves a lock of curly hair behind her ear. Rearranges her silverware. Basically does everything but look at me. "Just tell me!" I demand harshly. After everything that's happened, I feel like I'm about to shatter. I need to know the truth.

"It's an Anathema," she whispers and everything inside me freezes.

An Anathema. My eyes close and I shudder in horror. This is so much worse than I thought. "From the Council?" I whisper.

"Who else?" Lily answers impatiently, and I know she's right. No one else is powerful enough to lock an Anathema on to a warlock of Declan's power. Maybe my family could manage it, but it would take my mom, dad, Donovan and Rachael all working together to make something like this stick. And it can't be them for two reasons.

One, my parents don't dabble in things like this. And

two, they would never deliberately do something to hurt me—and everything inside me is screaming that before this is over, I'm going to suffer a lot more than I already have. We both are.

I think back on what Declan told me in the middle of the night and for the first time, truly understand why he came to kill me all those years ago. Anathemas are dark, dark magic. The most powerful curses in existence, they are strictly forbidden in my coven and all the others we associate with. They are also forbidden by the ACW (except, it seems, by their own hand), outlawed centuries ago because of the magic it takes to conjure them—and the blackness they bring to the wizards, witches or warlocks struck by them.

I think of Declan, of the darkness that surrounds him all the time. And I want to scream, to rage at the ACW for doing such an awful thing to him. I've researched him, talked to him, held him in my arms and I know that there is nothing he could have done to deserve such a curse.

Yes, he's shadowed. Yes, he sometimes walks the line between right and wrong, but how could he not with an Anathema hanging over him? How much strength, how much power, does it take for him to resist the black call of it every single moment of every single day of his life?

And yet he's done it. For twenty-seven years, he's done it, when he could have ended it years ago by simply murdering me. By taking my soul out of the equation. That he hasn't, even with its darkness embedded so completely inside him, is the mark of greater strength than I have ever known.

"You have to stay away from him." The urgency in Lily's voice pulls me out of the horrified stupor I've descended into. "If he recognizes you, if he knows—"

"He does," I tell her. "He already knows that we're bound."

"Then he'll kill you," she breathes, and this time the hand she reaches out for me is trembling wildly. "Declan Chumomisto isn't known for his compassion."

And yet he should be. For the hundredth time, I find myself reliving those long, slow, torturous moments with Declan last night. He'd healed me, comforted me, aroused me . . . and taken nothing for himself. "He's had plenty of opportunities to hurt me and he hasn't yet, Lily."

"Then he must want something from you, Xandra. There's no other explanation. No other reason that a warlock with Declan's magic would keep you around when you have the power to hurt him."

"Me? Hurt him? With what? My magic isn't exactly in the same class as his."

"It doesn't have to be." She shakes her head. "I've been researching all morning—I even called my grandma and talked to her about being soulbound. And she told me the same thing all the books did. That there's no way for both partners to escape being soulbound. The only way the curse breaks is for one of you to die."

"And if we don't try to break the curse? If we just live with it?"

"Then the curse breaks you." She looks sick. "One of the books I was reading last night said that people who are soulbound hurt each other over and over again, until they are completely destroyed, their souls utterly consumed by each other. It's one of the worst parts of the curse."

"*One* of the worst parts? What could possibly be worse than that?"

"The fact that even then you don't die."

"How is that possible? How do you live without a soul?" But even as I ask the question, I know. I've seen them. We all have. Empty-eyed witches and warlocks who have sold their souls, who spend the rest of their wasted, empty lives weaving shadowy spells to skim power, magic, emotion, from those who have not forsaken their gifts.

My stomach revolts and for a second I fear that I'm going to be sick, all over the eggplant and zucchini pizza our waiter has just placed in front of us. "Don't follow me," I tell her as I grab my purse and drop forty dollars on the table.

"Xandra, wait!"

She reaches for me, but I elude her, bolting for the door at a dead run. I don't know where I'm going, don't know what I hope to find. I know only that I want away from Lily with her sad eyes and copious knowledge.

But no matter how fast I run, I can't get away. The truth of what Lily told me has taken up residence deep inside of me and already I feel it twisting me up into something—someone—unrecognizable.

I dash like a crazy woman through the streets of downtown Austin.

Flee like a wild animal whose only thought is escape.

Run until I can't run anymore.

I stop when my legs are rubber and my lungs feel like they're going to explode. The stitch in my side is so bad that it feels like it's taken over my entire body, so I brace my hands on my thighs and concentrate on dragging deep breaths into my lungs.

But as my breath returns, so does my capacity for thought. And fear. And pain.

Whipping out my cell phone, I fire off a quick text to Lily telling her I'm fine, even though I'm not, and thanking her for not following me. Then I dial Declan's number, which he programmed into my phone last night while I was in the shower.

The phone rings only once before he snatches it up. "Xandra. Are you all right?"

"Why didn't you just kill me when you had the chance?" I demand. My breath is still coming in fits and spurts, but by now I think it's more from emotion than exertion.

He's silent for the beat of one second, two. Then, "Where are you?"

"Does it matter?"

"Of course it matters," he snaps out. "I'm coming for you."

"I don't know where I am." It's the truth. I haven't even tried to get my bearings yet.

"Stay where you are. I'll find you."

"Why? Why does it matter if you find me? Won't that just make things worse?"

"Who told you?" His voice is strained, his breathing quicker than usual and I realize that now he's running too. Only he's not trying to escape. He's trying to rescue me.

Only I'm not ready to be rescued, and I'm certainly not ready to see him. "Good-bye, Declan." I hang up the phone, prepare to take off all over again. But then I look around, try to figure out where I am. That's when I realize I'm back where so much of this nightmare I'm currently caught in started—on the slope leading down to Town Lake.

The yellow crime scene tape still cuts a wide swath across the trail leading down to the lake and I feel myself drawn to it. Drawn to the spot where I found her. Lina. It's not the same as the compulsion. I can fight the pull if I want to, but I don't. I want to see if—I don't know what I want to see. I just know that I do.

I cross the grass, stumble down the rocky slope to the trail that leads around the lake. My new cowboy boots are slick, but at least they're not five-inch Jimmy Choos, and I make it to the tape without any major catastrophes.

At first, I just stand here, looking out over the water. It's a gloomy day, overcast, with just a touch of wetness in the air from the rain that's been that threatening all day to fall. It's a perfect day for death, if there is such a thing, and I feel it calling to me. Again, not a compulsion so much as a whisper directing me down, down, down to the water.

I glance around, make sure I'm alone, then duck under the tape. I don't know what I'm looking for, what I'm supposed to find down here, but there has to be something. Otherwise why would sparks of power be bouncing around inside me like Pop Rocks?

I creep forward slowly to the spot where I found Lina's body. Instinct has me crouching down, peering into the cloudy water. Part of me expects to still see her there, staring up at me with sightless eyes. But there's nothing there, not even my own reflection. The day is too dark for that, the water too murky.

Seeking something—a connection, maybe—I brush my fingertips through the freezing water. And that's when I feel it, an ominous gloom spreading through the water straight at me. I immediately pull my fingers out of the water and dry them on my jeans. The last thing I want is to feel what I felt the last time I was down here.

But it's too late. The whispers are louder now, the sparks brighter, and I know I can't walk away until I've listened to what they want to tell me. It takes every ounce of courage I have—and a little extra, to boot, but I thrust my hand back into the water.

It takes only a few seconds before my bones begin to ache from the cold and soon after my fingers start to cramp. I feel the pain, but it doesn't matter. Nothing does but figuring this out.

The sinister feeling is back, and it's heavier now, more oppressive. It crushes down on my back and shoulders, circles around and presses against my chest until I'm struggling to draw a breath. And then it's like it starts to sprout fingers, fingers that curl around my throat and squeeze against my windpipe.

I start to panic even as I tell myself that what I'm feeling isn't real, isn't really happening. There's a flash of black in front of my eyes, and I glance around wildly—though I have no idea whether I'm looking for friend or foe. There's no one there, and that's when I realize what I'm seeing is him. Or at least, echoes of him.

I close my eyes, try to see what I can. What I'm supposed to. There's a thin arm, covered in a chunky black sweater. A slender hand encased in an elegant black glove. A wicked looking athame—ceremonial dagger—clutched in long, leather-encased fingers. I concentrate on the dagger, stretch my powers and my mind as far as both can go as I try to distinguish what it looks like.

In the Heka community, athames are very personal things—and very unique ones. Witches of power have their daggers specially made for them by artisans with incredible talent and power themselves, out of enchanted materials chosen specifically for the buyer. Athames created by the top makers aren't tools so much as actual extensions of a witch's power.

While young witches, and lesser witches, make do with less expensive daggers, the rule of thumb has always been to put as much money into one as you possibly can. Something tells me that this bastard's athame will be one of a kind, made of the finest materials available. If I can see it—really see it—it will be the first real clue to his identity that we have.

I concentrate harder, push a little further, and there it is. The blade is long and wicked looking, engraved with some of the darkest symbols Heka has—symbols that none but the darkest warlocks and witches dare make. It's smooth on one edge and curved and pointed on the other, designed—I know—to cause the most damage possible. My own body aches at just the thought of that blade being thrust inside of someone, then twisted so the wound can't close itself up. After all, that's what the jagged edges are for. They certainly don't help with cutting plants.

I move on to the hilt, try to see past the nightmare-inspiring blade. The hilt is silver and ornate, a lot of separate swirls diving in and out of each other to form an elaborate dragon. There's a jewel embedded in his eye, but I can't quite see its color. Not yet.

Either way, the dagger is definitely expensive. Definitely one of a kind. There aren't that many athame makers in North America who could create something like this. Surely, if one of them made this, they would remember for whom.

I strain to take a mental picture—maybe Declan will recognize it. But the more I concentrate, the harder it becomes to breathe, even as I get a clearer picture of the athame. The very air around me feels threatening now and my instincts—the same instincts that had me dipping my fingers in the lake to begin with—are now screaming for me to stand, to run, to get away.

Not yet, I tell myself. Just a couple more seconds to see the eye so I can identify what jewel is embedded in its decorative hilt. I've almost got it, almost—

My magic goes crazy, nearly blasts me apart. I yank my hand out of the water in self-defense, stumble to my feet. And that's when I see him—Ryder Chumomisto standing right beside me, his dark eyes more serious than I have ever seen them. He's dressed entirely in black, though he isn't wearing gloves. Blood drips down his left palm, coats his finger.

My first thought is that Nate was right. I reach forward to touch him, expecting him to be a vision like everything else I've seen today. But my fingers don't pass through him like I expect. Instead, they bounce against his chest. His very warm, very hard, very solid chest.

I scream then, scramble backward. I trip on a boulder and start to take a header into the lake but Ryder reaches out with his uninjured hand and snags me out of the air. For long, precarious seconds I'm dangling over the water, and then he's reeling me in. Pressing me against his side.

"Jesus, Xandra, are you trying to kill yourself? What are you doing down here?" Ryder scowls at me as he drags me a little farther from the edge.

"What are you doing here?" I counter.

He shrugs, looks out over the lake. "Lina was my friend. I've been here a couple of times since you found her body. I don't know what I'm looking for, but I have to try."

It's a reasonable excuse, certainly believable. But the oppressive feeling is still all around me, warning me of something I can't quite figure out. Ryder doesn't act like he feels anything, though, and I'm not sure if that's a good sign or a bad one.

"What happened to your hand?" I ask, pointing at where the blood continued to run down his fingers and onto the ground.

He flushes, looks a little embarrassed. "I was doing a spell and got so caught up I forgot to close it."

"Blood magic?" I whisper. I know there are witches and warlocks—even some wizards—who dabble in blood sorcery, but in my coven they are few and far between. My parents don't approve of it, refused even to let my siblings or me learn the basics of it.

"It's what I'm best at," he tells me, casually pulling an athame out of his back pocket and running the flat part of the blade across his palm as he murmurs a few words. The wound closes up instantly, leaving only a pale pink scar where the cut used to be.

But his cut isn't what I'm interested in. His dagger is. Long and curved . . . it looks nothing like the one I saw clutched in the murderer's hand.

I relax a little. Tell myself I'm just letting my imagination get the better of me because of the situation. Nate doesn't know Ryder, not the way I do. It's crazy to think he's out here up to no good.

And yet . . . I glance down at the crimson blood that has pooled on the ground. It makes me uncomfortable to look at it and the oppressive feeling gets worse. Though I'm not a witch who can feel the earth—or any of the elements for that matter—I swear I can feel it now. Shifting and trembling just under the surface as it seeks to rid itself of the dark magic done here. Ryder's magic? I wonder as I take a judicious step away. Or the killer's?

"Hey, you never told me what you were doing here," Ryder says, matching me step for step as I make my way back up the trail to the street.

"The same thing you are. Looking for something to tell me who did this to Lina."

His eyes narrow and the air around us grows even more menacing. I'm starting to panic now, even as I tell myself that there's nothing to be afraid of. That Ryder would never hurt me. Still, it's obvious that something's not right. I need to get the hell out of here. Now.

I scramble the last few steps to the grassy knoll, then all but run across it in an effort to get to the street. Why the hell didn't I bring my car? Why the hell did I let myself be drawn out here, again, with no way to get home?

"Hey, what's the hurry?" Ryder asks, and his hand closes around my elbow, drawing me to a stop whether I want to keep going or not.

I turn to face him and he's watching me carefully. I try to make up an excuse, but everything that flits through my mind sounds lame. I've got nothing.

Ryder steps even closer. "Hey, Xan, calm down." He wraps an arm around me and starts walking me toward the curb. "You look like you're about to jump out of your skin."

I feel like I'm about to jump out of my skin. I don't know what to do. My instincts are screaming at me to get out of this, to get away from Ryder, but the rest of me thinks it's insane to even suspect him. This is Ryder, the guy who helped teach me how to ride a bike. Who gave me boy advice when I was thirteen and in love with the biggest jerk at school. He's no threat to me.

Except at this moment, it kind of feels like he is.

I pull away and make a mad dash for the street. There has to be a cab around here somewhere, have to be some people walking their dog. If I can just get there—

"Hey!" Ryder yells and then he's running after me. "Xandra? What are you doing? You're going to hurt yourself!"

I don't care. Everything inside of me is yelling for me to get the hell away from him. I don't know if it's the cowboy boots or my reawakened magic, courtesy of Declan, or simply my subconscious run wild. And frankly, I don't give a damn right now. If I'm acting like a maniac I'll deal with it later. Right now, I just want to get away.

I'm almost to the relative safety of the street when I hit a slick patch on the still wet ground. My boots, with their flat, not-yet-broken-in soles, skid out from under me and I go flying. I hit the ground hard.

Adrenaline races through me and I scramble to my feet, despite the stabbing pain running down my right knee. Behind me, Ryder curses and he's close enough that I can feel his fingers brushing against my jacket. I try to lay on the speed, but I'm hobbling now—adrenaline or not—and I know that whatever escape I was mounting is over. There's no way to evade Ryder now.

Just one more reason to tell my mother where she can put these damn cowboy boots.

"Xandra, stop!" Ryder's hand closes around my elbow and yanks me to a halt. "What the hell is going on?"

Every self-defense move Donovan has ever taught me flits through my brain. I twist my arm away at the same time I hook my ankle behind his and kick through. It's his turn to stumble and his grip loosens—just as I intended.

I pull my arm from his grasp and back up, making sure to keep him in my sights. My heart is beating wildly and my brain is screaming at me that I'm making a mistake. That I've got this all wrong. But I don't care, can't afford to care. Not right now. I'm not going to end up like Lina and Amy and Jacqueline. Not if I can help it.

"What the hell, Xandra?" Ryder sounds exasperated and a little concerned. "Are you okay?"

"I'm fine." I continue backing away from him. "I need to get home."

"Let me take you. My car is just around the corner."

I shake my head. There's no way I'm getting in a car with Ryder. Not right now, not when I can't tell what is real and what is a figment of my overstressed imagination. "I'm good. It's not that far, just a block or two."

He sighs, thrusts a hand through his hair in exasperation. "I know where you live. It's more than a couple blocks. And look, it's starting to rain."

He holds a hand up, as if to show me the nonexistent raindrops. At that precise moment, lightning flashes and thunder rumbles across the sky. Seconds later, it opens up and rain pours down on us.

Damn magic. And damn Ryder, too. "It's fine," I tell him. "I like the rain."

"What the hell is going on with you?" He sounds bewildered, and something else. Something I can't quite put my finger on. It's enough, though. I turn and flee.

I've gone only a few steps when he catches up to me—his hand wrapped around my upper arm. That's it. I've had it.

I turn around, my hands bent into claws and I go for the eyes. Only it's not Ryder who's holding me. It's Declan.

Twenty-two

What the hell? Where did he come from?

I try to check my lunge, but it's too late. The thought must register in Declan's mind too, because at the last second he turns his head and my nails rake down his cheek instead of gouging out his eye. And even though I do my best to stop, I come away with a few layers of skin anyway.

"Shit!" I get a quick glimpse of blood dripping down Declan's face as he twists me around so that my back is to his front. Then he wraps his arms around me and holds me in place, my own arms crossed over my chest.

His hold is gentle, tender even, and it keeps me from freaking out at being so completely immobile. At the same time, though, there's still a small part of me that wants to go for his knees. I control it. Declan isn't hurting me—in fact, he's going out of his way to make sure neither one of us gets hurt. That knowledge is enough to let me breathe.

"You want to tell me what the fuck is going on?" The words are deep and growly and at first I think they're directed at me.

I bristle, start to twist against him—for all the good it will do me—when I realize it isn't me he's upset with. It's Ryder.

"How should I know?" Ryder answers, a wary look on his face that shows that he, too, is aware of the danger crackling in the air all around us. "We were down by the lake and she freaked out. I was only trying to help."

Is that true? I wonder frantically. Was the threat I felt from him completely in my head? It didn't feel that way at the time, but now that I'm safe I just don't know. I hate the uncertainty, the sudden inability to trust my instincts. I don't have magic, or at least, none that I can actually rely on. If my instincts are shot, too, I'm not sure what I'll do.

Declan finally realizes that I have no plans to attack a second time and lets me go, slowly. But before I can do more than wipe the rain from my face, he steps in front of me and blocks me from Ryder's gaze. Then, with one wave of his hand the rain disappears, as does the moisture in my clothes and hair. In fact, I'm perfectly dry when Declan turns to me and points toward the street. "My car is up there. Go wait in it and I'll drive you home."

I start to argue on general principle but the fact is, the car is looking pretty damn good right about now. Especially when I know Declan and Ryder are about to come to blows.

I should stay and listen to whatever they say—maybe it will help me figure things out. But the look on Declan's face says that I don't have a choice. Either I get to the car under my own power or I'll get there under his. That kind of high-handedness would normally get him a knee in the groin, but I'm beat right now. The emotion and adrenaline from earlier is crashing down around me and all I really want is to get someplace safe. Someplace where I can't feel the violent lash of the wind against my skin or see the hurt in Ryder's gaze.

The irony of Declan being my safe place is not lost on me as I turn and trudge to the car. The ground is still wet, a sign that he's even more upset than I thought. Or conserving his magic for something more important. Like a battle with Ryder.

The thought makes my stomach hurt. I've lived with magic my whole life, but I've never been comfortable with that aspect of it. I glance over my shoulder as I climb into the car. Though I can't hear what they're saying, it's obvious that the two of them are arguing. Declan's back is to me, but the air around him crackles with his rage. Ryder's holding his ground, but his face is pale and his hands are raised in the universal sign for surrender.

The wind picks up—ice-cold and ominous—and I have to wrestle against it to get the car door closed. I'm still catching my breath when the driver's-side door flies open and Declan slides smoothly behind the wheel. The already frigid temperature plummets inside the car.

"Did he hurt you?" he demands as he jams the key in the ignition.

"No. He didn't touch me."

"But he upset you." He turns to me, brushes a stray lock of hair out of my eyes. "I felt it the second I got out of the car."

"I think it was the place more than Ryder. I was already freaking out, feeling like something sinister was closing in on me, and then there he was, dripping blood." I flush, embarrassed by my earlier fear now that I'm safely ensconced in Declan's car. "I'm not used to blood sorcery and I overreacted."

He studies me. "Are you sure that's all it was?"

Can't he see that I'm not sure of anything? I haven't felt this insecure since my nineteenth birthday and I'm really not enjoying it any more the second time around. Banishing the confusion—or at least locking it away in the back corner of my mind—I nod. "I'm fine."

He relaxes at my reassurance, the car temperature warming just enough to defrost my fingertips. "I'm glad." He cups my face in his hand, runs his thumb gently over my lips. "I don't like it when you're upset."

The heat ratchets up another twenty notches, until frostbite is the last thing on my mind. The irony of his words isn't lost on me, considering the fact that I'm usually at my most upset around him, because of him. But right now that doesn't seem to matter. Nothing does, not when he's touching me like I'm fragile. Like I'm somehow precious to him.

I don't know what makes me do it, but I part my lips and nip sharply at his thumb.

His eyes darken, his fingers sliding around the back of my head to tangle in my hair. He tugs a little, urges my face closer to his and I know he's going to kiss me. More, I welcome his kiss despite all the mixed-up emotions pinging around inside of me. Or maybe because of them. I don't know. All I know is that I want Declan's mouth on mine more than I've wanted anything in a very long time.

I lean toward him, my eyes closing of their own volition. But the sound of a car door slamming close by yanks me out of my reverie. Tires squeal and I look up just in time to see Ryder burn rubber down the street. His obvious distress makes me feel terrible.

"I'm really sorry," I tell Declan. "I didn't mean to cause trouble between you and Ryder."

He studies me for long seconds without answering, his eyes cataloging every inch of my face. And when he finally does speak, his voice is low and smoky with unmistakable desire. "We've gone around before and we'll go around again. It's you I'm worried about."

I feel a tug deep inside of myself, an invisible thread pulling Declan and me closer and closer with each second that passes. Not just physically, but mentally and emotionally as well.

Is this what it means to be soulbound? I wonder a little frantically. This overwhelming compulsion to press myself against Declan until I'm all but inside him? Until he's inside me? Until we're both so wrapped up in each other that nothing else matters? Maybe then this emptiness inside me will be filled, the loneliness gone forever.

The thought frightens me, has me pulling away to stare out the window. Declan makes a frustrated sound deep in his throat, but I don't let myself care. I can't afford to, not when everything in my life is this mixed up. The murders, the compulsion, my magic, my response to Declan. How much of what I'm feeling is because of him and me and how much of it is because we're soulbound?

I don't know the answer, and until I do, I can't afford to let anything happen between us. Eight years ago I fell for him hard and ended up with nothing but a broken heart to show for it. I'm older and wiser now, or so I like to think. I won't make that mistake a second time.

Declan must be able to read my changing mood, because he swears bitterly under his breath before starting the car engine. Seconds later, we're slipping into traffic, cruising toward my house.

I don't say anything else, and neither does he. At least not until we're turning the corner onto my street, and when he finally does speak, his voice is so low that I have to strain to hear it. "I would never have done it."

"Done what?" I ask, mystified. Is he talking about the murders?

"Hurt you. I know I said I'd planned to kill you, but even before I saw you, I knew I wasn't going to go through with it." He pulls to the curb in front of my house, but doesn't turn to look at me. Instead, he stares straight ahead, his jaw working furiously. "From the moment I knew you existed, I searched for you. I told myself it was to do what had to be done, but even then I knew.

"I could feel you—all that warmth and compassion and determination to succeed—deep inside me and I knew I would never be able to harm you."

"Even though I might end up destroying you?"

"What do you know of destruction?"

I think of all those hours, months, *years* up in my room, practicing magic. Trying to be someone my mother would be proud of and losing a little more of myself every time it didn't work.

Declan doesn't need to know that, though. No one does. Besides, I know evasion when I see it and I'm not about to let him get away with it. Not this time.

"I know we're soulbound," I tell him, laying my cards on the table.

He does turn his head then, his obsidian eyes blazing into mine. "Where did you hear that term?"

"That doesn't matter—"

"Tell me, Xandra." He looms over me wearing his darkest warlock face, but I refuse to be intimidated. It's been eight years since we first met and I barely know any more about our situation now than I did then. When I was nineteen, my ignorance wasn't my fault. Now, if I continue to keep my mouth shut, continue to live without answers, it most certainly will be.

With that in mind, I lift my chin, keeping my eyes locked with his. "You know a hell of a lot more about it than I do, so why don't *you* tell *me*?"

For long seconds, he doesn't answer—so long that I begin to think that he *won't* answer. But then he surprises me by saying, "The truth is, I should have told your parents about it as soon as I'd found you. I didn't because . . ."

He has trouble finishing, so I do it for him. "Because you didn't want them to be prepared when you came to take care of the problem."

He glares at me. "No offense, Xandra, but the warlock I was then wouldn't have been afraid of what your parents could do to me."

"You were really that powerful?"

He lifts an eyebrow, looks impossibly arrogant and appealing. "I'm still that powerful. But back then, I was untouchable. That's what started the whole mess to begin with. It had nothing to do with you or your family and everything to do with me."

"Why? What did you do the Council that pissed them off so much?"

"I didn't listen to them, refused to let them control me. They didn't like that, especially considering the magic I commanded."

"So they cursed you?"

"They bound me, and my powers, to one of the few Hekan families that would have a chance against me."

"But you just said they wouldn't have stood a chance."

"The Council didn't know that." His smile flashes, as wild and wicked as I've ever seen it. "For all we know, they could have been right. Your family might not have been able to destroy me, but you're a different story."

"Because we're soulbound."

"No. Because of you, and the power you wield."

I start to give him my same old tired spiel—the one I've spouted to my mother for nearly a decade—but I stop before any of it leaves my mouth. Because it isn't true, not anymore. My power may be unconventional, and untrained, but it exists. Even now, I can feel it seething right under my skin, waiting for another chance to strike.

Still, what he's suggesting is absurd. "There's no way I can destroy *you*."

"You don't think so?"

"Please. I can't do one-twentieth of what you can do."

"Magic tricks aren't everything, you know."

I snort, refusing to buy what he's selling. "I wouldn't exactly call what you do magic tricks."

"I stand on a stage and perform for an audience. What would you call it?" He sounds self-deprecating, but he's watching me closely and I know my answer means more to him than he's letting on.

"Amazing. I've never seen anything like your show the other night."

"Really?"

I roll my eyes. "Stop fishing for compliments. You just finished telling me how powerful you are, which means you know exactly how astonishing your magic is. Besides, it's obvious how much you enjoy what you do."

When he doesn't respond, I ask, "What did I say wrong this time?"

"Nothing. I just never thought of it that way—as something I enjoy."

Now I'm confused. "Why else would you do it, then? You can do anything."

He ducks his head, and for the first time since I've known him, Declan's cheeks are pink—like he's blushing. Then he admits, "If you want the truth, it started as a kind of fuck you to the ACW. You want to take my powers, you want me to keep my magic hidden? Screw you, look what I can do."

"And now?"

He shrugs. "I don't know. I haven't thought about it in years. It's just something I do because . . ."

"Because you like it. You like sharing your magic—"

"I don't *share* my magic. With anyone." The darkness is back, causing a shiver to work its way up my spine.

Despite my fear—or maybe because of it—my tongue is firmly in my cheek when I say, "Except for me, you mean."

His teeth grind together, but there's a light in his eyes that tells me he's not as upset by the prospect as he lets on. "Except for you."

The lamp on my front porch flickers on and I can see Lily standing there, watching me anxiously. It won't be long before she's storming the car, ripping me out of Declan's "evil" clutches. And I find I'm not quite ready to say good-bye yet. Not when I'm getting glimpses of a Declan I've never seen before.

"You want to come in?" I ask impulsively.

He raises a brow. "Come in?"

"For dinner. I'm not sure what we've got, but I'm certain I can whip something up fairly quickly."

Now both brows are up. "You're going to *make* me dinner?"

"Well, not if you look at me like that, I'm not. I have been to culinary school, you know. I won't poison you."

His flush deepens. "That's not what I meant."

Exasperated, I start to ask what he did mean when it occurs to me that Declan might not have had anyone make him dinner in a long, long time. I try to discount the thought—after all, he's rich, handsome, charismatic, powerful. Everywhere he goes women stand in line for a chance to get to him. And yet, there's a loneliness about him, a solitary vibe that tells me he rarely lets anyone get as close as I've gotten these last couple of days. Which makes the way he defended me against Ryder—his brother and best friend—even more significant.

Suddenly, I'm a little shaky myself. I'm also completely resolved to getting Declan to stay for dinner. After everything he's done to keep me safe these last couple of days, a home-cooked meal is the least I can do.

Climbing out of the car, I head around to the driver's side and open Declan's door as well. Then I tug him out of the low-slung automobile and up the walkway to my house. "Come on," I urge as he puts up what feels like a token protest. "I have a couple of great bottles of wine I've been saving. We'll pop them open, cook something delicious and pretend this whole nightmare is behind us. At least for tonight."

Declan slips an arm around my waist, pulls me close.

And I know that, at least for a little while, everything is going to be all right.

That is until I look back toward my front door and realize Lily's no longer standing there. Donovan is. And he doesn't look happy.

Twenty-three

Beside me, Declan stiffens. His arm tightens around my waist, but I'm not sure if he's doing it because he thinks he needs to protect me or if he's staking some kind of claim. To be honest, neither motive impresses me. I start to shrug him off, then stop because I'm afraid it will be the excuse Donovan needs to pounce. And the last thing I need right now is a throw-down on my front walkway—especially between two of the most powerful beings I know.

"Let go," I hiss at Declan as we approach the steps. He does—after several excruciating seconds—but he doesn't look happy about it. Not that I care, as I'm more than a little pissed at this point myself.

I take the stairs two at a time, start to brush by Donovan. But he grabs my arm before I'm halfway through the door, anchoring me in place. "Where the hell have you been?" he demands. "Lily and I have been worried sick about you."

Behind me, I feel Declan shift menacingly, and I hold out a hand to him in the universal stop gesture. I don't need him to fight my battles for me and the sooner he gets that through his thick head, the better off we'll all be.

Surprisingly, it works. Declan doesn't move, though I can feel his power seething in the air around us. It's more than a match for the angry magic pouring off Donovan.

"I was down by the lake, checking out the crime scene

again. Declan was doing the same thing and he offered me a ride home." It's not quite the whole story, but enough of it's there that Donovan shouldn't be able to sense an untruth. "If you were worried, why didn't you scry my location?"

"I tried," he answers. "I couldn't get a lock on you. It was like something, or *someone*, was deliberately hiding you." He glares at Declan as he says the last and it's obvious who he blames for the spell's failure. Declan just shrugs, keeps his face blank. But I can feel the tension rolling off him. He isn't taking Donovan's revelation any better than my brother had. Of course, Donovan's too tied up in his own distrust and anger to realize that Declan's no threat to me. At least for now.

I try to slip past Donovan a second time and once again, he blocks me. Annoyed now, I get in his face. "This is my house. I'd like to come in."

"And you're my sister. I'd like to know you're safe."

We stand there, nose to nose, for long seconds until Lily finally breaks it up. "The delivery guy from Z'Tejas just pulled up. Unless you want him to call 911, I'd suggest the two of you back the hell off each other."

Though the words, and the tone she delivers them in, are casual, there's a look in her eyes that says enough is enough. Suddenly, it's like a clean breeze invades my consciousness, driving out the anger and aggression and letting me see myself, tensed up and braced for a fight with my beloved brother.

This isn't me. I'm no pushover by any means, but all this crackling aggression without purpose is so not my style. Nor is it Donovan's really. The worry is obviously getting to us.

I take a deep breath, step back. Lay a gentle hand on Donovan's arm. "I'm sorry I didn't call. The last thing I want to do is worry you."

He blows out a long breath, then pulls me in for a

quick hug just as the delivery guy makes it onto the porch. He's carrying two big bags and the smell emanating from them is amazing. I reach for my wallet, but Declan already has his money out.

"I invited you to dinner," I tell him. "I've got this."

He hands the money over—two hundred dollar bills, which is obviously too much for our order—then takes the bags. "Too late," he tells me, heading for the kitchen without a backward glance.

"I don't like him here," Donovan hisses at me as we watch his back.

"Well, I do. So get over it."

Dinner can only be described as a tense affair, what with Donovan glaring at Declan, me glaring at Donovan and Lily glaring at me. My roommate hates tension in our home and right now, the air around us is so taut that I think a deep breath might shatter it.

The only one who seems unaffected by it all is Declan, who eats his steak and drinks his red wine while grinning across the table at me—like he doesn't have a care in the world. Like he isn't the main focus of a police investigation determined to run him to ground.

I spend most of the meal pushing my food around my plate and praying for the excruciating experience to end. Neither Declan nor Donovan seems in any hurry, though, so by the time my brother finally lays down his fork, I'm wound more tightly than a jack-in-the box.

Springing up from the table, I start clearing away the dishes.

"Don't worry about it, Xan," Lily tells me, a steely look in her normally placid eyes. "Donovan and I will get this before I leave for Brandon's."

Normally, I'd argue—fair division of labor and all that—but tonight I just nod. Then grab Declan's hand and all but drag him down the hall to my room.

"Can you enchant this thing?" I demand as I slam the door shut behind us, suddenly furious. How is it my brother can make me feel like a recalcitrant teenager with nothing more than an arch of his brow?

"What thing?" Declan asks, obviously amused.

"My door! I don't trust him not to barge in here in twenty seconds with the suggestion that we all play charades or something."

"Charades?"

"It was my favorite game as a kid." I switch on the lamp next to my bed, then turn to face him. He's leaning against the wall near the door and in the dim light, he looks even darker and more dangerous than usual—if that's possible. My heart jerks a little in my chest, skips a beat, and I wonder vaguely if I need to get it checked. In case the virtual beatings I've received in the last couple of days have somehow knocked it off-kilter.

But then the left side of Declan's mouth kicks up in that little half smile of his and I admit that the skipped beat has nothing to do with anything but him. It's a big admission for me, and it scares me a little. I can feel myself falling for Declan, surrendering to the sexual tension that stretches between us, taut as a circus high wire. But I've been here before and last time it ended with me so emotionally devastated I could barely get out of bed in the morning.

Which, I admit, is better than dead. Still, is it stupid of me to run straight back into his arms? Am I just setting myself up for the kind of heartache I promised myself I would never feel again?

I am. I know it as surely as I know that I'm not going to do anything about it. That I can't do anything about it. Not at nineteen, not now and probably not ever. I don't know if it's because we're soulbound, but Declan feels like the missing piece of me. Like I've been walking around for twenty-seven years with a chunk of me not there. Suddenly, here it is, filling me up, making me whole, and I know that no matter what happened eight years ago, I'm not going to turn my back on him now. I can't, any more than I can turn my back on the power that has so recently begun to manifest inside of me.

What I'm thinking—and feeling—must be written all over me, because the smirk abruptly fades from Declan's face. Then he's pushing away from the wall and stalking toward me—stalking me—with a single-minded intensity that takes away the last little bit of breath I have.

He stops at the end of the bed, rests a hand on the ornate, iron footboard, and just looks at me. Like most predators, he likes to play with his prey before pouncing.

But I'm no one's prey, and haven't been for a long, long time. I stand up, start to close the distance between us.

Declan holds a hand up—whether to stop me or beckon me closer, I don't know. And I don't care. If he's warning me off, I don't want to hear it. Not now. Not tonight.

I'm only a couple of inches from him when I stop, close enough that if I take a deep breath my breasts will brush against his chest. Too bad I'm incapable of anything but the most shallow panting right now.

Heat is sweeping through me, from my toes to my sex, from my arms to my breasts, until just the simple act of existing becomes an erotic event. I don't know what's going on, can't figure out what's happening. I want Declan, I know that, but I've wanted men before. Wanted him before. And it's never felt anything like this.

Like my clothes—and my skin—are too tight.

Like even the most simple movement will shatter me.

I know Declan feels this strange, inescapable draw as well. I can see it in the darkening of his already midnight eyes. Hear it in the ragged breaths being torn from his chest.

I reach for him — I can't help it — and he flinches away from me.

The agony of rejection slices through me and I start to pull away, but it's too late. Magic — swift and unexpected — whips through me. It snakes out of my fingertips, winds through the inches between us and arrows into Declan.

Seconds later, an answering power — dark, rich, overwhelming — slams into me. It envelops me, overtakes me. Wraps itself around me and fills every corner of my being until all I know, all I am, is Declan.

I have a brief flash of clarity — realize that this is a power exchange at its most mystical and elemental — and then Declan is on me. Or I'm on him. I'm not sure who moves first, and I don't care. All that matters is getting Declan inside of me.

Our mouths meet in a frenzy of lips and teeth and tongues that weakens my knees even as it sends heat tearing through me. I stand on my tiptoes, press my body against his, wrap my arms around his shoulders. I want to be closer, need to be closer. If I could climb inside him, at this moment I swear I would do it. Declan must feel the same way, because he turns, backs me up against the wall. Pins me against the wall and plasters his body to mine.

I feel him, hard and hot, between my legs and I squirm in an effort to get closer still. He groans a little at the contact; then his hands are on my ass and he's boosting me up so that I can wrap my legs around his waist.

I jerk my mouth from his, rain kisses over his cheeks, along his stubbled jaw, down his warm neck until his shirt gets in the way. Frustrated, I yank at it, and to my shock it tears, right down the middle. I barely have time to register the fact that I have actually ripped his shirt — magic had to be involved because I know I'm not that strong — before he's doing the same to my own. Seconds later my bra follows the shirt and then he's back, his broad, muscular chest pressed against my breasts.

"I need—"

"I know what you need," he growls, and this time it's his mouth racing over every part of me he can reach. He pauses at the sensitive spot behind my ear, at the hollow of my throat, before sliding lower. He captures one of my nipples, pulls it into his mouth, and I explode, orgasm tearing through me on a ragged scream.

He doesn't stop, just keeps kissing and licking and touching and nipping at me until I'm worked up all over again. "I need you," he whispers against my mouth. "I need you, Xandra."

"Then take me," I tell him, tangling my fingers in the cool silk of his hair. "Now."

His control snaps and he reaches for my jeans, rips them off as easily as he did my shirt. Then he's fumbling with his belt, tearing open his own jeans. And he's inside me, filling me up with his heat and magic and the deep, dark power that's so essentially Declan.

I cry out at the feel of him—it's like nothing I've ever experienced before. My own magic rises up inside of me, tangles with his. It blends and grows and changes until all that I am, all that I have inside of me is somehow twisted up with all that he is.

It's powerful, overwhelming, exhilarating, terrifying all at the same time. "Declan!" I clutch at his shoulders, hang on to him with every ounce of strength I can muster. "I'm—"

"I've got you, baby." His eyes meet mine. "I've got you."

And just that easily I shatter. His lips crash down on mine and seconds later, he follows. As he does, the magic blasts through me. Rich, intoxicating, irresistible.

Just like Declan himself.

Twenty-four

When we can move again, which takes a few minutes as his legs are as shaky as mine, Declan stumbles to the bed, throws back the covers and then places me in the middle of the mattress. He climbs in beside me, pulls me back into his arms.

"Don't leave," I tell him, resting my head on his chest so that I can feel the rapid beating of his heart.

"I'm not going anywhere."

"Promise?"

He brushes a kiss over my forehead. "I promise."

I hear the truth in his words and relax, let myself slide softly into sleep.

I wake hours later, clawing desperately at the hands wrapped around my throat. Someone's on top of me in the darkness of my room, his hips between my legs, his large callused fingers around my neck.

I try to scream, but there's little air in my lungs—and no way to get the sound around the hands slowly strangling me to death.

Panic shudders through me. I buck and twist, claw and pinch, but he's immovable. Resolute. Even when I manage to grab on to his index finger and pull back until I hear a very distinct crack, he doesn't falter, though he does curse in a low, agonized whisper that sounds vaguely familiar to me.

I scratch at his hands some more, arching my back and

lifting my hips in an effort to dislodge him. And that's when I feel him—really feel him—for the first time, naked and aroused between my legs.

I scream.

I scream and scream and scream, but it doesn't matter. Barely a wheeze passes through my compressed throat.

Declan. Where's Declan? I reach a hand out to the other side of the bed, but it's empty. Once again, I'm alone with a madman.

My attacker laughs, even as his fingers tighten, squeezing the last drops of air out of my lungs. Then he's slamming himself inside me, ripping me apart with heavy, nightmarish thrusts of his hips, over and over again.

I reach for my magic, but it's not there. Nothing is but the pain and the horror.

I fight anyway, digging my nails as deeply into his skin as they can go. He curses, but doesn't pull away. Instead the pressure around my throat gets worse. And I start to fade away.

My heart, which has been pounding like a metronome on high since the moment I woke up, falters.

My vision, already impaired by the darkness of the room, goes gray.

My head spins, my brain working frantically up until the moment it seems to shut off.

And my body, my terrified, trembling body, releases, the tension draining away even as he continues his assault.

The entire world goes black.

I wake to darkness, a scream trembling in my abused throat.

For long seconds I don't move. I can't. I just lie in the dark, sucking in gulps of air, with fear a wild-eyed monster inside of me.

Everything hurts. My throat, my arms, my already abused ribs. My upper thighs. My—

I cut off the thought, refusing to go there now. I can't. Not if I want to hold on to the tiny strip of sanity I've still got.

My breathing finally evens out and I hold my breath, listen intently. If there's someone else in the room, I want to know about it before I do anything stupid. I don't hear anything but my pounding heart and the wind whistling by my bedroom window. Still I don't relax. I can't.

Reaching a hand out to what I hope is my nightstand, I fumble it up the lamp until I get to the switch. It's right where it's supposed to be, and as I click it on, I'm both thrilled and horrified to find myself in my bedroom. In my bed. Alone. The room looks exactly as it did before I went to sleep, except my clothes are folded neatly on the chair near the window and Declan is gone.

But I knew he was gone before I even regained consciousness. If he was still here, the attack never would have happened. He wouldn't have allowed it.

I try to think, try to reason things out, but I'm dizzy and confused and more terrified than I want to admit. I can still feel him on top of me, inside me.

Shoving the covers off, I shift so that my feet are on the cold cement of my floor. Then I push myself up and stumble to the bathroom on trembling legs.

As I splash cold water on my face, I tell myself that it was just a dream, just a nightmare. That it didn't happen. But when I glance down at my naked body, I see twin rivers of blood sliding down my inner thighs and I know better.

I want to cry, want to rage. Want to turn on the shower and step inside, letting it wash away everything that has just happened to me. But I can't. Because it didn't just happen to me. It happened to someone else, too. Some other woman lived through what I just did, only it was worse for her because he was actually there. Actually inside her. For me, it didn't really happen.

I repeat the words again and again, turn them into my mantra.

It didn't really happen.

Didn't really happen.

Didn't happen.

It just feels like it did.

Why wasn't Declan here? Why didn't he protect me from—

I slam the thought back, lock it away. I can't afford to go there. Not when the compulsion has just started burning inside of me. Declan must have had a good reason for leaving, could even now be on his way back to me. Besides, I don't need him to take care of me. I can take care of myself.

I grab a washcloth from the towel rack, wipe the blood and other fluid up from between my thighs. As I do, I refuse to think about what that other fluid is.

When it's gone, I grab a towel, wet it. Rinse myself. Again, the need to dive into the shower overwhelms me, but I ignore it as surely as I'm ignoring everything else. Because this time, while I don't know how or why, I do know that what I felt was different. It wasn't an echo of the past, wasn't bruises after the real damage had been done.

This time what I had felt had happened in real time. I don't know how I know, but I do. Which means that while I felt that bastard strangling and raping me, he was actually strangling and raping someone else. Which means, if I wasn't out that long, that he is probably still with the body. Which also means, if I'm very, very lucky, I have the chance to end this tonight. Now.

The compulsion is already on me and I know I'm minutes away from being dragged out of the house by it, whether I want to go or not.

I head back into my bedroom, call Nate. When he answers, sounding wide awake and completely pissed off, I tell him, "I had a vision."

"What? When? Why didn't you call me?"

"I'm calling you now. Come get me and I'll take you there."

"Is she already dead?"

"I think so." My heart breaks as I admit that I've failed again. "But I think it just happened. He's probably still with her."

"I'll be there in ten minutes."

That might be too long. Already, pain is burning through me, sizzling along my nerve endings. "Hurry."

"I am." He's breathless and I know he's running.

I hang up and dash for my closet. After dragging on a pair of jeans, a turtleneck and the heaviest jacket I own, I debate between cowboy boots and running shoes. In the end, I choose the running shoes. I tell myself it's because I need the traction, but the truth is I'm really shaken up. The last thing I need right now is anything that might better help me channel what just happened to me.

I cut the thought off again, then run into the bathroom and grab the bloody washcloth. I hit the kitchen, pull out a Ziploc bag and shove it into it, and then I'm out the front door. The compulsion won't wait any longer.

As I head down my front walk, I fumble my cell phone out of my pocket and call Declan. Not that I don't trust Nate, but in a situation like this, I'd much rather have Declan at my back, even though I can't figure out why he left when he promised that he wouldn't.

There's no answer. Damn it. I start to turn around, to go back inside and wake up Donovan, but it's too late. The compulsion has taken over and the only way my feet will move is forward.

I try to push through it, but I can't. The pain is worse— like someone's shoved razor-sharp talons straight into me and is doing his best to shred my insides.

In the end, I keep walking. There's nothing else for me to do. I try to call Donovan, but it's hopeless—he always turns off his phone before he sleeps. And Lily is miles away, tucked up in bed with Brandon.

I'm on my own, again.

Hunching my shoulders against the wind, I start to jog down the street. The burning is worse. Everything is worse, especially the urgency inside of me, screaming that I need to hurry or it will be too late. But I'm afraid it's already too late.

I break into a full-out run, not knowing where I'm going. Knowing only that I have to get to North Congress Avenue.

Where is Nate? I scan the nearly deserted streets for his car, but he's not there. Surely it's been close to ten minutes, so where the hell is he?

The thought has barely formed before Nate's car comes careening around the street corner in front of me, lights blazing. He must see me, because he slams to a stop in the middle of the road. Before he can even roll down his window, I'm there, hurtling myself into the car and yelling, "Go!"

He takes off.

"Where are we going?"

Here's where it gets tricky. How do I tell Nate, who is already having a rough time with this whole psychic thing, that I don't know where we're going? That I can only follow the feeling inside me, which directs me where to go?

Before I can come up with a suitable answer, we pass Sixteenth Street and the compulsion gets heavier. We need to—"Turn on Seventeenth Street," I tell him.

My voice is strained, sweat dotting my forehead and upper lip despite the cold. Nate looks at me sharply, but he doesn't say anything. I guess he doesn't want to risk upsetting the crazy psychic lady.

"Left on Trinity," I call out a few seconds later and Nate makes the turn, tires squealing.

"You know, this might be easier if you tell me where we're going," he says. "You're not giving much warning on where I'm supposed to turn."

"I don't have much warn—turn right here!" I tell him as we approach Martin Luther King Jr. Boulevard, pulling my legs to my chest and wrapping my hands around my knees. Maybe, if I make myself small enough, the pain will shrink as well.

We're getting closer—I can feel it. There's a part of me that's thrilled that this might be it, that we may finally have a chance to stop this monster from hurting anyone else. But there's another part of me that's terrified, as terrified as any one of the women he's killed. I know what he can do, have felt his blows as surely as any of his victims have. After what happened this morning, after what it felt like to be—

I stop the thought before it can fully form. I'm shaking already. If I go down that path, then I'll be no use to anyone. And I can't stand the idea of him getting away with one more murder. Not when I know it's within my power to stop him.

"Turn left here!" I say as we start to cross Red River.

Nate shoots me a fulminating glare, but does as I say—even though he almost runs a car off the road in the process. "We can't keep doing this, Xandra! Tell me where the fuck we're going."

And just that easily, I know. "UT."

"There's been a murder at UT?" Nate's voice is urgent and I know he's imagining the nightmare of trying to search one of the largest universities in the country. Not that I blame him. Over a hundred thousand people are on campus on any given day—between students, faculty and staff—and if it wasn't for this compulsion, I don't have a clue how we'd find her. Or him.

Following my instincts—and the pain—I direct Nate into one of the parking lots closest to campus. When I climb out of the car, I'm still not sure where we're going. But I take only a few steps before it hits me. He's taken her to the tower.

The most infamous building on UT Austin's campus, the tower stands in an area of UT called the Mall. Made famous by Charles Whitman in 1966, the tower is the site of one of the first—and most notorious—sniper attacks in American history. Standing on the observation deck at the top of the tower, Whitman killed fourteen people and injured dozens more.

Though the observation deck was closed for nearly thirty years, it's open now—and has been for over a decade. And I know, with everything inside me, that that is where this bastard has killed again.

"He's there," I say to Nate, pointing at the top of the tower, as I start running.

He looks at me like I'm crazy, though he's keeping pace. "There's all kinds of security. Plus it's closed—how could he get her up there?"

"I don't know. But she's there."

I can tell Nate wants to argue more, but he doesn't. He just stays beside me as we dash down Dean Keeton Street and across the East Mall to get to the base of the tower.

Once there, we look around for the security guard who should be on duty, but there's no one there. The burning intensity deep inside me gets worse—even before Nate pulls his gun. "Stay here," he hisses at me as he tries the front doors. They're unlocked.

I ignore him—it's not like the compulsion would let me stay even if I wanted to—following behind him as he moves cautiously through the lobby. Most of the tower is used for university offices, which means that the killer could be anywhere. But I know—and Nate seems to guess — that he's hundreds of feet up, on the observation deck. With the tower's history, that spot would make the most impact.

It's probably smartest to take the stairs — more chance of surprising the bastard with our presence — but twenty-seven stories is a damn long way up. In the end, we head for the elevator, but get off on the twenty-fifth floor, where we make our way down the hallway to the stairwell.

"Will it do me any good at all to demand you go back down?" Nate asks me as he leads the way, his face fierce with concentration.

"I can't."

"At the first sign of trouble, I want you to run."

We're whispering now, only a few steps away from the door that will let us out onto the observation deck.

I don't answer him, and he turns to face me. "I'm serious. Tell me you will or I'll handcuff you to the damn banister right now." His green eyes are furious, his mouth twisted into a snarl that means business.

"I promise." Even though I don't. I can't. There's only so much I can do when the compulsion is pushing at me.

We're at the door to the observation deck now and Nate reaches out, tries to turn the handle. It doesn't budge. Looks like we were better off taking the elevator. It's not like they can lock those doors.

I'm about to suggest that we go back down one floor and catch the elevator up, but Nate has his own ideas. The last fifteen minutes have obviously been as trying for him as they've been for me, because instead of doing the logical thing and going at this another way, Nate shoves me behind him with his left hand even as he uses his right to point his gun at the door handle.

Then he fires.

The sound echoes in the stairwell, hurting my ears and making them ring. But I don't have time to worry about that—don't have time to worry about anything except dying because Nate is through the door in an instant, his gun raised and ready.

I follow, terrified but unable to do anything else, and find myself in what is obviously a reception area. There's a small desk in the center of the room, with a computer and two picture frames on it. There's a couch and a few chairs scattered around the room, along with numerous plants.

What there isn't is a dead body. Or a psychopathic killer.

I don't have time to be relieved because the compulsion is going crazy. The pain is excruciating and I know that we're close. I follow the tugging toward the open door across the room, but Nate sees it too and puts himself in front of me.

His gun is raised and I pray this is it. I pray that murdering bastard is out there and we can end this. Now.

Nate sidles up to the open door, sticks his gun and his head out of it. And curses softly. Then he's stepping back, radioing for backup in little more than a whisper.

My heart goes crazy. This is it. This is really it. The compulsion is screaming at me, tearing me apart with the need to get to the body, but Nate isn't going anywhere— at least not with me.

"Get back downstairs," he hisses.

I don't move, I can't, and he repeats the order, following it up with a definite shove back toward the stairwell.

I want nothing more than to do as he says—the last thing I want is to see another dead woman, let alone be caught in whatever battle might rage up here before this thing is done—but I'm not going anywhere.

I can't.

"Damn it, Xandra. Go!" Nate wraps a hand around my upper arm and starts trying to drag me backward. I gasp— I can't help myself. It feels like I'm being pulled apart.

The high-pitched sound echoes in the empty room. Seconds later, there's a noise from the patio and Nate curses. Shooting me a disgusted look, he lifts his gun and steps back toward the open doorway. Then, before I can so much as blink, he's stepping outside, his voice loud and firm as he says, "It's over, Chumomisto. Get your hands up."

My heart sinks as he confirms what I'd been so afraid of at the lake yesterday. Declan is going to be devastated when he finds out Ryder killed four women. I know him. He'll blame himself and nothing I say is going to make any difference.

Part of me wants to stay right where I am. The last thing I want is to see Ryder standing over another poor woman's mutilated body. But the compulsion is in full gear and what I want is nothing compared to what I have to do.

There's no noise on the observation deck, save Nate's harsh, seesawing breath as he cautiously walks toward Ryder.

Taking a deep breath of my own, I step outside. And nearly pass out when I realize it's not Ryder Nate is talking to. It's Declan. And he's covered in blood.

Twenty-five

For long seconds I can't think, can't breathe. Can't do anything but stand here and gape.

I try to internalize what I'm seeing, to figure out what's happening here, but nothing's connecting. Nothing makes sense.

Declan out here on the observation deck, instead of Ryder?

Declan covered in an innocent woman's blood?

Declan, the man I'm soulbound to, a rapist and a killer?

Declan, not Ryder?

Against my will, I flash back to those moments when I first woke up. When I felt someone strangling me, brutally slamming into me. I'd thought then that it never would have happened if Declan was there, that he wouldn't have allowed it. Instead, all along, he's been the one hurting me. The one killing those other women.

It barely computes.

But it's impossible to argue with what I'm seeing. Declan kneeling next to a woman's tortured, mutilated body. His hands—covered in her blood—held out in front of him. His face a grim mask as he slowly turns his head and looks at me.

When our eyes meet, his are endless pools of black obsidian, so dark and shadowed that I can't read anything in them. It's surreal—this whole thing is really—

but especially that. I've always been able to read Declan's eyes and the fact that I can't now makes me realize that everything, every bit of these past few days, has been an act.

I want to scream, but my throat is so tight I don't think any sound will come out. It's like I'm being strangled again—this time by my own horror.

"Lay down on the ground," Nate tells him.

Declan doesn't move, just continues to stare at me—like he's waiting for some kind of sign. But I'm tapped out. I don't know what to say or do to get him to follow Nate's directions. Don't know if there's anything I can say.

"Don't make me shoot you, Chumomisto." Nate's voice is as steady as his hands and I can see it in his eyes. If Declan doesn't do what he says, Nate will shoot him. And it won't be to wound.

There's a part of me—the same part that is reeling with betrayal—that thinks I should step back, let this play out how it will. But I can't do that. No matter what he's done, I can't stand here and let Nate kill Declan. Not like this. Not if there's anything I can do to stop it.

"Do what he says, Declan." My voice is barely a croak, so I clear my throat before starting again. "Please, Declan. Don't make him shoot you."

For long seconds, Declan still doesn't move. And when he does, it's to stand not lie down. Nate's hand tightens on the gun and Declan's eyes narrow. For a second, I think he's going to do it. He's going to break the cardinal rule in the Heka community and reveal himself as a witch to a human.

If that happens, I don't know what I'll do. Hell, I don't know what any of us will do then.

"Goddamn it, I said get on the ground, asshole!" Nate yells.

Again, Declan doesn't answer him. Honestly, I'm not

sure if he even heard him. For the moment, his entire focus is on me.

"Declan, please." I'm pleading now, convinced that if he doesn't give in, this is going to end with either his death or Nate's.

For a moment, just a moment, there's a flash of something in his eyes—hurt, betrayal, anger, denial? It's gone so fast I don't have time to identify it, and then he's turning to Nate.

"I didn't do this." He's clearly speaking to Nate, but I know the words are for me. I just don't know if I can believe him.

"Fine," Nate answers. "Get on the ground and we'll sort it out after I get you down to the station."

"I'm not going anywhere with you." It's as if he's talking about the weather, so reasonable and unaffected is his tone.

Then, he takes a step back. Nate's hand tightens on the trigger and I know, I know, he's going to shoot Declan.

Instinct takes over and I dive forward—right between the two of them as the gun goes off—and straight into the path of the bullet.

It never touches me.

Instead, Declan throws out a hand, his magic slamming me into the ground as the bullet whizzes by. At the same time, he's shifting, turning, so that the bullet hits him in the shoulder instead of the center of his chest, where Nate was aiming.

I hit the ground hard enough to knock the breath out of me, and by the time—long seconds later—that I finally draw air into my constricted lungs, Nate's on the ground and Declan is gone.

Swearing, Nate stumbles to his feet and takes off after him. I don't move. One, because the compulsion won't let me leave the body now that I'm this close and two—maybe more importantly—I know my chasing after Declan won't matter any more than Nate's will. I feel his absence keenly, know that he's long gone. The second he was out of Nate's sight, he probably used his magic to dissolve. Depending on how good he is at disappearing—and judging from his show the other night, he's pretty damn good—he could be anywhere by now.

Hell, he could be in Europe by now.

For long seconds, I lie, faceup, on the observation deck. It's still nighttime, and the stars are twinkling merrily in the sky—if I pretend hard enough, maybe I can imagine the last hour never happened.

Except I can hear sirens in the distance, the backup Nate so frantically requested. I can also hear his footsteps pounding on the observation deck as he rushes around the last corner and stops in front of me.

"Are you hurt?" he demands.

I shake my head.

"Stay here," he orders.

Not a problem. "Where are you going?"

"To find that bastard who knocked you into the path of my bullet. He might have slipped past me, but he can't have gotten far."

I want to tell him that he's on a wild-goose chase, but I know it won't matter. Already, he's rewritten what he saw out here.

Magic didn't knock me to the ground. Declan did.

Declan didn't disappear into thin air; he just slipped past him in all the confusion.

As Nate runs toward the stairs, he's spewing a bunch of codes into his phone—codes that I'm guessing mean dead body and suspect on the loose. I just hope he and the backup he called for don't end up killing each other in their haste to get Declan.

The stairwell door bangs shut behind Nate, and I push myself slowly—painfully—to my feet. Declan wasn't fooling around when he sent me slamming to the ground.

In doing so, he saved my life — which is nearly impossible for me to comprehend, when I'm standing here with another body. Another victim . . . of Declan, it would seem, if my eyes can be believed.

But if torturing and killing women is really Declan's thing, then why the hell did he bother to save me? Especially when my death would make things infinitely easier for him? If he wasn't soulbound to me, his magic would once again be unbound . . . and there would be no chance of me destroying him.

So why did he save me? It's a question I can't answer, not now when I stand next to his latest victim. Maybe not ever.

Except there's a little voice inside of me whispering that everything is not always as it appears. Yes, it's hard to argue with the fact that I felt this woman's death. Harder still to argue with the fact that Declan is covered in her blood. And yet, I just can't reconcile the man who made love to me so tenderly tonight with the one who did this. How could anyone this sick, this depraved, be so sweet, so gentle, so giving?

It doesn't make sense.

The sirens are closer now and I know I should make an effort to fight the compulsion. If I back away now it will save me trying to do so later with an audience.

But something doesn't feel right. Or should I say, something feels more wrong than usual. That weird, oppressive energy is back — the same energy I felt down by Town Lake. And by the Capitol. Even in the forest near my house. I didn't recognize it then, didn't understand it, but standing here now, I feel it keenly — pressing down on me from every side — until it's impossible to ignore.

The need to stop the murders, and to determine once and for all whether Declan is the killer, has me moving. I crouch over the body, being careful not to touch her. She's naked, like the others. And like the others, she has my symbol—the goddess's symbol—branded onto her breasts.

But even as I acknowledge it, I realize that something's a little different, a little off, about it. The circle is more of an oval, the line that created it wavy in parts—like the person doing it was in a hurry. Or couldn't keep his magic from spinning out of control.

I think of Declan, of how calm and collected he was with Nate. There wasn't anything shaky about him, or his magic. I have the bruises to prove it.

So what am I dealing with here? Someone brave enough—and stupid enough—to frame Declan Chumomisto for murder? I can scarcely imagine it.

Maybe I'm the stupid one, searching for clues that aren't here. Imagining an alternative killer because I can't stand the idea that I let a murderer touch me. Any more than I can handle the concept of Declan being the one who nearly strangled me earlier. The one who raped me.

I shut the thought down as fast as I can, tell myself that I wasn't raped. I just felt what this poor girl was going through in her last minutes alive. I'm fine, whole and in one piece. Nothing actually happened to me.

So why does it feel like it did?

That's another question I don't have an answer to, so I ignore it. The sirens have stopped and I know I have only a few minutes—maybe less—before the observation deck is crawling with cops. Whatever imprint I'm picking up, whatever magical signature I'm feeling, will be gone then, muddied under the emotions and experiences of people who deal with death for a living.

Closing my eyes, I block out the world—and myself. I have no time to wallow in my own pain and grief, no time to think about Nate or Declan or even what this woman's last minutes on earth were like. I need to focus on the energy surrounding me, to garner as much information from it as I can. Maybe then I can figure out if Declan really is the killer, or if he's merely being framed.

The energy is all around me, but nowhere is it stronger than around the body. I extend my arms over her bare torso, shoving them elbow deep into the seething, roiling mess of dark emotions and darker magic.

Immediately, I feel him inside me, oily strands of black magic wrapping themselves around my fingers, my hands, my arms—any part of me they can reach—and sinking slowly through my skin. My first instinct is to shake them off, to do anything and everything I can to get rid of them.

But that won't help Declan and it sure as hell won't help this girl.

Ignoring the disgusting greasiness of the imprint, I keep my arms where they are. Then force myself to look deeper—to dive deeper—into the nightmare of this bastard's magic.

I'm struck first by the oddly mismatched threads of power. It's a subtle thing, something most people wouldn't even notice, but I grew up in a house the youngest of eight witch and wizard siblings. If I wanted to know who had pulled a prank on me, the only shot I'd had was unraveling the spell to see whose power was underneath it. I might not have had magic of my own, but I did have a strong sense of self-preservation—not to mention an unquenchable thirst for vengeance against my older siblings—and I'd learned early on how to distinguish the weave of one person's magic from another's.

Donovan's magic is clean and bright and straightforward—more of a simple back and forth weave that speaks clearly of the honesty and integrity that is so much a part of who he is.

Lily's magic is different, more subtle and more complicated than my brother's. Every spell she weaves is made up of multicolored strands of power that zig one way, then zag another before tangling around everything in their path. Sweet and exuberant and brimming over with life and happiness, her magic lights up everything around it.

And then there's Declan's magic. Though I've tried numerous times, he's usually really protected, the pattern of his magic spells impossible for me to get a grasp on, no matter how hard I tried. At least until last night, when we were making love, and his magic shot straight into mine, tangling itself all up in the basic, rudimentary strands of my own recent power surges.

His magic is dark—no doubt about it—but it's also sophisticated and elegant and restrained, using no more energy to complete a spell than is absolutely necessary.

Another way it's different is its color. The strands of Declan's magic are mostly silver—like the tattoo in the center of my hand—and they form a pattern, a weave, that I'd never seen before he crawled into my bed.

Some of that weave is here, I realize, with a dawning kind of horror. It's wrapped around this woman's throat, decorates some of her most brutal wounds. Though I somehow manage to keep my hands steady, the realization sends me reeling. Though the evidence was damning, there was a part of me that wanted to believe Declan was innocent, that he couldn't have done these vile, terrible things.

But his magical imprint is here—unmistakable and irrefutable. He really did do this. He really did rape, torture and murder four women.

I push to my feet, stumble backward, just as a group of police bursts onto the observation deck. Nate must have told them about me, because no one pulls a gun, no one tells me to put my hands up. I do, anyway, just so there will be no misunderstanding. Then I find a bench to curl up on and wait out the compulsion.

*   *   *

I spend the first half an hour after the police arrive—after my realization—in a dazed kind of horror. But as the shock fades, the fury rises. Along with my determination to see this through, to find Declan and put a stop to this once and for all.

We're soulbound after all—and while I am truly horrified by that fact at this point, I figure I might as well use it to my advantage. Declan certainly has.

I still don't know much about this soulbound thing—though it's been the longest twenty-four hours of my life, it still has been only twenty-four hours since I found out what we were meant to be to each other. Has been much less than that since I trusted him with my body and my soul.

Now all I can think about are those poor women—raped, murdered, discarded. How could the man who touched me so tenderly, who healed me so carefully, be capable of that kind of mutilation? That kind of horror?

I want to go after him, to find him, but I can't move. Not until this poor woman's body is taken away. And so I sit and plot. Normally I would try to follow the magic, the imprint, but Declan is too clever for that. His imprint disappears in the same spot he did.

But I know he'll show up again. He has to. Already, I can feel the emptiness kicking in, my soul longing for the brush of his even as my mind recoils.

Dawn is streaking across the sky in shades of rose and ruby red before the compulsion finally eases. I stumble to my feet, stumble down the stairs to where Nate is watching the morgue van pull slowly away.

"Come on," he tells me. "I'll give you a ride home on my way to the station."

I nod, numb. Home is as good a place as any right now. Once there, I'll see what I can do about finding Ryder. He always knows where Declan is.

The drive home is the stuff nightmares are made of. Nate is stiff, suspicious, and I don't blame him. Not when Declan all but disappeared in front of him and I can't, won't, give him any answers. I'm not trying to protect Declan, but I am a member of the Ipswitch royal family. It's my responsibility to protect the ancient secrets of Heka and that does not include sharing them with Nate, no matter how much I'd like to unburden myself. There's a part of me that can't help thinking if I tell him, tell everyone, then the visions have to stop. Everything has to stop. Besides, there's no proof that it would happen and a hunch won't get me very far. Not with my parents and not with the ACW.

I try to call Declan when I get in the house. No answer, not that that's a surprise. Then I try Ryder, also to no avail.

I'm sitting in the kitchen, trying to figure out what my next move is going to be when Donovan stumbles in looking for a cup of coffee. I don't say anything to him — talking to him before his morning caffeine is like bearding a lion in its den — so I just wait until he's more lucid. It's not that much of a sacrifice. After all, I don't know what I'm going to say to him anyway.

When he's finally able to pry his eyes open, he looks me over. I'm sure I look like hell. God knows I feel like it. When he grunts and demands, "What happened to you?" my feeling is confirmed.

"I need your help."

He places his cup of coffee on the table. "Okay."

For long seconds, I don't say anything as I debate how much I want to tell him. But in the end, it all comes spilling out. I need him to cooperate and the only way that's going to happen is if he knows everything.

By the time I'm done, Donovan looks like he's about to explode. "Why didn't you wake me?" he demands. "You know how dangerous this is and you run off in the middle of the night without so much as letting me know you were going?"

I explain about the compulsion, but he just shrugs it off. Not that I blame him. Going outside last night had been a stupid move on my part. Obviously. But when the compulsion is on me, I can't do anything else. I don't know how to explain that to him, how to make him understand what I feel at times like these.

"How are we going to find him?" I ask after Donovan finally stops swearing. "Do you think a locating charm will do it?"

"On Declan?" he asks incredulously. "Not a chance."

"Then what do we do?"

"*We* do nothing. *I* will head back to UT, check out the crime scene, see if I can find any traces of magic that will point me in his direction."

"This isn't your responsibility—"

"You're my sister. It doesn't get any more my responsibility than this."

I sigh. Donovan is nearly impossible when he throws on the big brother act. I could make all the sense in the world and it wouldn't matter in the slightest.

"I need to help with this," I told him. "I should have known, should have been able to do something to stop it earlier. Four women are dead—"

"And you aren't going to be the fifth," he shoots over his shoulder as he walks down the hall to his room, presumably to change clothes.

I glance down at myself, realize for the first time that I am covered in blood and muck from the crime scene. I dash down the hall to my own room, whipping my shirt off as I go. There is no way I'm being left out of this. If something happened to Donovan, I would never forgive myself.

I change like a whirlwind, flinging the dirty, disgusting clothes everywhere as I race to get dressed. I wouldn't put it past Donovan to simply disappear on me, and that I can't allow.

It turns out my racing pays off, because even after brushing my teeth and splashing water on my face, I'm ready before he is. I go outside and sit on the hood of his car.

Better to be safe than sorry.

Donovan comes out a couple of minutes later and I know he wants to argue with me. But I throw up a hand, stop him at the beginning of what promises to be one hell of a rant.

"I get it," I tell him. "I know you want to protect me. But you can't protect me from this—he's inside me and I can't get him out. I'm terrified, unless I do this, unless I catch him, that I'll never get him out. If you leave me here, I'll just follow you—you know that I will—so we might as well work together. Maybe it will keep us both safe."

Speech over, I take a deep breath, dart a glance at Donovan's face. He looks pissed, but I know that's just because he feels like I've outmaneuvered him. He knows I'll leave right after he does and nothing, save an imprisoning spell, will stop me. And he won't do that. He's an overprotective older brother but he's not a dictator. He won't lock me in against my will.

Except he does, with a flick of his hand and without a flicker of remorse. I find myself standing on my front porch, an invisible wall preventing me from taking one step off of it.

"Damn it, Donovan!" I'm screaming now as panic overwhelms me. "You can't do this. He'll kill you."

Donovan waves jauntily.

I flip him off, then go back inside and start pacing as I try to figure out what to do. Lily's already up and gone, so I can't ask her for help. If I call my mother, she'll be on my doorstep before I can take a deep breath, and knowing her, I would never step foot out of this house again. My other sib—

The phone rings and I make a mad dash for it, figuring it is Donovan. Maybe he's feeling bad—maybe I can change his mind—

"Hello?" I answer, pissed but more than desperate enough to play nice.

It isn't Donovan. It's Salima. And she has bad news.

Twenty-six

"**X**andra! Thank goddess I caught you. Don't go anywhere. I'm coming for you."

"Salima, now isn't really a good time—"

"I am well aware of that, Xandra. I just read my tea leaves. What have you been up to?"

"Salima—"

"There's death, Xandra. Death everywhere."

She's just figuring this out now? I've got to hand it to my mom—she sure can pick them. Before I can say anything else, she continues, "I can see it stalking you. Death wants you, Xandra, and I don't know if you're going to be able to cheat it."

I roll my eyes. Even if that was true—which it might be—it's not like there's anything I can do about it. If Declan wants to kill me, I'll put up a hell of a fight, but I don't know if I'm strong enough to stop him. If anyone is.

But then I think of the night he healed me, so carefully, so perfectly, and wonder if that's really what he wants from me. With me.

"Look, Salima, I appreciate your concern—"

"You're not brushing me off this time, Xandra." Outside a car screeches to a stop. I peer out the window and see her storming down the walkway. She's dressed in a bright red skirt with purple and green tights and a sparkly green shirt and looks like an escapee from the worst-dressed elf fashion show. But she's all but breathing fire. It's pretty obvious that she isn't going to go away.

My front door flies open before I can so much as reach for the knob. "Come on!" she tells me, suddenly in a huge hurry. "Let's go."

"I can't. Donovan's charmed the house. I can't leave."

"If you don't, you're going to die. You might die, even if you leave, but you absolutely can't stay here." Her voice quavers in outrage, though I'm not sure what has her so upset. The idea that someone might kill me or the worry that he'll do it on her watch.

"Well, then, we have a problem, because I can't leave."

She snorts, waves her hand and mutters a few unfamiliar words. As she does, I feel Donovan's spell lift. I'm free.

I'm more than a little shocked that someone like Salima can take on a spell of Donovan's, but I'll think about that later. Right now, there are more important things to do.

"Come on," I shout to her, barreling out the front door. "We have to catch up with Donovan!"

She doesn't argue, just throws herself into the driver's seat of her car and floors it. I don't live that far from UT, but suddenly it's the longest drive of my life. If something happens to Donovan . . . if he goes up against Declan . . . I have every faith in my brother's talents and if he was going up against anyone else I wouldn't even be worried. He's that good. But this is Declan. Dark, powerful-beyond-imagination Declan. And I'm terrified.

We pull into the parking lot nearest to the tower—the same one where Nate and I parked earlier. There are no spots available, but Salima doesn't let that stop her. She just waves a hand and somehow manages to create a spot from nothing.

"That must come in handy," I mutter even as I reach for the door handle.

"You have no idea."

And then we're running, straight through campus to the tower. Salima is wearing lace-up witch boots with high heels, but she manages to keep up—more magic, I'm sure.

The tower, when we get there, is surrounded—by yellow crime scene tape and a crowd of students and professors who are looking up at it in disbelief and horror. I feel bad for them. I know exactly what happened up there and still it seems reminiscent of the tower shooting. I can only imagine what it feels like to them.

Salima does whatever she does—who knew she'd actually be semi-useful to have around?—and we manage to duck under the tape without drawing attention to ourselves. We take the elevator this time, and even though she says it's safe, I'm fidgeting the whole time. Terrified. I want to find Declan with every inch of my being, but I'm praying that he's not here. That Donovan hasn't run into him yet. That—

The elevator doors open and disgorge us back into a scene that belongs in a horror movie. As we step onto the observation deck, there is blood everywhere. I thought I was prepared for it—after all, I was just here a couple of hours ago. But in the clear light of day, everything looks worse. More brutal.

My brother walks over to where the body was found, to where the blood is the heaviest, hands up and eyes closed. I don't know if he senses us or not, but I walk up to him hesitantly. Magic can be unpredictable—the more power you use, the more unstable it becomes, and the last thing I want is to cause any problems for Donovan.

I needn't have worried. He doesn't even look at me. Instead, his focus is completely on the outline of where the body used to be, and as I watch, I see the strings of color swirl up and out of the ground. The same strings I had used earlier to see who had been here, whose magic had touched the victim.

Donovan is doing something a little different, though. He's done a spell that separates them all out in front of him, a long series of lines of psychic energy that would be beautiful if not for what they represent. As it is, they're eerie as hell. And just as compelling.

I can see most of the colors, identify them as I did earlier. Declan's magic is the strongest, brightest, and I ponder that. Shouldn't his be the darkest and most dull? Every second that passes since the crime is a bigger stain on his powers, on his soul. Why hasn't that manifested itself on his string?

Donovan twists and sorts, and out of the pile of mismatched energies that have come into contact with this poor woman in the last hours of her life, and death, one more emerges. White, clear, sharp as a diamond, it's as fascinating as it is horrifying. I'm compelled by it, the feeling rising inside of me, and I step forward before I know what I'm doing. Reach out a hand to touch it.

"Are you crazy?" Donovan snarls. "Do you know what that is?"

I do know. It's the strand that represents the killer's power and it is absolutely beautiful. In a frigid, inhumane way. I also know if I pull on it, he'll feel it, wherever he is. He'll know that I'm closer than I've ever been.

I reach for it again, determined to show him I'm not afraid. But Donovan knocks my hand away. "No! I mean it, Xandra. This is dangerous."

Of course it is. Everything about my life is dangerous these days. This is nothing new. I start to fight him, but then I realize I don't have to. I can see the trail. Can follow the strand out of the tower, down the stairs and goddess only knows where else. With enough patience, I can follow it all the way to the bastard who did this.

I turn away, start to do just that.

In the back of my head is the realization that Donovan and Salima are following behind me. There's also the knowledge that this means Declan is not responsible. I don't know why he was there, standing over that body, but I know now it wasn't because he'd killed her. The pure, sweet relief of that is enough to make my knees tremble even as I take the stairs two at a time.

I follow the bright white strand down the stairs, across campus to another parking lot. Suddenly, I'm afraid I'll lose it, afraid I'll lose him. There are hundreds of cars parked here now and it's getting harder to follow it through all the psychic energy, all the echoes of people who are here every day. The white is getting muddied, blending in, until I can barely see it anymore.

But then I look up and tracing the power strand doesn't matter much anymore. Nothing does. Because there he is, sitting on the hood of a car, legs crossed casually in front of him.

Kyle.

The evil is literally radiating off of him. I can see where it's eaten away at his aura, at his soul, until all that is left is this rotten, terrible, slightly crazy thing in front of us.

How could I not see it? How could I not know? I'd spent a lot of time with him in the last few days. How had I missed it so completely?

I glance at Donovan and Salima, wanting to make sure they saw what I did. But neither of them looks alarmed as they scan the parking lot for I don't know what. "Don't you see him?" I hiss out of the side of my mouth. "Don't you—"

I don't get the chance to finish. Before I can so much as take a deep breath, Kyle has pulled out a gun. He fires three shots.

One goes wide.

The second one slams into Donovan's chest while the

final one hits Salima's stomach. They both crumple to the ground.

I waste precious seconds staring at them in shock. Then I'm falling to my knees, desperately trying to call forth the magic that remains stubbornly out of my reach. I'm on the verge of hysteria now, but I try to tamp it back. Try to focus on my brother. On Salima. On saving their lives. Dear goddess. They were here because they were trying to save me and instead I should be the one saving them. But I can't. I don't have the power to do it.

Desperate, knowing that it's too little, too late, I fumble my cell phone out of my pocket. Dial 911. Before I can say anything, Kyle hits my hand, knocks the phone onto the ground where he crushes it beneath his boot. Then his hand is wrapped in my hair, his gun pressed against the side of my face.

"Let's go," he mutters and he sounds as manic, as crazy, as he looks. I start to fight him, but he points the gun straight at my brother's head. I am paralyzed by the certainty that he will kill Donovan.

"Please," I beg. "Don't hurt him. Don't—"

He backhands me with the gun and my head slams against my shoulder. "Now you've got time for me," he snarls. "Now you aren't so wrapped up in that excuse for a warlock. You see me now, don't you?"

I force my aching jaw to move, to form the words he wants to hear. "I've always seen you."

"Bullshit. I was just some pesky fly buzzing around your head."

"Is that what this is about?" It doesn't make sense. The first murder happened before I ever met Kyle.

He laughs. "Don't be so full of yourself, Xandra. You're just a means to an end."

What does that mean? I start to ask, wanting to keep him talking long enough for me to come up with a plan to get us out of this. But my brain is frozen, the sight of

Donovan and Salima on the sidewalk too horrifying to get past.

But then I don't have to say anything. I feel a prick on my arm, followed by a burning sensation. A strange lethargy overtakes me. My legs tremble. My breathing feels funny. My body is out of my control.

He catches me right before I fall to the blood-soaked sidewalk.

Twenty-seven

I wake up slowly, with the overwhelming feeling that something is wrong, but I just can't quite figure out what it is. I try to put my finger on it, but my brain is fuzzy. The last thing I remember is Kyle sitting on the hood—

Kyle. Donovan. Salima. It all floods back at once. Panicked, I try to sit up, but I can't move. Again. Except this time it's not just magic keeping me in place. I'm actually strapped, spread-eagle, onto a black machine of some kind. It's tilted so that my legs are higher than my head, the blood rushing downward so that there's a throbbing behind my eyes.

As everything registers, I go crazy. Become an animal, flailing and screaming and straining in an effort to get out. Even as I'm doing it, I tell myself to calm down. That I'm not helping anything. That I'm just making things worse.

It doesn't matter. I can't stop. It's too close to that time in my bedroom, too similar to all those rapes I've suffered through psychically. I want out. Now.

Eventually, the panic recedes and exhaustion sets in. I quiet down, take deep breaths. Try to settle. As I do, I become aware—for the first time—that I am not alone.

"Kyle?" My voice is hoarse, rusty from screaming and dehydration. I hate that I freaked out, hate even more that he saw me like that. It's hard to be strong when your weaknesses have been on display for the world to see.

"Hello, Xandra. Welcome back." He moves closer to me, until he's just inches away, and I long to lash out at him. To rip him to pieces. But the only part of my body I can move is my head and he's standing by my feet.

He has a knife in his hand and he's turning it end over end, end over end, end over end. The motion is hypnotic, spellbinding, as—I think—he intends it to be. I can see all those women, their bodies cut to hell and back, and I know that however this ends up, it isn't going to be good for me.

And then suddenly he's moving, slashing the knife across my upper thigh in a shallow but painful cut. I bite my lip to keep from screaming. He's already seen me lose it once and I have no doubt I'll lose it again before this is over. But not yet. Not yet.

As I lie there, bound, helpless, waiting to see what he'll do next, I feel the blood trickle up my thigh to my abdomen and that's when I realize something else.

I'm completely naked.

That's when I start to scream again. Not out loud, not where the sick fuck can hear me and get satisfaction from it, but deep in my head on a psychic plane.

Xandra! Declan's voice snaps through the hysteria, grabs my attention. *Where are you?*

I don't know.

Look around. See if you can figure—

Kyle slices at me again, this time drawing a line across my abdomen. It burns. He follows it with a shorter, deeper cut to the fleshy part of my left arm, right above the elbow.

I bite my lip until it bleeds to keep from showing him the pain. Inside my head, I can hear Declan demanding that I answer him. He sounds nothing like he usually does. His normal cool, sardonic attitude has been replaced by a panicked rage that mingles with my own.

But all that emotion inside my head makes it hard to

think. I slam a door between us, try to lock him out. Not for good, but just enough that I can think. I can't get through this if I feel his emotions too. Besides, he doesn't need to live through what's about to happen. I've been on the other end of this and it isn't much better than actually having it happen. In some ways, it might even be worse.

"I don't understand," I tell Kyle, when I finally find the strength to unclench my jaw. "Why are you doing this?"

"Don't worry." He smiles but it doesn't reach his eyes, which still look just a little off. "It's nothing personal."

"It feels personal."

He lashes out, makes another cut on my leg, this one shallow and long. I jerk despite myself. "Hurts, doesn't it?" He does it again on the other leg. That's five cuts. I think of the women I found. Only seventy-six cuts left to go if he stays on pattern. The thought is as enraging as it is terrifying.

"If you keep this up, you'll lose everything. My family won't stop until they know who did this and the Council will have to—"

"The ACW will do nothing!" Another slash across my abdomen, but higher this time.

"You know that's not true. My family will demand—"

"Your family. Your family. Do you think I give a shit about your family? Do you think the Council does? Who do you think put me up to this?"

It takes a moment for his words to sink in, and even after they do, I replay them in my mind again and again, trying to make sense of what's going on. He can't be saying what I think he is.

"The Morgans. The Morgans. The Ipswitch throne." He says the words mockingly. "Do you have any idea how tired we are of hearing about you guys? About all your power? About how important you are? I don't give a shit how important, how untouchable you are." He clamps a hand down on my thigh, over the first cut. Squeezes until all the willpower in the world can't keep me from crying out.

"I'm touching you now, aren't I? And there's not a damn thing you can do about it." And then the real horror begins as he slides his hand to my inner thigh and then up—

I jerk, twist, kick out in an effort to make him stop. He finally does, then lashes out with the other hand. A quick slice of the knife across my ribs.

I swallow back the pain, wait until the light of madness fades from his eyes a little. Then ask, "What did you mean when you said the Council put you up to this?" He wants to talk, I can see it. Wants to tell me how brilliant he is. And I want to know. Just in case I get out of this. And even if I don't. I want to know how deeply we've been betrayed.

"It's the perfect solution. Even more perfect than the soulbinding, because Declan won't be able to use his will to run away from this. When he's blamed for the murders of five women, including the precious, precious seventh daughter of Ipswitch, it won't matter how much power he has. He'll be weak from losing you, his magic and soul adrift without your connection, and they'll strike then. They'll strip him of every bit of his magic and your parents will lead the charge."

"You won't be able to frame him for this."

"I already have. Even you, who are *soulbound* to the man, believed he was guilty. The ACW wants him to be guilty. Believe me, by the time they're done with him, no one will be looking too closely. They'll be too busy demanding his blood."

He lashed out again. A quick, deep slice across my breast. I did scream then. I hadn't been ready for it.

"Tsk, tsk, Xandra. I expected better from a princess."

"And I expected better from a Council bodyguard. I guess we're both doomed to disappointment."

That pisses him off and he plunges the knife into my thigh, twisting it so that the wound will bleed copiously. This is it. I know it. I can see it in his eyes, feel it in his hands as they squeeze my breasts.

I am going to die.

I think I knew we were headed here all along, from that very first body. But this plan, this determination to use me and my family to destroy Declan . . . it breaks my heart. Hell, it just breaks me.

I can't let him do it. Declan, who I've been so cruel to. Who I haven't trusted. Who I was ready to accuse, more than once, of brutal, vile murder. I can't let him go down for this. For murdering all those women and Donovan and Salima. And me. My parents, with the help of what looks to be a very corrupt Council, will wipe him off the face of the earth.

The thought galvanizes me and I renew my struggles, though I know they will do no good. But I can't just lie here and die, not when Declan is at risk. Not when—

Another slice of the knife.

Then another.

And another.

Kyle unbuckles his belt.

Slashes at me once again with the knife.

Pulls his belt loose from his jeans.

Cuts me again.

Then slaps the belt, buckle side down, against my abdomen.

I scream and deep inside myself I feel power welling up. Power like I've felt only once before—when I was making love to Declan. It's huge, raw, unimaginable.

Some of it is mine. I know it. I can feel it. But most of it is Declan's. I may have locked him out of my mind in an effort to save him my pain, but I haven't locked him out of my soul. Bound as we are, I'm not even sure such a thing is possible.

I close my eyes and open my mind, let him pour into me. Through me. I'll take as much of his power as I can if it means saving him from the fate the ACW has in store for him.

I can feel Declan inside of me now, can feel him searching for an outlet. Searching for a way to get to Kyle. I open my eyes, look straight at Kyle, and suddenly, he has one.

Power explodes out of me. It slams into Kyle, throws him across what I realize for the first time is a stage. At the same time, it rips away the ropes binding me and sends them hurling away from me as well.

Adrenaline races through me, mingles with the power surge, and I push myself off of the strange machine I've been tied to. I look around and for the first time realize I'm in the Paramount Theater, back where so much of this began. Deep inside, I feel Declan register this and know that he's coming for me.

But Kyle is back on his feet and coming toward me, murder in his eyes. I throw a hand out, try to wield the power flowing through me the same way I've seen Declan do. It doesn't work though—it's not my power—and Kyle figures this out pretty quickly.

Then he's running across the stage straight at me.

I scramble backward but my injured leg is unsteady at best. Add in the blood on the floor, and I go flying, landing on my ass with a painful thud. He's on me then, his hands wrapped around my throat as he squeezes and squeezes and squeezes.

Things are going gray, but I fight him anyway. I buck and kick beneath him, claw at his hands. But he's gone completely mad and I know this is it. My last chance.

I reach a hand out, search frantically for a weapon. But there's nothing around us. Nothing but the knife Kyle dropped several feet away as he dove for me.

Panicked, I reach for it, but of course it's too far away to do me any good. Not expecting it to work, but desperate enough to try, I mutter the words to a simple retrieving spell my mother used to use.

It works. The knife flies across the room and into my hand. I don't think, don't plan. I just react. Rearing up, I plunge it straight into Kyle's back. Pull it out and plunge it in again one more time. He rolls off of me, lifts a hand to finish me off with magic. But I'm ready for him and I lunge, slicing his jugular wide open.

He's dead in seconds.

Shuddering, I drop the knife, then crawl away from him. He's dead, I know he's dead, but I can't stand to be near him. I need to find a phone, need to—

One of the doors of the theater crashes open and Declan rushes in. "Are you all right?" he shouts as he races through the front of the house. I stretch out on the stage, dizzy from blood loss and residual terror. And then he's there, scooping me onto his lap so he can rock me in his arms.

"Thanks for the help," I tell him, glancing up at his face. I owe him an apology for thinking the worst of him, but the words get lost in the tears I see burning in his eyes.

"I almost lost you," he murmurs, pressing kisses to my head and cheek and eyes and lips. "I almost lost you."

"Only because I didn't trust you. I thought—"

"The way you found me was pretty damning," he says with a shrug. "I've been using my power to try to monitor as much magic usage as I could in the Austin area. I felt something last night and rushed to UT, trying to get there in time to save that girl. And catch the killer. I was too late." He says the last like all of this is his fault.

"You saved me."

He shakes his head. "You saved yourself."

"I couldn't have done it without you. I'm so sorry."

"You should be. You scared a century off my life." He cups my face in his hand, brushes his thumb over my lips. "Don't ever do this to me again."

I snort. "I can't exactly control whether or not a madman comes after me."

"Yeah, well, you can try." He puts a hand on my leg, on the really bad cut that is leaking blood all over. Within seconds, I feel it getting warmer and know that he is healing me.

I look around. "We need to call the police."

"Nate is on his way."

I gasp. "My brother. Salima."

"Already at Brackenridge Hospital. A student at UT found them, phoned it in. They're both in surgery as we speak."

I relax back against him. "So what happens now?"

"Now the ambulance comes and takes you to the hospital. Once you're cleaned up, I'm sure the police will want to ask you some questions."

I nod, though he's not telling me anything I don't already know. "I meant with us," I told him. "And the Council. You know they did this."

"I had already figured that out, though hearing it out loud makes it more real."

And more awful. Anger crawls through me as I think of the group that sentenced Declan and me to death—not to mention lives filled with misery—simply because they could.

I feel the fear start to slip back in, but then Declan's arm is around me, his breath a scant few centimeters from my ear. "They're not going to win," he tells me.

"Oh, yeah?" It's my turn to raise my eyebrows. "And how do you figure that?"

"Because we won't let them."

"The curse?"

"Fuck the curse. And the ACW. I'm keeping you."

"And I'm keeping you." I wrap my arms around his neck and pull him in for a kiss. The road in front of us is a messy one. Filled with problems and uncertainties and what I have no doubt will turn into a war against the ACW. It should terrify me, but as I sit here in Declan's arms, surrounded by his strength and his feelings for me, I'm not even nervous. Not when I know that cursed or not, we'll find a way to make things right.

We'll find a way to be together.

As Nate rushes in, paramedics and police officers at his heels, I rest my head on Declan's chest and wait for whatever comes next.

About the Author

Tessa Adams lives in Texas and teaches writing at her local community college. She is married and the mother of three young sons.

Also available from

TESSA ADAMS

THE DRAGON'S HEAT SERIES

Dark Embers

Prince Dylan MacLeod is one of the last pure-blood
dragon shape-shifters—and ruler of a dying race, the
Dragonstar clan. It falls to him to protect his people and
their ancient magic. But he has one important duty:
provide an heir...

Hidden Embers

In the New Mexico desert there is a secret race on the
brink of extinction—the pure-blood shapeshifters of the
Dragonstar clan. Their last hope for survival lies in the
hands of Quinn Maguire, the desperate clan healer lost in
love with a human.

Forbidden Embers

Desperate to save his clan from deadly biological warfare,
Dragonstar sentry Logan Kelly infiltrates the dangerous
Wyvermoon clan by posing as a rogue dragon. But his
plan is compromised when he falls for Cecily, the
Wyvermoon queen...